I0662313

This novel is a work of fiction. Names, characters, places, and incidents either are the product of the author's imagination or are used fictitiously. Any resemblance to actual persons, living or dead, events, or locales is entirely coincidental.

ISBN 978-0-9982946-3-6

Healing Bird

Written By

Dawn DeRamón

I would like to give a special thanks to my husband and kids for sacrificing their time with me so that I could dive into this book. A special thanks to my parents for their support and praise.

Kristen, thank you for all of your support, hard work, and friendship.

Author's Note

I enjoy listening to music while I work, and writing is no different. If you are wanting to set the mood for this novel, you can tune into Pandora and create the station for *Lindsey Stirling*.

You might find that the music suits the story well.

Enjoy!

Bird Family Tree

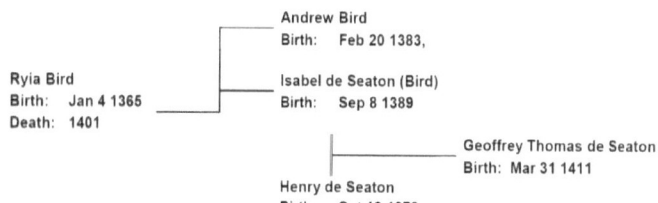

Andrew Bird
Birth: Feb 20 1383,

Ryia Bird
Birth: Jan 4 1365
Death: 1401

Isabel de Seaton (Bird)
Birth: Sep 8 1389

Geoffrey Thomas de Seaton
Birth: Mar 31 1411

Henry de Seaton
Birth: Oct 13 1378

de Seaton Family Tree

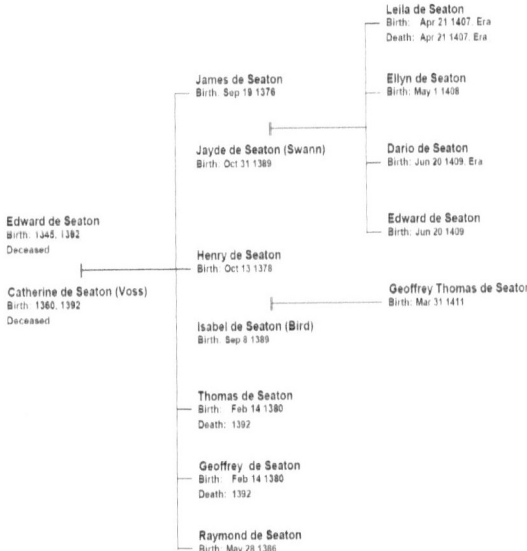

Leila de Seaton
Birth: Apr 21 1407. Era
Death: Apr 21 1407. Era

James de Seaton
Birth: Sep 19 1376

Ellyn de Seaton
Birth: May 1 1408

Jayde de Seaton (Swann)
Birth: Oct 31 1389

Dario de Seaton
Birth: Jun 20 1409. Era

Edward de Seaton
Birth: Jun 20 1409

Edward de Seaton
Birth: 1345, 1382
Deceased

Henry de Seaton
Birth: Oct 13 1378

Catherine de Seaton (Voss)
Birth: 1360, 1392
Deceased

Geoffrey Thomas de Seaton
Birth: Mar 31 1411

Isabel de Seaton (Bird)
Birth: Sep 8 1389

Thomas de Seaton
Birth: Feb 14 1380
Death: 1392

Geoffrey de Seaton
Birth: Feb 14 1380
Death: 1392

Raymond de Seaton
Birth: May 28 1386

Chapter 1
August 1410
Windsor Castle

Izzy trembled as she waited for the King to call her into the Hall. She had received a summons to court four days earlier regarding the annulment of her marriage. Her eyes were still swollen from so much crying. Nervously, she smoothed her gold dress once more, hoping that she looked perfect. The guard before her signaled for her to stand and follow him. Doing as she was told, her legs shook beneath her. Entering the hall, she heard her name being called. She took a deep breath and walked the entire length of the Great Hall, barely noticing its opulence. As she approached the steps where the King and Queen sat, she noticed a third seat, empty, next to the King. Izzy curtsied deeply and waited to be told to recover herself. As she stood she was aware that the sweet little bump protruding from her stomach was indeed noticeable. Her heart beat faster. How could she explain her lies to the King?

"Are you Lady Isabel de Seaton?" the King asked.

"Yes, your Majesty I-" Izzy was cut off when the King held his hand up to stop her. She could hear footsteps coming from behind her. "Excuse me," said a familiar voice. As the person walked past her and took his seat next to King Henry, she waited for Prince Henry, or Hal as she knew him, to face her. He leaned towards his father, "Please excuse my tardiness. There was business I had to attend to." He then turned his attention to the beautiful woman standing before them and recognition immediately lit his eyes.

"Izzy? What are you doing here?" he asked as he jumped to his feet and bounded down the steps to her side. He could see that she had been crying. "What is the matter? Are you well?" he asked as he looked her up and down, then back to her face. Quietly he whispered, "Izzy, are you expecting?"

Izzy bit her lip, desperately trying to fight the tears that once again welled up in her eyes. She nodded subtly.

The King cleared his throat drawing Hal's attention back to the etiquette of the court. "Excuse me Izzy," Hal said, quickly returning to his seat next to the King.

"As I had asked, are you indeed Lady Isabel de Seaton, the wife of Lord Henry de Seaton?" the King asked again.

"Yes, your majesty, I am," Izzy answered. The King looked from Izzy to his son and back again. "How do you know my son?"

"My services as a Healer were requested by His Royal Highness for the past four months," Izzy replied.

"I thought Healing Bird, a Lady Isabel Bird, was the healer?" the King asked both Hal and Izzy.

"Yes father, that is correct. You see, Lord Andrew Bird, one of your knights, is Lady Isabel's older brother," Hal informed his father.

"Your maiden name then is Lady Isabel Bird?" the King directed back at Izzy.

"Yes, your Majesty," she answered.

The King studied her a moment. "You seem quite familiar with my son how well do you know him?" The King noted that the woman before him was pregnant. Was she pregnant with his son's bastard?

"I would consider His Royal Highness a close friend," Izzy articulated carefully.

"A close *friend*? What do you call your friend when you are not in my court?" the King inquired with accusation in his tone.

Izzy nervously looked from the King to Hal. Hal nodded to her, giving her his silent permission to tell him. "I address His Royal Highness as Hal."

"Henry, I will not stand for this. I am going to ask you only once, so you had best be honest with me. Is this woman before me expecting your child?" The King's face grew redder with each word.

"Father, while I admit that Lady Isabel is exceptional in beauty, grace and intellect, she would never betray her husband, no matter the offer. I should know, I

3

tried to tempt her shortly after first meeting her." He spoke the last sentence quietly, a hint of disappointment and shame tingeing his tone. When he looked back to Izzy, he could see that he had embarrassed her. It was evident by the pink in her cheeks and her downcast eyes. "Forgive me Izzy, but you are hard to resist," he confessed.

The King sat back, disconcerted by his son's admission. When he finally turned to face Izzy again, the accusation in his tone had deepened. "You have lied to someone. You are either lying to me now or have lied to my son. Which is it?"

Izzy stood in shock, unable to believe that he could think she would dare to lie to him, the King of England. She shook her head trying to catch her breath. Everything began to spin and she threw her arms out, desperate to grab hold of anything as she felt herself falling.

Hal watched her go pale with his father's accusations and rushed down the steps, catching her in his arms as she fainted.

"My lord, I have met and spent a decent amount of time with this woman. I do not know her as the type of person to lie. She is very dedicated to her people and her craft. I think you have misjudged her," Queen Joan defended the unconscious girl.

With Izzy cradled in his arms Hal turned to the king. "Father, where is her chamber? She needs to rest."

King Henry sighed, "She is in one of the guest rooms. The guards can show you the way."

4

December 1407
Adonia

Henry was nervous about returning to Era for Christmas. He had left abruptly writing only a note to James and Jayde explaining that he had felt it was time for him return to Adonia. He could not have told anyone the truth; that he was jealous of the love and loyalty between James and Jayde. Henry had been amazed at how much James had changed, from the cold man that he had once been to the devoted husband with an equally devoted wife. Raymond had sent a letter updating him of the progress and changes he had made to Iole. Iole was their mother's favorite estate and she had often spent summers there. Raymond had written about James handing over papers and full control of Iole to him, and about the positive response the town had showed him. He had asked what day Henry intended to return to Era, offering to meet along the way, but Henry had been too deep in self-pity to respond immediately. The reality had been, though that he had been so deeply consumed by self-pity that he did not want to return to Era at all. When he finally had responded to Raymond, his note was brief, simply stating that he was not sure of the exact date but promised to be there for Christmas.

Raymond, of course, arrived in Adonia one week later. He traveled light and quickly with only his three most trusted knights. Henry was hiding something and Raymond was determined to learn what it was before Christmas. He arrived midmorning surprising Henry by walking onto the training fields.

"Raymond? What are you doing here? Is everything okay?" Henry was immediately concerned at the unexpected sight of his brother. Raymond never traveled without sending word first.

"I am fine Henry; it is you that I worry about. Would you like to discuss your problems over swords here on the training fields or in the hall with wine or ale?" Raymond was not about to give Henry any opportunity to deny that there was a problem.

"Raymond, I do not know what you are talking about. There is no problem." Henry felt more irritated than he had all week. It bothered him even more that Raymond had picked up on his distress

"Henry, I know you value family above everything. So, when I ask you if you would like to meet and travel together to Era, the usual you would agree and talk about some crazy plan. This is not the usual you and I need to know what is causing this compromise of values. So, tell me Henry. Tell me everything." Raymond tried to be firm, yet somehow still sounded gentle like their mother.

Henry heard their mother's gentle and caring tone in the way that Raymond spoke and for a moment, he felt like a little boy again, upset that James took a toy or got special privileges and he did not. Sighing, Henry said, "If you are going to insist on discussing this, then let us go inside to speak." Henry did not want to unload his worries to Raymond but knew that it would be better to work it out. He also knew that Raymond would not rest until he knew everything.

Raymond followed Henry into the magnificent hall at Adonia. Even Henry's gait seemed weighed down, Raymond saw. The two each grabbed a pitcher of ale and a mug and sat down at a small table in two large chairs before a roaring fire in the far corner of the hall. Raymond poured ale into their mugs, offering one to Henry and leaned back in his chair, waiting.

Henry accepted the mug of ale and took a drink. He stared into his mug not wanting to look into his brother's eyes. Maybe if he did not make eye contact with Raymond then he could just avoid all of this. He heard Raymond shift in his chair and instinctively looked up. Their eyes locked and Henry sighed allowing the words to tumble out of his mouth.

Raymond sat quietly attentive as Henry started from the beginning. The guilt he felt for doubting Jayde's fidelity to James, the pride and respect he had for her for training so hard and never giving up. Finally, he admitted to the anger he held towards James for being so closed minded, and treating Jayde like a child. "I think I am just jealous of what they have. Raymond, I am twenty-nine years old. It is my time to have a family and make a life of my own."

Henry stared at the fire in the corner and thought of Era, James and Jayde. He could see Jayde racing that damned horse of hers down the field and could not help but smile. Raymond's voice interrupted his thoughts.

"Is it possible that you are not jealous of what *they* have but are more jealous of what James has? Specifically, *who* James has?" Raymond did not want to spell out what he already knew.

"What are you trying to say Raymond? I think I know exactly how I feel." Henry became immediately defensive and regretted saying anything to Raymond.

Taking a deep breath, Raymond pushed on, despite his brother's sudden hostility. "It just sounds like there are deeper emotions. Henry, you talk about Jayde as though you are in love with her." Raymond waited for the explosion. When there was none, he asked, "Henry, *are* you in love with Jayde?" Raymond again waited again with no immediate response.

Henry could not believe what Raymond was insinuating. No, not insinuating, but declaring! Jayde was his brother's wife! She loved James! She risked her life to save him, and led two hundred fifty

knights to war! Of course, he could see why
Raymond could think this of him. After all, Jayde
was brave, beautiful, strong, and powerful and had
more skill with a sword than many knights he knew.
Henry braced his elbows on his knees, and let his
forehead fall into his open hands. "Oh my God. I
have fallen in love with Jayde. What have I done?
Raymond, what have I done?"

Raymond sat silently while Henry wallowed in the
guilt of his realization. Henry was right about it
being past time for him to want to settle down.
Henry would never seek out a bride though, he was
far too romantic, believing that the right girl would
come into his life when the time was right.

Raymond had a plan, but he would need to speak to
James about all of this first. and if James would not
go along with his plan, he knew that Jayde would.
He would however need to be careful what he said
regarding Henry and make sure not to mention his
affection for Jayde.

"Raymond, I cannot go back to Era now for
Christmas!" Henry finally erupted in a sudden panic.
He had ruined everything for his family by falling in
love with his sister-in-law. He had ruined his
family! How was he supposed to repair this?

"Calm down Henry. Of course you can and will
return to Era. You have not ruined our family. You
have just added an interesting obstacle. This shall
pass, and in time you will see that." Raymond could

not help but allow his mind to wander and get lost in his idea.

Henry's panic waned and he looked up at Raymond. Could he be right? Would this eventually pass? Taking a deep breath, he asked "When do you leave for Era?"

"As soon as I return home to Iole. I will pack a wagon and leave the next day. When do you plan to leave for Era?" Raymond wanted to get to James as quickly as possible.

"I will leave here in seven days." Henry spoke quietly. He knew that his brother was right, he must face his problem head on and not allow a rift to separate their family.

"Wonderful. I intend to rest then leave for Iole in the morning." Raymond put down his ale and left Henry in the hall alone to worry about the impending visit.

Raymond left Adonia at dawn and raced home to Iole. He was anxious to pack a wagon and leave for Era as soon as possible. Racing through the gates of Iole, Raymond saw a familiar face waiting for him. "Andy? Is that you?" Raymond called out as he slowed his horse and dismounted. Smiling, Raymond embraced Andy and led him into the hall. "What brings you to Iole my friend? Is everyone well?"

"It is good to see you again Raymond. Everyone is well, for the most part. I hope it is not bad timing for my unannounced visit. I am traveling to the King's court, and was in dire need of a place to stay for a few days and rest my horse." Andy walked alongside Raymond into the estate.

"It should be just about time for the midday meal, sit with me and bring me to date with your family." Raymond could smell the baking bread and heard his stomach growl. He led Andy into the great hall, over to the roaring fire where they sat in two carved wooden chairs. Once seated, a servant appeared to serve wine to the waiting men.

"Raymond, I heard there was trouble with your brother recently. Is everyone well now?" Andy asked before taking a drink.

Laughing a little, Raymond replied, "Andy, when is there a moment when one of us has not been in trouble?" Both men laughed heartily in agreement. "James was married last year, then his wife, Jayde, was abducted, rescued, James was abducted, Jayde lost the baby, slaughtered the man who abducted them both and rescued James. James is now a reformed man who dotes on his wife and bends any rule to fit her needs. Henry however, is a different story. He is feeling sorry for himself, and needs to be married, to focus on his own family. As for myself, well, I plan on making a few more changes to Iole this winter and spring and then I might spend the summer traveling the countryside. First, I will be traveling to Adonia to see James and Jayde. I leave in the morning. Once there, I intend on speaking

11

with James to arrange a marriage for Henry. You have not been to Adonia in a while. Would you like to travel with me or perhaps you would prefer to stay here and rest a while longer?"

"Do you have someone in mind for Henry? Obviously, there would need to be a dowry as I do not imagine that James would part with one of his own estates." Andy mused, ignoring the latter portion of Raymond's question.

"I do not have anyone in mind for Henry yet, and a dowry I think would be the least important, as he lives at Adonia. It was one of the estates that Jayde brought to the family that she and James gifted to Henry. Why do you ask?"

"Well, to be honest, since my parents passed away, Ackerley has slowly deteriorated. I have no desire to run Ackerley, which leaves my sister, but she is not allowed to run an estate without being married. Not to mention that Isabel is getting older. Ackerley needs an experienced hand, Isabel needs a husband, and Henry needs a wife and could benefit from owning Ackerley. Do you think that Henry would consider it? A marriage to my sister?" Andy asked, hopeful at the prospect. He felt ashamed for not wanting any part of the politics that came with being Lord of an estate. Since he was a child he had only wanted to train with the King's knights and he wasn't about to miss that opportunity.

Raymond thought about Andy's proposal. He searched his memory but could not remember Andy

Healing Bird

having a little sister. "Andy, how old is Isabel?"
What if she was just a child?

"Izzy has just turned eighteen. Recently she has
been learning of herbs from the nuns. I think she has
resigned herself to never marrying. I do not know
why mother and father never accepted an offer for
her hand. She is quite beautiful and used to always
fantasize about having a family." Relief began to fill
Andy at the possibility of such an easy solution to
both of their dilemmas. He had known the de Seaton
family his entire life and felt that all of the brothers
were good men. He wanted his sister to be treated
right, and with Henry she would certainly be well
loved and cared for.

Raymond's worried expression had disappeared at
the mention of Izzy's age and the idea of a marriage
between her and Henry intrigued him.

"I do not want to delay your travels to the King's
court, but could you spare time to come with me to
Adonia? James would be happy to see you again and
we could propose this plan to him. James could
force Henry to marry Isabel, citing financial gain for
the family, and you can arrange the marriage contract
for Isabel."

Raymond hoped that James would accept this plan
and enforce it. He knew that he would have to tell
James the truth though, about the sudden urgency for
this plan and he hoped that James would not be
angry.

13

Andy knew that he could spare the time and take a detour to Era, especially if it meant security and safety for Isabel and Ackerley. "It would be a pleasure to travel with you to Era. Thank you, Raymond. Thank you for considering my sister for Henry and your willingness to help me out."

Chapter 2
Era

Jayde was thrilled; both Henry and Raymond were returning to Era for Christmas. She and James had so much to be thankful for and getting to spend time with the whole family would be immense fun. Raymond was supposed to arrive tomorrow and Henry the day after. There was still so much to do. Decorations to hang still, fresh linens for the guest rooms, and meal plans to finalize. Fresh cut pine boughs had been brought in and tied together to make garland and were being hung around the hall. Beautiful red and gold, and green and gold ascots were being hung in the Great Hall with the pine garland. Jayde wanted everything to be perfect! This would be her first Christmas with James, and she was thrilled with her surprise for him.

James watched Jayde run around the castle ordering decorations to be hung and rooms to be cleaned, bubbling with joy and energy. He constantly worried about her health though. Recently she had been very ill and despite the surges of energy, Jayde usually ended the evenings early, retiring to their chamber pale and exhausted. Although Maggie did not seem to worry, he knew that something was wrong. James watched as Jayde tried to climb a ladder in the hall to show exactly how she wanted the ascots and garland placed. He could not just stand by anymore. This was driving him crazy. Turning his back, he turned to walk out to the stables to make sure that they were ready for his brothers' arrivals. He heard the gasp and knew before even turning around that Jayde had fallen. Running to her, he immediately began to check her for injuries.

"I am fine James, I promise. I simply missed a rung and slipped. I am fine," Jayde tried to reassure him. "Good, I am glad that you are not injured. Now, you will rest for the remainder of the day upstairs? You will not lift a finger. If you need anything, you will ask for it and you will not argue with me." James was a little gruffer than he meant to be, as he lifted her up and carried her upstairs. James had learned that he could not fight her mind or her mouth, but she was small, and he was both bigger and stronger. When words failed, brute strength won. He would simply carry her away from whatever situation was causing the problem. She could not argue with that. Jayde argued the entire way up the stairs even at one point going completely limp in his arms hoping to squirm away and return to her task.

"If you do not stop squirming, I shall give you reason to squirm," James said as he nuzzled her neck growling in her ear.

Jayde could not help but laugh and taunt him just a little by squirming more in his arms.

Closing the door to their chamber, James set Jayde down on the bed and said, "Now, I shall have to teach you a lesson." James wiggled his eyebrows as he began to tease and tug at the ties to her dress. Jayde could not help but giggle while she tried to escape him. She rolled off of the bed and ran around the post trying to run past him and out the door laughing the entire time. James wrapped his arms around her waist, lifted her off of the ground and fell back onto their bed tickling Jayde until she cried. Her laughter was contagious and James found himself laughing right along with her. Sliding out from under her he straddled her, placing a hand on either side of her shoulders. Smiling he leaned forward to kiss her forehead then her mouth, her ear and her neck. Sitting up he looked her square in the eyes, "Jayde, please, promise that you will stay in bed today. I do not know why you have been ill or so exhausted, but I worry. Please, do as I ask?" Jayde was about to tell him that she would not stay in bed but would promise to let someone else climb the ladder when a familiar sound came from the hill. It was Geoff's song. A smile spread across her face and a giggle escaped her mouth when James rolled off of her and groaned. Jumping to her feet, Jayde grabbed James' hands and pulled him with all of her might until he finally helped her and stood up on his feet.

"I thought they were not supposed to arrive until tomorrow or the next day," James groaned Unable to keep from smiling, he let Jayde lead him out of their chamber, through the hall and into the courtyard

17

where they waited for one of his brothers to arrive. "What, you are not going to jump on your beast, Galavant, and go racing up the hill to greet my brother?" James laughed at the look on Jayde's face. Jayde thought for a moment about this statement and gave it serious consideration. It had been nearly a month since she had taken Galavant out for a run, but she did not want to risk injury. Only Maggie knew her secret and until Christmas she was going to keep it that way. So she remained at James' side waiting to see which brother was arriving early.

Raymond waited for the responding call from the watchmen in the woods before proceeding into town. He hoped that his surprise would be a welcome one. Not only was he a day early, but he had brought a guest with him. Raymond spurred his horse forward racing down to the streets, slowing through town and then pushing his horse forward once he cleared the houses. He could see Jayde and James standing in the courtyard waiting for him. Once he had arrived, Raymond jumped down and handed his horse to the stable boy. He then went to James and Jayde to hug them both. "It has been too long!"

James laughed and hugged his brother back. "It has only been three months! How are you doing? How is life at Iole?"

"Good! Great actually! But we can talk business later. Now, I get what I came for." Raymond turned to Jayde and gave her a hug and a kiss on the cheek. "How are you getting along without Henry and me here to help tame my brother for you?" Raymond teased.

Laughing, Jayde joked, "I cannot manage without you two boys. Thank goodness I will finally have help!"

Turning to face both James and Jayde Raymond appealed, "I hope you do not mind, but I had an unexpected visitor in Iole and invited my guest to join me for Christmas here at Era." Just as Raymond was finishing his sentence a solo rider arrived in the courtyard.

"Andy! It has been far too long!" James said as he approached the rider.

Raymond stood back with Jayde as James greeted their family friend. "Andy, well, Lord Andrew Bird, has been friends of our family since we were all kids," he explained to her. "Andy trained with both Henry and James until everyone became ill. We occasionally saw him when we lived with our Uncle, but it was not nearly as often as we would have all liked. He has a baby sister, and she is the same age as you."

James walked over to Raymond and Jayde with Andrew in tow. "Lord Andrew, this is my wife, Lady Jayde. Jayde, Lord Andrew has been a family friend of our since we were small children. It has been nearly four years since I last saw him. Let us go inside and enjoy some ale and warm ourselves by the fire while we wait for the midday meal." The group turned to go in as the ten knights that

Raymond traveled with dismounted and led their horses to the stables.

James and Andrew walked ahead of Raymond and Jayde, talking of people they had known and if either of them kept in contact with those people.

Jayde could not help but smile. Watching James walking with Andrew, he acted like a young man. She was curious to see who this man was that Lord Andrew had awakened.

Raymond saw from the corner of his eye the smile on Jayde's face. "What makes you smile so softly?"

"I cannot help but be in awe at the youth that Lord Andrew brings out in James. I feel like James has been missing this piece of his soul for too long," Jayde responded quietly.

Shortly after their arrival in the hall, knights began to fill the empty space and Maria had the midday meal served. Jayde sat quietly through most of the meal listening to James and Lord Andrew reminisce of younger years.

After the meal was done, James pulled Jayde aside. "Would you mind if I spent the afternoon showing Andrew around Era and the changes that have been made since we were kids?"

"You two boys go on and enjoy yourselves. Just be sure to be back in time for the evening meal," Jayde teased.

"Yes mother dear," James teased back and for a moment the sentiment provoked an idea that hadn't occurred to him before. He paused in thought, considering his statement and wondered if it were possible for Jayde to be pregnant. He shook his head, he would have known, then he pushed the thought far from his mind. He turned and raced from the hall to take Andrew around all of Era.

After the evening meal, Raymond and Andy told James and Jayde about their idea to marry Henry off. Jayde missed most of the conversation though, exhausted and nearly falling asleep from the excitement of the day. James carried Jayde upstairs promising to return back to the hall to continue their conversation soon.

"What do you think James will say?" Andy asked Raymond anxiously.

"Honestly, I do not know. The fact that he intends to come back down after he gets Jayde to bed seems like a good sign though. You should go get some rest, I will continue to talk to James tonight. He might be more open without worrying about saying something that might not be agreeable with you if it is just he and I. In the morning, I will tell you everything." Raymond needed Andy to leave so that he could fully explain to James his reasoning for trying to marry Henry to Isabel.

"I do not want him to feel pressured, or obligated. Please make sure he knows that there would not be any bad blood between us should he refuse. Good night my friend." Andy was indeed tired and promptly left the hall to his guest room to get some sleep.

Time passed and Raymond waited alone wondering if James had forgotten or if he had become distracted. He was just about to get up and retire for the night as well when James returned to the hall.

"I am sorry to have kept you, Jayde woke up and was ill. I wanted to make sure she was alright and back in bed before returning. Did Andy go to bed already?" James asked.

"He did. He had been traveling for several days before reaching Iole and then there was the journey here. James, I must tell you something, but I am worried that it will cause a rift between you and Henry. There is no gentle way to say it though." Raymond waited to see what James' reaction would be.

"Well, we will not know until you talk Raymond. I know that you keep secrets well, so if this is something that you feel you need to reveal to me, then I will do my absolute best to control my temper," James promised.

"You see, Henry believes his affection for Jayde is inappropriate and because of this he was planning on not returning to Era. I know that family is everything and I am trying my best to help fix this." Raymond spoke quietly so that no one could overhear and spread gossip.

James smiled contemplatively. "Well, this is important information, but it is not anything that I did not already suspect. Do you really believe that a marriage between Henry and Lady Isabel could change this?"

"If not right away, then with time, yes. Also, Ackerley is a rather large estate and although I do not know in full its condition, I know that with hard work, it could be beautiful. I know that if you ask Henry if this is something he wants, he would refuse you. You do however have the power to force the marriage as you are the eldest brother and if you tell a small lie, explaining that it is for financial gain, Henry will not refuse. Henry would never intentionally do harm to our family."

James thought about this for a while. "I will speak to Jayde about this in the morning and we will talk more after the midday meal."

"Do you think it would be wise to include Jayde in this decision?" Raymond was worried that if Jayde knew of Henry's affections, that she might be uncomfortable and that could make an already awkward situation much worse.

James laughed. "Raymond, if you marry someone like Jayde, I will wish you all of the luck in the world at trying to keep her out of your business. Jayde will demand to know everything she missed, and with regards to Henry and his fondness for her, she will be flattered but not swayed. You should go and get some rest now. I need to go back to Jayde. She has been ill for quite some time now and I am very worried about her." The brothers said good night and went their separate ways.

When morning came, Jayde insisted James explain everything that she had slept through. She had noticed that Henry had pulled away from the family since he left Era in September. Now, she sat patiently on the bed staring at James waiting for him to start talking.

James tried to pretend that Jayde was not staring at him, but she was like Raymond and could extract a secret from any person just by sitting quietly. Finally, he could not take her penetrating eyes anymore. James told Jayde everything, including Henry's feelings. Jayde was flattered and admitted that it had crossed her mind that Henry might have feelings for her, but that it didn't change anything. They agreed that a marriage would be good for Henry, though James hoped that Henry would not put up too much of a fight, and Jayde worried that Henry would be too harsh on his new bride.

Andrew and James signed a contract that afternoon and a messenger was sent to Isabel in Ackerley explaining that she was to pack and arrive in Era within the week.

Henry arrived at Era that evening filled with dread with no idea of the plans his brothers and sister had made for him.

The evening meal had just begun when he arrived. As he walked into the hall, James, Raymond and

Andy stood shouting a greeting to him that was immediately echoed by the room filled with knights. Henry smiled as he approached the standing men. It felt good to be loved and wanted. He embraced his brothers then turned to Andy expressing his surprise and happiness to see him again. Then he turned to Jayde. As she stood, he noticed there was something different about her but wasn't certain what it was. He hugged her gently and gave her a quick peck on the cheek, then took a seat next to Andy and spent the meal laughing, eating and drinking while catching up on family news. At the end of the meal, Jayde excused herself, declaring her exhaustion and retiring to her chamber. She leaned over James' shoulder and kissed him before leaving the hall. Henry watched her walk away realizing abruptly what was different about Jayde. She was expecting. He felt simultaneous jealousy and joy. The small bump further confirmed that his love for her would forever remain unrequited and yet also realizing that she would have what she deserved; the opportunity to be a mother again. Feeling awkward, he turned back towards the table and realized that both James and Raymond were watching him. He grabbed his cup of ale and drank it all in one gulp. He would get through this even if he had to spend the entire visit drunk.

James could not help but watch his brother as Jayde walked away. Henry had turned around and watched until Jayde had crossed the hall and started up the stairs. James struggled to keep his temper checked. It was only after Henry had turned back around to face the tables that James finally felt Raymond's hand and warning where it still rested on his shoulder.

"When should we talk to him? I do not think tonight is a good night," Raymond whispered to James. "If we tell him now then he could stop watching *my wife`*." James growled back at Raymond. "This is exactly why we should wait. We will speak with him tomorrow, after you are both sober." Raymond tried to soothe James' temper but could not argue with it. To look at another man's wife the way that Henry did was justification enough for a fight, but to look at your brother's wife that way could cause a war.

The evening remained charged between the brothers, finally ending when Henry could no longer stand on his own. Raymond helped Henry to his chamber before retiring to his own. The next day was going to be a rough one.

Jayde was taking her daily walk to the stables to visit Galavant when she ran into Henry.

"Good morning Henry! I am so glad you could make it back to Era this year. How is Adonia doing?" Jayde loved Adonia and missed it terribly in the winter. Even though it was so close, there was just so much else to do that a visit there just never felt possible.

Henry was startled to see Jayde. "Good morning Jayde. How are you feeling? When are you to deliver?"

Jayde's face turned white and she rushed forward to hush Henry. "Shh, please," Jayde whispered as she pushed Henry away from the garden towards the breeding stables where she kept Galavant. Once they were a distance away, she asked, "How did you know?"

"I can see the bump. Does James not know?" Henry asked.

"No, no one knows. I am keeping it a secret until Christmas," Jayde whispered with an endearing smile.

Henry felt a great deal of satisfaction knowing that he knew before James. "Well, then I shall keep your secret too. What are you doing out here this morning? It is very cold and you do not have a cloak on." Henry thought for a moment how nice it would be to pull her into him and hold her tight, keeping her warm. Then the reminder that she was married and pregnant brought him back to reality.

"I am visiting Galavant. I do not want to ride him and risk harming the baby." Jayde lamented as she placed a hand on the bump at her midsection. "I should have the baby around the end of April or beginning of May."

Henry swallowed hard. Watching her, being this close to her, and in the state she was in was much more difficult than he had imagined. He needed to leave but could not leave Jayde out here in the cold alone. "We should return to the hall. It looks like it might start to snow again," he insisted.

Jayde took another minute to rub Galavant's nose before turning and walking back to the hall where it was warm. Once they were inside, Jayde excused herself and went to the solar where she was working on a project for the knights. She had wanted to give them all something useful but could not think of anything that they might need. When she had found the green silk however, she decided to make them all pouches. She was making one for each knight, embroidering their initials on one side and swirls to represent Era on the other side. She had started this project in October and was nearly done. There were only eight pouches left to embroider. Jayde was deep in her project when she heard the scuffle from below.

"You did WHAT?" Henry screamed. "How dare you decide what I need in my life! You cannot do this!"

"Henry, this is business, and you know it. I must do what is right for our family," James tried to remain calm.

"So have Raymond marry her then! I will not do this!" Henry objected loudly.

"Raymond is not ready to marry. The contract has been drawn up, and she is on her way now. You will be married the day after Christmas." It was apparent in his tone that James was struggling to not attack Henry.

Jayde came hurrying down the stairs just as Henry slammed his fist into James' face, sending him to the floor. "James!" Jayde screamed rushing forward. She knelt down over him to shield him from another blow and to check if he was injured.

James was stunned for a moment after Henry knocked him to the ground and he watched Henry raise his fist again as Jayde came rushing to him. Without thinking, he shoved her to the ground, jumped up and slammed Henry against the wall. "Let this sink into your thick head. You will marry Lady Isabel Bird, you will never raise your hand to strike when my wife is in your way and you will cease your inappropriate feelings for *MY WIFE*!" James took a deep breath struggling to regain control. "Do you understand me?" he growled.

Raymond and Andy both stood back. This had not gone the way either of them had anticipated.

"I do not remember Henry having any temper. Is this normal?" Andy asked, worried about his decision.

"Henry rarely gets angry, but like James, when he does, it is explosive," Raymond responded.

Raymond remained unfazed by the scene before him. He had grown up watching drama play out between

James and Henry and this was no different than any other fight between the two men.

Henry was seething, though. He stared into James' hard, cold eyes until movement from behind distracted him. It was Jayde picking herself up from the floor. The look on her face betrayed her heart. He could see the sadness as clearly as he could see her. Slowly she approached the two men and laid her hand on James' shoulder.

"This must end now. James, put your brother down. Henry, lower your fist. Henry, there are two choices. You can leave and return to Adonia. Lady Isabel will arrive and be humiliated and whatever financial gain there was to be had will be lost. Or you can stay, fulfill your duty to your brother and family name, and find a way to love. The choice is yours and you both must live with your decisions. However, I will not allow either of you to continue to behave like animals in my home. Henry, go take a walk and make your decision. Lady Isabel should arrive tomorrow. Christmas is two days away, and your wedding in just three days. James, come upstairs with me, and let me tend to your face. Raymond and Lord Andrew, go make yourselves useful. I am sure that Maggie or Maria have a list of things that need to be done and many of them require strong men. Go, all of you." Jayde waited for James to release Henry, then she shoved James up the stairs to their chambers.

"I am fine really I -" James began to protest.

"Yes, I am sure you are fine. I am going to wipe the blood from your split lip anyway." Jayde was a little rougher than she should have been causing James to wince. Sighing, she sat down beside him. "What do you think Henry will do?"

"He will pout, then honor the contract that Andrew and I made. Henry is an honorable man, but difficult," James relented more calmly now.

"Ah yes, a de Seaton boy being difficult, I am shocked!" Jayde said, leaning against James "I did not like seeing the two of you fight. You know I would have defended you to him. You trust where my loyalty is, right?" Jayde worried. She did not enjoy seeing James jealous.

Smiling, James wrapped his arm around her and kissed her forehead. "Yes, I know you are loyal to me. It is the knowledge that you *would* try to fight anyone, including my brothers, to protect me, that scares me. I will not allow anyone to put you in harm's way, including yourself. I love you Jayde."

Henry was angry and humiliated. How dare James arrange a marriage for him! If he did not value and honor his family's name, he would leave immediately and never return. He knew he should be angry at Raymond as well because Raymond had provoked all of this. If he could only learn to keep his mouth shut. The worst part of all though, was

Jayde seeing him punch James. No, the worst part was James being right and him not realizing that Jayde was protecting James with her body when he raised his fist to strike James a second time. He knew that the only way out of this mess was to marry this Lady Isabel. Maybe he could learn to like or even love this Isabel woman … wait, how old was she anyway? Dear god, if this was a financial gain, was she an old widow? No, she was probably hideous. It didn't matter. He worried that no matter how beautiful she was, he would always compare her to Jayde.

Henry managed to hide and stay out of view for the remainder of the day. He notified Maggie to have his evening meal sent up to his room. He would need to calm himself. Tomorrow he would face James, and they would move forward. He would however, refuse to meet his future bride until he had to face her for their vows. If he met her prior to their vows, he knew he would find a way to run.

Chapter 3

Henry woke with the sun on Christmas Eve. He could smell the beginnings of the feast that was being prepared below. Traditionally, their family began to celebrate on Christmas Eve, and did not end until the end of the day following Christmas. Christmas Eve was always about playing games, eating, drinking and telling stories. Christmas Day began with warm wine, an exchange of a gift, music, more games, more feasting, dancing and lighting of candles for loved ones that were not able to celebrate. The day following Christmas was always quieter. Pies were the only foods served this final day of celebration. Their mother, Lady Catherine, would always write a note to each member of the family, and servants as well, about why she was grateful for them, and pass them out on this day. Henry still had every note that their mother had ever written to him. He wished he could talk to her now. She would tell him that everything would be fine, that James was wrong for doing this without consulting him. Was this punishment for caring for Jayde? Caring? Who was he trying to kid? He was in absolute awe of Jayde. What was he thinking? He needed to stop. Jayde was his brother's wife, his WIFE. In two days' time, he would have a wife as well. Groaning, Henry got up and snuck down stairs to steal one of Maria's delicious morning rolls filled with soft sweet cheese and candied fruit from the end of summer. Peeking around the corner, Henry made sure there was no one around, then walked into the kitchen and saw two morning rolls on a linen. Smiling, he grabbed them and headed back to his chamber. Tomorrow he would be sure to leave his gift for Maria. This year, he had commissioned Diane to make a fur lined cloak for her. He knew that it was much nicer than anything she owned, but she deserved it for all of her constant hard work. Henry waited until everyone else had woken and ate their morning meal before finding James and speaking with him.

"James, I would like to have a word with you please." Henry motioned for the two of them to go into the office upstairs.

James nodded and followed Henry upstairs. Jayde had given him an earful last night and he was going to try like hell to remember everything that she said.

"James, yesterday caught me off guard. I need to know what I am to expect when this Lady Isabel arrives." Henry was giving his best effort to accept his fate and move forward.

"I know, and I should have spoken to you first, but it is a good arrangement and with time, you will come to like this woman. I am not sure what you mean by 'expect' however, so I do not have an answer for you." James followed Jayde's instruction and used 'I' to help keep both of them calm.

"I want to know how old she is, if she is good and kind, pretty, or smart? Honestly, I do not want to spend any time with her before I marry her. If I meet her and find something I hate, I fear that I would be willing to smear our good name and run away. Does that make any sense to you?" Henry was still hoping that James would tell him he did not need to do this, that it was okay if he humiliated this girl, or woman. James understood all too well what Henry was going through. He had the exact same worries when he had married Jayde. "I believe Lady Isabel is eighteen. I do not know if she is pretty, or good and kind, but I do know that she is smart. She has been studying with the nuns in Ackerley and from what I understand is very knowledgeable about herbs. She is considered a healer at her home. If you do not want to meet her prior to your vows, I will not object. I felt the same way when Jayde and I were to wed. Listen, her family is a good family. I cannot imagine that she would be any less kind than they. You should know though, that she will have no family at the ceremony. It will be a very small and private affair.

Henry tried not to be dramatic. A 'good family' and 'any less kind than they.' He sounded so flippant, but this was his life! Henry took a deep breath. There was no point getting worked up, there was nothing that he could do. "Very well. Thank you for your time. I will see you around." Henry left James and the office behind. The next two days were going to be torture.

James waited a moment after Henry left before leaving his office as well. Hopefully, there would not be any more trouble about this wedding. He thought for sure that Henry was going to question him about his knowledge of his feeling for Jayde. Should he have brought it up? Really, how did Henry expect him to feel? He had to remind himself that this was a waste of time to get worked up about. Henry had not even mentioned it in conversation. Taking a deep breath, he went back downstairs to play a game of chess with Jayde. She had promised to teach him how to play the game last year when they were first married.

Henry went into Jayde's solar and searched the books his mother used to keep. He found a small black bound book labeled *Apothecary*. He should try to have something in common with this woman before she arrived. Leaving the solar with the book, he nearly knocked Maggie over in the hall. "Oh, Maggie, please have all of my meals brought to my room today. I have some important reading to do. Also, please make sure that I have ale as well, lots of ale. Thank you." Henry turned and walked briskly to his chamber. He began to read immediately and found that he did not understand anything in the book he had chosen. What on earth would you need something called *blue tansy* or *mug wort* for?

By the time his midday meal had arrived, Henry had already drunk enough ale to become inebriated. He had put the book down a while ago and started to consider what his options were with this woman. He would marry her and send her back to whatever town she was from. He would give her an allowance and never think twice about her otherwise. All he had to do now was get through the next couple of days. He would not be truly required or missed until tomorrow and he intended to avoid James and Raymond until then.

Though Henry continued to drink, at one point he heard a commotion from the hall and could only assume that Lady Isabel had arrived. He took another long drink of ale. Tomorrow would be torture, but James had agreed that it would be best for him and Lady Isabel to wait to meet until the day they were married. Still, he felt like a prisoner in what used to be his own home. All that he could think about was how he could never keep his damn mouth shut. What he still did not understand, was why Raymond had said anything to James at all in the first place? What was it that Raymond got out of this? He shook his head and closed his eyes, too tired and drunk to think about it anymore. Sleep would surely clear his head.

Henry woke Christmas morning with his head hurting horribly. He had drunk too much the day before and now was going to pay for it all day. Hoping that food would dull the pain, Henry quickly and quietly snuck down to the kitchen where another sweet cheese filled roll was waiting for him. He took the roll, leaving the wrapped cloak in its place and dashed back upstairs. He waited until he heard Raymond leave his chamber to go to the great hall below and followed his brother, catching up to Raymond at the top of the stairs.

"Henry, you startled me. How are you feeling today?" Raymond was worried for his brother. Since Henry and James had fought, Raymond had not seen Henry at all. Looking at him now, Raymond could see that his assumptions were correct and that Henry had been drinking heavily.

"Were you expecting someone else?" Henry chided. "I thought I would join you for a feast if I am still welcome." Henry's head pounded with each word. Raymond wondered fleetingly how Henry intended to treat Lady Isabel. He had the opportunity to meet her, and although she remembered the three of them, neither he nor James seemed to remember her.

"Is Andy ready to lose game after game today?" Henry grinned. He would enjoy today despite what his future held.

"Andy left yesterday after the morning meal. He was on his way to the King's Court to train. He offered his congratulations to you," Raymond offered, knowing that he told a lie. Andrew had left worried and hoping he had not made a mistake agreeing to a marriage between Henry and Isabel. Henry frowned. He had not realized that Andy was not staying with them longer. He should have taken the time to socialize with him rather than hide in his room. "Well, shall we go downstairs and enjoy some spiced warm wine then?" Henry and Raymond went downstairs without speaking, both lost in their own thoughts.

Henry sipped the spiced wine. He wanted to be careful not to overindulge as he had the day before. Finally, Jayde and James came down to the hall and the morning meal was served. Despite everyone giving their best effort, the tension was thick and everyone felt uncomfortable. Henry avoided looking at Jayde and resented James for his discomfort. By the time the midday meal was served, Henry had quit caring about slowly sipping spiced wine and was now trying to drink this day away as well. He huddled in the corner near the fireplace drinking and hating his life. Before long, he fell asleep.

James watched with some guilt as Henry drank the morning away and fell asleep shortly after the midday meal. Isabel had come down into the hall as arranged, and tried to excuse herself back to her chamber so as to not disturb or cause any more trouble for her soon to be husband.

"Nonsense. Please, Lady Isabel, come with me to distribute a few notes. By the time we return, James and Raymond will have carried Henry off to bed. I promise, I will not let him ruin our day," Jayde insisted, linking arms with Lady Isabel before leading her up the stairs to her solar to collect the notes she had written last week.

Isabel began to protest, "I do not want to separate family on such a special day. Lord Henry should be able to spend the day with you rather than retreat to his chamber because of me." Isabel was nervous. Andrew had sent a messenger to her with word that a marriage was arranged for her to Henry de Seaton. She was furious! She remembered the brothers well, and knew them to all be good and kind, but could not believe that Andrew would arrange a marriage for her without discussing it with her first! They had always been close and Andrew had let her run Ackerley after their parents had passed. He had never had a business mind and had been happy to let her take control. He had promised to take care of her and promised that he would never sign her life away. Isabel knew that she was getting older and that in three or four more years she would be considered an old maid. In fact, her proposals were already becoming fewer and fewer. She had considered ignoring her brother's message. She thought about staying home in Ackerley and just joining the nunnery, but then Ackerley would be lost to the King and everything that their parents had struggled for would be lost as well. In the end, Isabel had chosen to let go of her anger and trust her brother. She packed her belongings and began the journey to Era, where she was to wed Henry de Seaton, a man she had known when she was a young girl, but had not seen in ten years. Ten years could change a person. They had changed her. Ten years ago, she became an orphan and was blessed to have the Abbess take her under her wing. The Abbess made sure that she had learned to read and write. Then she had the Infirmarian teach her everything she could of herbs and their healing properties. Isabel had been considered a healer by many of the townspeople in Ackerley and spent a great deal of her time creating teas and poultices from the many herbs in her garden.

Jayde refused to allow Lady Isabel to run off. "Lady Isabel, by this hour tomorrow, you will be my sister-in-law. I think we are close enough to that time to consider ourselves family. We will not allow Henry to spoil our good mood because he wants to pout and throw a fit." Jayde led Isabel into the solar where she had been keeping all of the notes she had written to the servants. James had told her how his mother used to write a thank you note to the main servants and usually included a small amount of money as a gift as well. Jayde had decided to continue with Lady Catherine's tradition.

"What are all of these notes for?" Isabel asked as Jayde began to make two stacks. She handed one to Isabel.

"These are for some of the servants. It was a tradition that Lady Catherine started and I am hoping to be able to continue it." Jayde smiled with the hope that her attempt at tradition would be welcomed.

Isabel did as she was asked and followed Lady Jayde around as notes and coins were passed out. Most of the notes and coins were greeted with smiles and tears and words of gratitude for thinking of them. There was one especially meaningful note however; the recipient was the blacksmith. He was a middle-aged man and he gave Lady Jayde a hug upon its receipt. Isabel was curious what was so special about the relationship between Lady Jayde and the blacksmith but knew better than to ask. Instead she smiled and continued to quietly follow.

As Lady Jayde had promised, by the time they returned to the hall, Henry was gone and the atmosphere in the hall had been lightened. Isabel relaxed a little and began to enjoy the rest of the day with her new family. She wanted to know what it was that bothered Henry so much but dared not ruin the contentment with such an impulsive question. She allowed herself to be absorbed into the joy and family games, laughing and sipping spiced wine. She noticed that Lady Jayde did not run around or dance as much as everyone else. She noticed the small bump of her stomach. Isabel waited for there to be a break in the games and laughter before sitting down next to Lady Jayde. Quietly, she asked,

"When are you expecting to deliver?" She guessed by the shocked look on Lady Jayde's face that not many people knew, if any of them did.

"Is it really that obvious?" Jayde asked quietly, careful not to cover her stomach with her hands and give away what she hoped was still a secret.

Smiling, Isabel answered, "I have been training with the nuns back home in herbs and midwifery. I notice the small details."

Smiling back, Jayde whispered, "I am due near the end of April or beginning of May. I am waiting to tell James until I know this baby will survive."

Jayde thought of her sweet baby in the rose garden and fought the tears that burned her eyes.

"You might not have to tell him if you wait much longer," Isabel teased. "Please forgive my ignorance, but have you lost many children?"

"Just one. My sweet Laila. I gave birth too early, and she just could not survive." Jayde's mind began to wander back to that night.

Isabel watched with regret, the pain that crossed Lady Jayde's face. There was more to this than Lady Jayde was sharing and she wished she knew a way to ease her pain and worry. "If you would like, I can blend some herbs together to make a tea to help keep your strength up. Are you experiencing any illness with the pregnancy?"

Jayde was surprised at how well Isabel navigated through the conversation. "I would love to have some tea. Thank you. I am still experiencing some illness, but it is usually just in the mornings."

"I will make a blend of herbs for you to use for a tea to help with the sickness too." Isabel felt better about bringing up such painful memories. She also felt useful which of course made her happy. Quietly the two ladies sat near the fire talking and resting until they were both too tired to continue. Standing, they hugged and said good night to each other. Isabel watched as Lord James intuitively noticed that Lady Jayde was ready to retire to their chamber and instantly concluded his fun to walk with his wife up the stairs.

Raymond walked over to Lady Isabel. "Well, Lady Isabel, would you like me to walk you to your chamber as well? I hope that Henry's poor behavior has not soured your day with us. He is not usually like this. He was just as surprised by the marriage as I guess you were. I hope you will not be disappointed by an intimate celebration tomorrow." Raymond rambled on as he escorted Isabel to her chamber. Once they reached her chamber, he quickly gave her a peck on the cheek and waited for her to close the door behind her before checking on Henry. He could hear Henry's snoring from outside his chamber. He left his brother to sleep off the wine and retired to his own chamber. The following day was going to be a painful day for Henry.

Isabel waited until she heard Raymond walk away from her door. Taking a deep breath, she walked over to the chest where she had packed her prettiest gown. She had not been prepared to be married and so she had picked out her prettiest dress, one she had planned to wear to the King's court in the spring. The kirtle was taffeta and the color was a rich shade of purple, like the juice from dark grapes. The silk over tunic was a warm lavender that matched the color of the flowers themselves. The neck of the bodice was square with delicate lace matching the color of the taffeta. There was not much money to be spent on clothing, and Isabel had decided she would rather spend the extra funds on the color of the fabrics rather than having jewels sewn onto them. It was a beautiful gown that made her pale skin glow and blue eyes even brighter. She did not have a veil to wear, but this was to be a small and private ceremony. She hoped that her new family would not think poorly of her or her lack of wealth. Isabel pulled the gown out of the trunk and laid it across the window bench to smooth out the wrinkles from being folded. Sitting on the edge of the bed, Isabel brushed her blonde hair before climbing beneath the blankets in hopes of quickly falling asleep.

Henry woke feeling as miserable as he had the morning before and he began to feel even worse when he realized it was the day after Christmas, the day he was to be married. Henry walked across the room to the fireplace and stoked the fire. He stood staring at the flames trying to think of any last-minute ideas to get him out of this marriage. There was a sharp knock on the door as the door was pushed open. Henry turned to see Raymond and James coming in. "Tell me, what do I owe for the pleasure of your company?" Henry asked dryly. James ignored his brother's condescension and smiled casually at Henry. "I am here to help you get ready for your wedding. I realized that I regretted having not told either of you when I was to wed Jayde and thought that you might enjoy some company before you go downstairs to meet your bride." James crossed the room and poured three cups of wine from the pitcher he had brought up. Raymond remained silent and pulled Henry's clothes from the chest laying them out on the bed. What could he say to Henry? 'Sorry that I betrayed your trust? It is my fault that you are miserable and being forced to marry a family friend's daughter?' Isabel was warm and full of personality. She laughed with them last night, ran around the hall, played games and fit in with the family. She would be a wonderful addition to their family and hopefully, Henry would see that too.

James realized that the only way that Henry would stop being angry would be to get him to drink more wine and relax a little. There were still a couple of hours before the ceremony and James was going to use his time wisely.

When Maggie arrived in Lord Henry's chambers
with three other servants the three men were slapping
each other on the backs and laughing. On the table
stood an empty bottle that had once held one of Lord
Edward's few bottles of Brandy. There were trays of
food and pitchers of wine brought in and set on the
table. As she turned to leave, she heard Henry
speaking to James, and could hear his slurred speech.
She could not tolerate when men abused the drink, as
it usually turned them into monsters. Maggie sent
the other servants back to their other jobs and went
to Lady Isabel's chamber. There she found Lady
Jayde and Lady Isabel getting ready after eating a
small amount of the food brought up earlier.
"Oh Maggie, thank goodness you are here. Would
you stay and help me with getting Lady Isabel
dressed?" Jayde being four months pregnant
struggled to get the corset as tight as it needed to be
without help.
Maggie quickly walked to Lady Isabel's side and
asked, "How tight do you need it to be?"
Isabel held up her hands and showed Maggie how
tiny her waist needed to be.
"Heavens child! How do you plan to breathe! Lady
Jayde, you just sit over there and rest. No use in you
and the baby getting -" Maggie turned to face Lady
Jayde, shocked at herself for the words that slipped
out. "My Lady, I am sorry, I did not mean to say
anything."

Jayde chuckled. "I guess it is getting harder to hide my little secret, is it not Lady Isabel? It is okay Maggie, I plan on telling Lord James today. If you could keep my secret just a little longer?"

Relieved, Maggie smiled and promised to not say another word. Turning back to Lady Isabel, Maggie helped her finish getting dressed. When she was done, she asked for the veil.

"I do not have a veil. I was not prepared to be married." Isabel felt embarrassed by the confession. Maggie thought for a moment. "My Lady, if you would wait here for a few minutes, I have something for you." Maggie then rushed off to the solar and dug through Lady Catherine's chest. There she found a beautiful silver comb and quickly returned with it to Lady Isabel's chamber.

Isabel saw the silver comb in Maggie's hands. It was exquisite and far too expensive for her to wear.

"Now before you begin to protest, because I can see that you are about to and it is your character to do so, this belonged to Lady Catherine. I am sure she would have loved to know that one of her beautiful daughters would wear this," Maggie said pulling Lady Isabel's hair back from her face.

"Oh Maggie! It is perfect!" exclaimed Jayde. It added just a touch of shine to Lady Isabel's blonde hair. Jayde wondered where Maggie kept finding such wonderful gifts. She would ask Maggie to show her these treasures another time.

Isabel took a deep breath and faced the mirror, staring at the woman before her. The purple and lavender of her dress brought a warm glow to her skin, and her hair pulled back opened up the frame of her face. This was a new woman, one she had never met before. She looked confident and poised, filled with grace and nobility, but still kind. She looked like someone that Isabel wanted to know. Taking one last look, Isabel finally turned to Lady Jayde. "I do not know that I am ready for this, but there is no turning back now."

Jayde stood and took Lady Isabel's hands into her own. Gently squeezing them, she said, "Isabel, you are breathtaking! I hope Henry faints when he sees you." Jayde smiled and giggled. "Shall we send for the boys?"

Maggie nodded and left the room to tell Lords Henry, James and Raymond that it was time. She knocked on the door to Lord Henry's chamber and then pushed the door open. When there was no answer. Raymond looked helplessly to Maggie as she walked in. James and Henry had managed to drink far too much wine and both were consumed by the drink.

"Maggie, what are we to do?" Raymond had no idea how to handle this.

"You help Lord Henry and I will help Lord James. The ladies are already expecting you and if we wait for these two to sober, we will be waiting for days. Let's go." With that, Maggie gestured for Raymond to assist her with Henry and began to push Lord James towards the door, then down the stairs and finally to the fireplace where it was warm. The priest was there to greet them and raised his eyebrows in surprise and disapproval when Henry and James arrived inebriated. With a huff, Maggie returned upstairs to help Lady Isabel down the stairs in her gown.

Jayde went down to the hall first. When she stood next to James, she turned to face him. "James de Seaton, what is wrong with you? How could you behave like this? Lady Isabel is nervous enough. You and Henry could not even have an ounce of self-control?" She was on the verge of tears. What was supposed to be a beautiful moment would be destroyed.

All eyes turned to the stairs except for Henry's. He continued to stare at the floor blankly refusing to face his fate. Lady Isabel was beautiful. She gracefully crossed the hall and walked herself to the priest and Lord Henry. She could smell the wine and brandy on him and was instantly livid. He probably would not have even noticed if she had been wearing peasant rags.

The priest began the ceremony. He began with a prayer, then a sermon on loyalty, trust, and ended with the importance of obedience. Isabel heard Jayde stifle a laugh and struggled to not burst into tears and laughter as well. Finally, the priest asked if they had rings to exchange with their vows.

Raymond brought both rings to the priest who in turn gave them to Henry and Isabel. Their vows were said though slurred on Henry's part, their fidelity to GOD and each other was pledged, and rings were clumsily exchanged. After the ceremony was finished, Henry finally looked up at Isabel.

Henry looked up from the floor finally and into the eyes of his new wife. She was mesmerizing. Her eyes were blue and her blonde hair reminded him of the rays of winter sunlight. Her lips were full and soft and the color was the softest shade of pink. He could see himself kissing those full lips and looking into her eyes searching for his soul. Her shoulders were broad but her frame still petite. She was nothing like Jayde; she was curvy, soft and absolutely stunning. Then for some reason, Henry thought it would be a wonderful idea to speak. Leaning unsteadily to the side to look at James, he said, "At least she is not a troll!" and then he spun away from them all and retched in the corner.

Isabel stood still trying her best to control her temper. A troll? Truly, a troll! She would show him a troll! When he turned to the corner and retched she could not hold her tongue any longer. "It serves you right to be ill. I hope that your head hurts so violently in the morning that you retch again! How dare you disregard me like this! I was not looking forward to this marriage either, and yet here we are. At least I had enough respect for you and the sanctity of our wedding vows to be coherent!"

Henry wiped his mouth with his sleeve as his wife began to yell. Shocked, he turned to face her again. It took him a moment to understand what she was saying. She hoped he would be ill again in the morning? Respect? What was she talking about? All he could do was stare at her with his mouth hanging half open. He saw Jayde shaking her head, saw James laughing, and then saw Raymond standing there with a look on his face that translated to 'you deserve this.' Then, just as suddenly as it had begun, it was over. Food was brought out to the table and his wife walked away from him and sat down. Unsteadily, he followed Raymond and James, where he took his place next to his bride. He tried with difficulty to focus on her but all he could see were the two tears that trickled down her cheeks. Isabel could feel the tears welling in her eyes. She tried to blink them away, but one from each eye escaped and fell down her cheeks. She wiped them away before they could reach her chin. There was absolute silence as the meal was served and eaten. Nearly an hour had passed when the meal was finally finishing, and without warning a messenger rushed into the hall. He carried a letter with the King's seal on it.

"Pardon me my Lords and Ladies, but I have an urgent message for Lord Henry de Seaton," the exhausted messenger wheezed.

Isabel stood up, resigned now to speak for her drunken husband. "I am Lady Isabel de Seaton, the wife of Lord Henry de Seaton. He is ill; however, I can accept his message on his behalf." The messenger crossed the hall and relinquished the message to her. Isabel proceeded to open the letter and read it to herself. She laughed dryly, then handed the note to Lord Raymond.

After reading the note, Raymond announced, "It seems that our Henry has been requested by Prince Henry himself. He is to leave immediately and travel to the King's court where he is to join the Prince's army and aid in squashing the rebellions against the King." At that moment, two of the King's knights entered the hall.

Henry had only begun to sober in the midst of the meal but was not quite yet completely alert. All he heard was that he was being summoned to leave immediately. When the two King's knights entered the hall, he registered the seriousness of the situation. Standing, he immediately went to his chamber to retrieve his sword, dagger, cloak, and satchel. Within minutes he returned to the hall. Before leaving with the knights, he went to Raymond. "Brother, see that my wife is taken care of, that she safely arrives in Adonia and is settled in. Oh, and brother, do not fall in love with her or you might find yourself being married off next."

Isabel sat in shock as Henry left the table, then returned within a few minutes. She watched as he spoke with Lord Raymond, then without even saying goodbye, just left. She felt lost, unsure if she was relieved or disappointed, grateful or resentful. Lost. The room was quiet and everyone sat staring at her. She could take no more of it and finally stood up, escaping upstairs to her chamber. She changed morosely out of the beautiful purple and lavender gown and back into a plain off-white kirtle and a beige over tunic. Gently she pulled the comb from her hair and placed it on the table. Taking a deep breath, she told herself it was going to be fine. No marriage started with love. It was something that had to be cultivated, like herbs in a garden. Finally, her strength left her and she threw herself on the bed sobbing until the sweet dark release of sleep overcame her. Isabel awoke to find Maggie stoking the fire and the moon rising in the dark sky.

"I am sorry Lady Isabel, I did not mean to wake you. Your room was growing cold, and I wanted to be sure that there was food in your room when you did wake. Would you like to eat something?" Maggie felt terrible for the poor girl. Married to a drunk man, then abandoned before the ring on her finger had even warmed with no promise of return or care. Isabel took a moment to decide if she was hungry enough to actually eat. Taking a deep breath, she said, "I suppose there is no purpose to me remaining angry at what I cannot change. Yes, thank you, I would love to eat." Smiling at Maggie, she walked to the table and began to eat the meats and cheeses that had been laid out for her. "Maggie, is there anyone that needs to return to Adonia?"

"I do not believe so My Lady, but I shall ask Lord James for you in the morning." Maggie was relieved that Lady Isabel had such a judicious head on her shoulder, she seemed very sensible.

"Oh, that is okay, I will ask him in the morning. Thank you for your help." Isabel continued to eat in silence, deep in thought about what she would do next. She waited for Maggie to finish with the fire and leave her chamber before she stood and began to pack her belongings into the trunk, including the beautiful purple taffeta dress. She laid out a brown wool kirtle and a beige over-tunic. The only other item she left out was the silver comb that she had worn in her hair earlier that day.

When morning came, Isabel was dressed and had already had her trunk sent down to a wagon. She went down to the hall and ate a morning meal, finishing when Lord Raymond, Lord James and Lady Jayde joined her.

"Good morning Lady Isabel, you are up early," Raymond greeted as he joined her at the table to eat.

"Good morning Lord Raymond, Lord James, Lady Jayde." Isabel waited until everyone was seated. "Lord James, do you know of anyone that needs to return to Adonia? I would like to leave today. With Lord Henry gone, the sooner I am able to get to know Adonia and her people, the better."

James was shocked. He would have expected a woman in her situation to be upset, lost, or just different. Here she was however, refusing to need

Henry, refusing to be vulnerable. He was impressed. "I do not know anyone that needs to return to Adonia but Raymond and I will travel with you. If you must leave today, then we will make that happen."

"I would appreciate it greatly. I have only the one trunk with me, and the wagon can travel alone at a slower pace. What time would you be ready to leave?" Isabel wanted to see all of Adonia and make sure that the people were not neglected, that they were growing the best crops, and were profitable in as many ways as possible. She refused to allow herself to be helpless or useless and knew that she would feel more at ease with a mountain of goals ahead of her.

Before the midday meal was served, Isabel, James, Raymond, and knights Fendrel, Luther and Peter, were saddled and leaving Era. Isabel had left a note for Jayde, offering her assistance when it came closer to the time that she was to have the baby as well as anytime that Jayde needed something. The group of six rode hard through the day into the evening before they finally stopped for the night at an Inn. They agreed that with the snow, it would be best for everyone and the horses to rest indoors for the night. James paid for the room and paid for an evening meal as well. Sir Fendrel, Sir Luther and Sir Peter chose to sleep in the stables to make sure that thieves did not steal the horses in the night.

Sitting down at a table they drank ale and waited for the meal to be served. The silence between the three of them was uncomfortable. Isabel observed James and Raymond and knew that the only way for the discomfort to dissolve would be for her to start a conversation.

"Lord James, tell me if you will, what was your family's true gain of the arrangement between Lord Henry and I?" Isabel was bold and refused to play the games that ladies of the court played. She found that if she shocked people with her boldness that she was more often able to get an honest answer.

James nearly choked on his ale. He had not expected for any conversation between them to begin like this. Once he recovered, he realized that Raymond was laughing at him though Lady Isabel remained quite serious. "Well, we did profit from the marriage. Land and an estate is a profit." James was grasping for anything other than the truth. He could not tell this young lady that her husband lusted after his wife.

"Lord James, I know that as a man, it is your duty to protect delicate ladies from such complicated matters, however I have been running Ackerley alone for several years and am very aware of what we have to offer and what we do not have to offer. Whatever it is that you are hiding, I hope that you will eventually come to trust me enough to tell me. I promise, I do not judge." Isabel would have to ask Lady Jayde the next time she visited. Turning to Raymond, Isabel changed the subject. "Lord Raymond -"

"Please, just call me Raymond. We are family, and I hope you regard me as much your brother as Andrew is," Raymond interrupted.

Isabel smiled. "Raymond, tell me about Henry. Explain to me the man he has become, please." Raymond sat back a moment, thinking carefully about what he wanted to say. "Well, Henry would like everyone to believe that he does not worry what others might think of him but the truth is that he honors the reputation of our family name above anything else. The man that he chose to be for you yesterday is someone that I have never seen before. I will not lie to you, he was not happy about this marriage either. He had just begun to settle in Adonia and was truly loving the wonderful changes he had planned for it. Henry had been trying to find a way to forge his own path. When James married Jayde, they gifted Adonia to him. Henry considered this his opportunity to finally be on his own. What James does not want to tell you is that Henry had discovered an obsession. To save our family and to save Henry in particular, James arranged your marriage to Henry with Andrew. Henry likes to joke and appear flippant to the world around him, but that could not be farther from the truth." Raymond took a moment to sip his ale.

"Henry is actually a very sensitive and passionate man. He does not give his trust or his love quickly or easily. If that love or trust is betrayed, he takes it quite hard. I believe that is part of the reason Henry

58

chose to drink himself stupid; because I betrayed him. I betrayed his trust when I arranged a marriage without speaking to him first. I do not know how to fix my mistake, but believe that you, Lady Isabel, are quite the opposite of a mistake. I believe with my soul that you are the missing element to Henry. I can only hope and pray that you can be patient with him and wait for him to return and come to his senses," James finished for Raymond.

Isabel took this bit of information in. Before she could ask another question, a tray of meats and bread were brought to them. Isabel sat quietly eating while thinking about the bit of information that James and Raymond had revealed. Henry was bound by loyalty and honor. Despite his anger regarding his marriage, he would not shame his family or her and therefore accepted his fate reluctantly. She was curious to know what this 'obsession' was that put not just himself, but his entire family as risk. Isabel also could not help but wonder how this sensitive and passionate man would act. She struggled to see him holding her hand gently, speaking to her with kindness and love.

Raymond saw how deep in thought Isabel was. "Lady Isabel-"

"Since we are family, the formalities should be dropped equally. Just call me Izzy. That was what my parents used to call me and what Andy calls me still today," Isabel said.

"I like Izzy! It is very sweet and suits you quite well. Izzy, Henry is not something you will be able to understand easily. It has taken our entire lives to understand him and yet there is still plenty of mystery even for us. Give him time to calm down. Let him fulfill the duties that Prince Henry has asked of him and when he returns, hopefully he will open up to you then." Raymond hoped that Izzy would trust him and try to not worry about Henry.

Izzy smiled at Raymond and nodded. Raymond obviously knew nothing about women. Telling a woman not to worry always had the exact opposite effect. The rest of the meal was silent. Izzy finished eating and felt the exhaustion take over. She looked at both James and Raymond who were both still very involved in eating. The sounds inside the inn were quiet and the fire kept the room comfortably warm. Letting her eyes gradually close, Izzy finally succumbed to sleep.

James looked up from his plate to grab his mug of ale. Sitting between himself and Raymond was Izzy, and she was fast asleep. "Raymond," James whispered. Raymond did not respond. "Raymond!" James whispered louder. Raymond picked his head up with a mouth full of bread.

"What?" Raymond replied. He saw James motion with his head towards Izzy and followed the cue. He looked over to Izzy and saw that she was asleep. "What should we do?"

"Just let her rest until we are finished eating." James thought of Jayde in Era. Before he had left, she seemed like she wanted to talk to him. He was so worried about her, her recent illness, and sudden change in behavior. It left him trying to figure out what was wrong with his wife. Lost in his thoughts, he did not see the brawl that was starting near them. Before James could react, two men came slamming down onto their table. Raymond was jumping up and out of the way, but James went flying backwards upon their impact and Izzy was trapped underneath the two brawling men until they rolled off of her and continued their fight.

Izzy was still trying to recover from the rude awakening when James came to help her to her feet. The brawl continued in front of Izzy and there was no place for her to go. Izzy watched James and Raymond stand aside and over heard them discuss if they should step in or not. More chairs, tables and benches were being broken, which would mean so much work for the inn keeper. Izzy calmly walked over to the two brawling men and placed one hand on the shoulder of each man. Startled, both men turned to look at the person belonging to the hands. "Gentlemen, what are you two fighting about? A woman? Ale? You both should go home, rest, and in the morning return here to help mend the items you have destroyed," Izzy spoke quietly and with authority yet somehow she looked as gentle as a lamb. As she spoke she had guided the two men towards the door. As she pushed them outside, she reminded them, "Now gentlemen, do not forget, to get your rest, I will be expecting you here to fix the destroyed furniture in the morning. Good evening gentlemen." Izzy returned to where James and Raymond were standing and staring. "James, Raymond, I am absolutely exhausted. Could we please go to our room and rest now?"

Raymond could only nod and James guided Izzy up the stairs to their room silently. Once the three of them were in their room with the door secured, James started to laugh. Izzy turned to face James and question why he was laughing when Raymond began to laugh as well. Confused, Izzy stood in the room looking from one man to the other.

"What is so funny?" Izzy asked.

"It is just that those two men..." Raymond gasped.

"...and you are so tiny!" James finished.

Izzy stood watching the two men wondering why they found the fight below so funny. "I do not see how two grown men fighting and ruining furniture is funny."

"Not the fight, you! In a room filled with large strong men, not one of them stepped in," James mused.

"You walked over to them and gently took each of them by the arm and walked them out of the Inn as though you were at the King's Court while the rest of us could only stare!" Raymond continued.

James and Raymond both realized that Izzy was not going to see the humor that they saw. Finally, after calming down, they gave Izzy her privacy to change for bed. After she had climbed into bed, James decided to ask her some questions.

"Izzy, how old were you when your parents passed?" James began.

"I had just turned eight years old," Izzy answered.

"Lord Andrew said you are considered a Healer. Tell me, how did you come to learn so much about herbs, and healing?" James asked.

"Oh, the nuns took me in, sort of. The Abbess made sure that I could read and write, then she had me studying with different nuns to learn different skills. I've helped to deliver several babies, I've studied plants, and learned how to use those plants to help heal. They started my teachings just a couple of months after my parents passed." Izzy thought back to her home at Ackerley and wished she could be going there now. She would go to Ackerley in a few months, in early spring and make sure that homes were repaired, drainage ditches dug, and baskets woven. She could only hope that the people of Adonia would be just as receptive to her being a part of their lives. Izzy was so deep in thought she did not hear James' question.

"Izzy?" James questioned.

"I am sorry, did you say something?" Izzy felt terrible. She hoped that her not hearing or responding to James would not give them cause to judge her.

"I was asking you what your plans are for Adonia," James repeated himself.

"Oh! Well, first I would like to meet the people and hear what they need most. I want to make sure that their homes have been as well repaired as possible and help in any way that I can. If I have to, I will help them repair their homes myself. Having sick farmers or families does no good for the town. I will want to encourage the women to weave, baskets are so important for everyday life but especially for harvest. Maybe I will invite the ladies into the hall to weave together..." Izzy got lost in thought again.

"Is that all?" James asked laughing, amazed at all of the positive plans she had for a place she had never been.

"What? Oh, no. I'll want to make sure that the irrigation ditches are dug properly and that there are the proper tools for the work. There will be tending to livestock, and preparing the fields for plowing and planting. That should keep me busy at least until spring." Izzy was curious what crops Adonia grew primarily, what they were lacking and what she could do to add a little variety if needed.

James and Raymond sat there and stared at her. James was impressed. She seemed to know as much about running an estate as he did, if not more. Why had he not thought to offer the large warm hall for the ladies of Era to use to weave? Ladies love to talk and laugh and having fun always helped the time pass more quickly as well as made dull tasks easier. He would need to mention this to Jayde.

Raymond sat quietly admiring Izzy's desire to be useful. He wondered if that was just a part of who she was or if it was something the nuns had taught her. The more he listened to Izzy speak, the more he believed it was written in the stars for her to marry Henry. Henry may not know it yet, but Izzy might just be the woman of his dreams. Raymond yawned and stretched. "Brother, would you like the first watch or the second?" Raymond asked, his eyes already struggling to stay open.

"I will take the first watch. You get some rest. I will wake you when I need to rest as well." James had much on his mind. He had his own estates to run and the thoughts of Jayde and everything they had been through played through his mind as they often did when he could not sleep. James dimmed the light, and listened as both Izzy and Raymond quickly fell asleep. Izzy was so different from Jayde. Where Jayde was timid, Izzy was bold. Jayde was fragile, but Izzy seemed strong. Neither of them had an easy childhood, but both seemed to have survived and were happy. He hoped that Izzy and Henry would be happy with one another. He wished it with all of his heart. James sat thinking and planning for Era and the season ahead. He would be sure to check in on Izzy frequently until Henry returned, and hoped that by Christmas of next year, he and Jayde could be expecting again. After several hours, James finally woke Raymond and laid down to get some rest while Raymond took watch.

Chapter 4

With the early morning sun, James, Raymond and Izzy awoke and readied themselves for the final push for traveling to Adonia. As the trio walked down the stairs to meet with their knights and leave, they were greeted by one of the two men who had been brawling the night prior. James and Raymond were as surprised as the Inn keeper had been.

"My Lady, please, accept my deepest apologies for my behavior last night. It was disrespectful and shameful, and I am mortified to have been so boorish in your presence," the man said as he pulled his old hat from his head exposing a balding spot.

The Inn keeper approached the group. In a shocked tone he said, "The brothers returned and the other one is out back working on tying the table they broke back together. I do not know how you did what you did, but I surely appreciate it. Thank you." He tipped his hat to Isabel before returning to his work.

Izzy smiled at the balding man. "I am so pleased to see that you and your brother have returned to fix your wrongs. It takes a true man to admit the error in his ways and be so willing to correct them. You have a good heart in you sir." Izzy gently touched his arm before she continued out the door trailed by Raymond and James who once again were left with their mouths hanging open.

Once they were seated on their horses, they kicked them forward and raced for Adonia. It was well past the evening meal when the six people rode into Adonia. The knights immediately took the horses to the stables while James, Raymond and Izzy stumbled into the hall. There was a servant rekindling fire in the hearth for the next day who startled when she saw them come in. James quickly explained who they were and only when the maid recognized Raymond did she believe them, running disconcertedly off to fetch another servant.
Alice was just about to leave for her own home when Sarah came rushing in.

"Alice, Lord Henry's brothers are here and they have brought a woman they claim is his wife but Lord Henry is nowhere to be seen. What should we do?" Sarah asked, panicked.

"Heaven's sake child! Calm down and go into the kitchen. Prepare a tray of meats, cheeses and breads. I will be in to help in just a moment." Alice rushed out to the hall to greet the small party. "My Lords and My Lady, you must be exhausted and famished. I am Alice and I am head of the staff here in Adonia. Would you like to sit here in the hall and eat or would you prefer to eat in your rooms?" She could see the exhaustion on their faces and took note of the filth of their clothes.

"Good evening Alice, I am Lady Isabel, I think it would be best if we could just sit here and eat before going to our chambers." Izzy spoke up declaring herself the one that would be in charge of the small group.

Alice nodded and scurried away to get food and drink on the tables. She passed Bess and instructed her to light the fire in the hall quickly then prepare water for baths in the Lord's chamber as well as two of the guest chambers. Walking into the kitchen she grabbed two pitchers and filled them with cold sweet wine and followed Sarah out to the table with them. As soon as Alice had placed the pitchers, she and Sarah gathered the baths and placed one in each chamber, lit the fires and turned down the beds. By the time they were done, the water down below was just about ready to be taken up for the baths. Alice instructed Sarah and Bess to find more servants to help fill the baths as she returned to the fatigued trio. "Lady Isabel, may I lead you to your chamber?" Alice waited for Lady Isabel to stand and follow her up the winding stairs to the chambers. "My Lady, this room belongs to Lord Henry, and you now as well. May I ask when Lord Henry will arrive?" Alice felt unsure of the situation she was in and hoped to get more information.

Izzy waited for Alice to show her the chamber before she spoke. "Alice, I wish I could give you an answer, but the truth is, I have no idea. About one hour after our vows were said, Prince Henry sent for him to leave immediately. I cannot imagine how this must look and how you must be questioning everything, but I hope that you find a way to trust me." Just then, Sarah, Bess and two other servants came filing into the chamber carrying buckets filled with hot water and began to pour them into the bath near the fire. "Oh my, Alice, a bath is exactly what I need after riding from Era! Thank you." She waited until everyone had left, including Alice before peeling the layers of clothing off, letting them fall to a pile next to the bath and without hesitation climbed into the scalding bath water. She sank into the tub until she was completely submerged. She held her breath concentrating on her heart beating under the water until she thought her lungs would explode. She emerged from the water only until her chin was above the water and allowed the dirt and filth to detach from her body. Just then, there was a gentle knock on her door.

"My lady, may I come in?" Alice called out.

Izzy was startled. "Yes, but I am in the bath still." Alice came in with a basket and knelt down next to the bath. She pulled out a bar of soap and lathered her hands gently, then massaging Lady Isabel's scalp and dutifully scrubbing her hair. Alice did as she always had and began to wash Lady Isabel's arms, hands and finally her feet. As she washed the soles of her feet, she could feel Lady Isabel tense until she violently jerked her foot from Alice erupting in laughter.

"I beg your pardon Alice, but I fear that I am dreadfully ticklish on my feet. Thank you for your help, but I think I am done." With that statement,

Izzy fully submerged once again scrubbing her scalp and hair under the water to rinse the soap out. When she came up for air, Alice was standing with a large soft linen open and waiting for Izzy to step out and dry off with.

"My lady, do you have a lady's maid?" Alice was curious from where this woman hailed and what she had planned for Adonia.

"I do not Alice. I have not had one since I was ten years old. Is there someone you would like to recommend?" Izzy was curious to see what Alice thought of her. If she had a maid in mind, would she be kind or cold? If the maid was cold, then she knew that Alice did not care for her and wished she would leave. If the maid was kind however, then she hoped that it would be a sign that Alice was willing to trust her.

"I know of a few maids that would love to be a lady's maid but let me interview them for you. I want to make sure that you get the perfect one." Alice would wait a bit until she knew the new mistress better before choosing a lady's maid for her. "Until then My Lady, I will fill in if that suits you."

"Thank you so much Alice; that would be wonderful." Izzy realized that her comb was in her trunk. "Alice, would there happen to be a comb that I could barrow until my trunk arrives? I was in such a rush to get here that I did not think to travel with it." Izzy hoped that the woman would be kind.

"Yes, My Lady. I will return in just a moment."
Alice returned moments later with a comb and began
to come Izzy's blonde hair. When she was done, she
set the comb on the table and asked if there was
anything else that she could do for her.
"Oh no, Alice, that will be all. You've already done
so much to help. Thank you. I will see you in the
morning. Sleep well." Izzy stood and crossed the
room to the bed. It was large and soft and took less
than a second for Izzy to fall fast asleep.
Alice watched as the young woman nearly fell asleep
still sitting up in bed. Lady Isabel seemed so tired
that she forgot to even put her feet up in the bed.
Sighing, Alice walked across the room, and lifted the
young woman's legs onto the bed. She pulled the
covers up and tucked Isabel in. Tomorrow would
tell so much more about this woman. Alice quietly
left the room and finally left for her own home.
Izzy awoke to a pale pink and orange sky that teased
of the rising sun that would soon grace the sky.
Quickly, she dressed, combed and braided her hair
and practically bounced down the stairs to the hall
below. The castle was busy with life already. She
could smell bread being baked from the bake house
and as she passed the kitchen, she saw several
servants working already on the day's meals.
Entering into the Great Hall, she found food being
set out on the tables for the small morning meal.
Izzy was eager to integrate herself into Adonia. She
hurried through her meal and then went to find Alice.

"Alice, could you tell me who I should speak to so that I may be taken through town and introduced to the farmers?" Izzy asked, after finding her in the courtyard.

Alice was affronted by Lady Isabel's request. She had not even been here a full day and already wanted to change everything. She had a lady's maid for her alright, a wild pig! "Yes, My Lady, I believe you will want to speak with Hugh. He is the Constable in Adonia. I will send for him immediately." She turned and left to get Hugh. What a retched woman! She was glad that Lady Isabel would be out of the way for the day!

Izzy waited patiently on a bench near the courtyard where Alice had left. After a short time, a stout middle-aged man walked in.

"Hello, I am Hugh, the Constable of Adonia. You must be the new mistress, Lady Isabel?" Hugh had already heard an earful from Alice about how this woman was going to change everything, how perfect Adonia was and did not need some uppity woman coming in to fix what was not broken. Honestly, he did not think too much of what Alice had to say. She had a tendency to exaggerate.

Izzy was impressed by Hugh's attitude. He did not seem arrogant, nor did he act timidly. She liked him immediately. "Good morning Hugh, you are correct. I am Lady Isabel. It is a pleasure to meet you."

"Good morning My Lady. What may I do for you today?" Hugh asked.

"I was hoping that you could introduce me to the farmers in town?" Izzy was hopeful that today would be the first of many great days here in Adonia.

"Of course, My Lady. It is cold outside, you should wear a cloak. Can I get you one?" Hugh asked. The cold outside nipped viciously leaving a chill in your bones that was hard to warm.

"You're right, but no. I will retrieve my cloak. Thank you." Izzy ran up the stairs to grab her cloak, put it on and fastened it as she ran back down the stairs to the kindly waiting Hugh. She had not been expecting that he would drop everything to take her about. Hugh led her out of the castle across the gate and to the stables. They waited while two horses were saddled for them. Hugh led Izzy along the outermost fields first. She could see that the field were in bad shape, and in desperate need of weeding and plowing.

"Hugh, is there an ox to help the farmers with the hard work in the fields?" Izzy asked.

"No, My Lady, there has not been an ox in Adonia for more than a decade. Lady Ethna sold it for profit. With the ground so cold, the farmers are not strong enough to pull the plow themselves and we are too poor as a community to purchase any good work horses," Hugh answered honestly. There was something about Lady Isabel that put him at ease. He knew that he could say anything to her and she would hear it rationally.

"I see. And the farmers' homes, are they well repaired or in similar conditions as the fields?" Izzy asked.

"Well, some of the homes are repairable for winter while others are not even livable. For those families, they usually group together and stay in the stables with livestock during the winter." Hugh thought of the many families in town forced to survive in the stables. Lord Henry had not been here long enough before returning to Era to make any changes, and he had not shared any plans for change either.

"Hugh, would you mind taking me through town to meet any of the families that are willing. I would like to hear what they need most immediately and see what I can do to help them. I would also like to see the homes that are not livable. Perhaps later, you and I can assess finances and create a plan for repair. I would like to hear from you what you feel our most immediate focus should be to help our farmers and families thrive. Would you be willing and able to work with me?" Izzy asked him.

Hugh was stunned by this woman's interest in her people but recovered as gracefully as he could manage. "Yes My Lady, it would be a great pleasure to work with you." He could only hope that she would have some useful solutions.

They continued through town and Hugh introduced Izzy to as any of the townspeople as possible. Izzy noticed that there were very few young children amongst the families. What infants she did see, she noted, all seemed sick. She would need to remedy this immediately.

"My Lady, that is most of the townspeople. There are a few who are ill or traveling right now and I would be more than happy to take you to them all as soon as they are able. We should return to the castle now." Hugh was freezing and he could not imagine that Lady Isabel was much warmer.

"Hugh, when we return, would you please join me by the fire to warm up and begin discussions about Adonia and its people?" Izzy did not want to waste any more time. The people were struggling. They were either too ill and poor to have children or were too ill and poor for those babies to survive.

"Yes, of course My Lady." Hugh was grateful for the invitation to warm up.

As soon as they returned to the castle, Izzy handed her cloak to a servant and immediately sought out Alice. "Alice, I need a pen and paper immediately. Then, send a messenger to me. I have a very urgent message to send." Izzy waited for Alice to answer her.

"I am busy My Lady, but I will tend to your needs as soon as I am able," Alice replied tersely.

"Alice!" Hugh scolded her. "You will tend to Lady Isabel's requests and needs immediately unless you wish to find new employment. You might think you rule this estate but you simply rule the servants. I take orders from Lady Isabel, and you take orders from us. Learn your place." Hugh felt compelled to defend Lady Isabel. He was angry and it was rare for him to be like this. Lady Isabel seemed genuinely concerned for the people of Adonia and they were in dire need of help. He would not stand by and allow someone so shallow minded to interfere.

Izzy had startled when Hugh had reprimanded Alice but was quite grateful for his support. Turning, she smiled at him and signaled him towards the roaring fireplace.

Alice murmured a coerced apology and turned immediately to take care of everything that Lady Isabel had requested.

When Alice brought paper and pen to Lady Isabel, Hugh asked her to bring them warm ale and meats. "My Lady, Alice will trample all over you and undermine you at every opportunity if you allow her to. You should be stronger with her, if I may say so," Hugh suggested as they ate.

"Thank you for your advice and help. I will remember that next time." Izzy bent her head and wrote her note, sealing it with a stamp and then blew on the wax to help it dry. When the messenger arrived, she handed it to him.

"Hello, I am Lady Isabel the new mistress of this estate, and your name is?" she greeted him.

"Gille, My Lady, at your service," he replied.

"Very well. I need for you to leave immediately for my hometown, Ackerley. When you arrive there, please deliver this to the Constable there. His name is Myles. Myles will take care of you. Do not leave Ackerley until Myles sends you with a note in return," Izzy instructed. "Be sure to pack provisions before you leave as well."

"Yes, My Lady," Gille obliged before sprinting out of the castle towards the stables to ready his horse.

"Provisions, Lady Isabel? Ackerley is barely a half day's hard ride from here," Hugh noted, confused.

"I know; however, he is traveling during the evening meal, at night in the cold, and I want to make sure that he knows I offer him whatever comfort I can to him while he takes this urgent message to Myles." Izzy stopped speaking when Alice and Bess arrived with meats and ale. Izzy smiled and thanked them before returning her attention to Hugh.

"Hugh, why have so many homes not been repaired?" Izzy inquired, hoping that Hugh would provide her with an honest answer.

Hugh sighed. "I would love to say there is a simple explanation, but unfortunately it is not. It started several years ago when Lord Dario remarried to Lady Ethna. She changed things, demanded higher taxes, and did everything within her power to make it difficult here in Adonia. I wish I knew what life had done to her to make her so hateful. I know she was a widow, perhaps losing her first husband made her a monster. It is a shame, she could have done so much for Adonia." Hugh took a sip of ale then continued. "Once the families became ill, they did not make repairs to their homes, very little digging, very little basket weaving, and by the time the spring and summer came, everyone was too busy to catch up from winter and the cycle still continues on."

"Are there supplies that can be gathered to make repairs to homes right now?" Izzy was concerned for the health and safety of the people of Adonia and wondering what Henry had done or was planning to do to help.

"Not much has been done to prepare for winter at all. It almost seems as though the town is giving up." Hugh knew that there was talk in the town of packing up in the spring and leaving. Maybe Lady Isabel could be the town's hope.

"I see, well, that leaves quite a bit for us to do. Whose home is in most need of repair?" Izzy did not want to waste a single moment.

Izzy and Hugh stayed up for hours discussing homes, families and farmers. They agreed that in the morning, they would go out and ask for volunteers to collect supplies to begin to repair homes. "Within a week, I would like for us to be done with home repairs, and I would like for us to meet again to discuss farming. As soon as we are done repairing homes, I would like all of the women in town that weave baskets to meet here and weave together. We need to bring Adonia back together. Friends and neighbors should never have let each other's homes fall into such neglect. Get some rest, tomorrow will be a very long and exhausting day."

"Thank you, My Lady. Thank you for giving Adonia a chance." Hugh stood up and said good night before leaving the hall and returning to his own home where his wife and kids were fast asleep.

Izzy waited for Hugh to leave before sinking back into the chair in front of the fire. She thought back to the note she had sent with the messenger. She figured he should be arriving by the morning meal. Myles would take about three days to get everything she requested and it would take another three days to bring it to Adonia. By the time everything arrived, they should be done repairing homes and ready to begin digging ditches and plowing the fields. Izzy took a final sip of ale and forced herself upstairs to bed. She was so exhausted that she felt almost too tired to sleep. Tomorrow would be the first day that she would be able to gain the town's trust. In her chamber, Izzy changed for bed and fell asleep within moments.

She woke the next morning and dressed in her warm wool under tunic and over tunic, then headed downstairs to the hall where she ate a large meal before pulling her cloak on and walking to the stables where she waited for Hugh. By the time he arrived, the stable boy had two horses saddled and ready with an empty wagon trailing behind one. Izzy and Hugh rode their horses to the edge of town where they began to collect sticks. The goal today was to repair just one house for one family. They had agreed to take it one house a day and then make new plans after that. Their hopes were that once the townspeople saw them repairing one house, they would start to pitch in and houses would be repaired that much faster. Hugh and Izzy started a fire so that they could take breaks and warm up when they needed to, getting to work right away on the first house.

Hugh and Izzy worked tirelessly through the entire morning not stopping for a single break. It was not until a neighbor came outside with half a loaf of bread did they stop.

"Hello, I am Adam. My wife baked bread this morning and wanted you to have some. She also said that I should come out here and make myself useful. So, here I am. Where can I start to help?" Adam asked.

Izzy grinned, grateful for the help and the bread. "Thank you, Adam. I am afraid that in our rush this morning, we forgot to bring anything to eat. You and your wife are incredibly kind to share. Would you join us and share this bread?" Izzy asked, wiping her brow.

Adam smiled, "No thank you, I have already had some. You two should take a break, enjoy the bread, and let me work for a while." He walked past them and picked up where they had left off repairing the house.

Izzy and Hugh broke the bread in half and stood by the fire enjoying the reprieve. Shortly after, a woman emerged from the same house as Adam carrying a mug. "We only have the one mug, so you will have to share with one another."

Hugh extended his hand to the woman. "Thank you very much." He took the mug and gave it to Lady Isabel who took a deep drink. He took the mug back after Lady Isabel was done and finished what was left. He handed the mug back to the woman and thanked her again. The woman took the mug and quickly went back inside the house. Izzy and Hugh exchanged a look before returning to the house they were repairing and picked up where they had left off assisting where Adam was working now. Silently, the three worked until the house was finally restored. The sun was about to set and it would be time for the evening meal soon.

"Adam, thank you again for working with us. I do not believe that we could have finished the house today had you not come out to help us. If there is ever anything that I can do to help you, please let me know." Izzy extended her sore, dirty hand to shake Adam's.

Adam reached forward and shook her hand without hesitation. "My Lady, I am glad that I could be a help. If you meant what you said, I will take you up on your offer of help sometime."

"Lady Isabel always means what she says. She is good on her word." Hugh stepped forward. He had only known Lady Isabel for one day and he hoped that she would be as true to her words in the future as she had been today. He trusted her. When Lord

Henry had taken over Adonia, he had not made the plans that Lady Isabel had made. He had grand ideas of a wealthy Adonia but no idea how to achieve it. Izzy and Hugh watched as Adam turned and went back into his home. They mounted their horses and made their way back to the stables.

"I will handle the horses and wagon, you go in and get warm," Hugh insisted as they reached the stables. He dismounted and took both horses by the reigns. Izzy climbed off of the horse feeling every muscle in her body ache. "Hugh, after you are done, please join me for the evening meal so that we may discuss where we are going tomorrow." She did not give Hugh an opportunity to object. She turned and walked away towards the castle. It was dark out and she could hear the owls calling out. Oddly, it sent a shiver down her spine. She hurried into the castle and down to the hall where a large meal was being prepared. Inside the hall were nearly one hundred knights standing, waiting for something before sitting down. Izzy slowed down and cautiously made her way to her chair near where James and Raymond were also standing. She looked around and waited for another minute until finally she could not wait anymore. Leaning to her left, she quietly asked, "Raymond, what are we all waiting on?" Raymond chuckled. "We have been waiting on you." He saw the confused look on her face. "Word travels fast here. Apparently, you were seen by several families repairing a house in town today.

What is more, you were seen sharing bread and a mug of ale with another family. No one can remember a Lord or Lady of Adonia ever getting their hands dirty for the families here. You are a hero in their eyes," Raymond explained with a large grin on his face.

"That is silly. How else will the houses get repaired if we do not pull together?" Looking around at the hall full of knights her discomfort grew. "How do I get them to sit down?" she asked quietly.

Laughing out loud, Raymond answered, "Simply sit down."

"Oh!" Izzy quickly sat down and was a bit in awe at the uniformity of the room of knights that sat down as well. Leaning towards Raymond again, she asked, "What now?"

"Whatever you would like. You can make a toast, a speech, or simply start eating," Raymond whispered back.

Izzy was nervous. She stood up and grabbed her cup. "Hello. You all must be used to seeing Lord Henry and wonder where he is and who I am exactly. I am Lady Isabel and the day after Christmas, Lord Henry and I were married. Currently, he is serving with his Royal Highness. I do not know when he will return, but he has entrusted you all to me. I have had the opportunity to speak with Hugh, and I think we have a great plan to help the families in this town to heal and eventually grow. I have great hope for all of you and Adonia. I also hope that you can find a way to trust me and work with me." Izzy looked about the room nervously. "That is all I guess. Um, enjoy your meal." Quickly she sat down.

"First time giving a speech?" Raymond asked.

"Was I that bad?" Izzy worried.

"No, you did just fine. There is a bit of history with these knights and Lady Jayde. These men are much different than other knights. They are not afraid to respect and follow a woman. Treat them with kindness and respect, and they will love and protect you with their whole hearts and lives," Raymond said proudly.

Izzy smiled and began to serve herself. She had made far more progress today than she had realized. She saw Hugh and waved to him. She watched as he smiled at her then took a seat with the knights. Her feelings were instantly hurt that he had not chosen to sit with her. Although his status was beneath her, she had thought that she had found a friendship with him. She tried her best to piece together the day and where she had gone wrong. He had stood up for her, a complete stranger, to Adam from town who Hugh had probably known for many years. She knew that she could not let the town down but more importantly she knew that she could not let Hugh down. So what did she do wrong? Had she offended him somehow?

James noticed Izzy's change in attitude. He stood and walked around and sat in what was Henry's chair. "Izzy, what is bothering you?"

Izzy struggled to keep her emotions in check and looked down at her plate as she answered. "I think I am just tired. I am not accustomed to the type of manual labor that I did today and am still adjusting to the idea that I am married... sort of."

"I wish you knew that you could trust me. You are my little sister and I will protect you as I do my wife. When you are ready, I will always have an ear to hear your troubles. My shoulders are broad, though not quite as broad as Henry's, but I can shoulder your burdens. Just remember that. Maybe you should rest tomorrow?" James worried that she would internalize all of Adonia's problems, her own problems, Henry's problems and anyone else's problems that came her way. She was strong, he could see that, he just wished she would share some of the load. To make it worse, she was married in the eyes of the law, but not necessarily in the eyes of the church because of Henry's unexpected royal draft. He could only wonder what her thoughts were on the subject.

Izzy quietly finished her meal and excused herself, retiring to her chamber. Walking up the stairs, Izzy knew that the next week and even the next month were going to be a physical strain. It would be worth it though. She could not wait to hear that the families were able to move back into their homes. Arriving at her chamber, she pushed open the heavy door and was pleasantly surprised that her chemise was laying on the bed and a fire was roaring in the fireplace. She had barely changed and climbed into bed before she was asleep.

Chapter 5
January 1408
Adonia

Dear Lord Henry,

It is the end of January and Adonia has begun to show signs of recovery. It has been an incredibly long and painful process, but it has been worth it. With the help of Hugh, many of the townspeople and the knights, most of the houses of Adonia have been repaired and are now inhabitable again! There are still a few families that want to remain in the main barn with the animals, and I cannot blame them. My plan for next winter is to have a few smaller stables and barns built around town so that families can stay in their homes and also be close to their livestock. I wrote home to Ackerley after I first arrived in Adonia and asked Myles, my Constable, to ask around and purchase an ox for Adonia. I was thrilled when two weeks later an ox was delivered to us! We have been hard at work weeding the fields and putting our new ox to good use. The winter fields have all been plowed and most of them have been planted with beans, peas and onions! I invited the ladies in town to weave baskets in the great hall in the mornings and it seems to be working well. The attitude of many of the women has begun to change. They smile to one another passing through town and just last week, Emma (Adam's wife) helped Catherine to churn butter. I know that must sound trivial, but Catherine's husband passed three weeks ago and now Catherine and her young daughter are both ill. Emma has been milking Catherine's cow daily so the milk does not dry up. In fact, many of the women have started to work together around town to help each other. It is such a beautiful change! I have begun to clear out the private gardens of the weeds and am preparing to plant herbs this spring. I hope you like what I am doing for Adonia. Lord James and Lord Raymond were kind enough to escort me from Era to Adonia the day after you left. Lord James returned to Era after three days and Lord Raymond stayed for two weeks. Oh! Lady Jayde is expecting! She is due around the end of April or early May. I am excited to get to visit with her next month when I travel to Era. I will leave on the fourteenth and return on the twenty-fifth. Do you think you will be home in time for the birth? How are you doing? Do you need anything? Do you know if you will be returning home to Adonia anytime soon? Everyone here asks about you

> *frequently, I wish I had more information to give them. As soon as there is an update to Adonia's finances, I will write to you again. I hope you are well and safe and I am hoping to hear back from you soon.*
>
> > *Take care.*
> >
> > > *Lady Isabel*
> > >
> > > > *January 1408*

Izzy folded the letter, poured wax on it and stamped it shut with Adonia's seal. She sat back in the chair and stared at the fire. She questioned herself; why would she write a letter to a man who did not want to marry her? A man who left her without saying good bye, and had not even bothered to write to her while he was away? She considered burning the note and not wasting the money to send the message. She knew that the right thing to do was to send it though. Did she really believe that he would write back to her? She felt like such a silly woman, hoping for some sign of affection from a man who did not know her, and she only knew him from when she was a child. Sighing, she stood up and carried the letter downstairs where the messenger was waiting for her. "You will need to travel first to the King. From there you will be told where to find Lord Henry. After you deliver this message, see if there will be a message sent in return. If Lord Henry does not have a message to send in return, please return to me regardless and inform me of his whereabouts. I will pay you twice your regular fee when you return. Does all of that make sense?" Izzy relayed to the messenger.

"Of course, My Lady," he said. He accepted the note and put it in his bag, then turned and left for the stables. Just to reach the King would be a three-day journey, then possibly another three days to Lord Henry and up to six days for the return trip. Izzy watch the young man race out to the stables before turning to meet with both Hugh and Alice. She could not help but wonder where the messenger would report Lord Henry at. She was once again lost in thought as she walked thinking of one hundred things at once.

"Lady Isabel, is everything okay?" Hugh asked as Izzy approached. He could see her mind was preoccupied. Alice sighed and rolled her eyes when Izzy sat down.

Izzy had dealt with enough of Alice's attitude and contempt. "Alice, is there a problem? Is there something you need to share with me?"

Alice was startled by Lady Isabel's boldness. "No, um, no My Lady," she stammered.

"Then can you explain to me what I have done to you to deserve your disrespect?" Izzy waited a moment to see if Alice would even try to respond.

"You have done everything within your power since I have arrived here to make me miserable. You found the 'perfect' lady's maid for me. I had to dismiss her. She pulled my hair out when she combed it no matter how much I asked her to stop and please be careful. The next woman you brought in was no better. She was worse actually. She ripped my hair out and pinched my sides when she would pretend to help me dress. I finally lost trust in you and sent for Sadie, my lady's maid from home. I know that she will not cause me any harm. You go behind my back and change my orders for the kitchen, meals, and general household. I do not know how Lord Henry handled the household or staff, but I am here now and I am working day and night to get Adonia back to a place of beauty and profit. So, you have two choices. You can either join me and help me or get out of my way and be dismissed. Make your decision right now." Izzy waited this time for Alice to respond.

"My Lady, if you feel like I am not qualified for this position, I shall leave. You are accusing me of sabotage and I will not stand for it," Alice huffed.

"Alice! How dare you speak -" Hugh began.

"You are dismissed effective immediately Alice. Please collect your coat and go home." Izzy was firm. She looked Alice in the face and watched as this new reality was accepted.

It took Alice a moment to actually hear the words before she reacted. She was being fired! Slowly she stood and began to walk away. How dare she? Who did Lady Isabel think she was? Stopping, she turned around and marched back over to the table where Hugh and Lady Isabel remained seated.

"You cannot dismiss me! You do not own Adonia! You are nothing, a nobody! You think you are something special because you married his Lordship! If you are so special, then where is your husband? How do we know you are who you say you are? I will not leave my post unless Lord Henry himself dismisses me!" Alice screamed at Lady Isabel. She was so irate, she did not notice Hugh stand up and place his hands on her, nor did she hear him call for the guards.

Isabel remained seated until Alice had finished yelling in her face. She then stood, straightened her spine and pulled her shoulders back making herself as large as she possibly could. She would not allow Alice to intimidate her. When the guards came in and grabbed Alice, Isabel seemed just as startled as Alice. Isabel tried to keep calm and regained her composure as the guards dragged away the now kicking and screaming Alice.

The room had begun to fill with several of the staff as the commotion escalated. The entire kitchen staff were clutching linens or aprons watching the scene as Alice was dragged past them. Bess had Alice's coat in her arms and handed it to a guard as he passed. Then she turned and went back into the kitchen to continue working on her chores.

Hugh waited until Alice's screaming could no longer be heard. Then, in a booming voice, he announced, "Back to work unless you would like to be next!" Hugh and Izzy took their seats once again and he watched as Lady Isabel took a deep breath. "Are you okay?"

Izzy gave a tight smile and nodded.

"You did the right thing. Do not doubt yourself." Hugh could see the entire scene bothered her greatly. Just then, Bess appeared with two mugs of ale and a cup of chamomile tea. "My Lady, I was not sure which drink you would prefer, so I brought both." Bess turned around and began to walk away. She stopped and quickly walked back to Hugh and Lady Isabel. "My Lady, if I may be so bold to say, thank you. Thank you for dismissing Alice. I look forward to working under anyone that you choose and I am confident that they will do a far superior job." She smiled and disappeared back to the kitchen. She had chores to do and someone needed to pick up the pieces that Alice had left behind.

Izzy looked at Hugh as Bess walked away. "Has Alice been torturing everyone in the castle?"

"You have no idea! I am sure that many more than Bess will be grateful for your decision. Are you okay to continue with our meeting?" Hugh asked.

Izzy gratefully took a sip of the tea. "Yes, let us continue and not allow our day to be ruined." Quietly the two of them discussed the town, the people, buildings, farms, and animals.

"Lady Isabel, have you heard from Lord Henry yet? Has he said when he will be returning?" Hugh asked. "I do not mean to be rude or intrusive, but the knights need more training, and it is usually Lord

Henry that would train them. There are a few knights that are far more experienced than others, and they could lead training for now in his stead. If you would like to see them, I can take you out to the training fields tomorrow?"

"Unfortunately, I have not heard from Lord Henry yet. I have sent out a letter to him, so it is possible that within the next week or two I will receive a letter in return. As for training, yes, I think tomorrow I should accompany you to the training fields. I would like to appoint a couple of knights to lead training and have monthly meetings with them. I am sure that Lord Henry will send for knights occasionally and they should be battle ready. Hugh, we need to find a replacement for Alice. I cannot add her job to what I am already doing. Do you have any recommendations?" Izzy was nearing exhaustion again. The non-stop physical labor of helping to repair homes, weed and plow fields, and now working on weeding and preparing the private gardens for herbs depleted her of energy and strength every day. She had lost count of how many times in the last month she had been awakened because someone in the village was ill. She desperately needed to get the herb gardens planted and growing. She had already sent word to Ackerley and had small barrels of planted herbs sent over to keep indoors near windows. She was using these and hoping to be able to transplant them come April.

"My Lady, Bess would be an excellent choice. If you would rather bring someone from your home, I would understand, but I know that Bess is well respected by everyone here. Perhaps you could give her a try?" Hugh suggested.

"Yes, Bess can try. She will have one week to prove herself. If she fails, I will search for a replacement. If she succeeds however, I will extend her opportunity to a full month and then make it permanent if everything works out well. Does that sound reasonable?" Izzy was relieved for a simple answer for once.

"Yes, My Lady, very reasonable. I know that Bess would be proud to show you her skills. Would you like to tell her or rather I tell her?" Hugh questioned.

"I will tell her, Thank you though." Izzy yawned. It was still morning, but she already felt exhausted. She needed to wake up, she had jobs to do today that could not be put off until tomorrow. As soon as their meeting was over, she found Bess and told her of her temporary promotion and the conditions that went with it. Then Izzy grabbed her cloak and walked down to the houses below. She wanted to check on Catherine and her daughter as well as a couple of other women in town who were pregnant. One of the ladies had been due to deliver the week before. Izzy felt inside the pocket on the inside of her cloak for the blue and black cohosh, as well as the red raspberry leaf for tea.

Izzy was happy to see that both Catherine and her daughter were recovering quickly. Catherine said that as soon as they began to rub the eucalyptus oil on their feet, the coughs had gone away. Izzy left promising to check on them again in a few days and went on her way through town to check on Edith. Edith was about eight months into her pregnancy and doing wonderfully. Izzy did not worry about the health of either her or the baby. Leaving, she went to Clare's house. Izzy could hear the screams from down the road. Picking up her skirts, she sprinted up the hill until she reached Clare. Bursting into the home, she immediately ran to Clare's side. Clare was very petite and her belly was so large, Izzy knew it would be a long day but prayed that she would be able to help Clare bring this baby into the world safely.

It was nearly dawn the next morning when finally, Clare was able to hold her screaming, large baby boy.

"Clare, he is beautiful! Do you and John have a name chosen?" Izzy asked quietly as Clare began to nurse.

"John likes the name William and I think it fits him well," Clare whispered. Izzy cleaned up while Clare and William rested. When the sun had crested over the hill tops, Izzy left the tiny house and slowly made her way back to the castle. She could smell the day's bread being baked and felt her stomach rumble. She could not decide if she was hungrier or more tired, neither of which she could resolve to take care of first. As soon as she walked into the great hall, Bess and Hugh were at her side.

"My Lady! We have been searching for you!" Hugh said.

"My Lady, where have you been? We were so worried!" Bess added.

"Are you alright? Where have you been?" Hugh's voice was swimming with concern.

Izzy felt irritated at the barrage of questions. "I do not need to answer to either of you regarding my whereabouts!" Izzy snapped. Rubbing her temples, she looked at both Hugh and Bess, their expressions dismayed, as if she had slapped them with her words. "I am so sorry. I am so tired. I went to John and Clare's home and Clare had a very long and difficult labor. Both mom and baby are healthy and resting now, but I have not eaten anything since yesterday morning and have not had any rest either. I did not mean to be cross with either of you. I just need to rest."

"Of course, My Lady," Hugh said and quietly stepped away towards the kitchen.

Bess took Isabel's hand in her own and started towards the stairs that led to the chambers above. Izzy was so tired she did not notice anything that was going on around her. Suddenly there was bread in her hand as she was being guided up the stairs. She took a large bite of the bread, chewing as she climbed. Before she realized it, she was at the door to her chamber and the bread was half gone.

Bess led Lady Isabel to her chamber and waited at the door for her to go in. When she did not open the door, Bess opened the door and continued to lead Lady Isabel inside. She helped Lady Isabel undress even as she finished eating her bread, Bess stoked the fire and turned down the blankets. As soon as Lady Isabel had finished eating, she was given a drink of tea and she laid down in the bed, falling asleep as her head touched the pillow. Bess pulled up the covers and placed two smooth rocks from the edge of the fire under the covers at Lady Isabel's feet. Quietly, Bess returned to the kitchen and gave instructions to get a thick stew started for Lady Isabel.

Izzy woke up to the aroma of beef stew in her room. Sitting up, she saw the fire was strong and the steam rising up from the stew on the table. Yawning and stretching she made her way to the table at the fire and sat down. She closed her eyes and inhaled deeply, the decadent smell filling her lungs. Lifting the ladle from the pot she poured the thick, chunky stew into a bowl. Dipping the spoon into her bowl she blew on the contents and slowly took a taste. It was amazing and warmed her very soul. She would need to be sure to request this for future dinners. As she sat enjoying every bite of the beef stew, she could not help but wonder if Henry had ever had the pleasure of eating this. Izzy found herself wondering if he was injured or not if he was warm or cold and wet. She wondered again if he would respond to her letter. As Izzy was ladling a second bowlful of stew, there was a gentle knock on the door.

"Lady Isabel? It is Bess," she heard Bess call gently. If Lady Isabel was still sleeping, she did not want to wake her up, but if she was awake, she wanted to make sure that she did not need anything.

"Come in," Izzy called out.

"My Lady, how are you feeling?" Bess asked as she carried in a pot of tea and a mug.

"I am still tired but am feeling so much better. How late is it?" Izzy wondered out loud.

"It is quite late My Lady. The evening meal was served a couple of hours ago. Is there something you need?" Bess asked.

"Oh dear, I did not intend to sleep so much! I had wanted to go back to check on Clare and baby William. I guess I will just have to wait until morning now. I did instruct John that if there were any problems or questions to send for me right away no matter the time." Izzy was hopeful that everyone was well.

"My Lady, is there anything else I can get for you?" Bess inquired. It had been a long day for her as well. It was her second day as head servant and she had already made several changes within the castle and out that she hoped would make life easier for everyone.

"Thank you, Bess, I think I shall be fine. I am going to ladle one more bowlful of stew and then go back to bed. Will you see the cook on your way home?" Izzy asked, referring to her wonderful cook.

"Yes, My Lady. I walk home with Abigail each evening," Bess answered.

"Would you be sure to tell her how wonderful her stew is? This is my third bowl! Also let her know that I would like for her to make this once each week if she can!" Izzy requested.

Bess smiled and laughed. "Of course, My Lady! Abigail will be delighted to hear that someone loves her cooking!" Bess bid Izzy good night and left. Izzy sat before the fire drinking the tea that Bess had brought up and allowed her mind to wander.

Grabbing a quill and paper, Izzy wrote a quick note to her brother Andy. She signed it and sealed it and left it on the table to remind herself to give it to the messenger when she saw him next. There really should be at least one other messenger she thought to herself. She stoked the fire and added another log before climbing into bed and drawing the covers up to her chin. Izzy fell asleep quickly but tossed and turned through the night. She dreamt of her wedding day. The scene played over and over in her dreams and each time she felt the rejection and humiliation grow deeper. By the time she awoke, she was not sure that she wanted to hear from Lord Henry at all! After visiting Clare and baby William, Izzy tried to distract from her sour mood by throwing herself into pulling weeds from the place she intended to plant her herber.

It took nearly three days to finally remove all of the weeds from the herber. She enlisted several men from town to help her repair the stone walls and lattice that surrounded the gardens. In the midst of repairing the walls and lattice, the messenger that Izzy had sent out to Lord Henry returned.

Izzy had been working alongside the townsmen strengthening the stone wall when Hugh came for her.

"Excuse me Lady Isabel, but the messenger has returned and insists that he must speak with you and only you," Hugh informed her skeptically.

Izzy stood up and stretched her back. Brushing her dirty hand on her apron, she followed Hugh inside the castle to the hall where the messenger sat.

Gille jumped to his feet as soon as he saw Lady Isabel walk into the hall. "My Lady, my apologies for taking so long to return to you, but I had to wait for two days for the rebellion to be squashed, then another day before Lord Henry would even see me and then another two days for him to tell me his message to you. He said it would be a waste of time to write a message so short and that I needed to just memorize it and leave. His message was, 'Have Hugh send five of my best knights, and I am fine, just leave me alone. I will send word if I need anything.' That was it My Lady." Gille was nervously wringing his hands. If he ever sent a message like that to a woman, he would imagine the poor messenger getting the slap that was meant for him.

Izzy plopped down dejectedly in the closest cold, hard chair. Really? That was all that her husband had to say? Nothing about his sister-in-law, nothing about Adonia. Just 'leave me alone.' He had dismissed her. She was nothing to him. Forget the fact that she was his wife, but she was making his estate better! Izzy realized that she had been biting her lower lip. She had not done that in years, not since her parents had passed and Ackerley had fallen into such a poor state with Andy running it. There was nothing for her to do in response to his message. Taking a deep breath, she stood up.

Gille's worry grew. Lady Isabel had not said a word and now she looked determined and was standing up. He took a deep breath and lifted his chin boldly. He could take it like a man. She could do what she must and he would not even flinch.

"Gille, what on earth are you doing?" Izzy asked, eyeing him. The poor boy was standing braced for something with his eyes squeezed shut.

"I am preparing to accept the slap that you are about to deliver to Lord Henry My Lady. It is okay, I promise not to cry, I can take it," Gille declared bravely. After waiting another moment, and still not receiving a slap, he opened his eyes. Standing before him were Hugh and Bess who looked perplexed and Lady Isabel whose face was turning red.

103

Izzy struggled to keep her amusement hidden. She had covered her mouth and was struggling until she thought she was going to burst. Finally, she could not hold back any longer. She burst out laughing, crossing her arms over her stomach and bending forward. Suddenly, every emotion that she had stifled, every ounce of stress, each day that had passed since Christmas, came rushing over her and she collapsed to the floor in a heap. She laughed so hard that she began to cry and soon began gasping for air. When she was finally able to regain control of herself she looked up to see three very concerned faces staring back at her. She could not help herself, she began to laugh again, and when at last it was done she leaned back against the side of the chair and took a deep, calming breath.

"My Lady, are you well?" Gille asked.

Smiling, Izzy responded, "Actually Gille, I have never been better. In fact, I have not laughed like that since before my parents passed. The nuns frowned upon such frivolity and I honestly think I had forgotten how to." She sighed again. "How wonderful. Well, if Lord Henry wishes to be left alone, then alone I shall leave him." She accepted the extended hands from Gille and Hugh to help her up. "Thank you both. There is no point being upset over the message so laughter was the best way to handle it I suppose. I cannot help but find it funny how childish he is acting though. Gille, please follow Bess to the kitchen to get something warm to eat. I will send Hugh to you in a moment with the price we agreed upon." Izzy smiled again and waited for Gille and Bess to walk away before leading Hugh to the chamber above where she kept money for the messenger. There she handed Hugh Gille's payment as well as the note she had written for her brother. She hoped that Andy would be in a better mood receiving her letter than Lord Henry had been. After thanking Hugh, she returned to her work in the garden alongside the townsmen.

The next morning, Izzy went to the training fields after the morning meal. There she found Sir Calvin and Sir Merek. As she approached, the two men stopped their conversation and stood facing her, waiting for her to reach them.

"Calvin and Merek, the two men I was looking for!" Izzy teased.

"How can we be of service?" Calvin fired back.

"Lord Henry has sent word that he requires five of his best knights. I know that the two of you are the best, and that you are who he is requesting, but I would prefer it if you two would remain here in Adonia and send five knights of your choosing. My reasons for wanting you two to remain here, are that I need strong knights to lead everyone else, to train and to protect. Would you consider my request?" Izzy wanted them to have a part in the decision, after all, they knew which knights were strong and who needed to train more.

Merek was flattered that Lady Isabel considered him one of the best knights in Adonia and he could not help but to allow his chest to swell with pride. There was no doubt how skilled Calvin was, so to be considered equal to him was a great honor.

Calvin could see the pride exuding from Merek and realized that he too was proud of Lady Isabel's acknowledgment. Grinning, he said "Thank you for regarding us so highly."

"I believe that Calvin and I could group five great knights to send to Lord Henry. They would be ready to go by dawn, unless it is imperative that they leave immediately?" Merek questioned.

Clasping her hand in front of her, Izzy was relieved that she would be well protected here at home.

"Wonderful! Dawn will be fine. The messenger, Gille, will take you to their camp on his way to the King's Court. Please, let me know if there is anything that will be needed." Izzy was thrilled.

Both men nodded soberly as Izzy turned and walked away, but then slapped each other on the back jovially, wearing wide goofy grins.

Izzy returned to the gardens and devoted to keeping herself busy for the next week when it was finally time for her to visit Lady Jayde in Era.

Chapter 6
April 1410
Outside of Winchester

Hal was trying his best but could not get the spear tip out of the wound. They needed a doctor to help, but there were none that he trusted. "We need to move him out of the rain. Help me to carry him into his tent. I will figure out what we need to do then," Hal ordered.

"Yes sir," said one of the men as they helped to carry Lord Henry to his tent.

"Leave me to think a minute, I will call for you when I come up with a solution." Hal paced the tent. As the flap to the tent blew open from the cold night air, a small stack of papers fell from the table and onto the ground. Hal bent down to pick them up and saw they were letters. Glancing at the first one, he saw that it was signed 'your wife' and he was shocked. He had no idea that Henry was married as Henry had never mentioned that he had a wife. Curiosity got to Hal and he sat down to read the letters.

Dear Lord Henry

  Winter faded into a beautiful spring here in Adonia. The fields produced an abundant quantity of crops and the ladies in town took special care to dry the many beans, and the onions have been braided and stored in the cellars. Since we were unable to grow a large variety of winter crops, I have arranged for Ackerley and Adonia to trade and exchange. This has saved quite a bit of money for both estates. Summer has been amazing. The cliffs nearby have been a wonderful treat in the evenings. I wish I would have known about the view in the spring, I can only imagine the beauty it would have shown. The flowers in the trees blooming, the green sprouts in the fields growing. Next year, I will have to remember this special place.

Jayde is doing well. She gave birth to a daughter, Ellyn, on the first of May. James is completely smitten with his daughter. Every noise she makes, he is at her side. Jayde is happy and is looking forward to Christmas with Ellyn. Jayde and James have asked if you will be home, but I have no news to give them. I understand you do not like me. That is okay but have some decency and write to your family. They miss you and worry about you.

Is there anything special you would like for me to plan for Adonia for the upcoming winter or spring? The town is thriving and already there have been four successful births in town. All four children are thriving as well. Sir Calvin and Sir Merek have the knights on a rotation in town as well. They rotate between the fields, making repairs and building. We have already rebuilt three homes to replace the mud and stick dwellings. Closer to the center of town, a large barn was built to help keep the animals safer from predators and to prepare for winter again.

I know that you requested for me to leave you alone, but I cannot help but look at Adonia and think that she is far more precious to you than you reveal. I am letting myself believe that you have a love for Adonia like the love I have for my home. I took a trip back to the other estate in May and will return there for the entire month of October as well. If you should come home, and I am gone, that is where I will be. I wish you would tell me the truth about why you avoid me. If I have done something wrong, I will try to fix it.

Your wife,

Lady Isabel

September 1408

Dear Lord Henry,

Merry Christmas, at least I hope your Christmas was merry. Abigail sends the fruit cake, Jayde the hat and gloves, and I, well, the finance reports. Adonia is doing well and preparing for the much-missed spring. We actually made a profit from hogs that went to slaughter! The wheat and rye crops were successful but could have been better. We will rotate the fields again this spring to see if it will improve.

Little Ellyn is growing so fast! She is crawling and Jayde is pregnant again! She should be due sometime in July! She and James are both so excited! Your family is growing and you are missing it! I wish you would come home, if not to Adonia, then to Era. I have not heard from Andy in a while. If you hear from him or anything about him, will you please send word to me? I worry about him. He is not nearly as war ready as he would like to think.

Take care of yourself. I will write again soon.

Your Wife,
Lady Isabel

December 1408

Dear Lord Henry,

I still have not heard anything from my brother, Andy, and equally silent is you. The messenger says you are alive, so I continue to write to you regarding Adonia, my estate and your family. I commissioned a passing artist to paint a pocket portrait of the blooming orchards here in Adonia. I hope you like it. I thought his work was amazing and thought you would appreciate it. Spring was slow to start this year, and summer was not nearly as hot as last year. Our crops at both estates continue to do well. James, Jayde and Ellyn were out visiting in the spring, and Jayde was thrilled to see how healthy Adonia is looking. I had forgotten that this was once Jayde's home! She loved the herber and was impressed if not somewhat jealous of the quality of homes that are in town. James, of course, gave me a sideways glance, but Jayde and I just giggled. Oh! Jayde went into labor early! The twentieth of June, to twins! Two boys, both with dark hair and strong lungs. James of course is bursting with pride. They have named the boys Dario and Edward. I can only wonder what kind of Uncle you would be.

Poor Hugh fell and broke his leg in February. I helped him with his recovery and although he healed without a limp and has been crutch free for several months, he still says it aches from time to time, usually when the weather changes. Sir Merek was married in May. He married a young woman that he met last October from Ackerley. Both Sir Calvin and Sir Merek accompany me to Ackerley each time I take a trip, so I was not surprised when I learned that Merek had met someone. Have no worries though, Sir Merek is very dedicated to you and he and his new bride are happily settled here in Adonia.

We are hoping to have a small carnival next spring to bring in new people to Adonia and help the little town grow. If we are successful in the spring we will most likely have another carnival in the fall. Right now, the ladies from town are gathering fabric and are creating a large quilt that they plan to sell in the spring.

The people of Adonia miss you, do not forget that. Your family loves and misses you as well.

> *Be well Lord Henry.*
> *Your Wife,*
>> *Lady Isabel*

>>> *August 1409*

Hal stopped reading even though there were two more letters in the stack. Henry had a wife who was a healer! She could help them! Using the quill and paper at Henry's table, he wrote a quick message and then stamped it with the seal on his ring. He ran out of the tent and called for the messenger. "Get this to Adonia. Give it to Lady Isabel only. How fast can you get there?"

"If I leave immediately, I can be there by dawn," the messenger said.

"Go then, go right now. Do not stop to rest. Henry's life depends on it," Hal said before returning to the tent. He knew that the injury to Henry's side would get infected and the longer he went without treatment, the worse he would be. Already the wound had caused a fever. If only Henry would have told him of his injury yesterday.

The messenger nodded and tucked the sealed note into his bag as he ran. He mounted his horse and left the camp at a full gallop. He did not stop until he reached Adonia.

Isabel was just finishing dressing for the day. Today she was to meet with individual townspeople to hear their needs and concerns and offer solutions as well as accept rent. She was wearing a pretty yellow linen gown with a cream over tunic. As she tied her braid, she heard a rider quickly approaching the castle. She rushed down the stairs praying that James, Jayde and the children were not injured. Izzy came into the hall at the same time as an exhausted and wet messenger who stood there pushing hands away from him.

"PLEASE! I must speak with Lady Isabel!" the messenger stated too loudly again.

Rushing forward Izzy placed her hands on the boy's shoulder. "I am Lady Isabel. Who is injured?" Her stomach sank as she spoke the words.

The messenger pulled the sealed note from his bag and handed it to her.

Izzy recognized the seal of the King and her worst fear came to her. It was Andy, he was wounded or dead or about to die.

Hugh grabbed Lady Isabel by the shoulders when he saw the color drain from her face and guided her to sit on the bench nearest to them.

Izzy's hands shook as she broke the King's seal and opened the note. She read it and finally sucked in air. Tears of relief rolled down her face. It was not Andy, but Henry. His Royal Highness was requesting her immediate departure from Adonia to travel to the campsite to save Henry's life. Izzy looked up at the messenger, "Are you well enough to travel?"

"Yes My Lady, but you should know, it is not an easy ride." The messenger looked at her frame as he spoke. He was not sure if she would be able to endure it. "I would also require a rested horse."

"Hugh, help him get three horses ready, I will be ready to travel in five minutes," Izzy ordered.

"My Lady, which knight should I tell to accompany you?" Hugh asked just as Sir Calvin and Sir Merek ran in.

"I will not need any knight to protect me. I am going as a healer," Izzy explained.

Without any hesitation both Calvin and Merek opened their mouths to object.

"Like hell you will travel alone!" Calvin's voice boomed.

"I would just as soon rot in my grave before you travel alone!" Merek shouted over Calvin.

"I do not have time to waste on arguments. Sadie, pack two garden gowns, needles and as much silk thread as you can find as well as several linen sheets. Be at the stables in less than five minutes." Izzy addressed her good friend and lady's maid who had been standing nearby. She then jumped up and ran up the stairs to pack her own garden gowns and needles. Shouting back down the stairs as she ran, "Bess! Get me a couple of bottles of brandy or bourbon!" Then she disappeared above. Opening the trunk, she found two garden gowns. They were identical. Plain, brown gowns with loose fitted sleeves, and beige aprons. She wore these when she worked in the herber or the fields to hide the dirt and stains. She grabbed her thick riding gloves and a clean kirtle. Then, digging deeper into the trunk she found a large messenger bag and laid it on the bed. She rolled her two gowns and stuffed them into the bag followed by her kirtle. Taking the bag and her gloves, she ran downstairs and began to pick herbs from the garden. She grabbed handfuls of clove, peppermint, lavender, cat's claw, and calendula. She ran back into the castle, straight to the cellar, where she grabbed garlic, ginger and licorice root. Adding these final items to her bag she went back to the hall where Bess had two bottles of brandy and her cloak waiting for her. Careful to protect the herbs in the bag, she wedged the bottles in as well.

"Bess, I will send word with a messenger in the next few days. Keep things calm here, please." Izzy turned and left as Bess nodded. She went straight back to the kitchen to alter the day's plans.

Izzy fastened her cloak over the full messenger bag as she ran to the stables. Everyone was waiting.

"Are these our fastest horses?" she asked.

"Yes My Lady. The other horses are war horses and will not run as quickly," the stable boy answered.

"Hugh, keep Adonia safe and happy. You have the note?" Izzy asked.

"Yes My Lady," Hugh nodded.

"Good, burn it. Do not let anyone see it or read it. I will send word in a few days. Say nothing to anyone, including Lord James and Lady Jayde." Izzy was clear with her instructions and trusted that Hugh would follow them.

"We need to leave now Lady Isabel," Sir Calvin reminded her.

"Go!" Izzy ordered. The group of five kicked their horses forward leaving the safety of the castle walls.

They stopped every few hours to let the horses breathe for ten minutes while they ate bread and cured meats, pushing their horses hard, they finally made it to the campsite outside of Winchester. Hal heard the group of horses as they came thundering through the woods. He had several archers in position and waiting for the order to fire at the intruders when he recognized the messenger. Behind him was a petite red head, fierce looking blonde and two large knights. The archers stepped aside to allow the riders through. Hal grabbed the horses that belonged to the two women while they dismounted. His breath caught when he got a better look at the blonde rider. She was beautiful, and her strength exuded from her like light radiating from a candle.

Isabel recognized His Royal Highness immediately and curtsied deeply while Sadie followed her lead. "Your Royal Highness-" Izzy began but was interrupted.

Her curtsy brought him back to reality. "Here, you must call me Hal, and please, no more curtsies. Are you Lady Isabel?" Hal asked.

"Yes, but please just call me Izzy," she replied.

"Izzy, I had no idea that Henry was married. I would never have allowed him to remain here without break to go home had I known. Please accept my apologies," Hal offered.

Izzy smiled sweetly, "Where is he now? Does he know that you have sent for me?"

"Right this way." Hal guided her towards Henry's tent by her elbow. "I have not told him that I sent for you only because he is delirious with fever and would not understand or remember any way."

"That is fine. Let us keep it that way for a while." Walking into the darkened tent, she could barely see. "I must have more light in here if I am going to help him." When she moved closer, she could see that his skin was flushed but dry as his body fought the fever. As Hal created more light in the tent, Izzy and Sadie immediately went to work. First, they extracted the spike that was lodged in his side. She cut the resulting gash open wider and when she did, a small amount of pus oozed out of it. She grabbed a bottle of brandy and poured a small amount on the wound then immediately soaked it up with a clean strip of linen.

Henry moaned as the brandy seeped into the wound. "I know, hush, this could not be as painful as having to be married to me. You will be fine, I promise," Izzy chastised quietly.

The two women worked carefully to stitch the deep wound closed, carefully stitching the inner layer of muscle with silk, and then tending to the outer layer. They had to stretch his skin to cover the wound but managed to do it very quickly. Using silk thread again, Izzy carefully tied each stitch with the hope that when she had to remove them, they would not be painful, but she had done this enough times to know that was wishful thinking.

Sadie washed her hands then began to clean up their tools. Izzy washed her hands as well then, she turned to Hal. "Hal, is there someplace that Sadie and I can put our belongings?"

Yes, I had a tent assembled for you while we awaited your arrival. My apologies for not having a second tent already assembled, I was not expecting two of you. I will have it taken care of in the morning. Until then, Izzy, I will show you to my tent and I will stay here with Henry.

Izzy smiled as she had so many times before when having to take control of the situation from a man. She knew that Hal's intentions were good, but this was not how she was trained and she had no intention of changing the way she worked any time soon. "Hal, would you escort Sadie to her tent, and Sir Merek and Sir Calvin as well. Thank you." She left no room for negotiations as she turned back around to face Henry who looked even worse than he had when they first arrived.

Izzy sat down and faced Henry, noticing that with the exception of a few added lines to his face, he appeared the same. She found him to be just as attractive as the day they met. Her fingers ached to reach out and touch his dark hair, to trace his jaw and caress his dark skin. The glow from the candles made the cold night feel a little warmer and for a moment, Izzy was back at Era, the day after Christmas, on her wedding day, hoping for a bright future. A gust of wind brought Izzy back to the present. Turning quickly to face the tent flaps, she saw that the wind was not the only thing that had interrupted her past. Henry came in rubbing his hands together.

"Hal, what are you doing back here?" Izzy asked as Henry walked towards her.

Hal watched her lips move envisioning them closer to his lips. "I, uh, thought I was escorting you to my tent so that you could rest."

"Oh, that is sweet, but I am here now and will stay up through the night with him. I am going to make a poultice to help with his pain and some tea for him to drink. Our next battle will be fighting the fever and infection. You should get some rest, tomorrow will be an equally long day." Izzy spoke quietly and kindly.

Hal nodded and was about to leave when he decided he had a question that must be answered. "I need to know why you are in no hurry for your husband to know you are here with him."

Izzy thought for a moment before answering him. She began pulling herbs from her bag and arranged them on the small table. As she worked she told Hal everything from the beginning.

Hal sat quietly listening as Izzy spoke, mesmerized by how graceful and strong her movements were. He continued listening while grinding herbs for her, and finally understood the letters he had read. The letters had felt loveless for the man, but not the land, but maybe he was wrong. If she did not have some love for him, then why would she be here? Then again, how could she love a man she barely knew? He felt more confused than he had before. What he did know was that Lady Isabel was a beautiful, strong and educated woman and he wondered if there was any chance that he could make her his.

"There is more to the story. I only recently discovered the truth behind the rush of our marriage. I played along with the story that Lord James and Lord Raymond told me but learned the truth from a maid in Era. It seems that Lord James had gone missing, bound and tortured by a vengeful mad man for months. During this time, Henry's sister-in-law, Jayde, searched and trained with her soldiers. When Henry was finally informed of his brother's abduction, he went to Era, and fell in love with his sister-in-law. Somehow, and I cannot explain why I feel this, but I do not believe he actually fell in love with Lady Jayde. I think he fell in love with the fantasy of being in love or being loved as much as Lady Jayde loves Lord James. This is partly why I continue to write to Henry. I hope that eventually he will realize that he never actually loved her, will quit punishing himself and just maybe accept me as his friend." Izzy continued mixing and grinding herbs while she spoke.

"He will want to know who you are. I do not want to lie to him. He has a right to know that you, his wife, were the one to save him. What makes you think that he will not recognize you? You are quite

121

unforgettable," Hal spoke honestly with lustful images crossing his mind while he hid his feelings as best as he could.

Although Izzy was flattered, his words did not charm her. "If he recognizes me, then of course I will tell him. However, he was so drunk during our vows, I doubt he will even remember me at all. He might know me, but not be able to put a finger on the memory."

"How do you want me to introduce you to him then, if he does not recognize you?" Hal asked.

Izzy thought about it. "Lady Isabel Bird will be fine."

Hal looked perplexed for a moment. "I know that name…"

"My brother is Lord Andrew Bird of Ackerley. Well, used to be of Ackerley. He gave it up as dowry when I was married. Do you know him?" Izzy asked anxiously now at the prospect of hearing any news of her brother.

"I know of an Andrew Bird, but have not met him. I do not know of his whereabouts now though. I am sorry. I can inquire for you if you would like," Hal offered.

"No, thank you. I do not wish to waste resources. If he were deceased, they would send word." Izzy began to mix tea with ground herbs to make the poultice, trying to take her mind from such a tragic thought as that of her brother passing. Then, with Hal's help, she lined up several long strips of linen under Henry's back. She applied the poultice to the wound, covering it with several layers of short strips of linen. She then covered it all up with long linen. "He needs to drink one cup of this tea three times a day for the next week." Izzy then applied the ground lavender across his forehead. She combined the peppermint with lavender and applied it to his spine and the soles of his feet. "Once I pull his stitches, I should probably return home."

"If you need to rest, I can bring in a cot for you. Then at least you can try and rest while he is resting," Hal said.

"I appreciate the offer, but I need to be awake through the night to watch his fever," Izzy explained as she continued to grind herbs.

"Would you prefer silence or some company?" Hal asked.

"I would love some company. Thank you." Izzy felt the awkward silence as he took a seat near her. She hated awkward silence. "Tell me Hal, what does Henry talk about?"

Hal thought of the random conversations they had shared over the past two and a half years. They had shared quite a few laughs, but mostly spoke of war strategy, moving and the training of troops. He frowned as he remembered when he learned about Henry's marriage.

Izzy stopped grinding herbs and looked at Hal. He had been silent for too long, and now he had a frown on his face. She waited for him to come back to the present.

Hal realized that Izzy was standing there just staring at him. "My apologies, I was just thinking. Remembering actually. I remember just this past October, what we did to him for his birthday." Hal forgot for a moment that Izzy was Henry's wife. "The men all pitched in and got him a, um, memorable night- um, well, nothing actually." Hal bumbled, realizing his mistake too late. He had no idea how to get himself out of this situation.

"I see. So, for his birthday, which is in October, you all bought him an evening of physical pleasure rather than send him home to his wife?" Izzy sighed. She was silly to have dreamt that rescuing him would change him or make him like her. "I have spent the past two and a half years imagining what it might be like if he had not felt obligated to agree to marriage. I cannot even begin to imagine how he must resent me. No, I think I can, he has not come home since we said our vows."

Hal watched Izzy speak and saw the wave of sadness and defeat that washed over her while she spoke. "This will probably not make you feel any better, but Henry has not spoken much of his personal life. I had no idea that Lord James had even been abducted."

Izzy laughed, "You are right Hal; that did not make me feel better at all. If I may ask, how and when did you find out that Henry was married?"

124

Hal studied her for a moment. She seemed genuinely curious, not angry. "I began to wonder at his last birthday but had not asked. As I said before, everyone pitched in for his, um, evening. We got him drunk to get him to loosen up first, then shoved her in his tent. After a few minutes, we could hear him yelling at her that she had no right and that she needed to leave. After he had sobered up, he simply said that he had obligations and that he could not participate in our gift, but did not go into any further detail. Yesterday, when we brought Henry into his tent, the wind blew against your letters. I was curious and read them. You can imagine my shock in learning that he was married. It was then that October made sense. Since he kept his marriage hidden, I can honestly say that I was not expecting you." Hal found it difficult to imagine keeping a woman as beautiful and confident as she was a secret.

"I guess we do not all meet expectations. I fear I am not the striking beauty as some other ladies are, but I am smart, honest and loyal to a fault. Nothing special." Izzy felt plain; blonde hair, blue eyes and pale lips, obviously nothing special. She looked up after minutes of silence to see a look of disbelief and shock on Hal's face. "I find that it is better to admit the truth than to live a lie." Again, the dumbfounded expression on Hal's face troubled her.

"Nothing special; I am not sure that those could be words used to describe you and I cannot believe that any man could be so incoherent that they would not remember you. It is interesting that you think that Henry does not care for you. I say this because of how weathered the letters are. You can look at them yourself and see how worn and soft they are. It is as though he has read them a hundred times each. So, if you are so plain, then why keep your letters and reread them so often?"

Izzy could not answer for fear of letting some childish hope or fantasy be revealed. She felt her heart flutter and bit her lip to keep from smiling and blushing.

Hal saw the faint smile on her face before she bit her lip. The smile gave her striking features a softness that warmed the tent.

Izzy felt her heart continue to beat wildly in her chest. She had to turn away from Hal. Facing Henry, she reached her hand out to his flushed face. She felt his cheeks and forehead. His skin was hot and dry. She took out one of the bottles of brandy and added it to the ground up herbs.

"Would you help me?" Izzy asked. "I need you to grab that linen there," she said pointing to a stack of them. "Then, once I take his boots off, I am going to rinse his feet and apply this poultice. As soon as I apply the poultice, I want you to place the linen over the poultice. I will tie it around each foot. Hopefully this will help with the fever."

Hal jumped up from his seat and did as he was asked.

"Next I need to roll him gently to his side and smear some of this down his spine," Izzy explained. Hal jumped to action again. He was grateful for something to do to help rather than just sitting and watching Izzy work. After that was done, Hal stood silently behind Izzy feeling uncomfortable and useless. "So, what next? What do we do now? How long until he is healed?" Hal fired off his questions. Izzy spoke softly as she sat down on a chair near Henry. "Now, we wait. Depending on how severe his infection is will determine how long it will take for him to heal. The herbs we just put on him will hopefully help lower his fever. The poultice on his wound will help fight the infection and keeping it clean will prevent any future infections. When his fever drops, he will probably try and be tough and swear he can resume activity. He *must* remain in bed and rest so that he will heal. He could reopen his wound and the chances of him recovering from a second infection are slim. You must command him to rest. I doubt he will listen to anyone else." Hal nodded his understanding. Then the two sat in silence for over an hour both lost in thoughts, both not wanting to reveal their awkwardness, or vulnerabilities. Finally though, Hal could take no more. "Izzy, in the letters that you wrote to Henry, you seem to love Adonia and seem to only write of the happenings of the town and Henry's family. Does Adonia truly keep you that busy?"

Izzy answered cautiously. "I do like Adonia and the people are wonderful. There has been such a wonderful change these past two years for the town. The people have come together, and they help one another, as well as give their help to me without hesitation. I do miss home though and have tried to visit Ackerley at least three times each year. The beginning of fall is my favorite time to visit."

"Ackerley? I've heard of it, but never visited. Tell me more about it and how you grew up." Hal mused. He watched as Izzy's eyes lit up at the opportunity to talk about Ackerley.

"Ackerley is beautiful. It is so different from Adonia. Adonia is just starting to heal, but Ackerley has been a healthy community since my parents took it over. When you take the road up to the castle, it is lined by dozens of giant oak trees. During the winter when the snow has fallen, the lines from the dark, naked branches cut across the grey sky so gracefully. The beautiful bright new leaves in spring could put a smile even on Henry's face, if he would visit. Then the large leaves offer a cool cover for the hot summer months. In the fall, the big beautiful leaves change colors. There are shades of red and purple, light yellow and rich golds. It is breathtaking. Once through the gate, there is a beautiful duck pond. I used to sneak away as a little girl and sit at the water's edge soaking my feet in the cool pond. Andy and I spent many hours hiding in the tall reeds around the pond avoiding our parents and causing quite a bit of trouble. Once my parents passed, Andy threw himself into training and I was left alone. Finally, the nuns took me in and taught me everything I know about herbs, healing, midwifery, and running the estate. By the time I was fifteen, I was being called a healer by the nuns and the townspeople. It is hard to be away from home, but I feel like Adonia needs me more than I need Ackerley. I would not write at all, but it seemed as though Henry really loved Adonia. So, I stay there and hope to bring it to its full potential of prosperity and life." Izzy took a moment. "I write of nothing but Adonia and his family to Henry because I do not think he cares to hear about anything else; mainly not me. Truthfully, he does not care for me. I was not in his plans and I think he would rather die on the battlefield than have to come home to Adonia if I am still there. When he is done fighting, and he wishes to return home, I will hand over Adonia to him and my only request will be for him to allow me to continue to manage Ackerley. I truly believe that Henry loves Adonia the way I love Ackerley and I doubt that there will ever be room in his heart for me." Izzy became quieter having reached the end of her story. She sat silently, staring at Henry but not actually seeing him. Her mind was far away, on the hill with summer ending and fall beginning, feeling the cool breeze catch her hair, and listening to the sharp rustle of the oak leaves as the wind dashed across their surface.

Hal wanted to know why it was that Izzy cared so much for land that belonged to a man that she believed did not love her and how she could be so willing to give it up. Hal continued to ask questions through the night about Adonia and Ackerley. He suspected that Izzy hoped for true love and a change of heart from Henry.

"I know that your wedding was rushed but tell me about it. Who was there, were there any gifts, what did you eat?" He listened until she finished telling him about giving Henry a tongue lashing and he burst out in laughter.

Izzy had been hesitant to share of how she had spoken to Henry, but when she heard Hal's laughter in the quiet night, she could not hold back any more either. She heard the familiar sound of her own laughter escape her lips and started to laugh so hard that she began to cry. Her tears of laughter became tears of anguish until she buried her face in her hands and released the past years of hate, hurt, and feelings of inadequacy.

Hal's laughter quickly died as Izzy's laughter turned to tears. He felt uncomfortable and unsure of what to do, just sitting and staring at her. Should he reach out to comfort her or let her have this moment of despair? He sat quietly, listening to her pain escape from the protective shell she had kept for so long. He watched as this young woman became even stronger by being vulnerable to him. He had learned from King Richard II that sometimes strength came from weakness. So he waited until Izzy's tears lost their power. When they slowed, he reached out his hand and wiped away the remaining tears that slid down her cheek. Realizing what he was doing, he drew his hand back quickly.

Izzy felt a crimson blush of embarrassment creep into her cheeks as she struggled to compose herself. "Please forgive me, I did not mean to be so weak and make you uncomfortable."

Hal studied her as she spoke and after she was finished, he observed her pulling herself together and tucking everything back into the protective shell that she had built up over the years. She became the healer that she was trained to be; controlled, strong, and yet there was this bit of childlike hope that struggled to survive. There was much more to Lady Isabel de Seaton and he could not help but wonder if Henry would ever recognize it. "Izzy, I know that I asked you to come here to heal Henry, but do you think you would mind tending to some of the other men in camp? Last week, one of the men was cut and now it is severely infected. I worry that we will have to cut his limb. Is that something you could help me with or is that too much to ask?" It would be such a great help if she stayed on and helped, and it would give him time to get closer to her.

Izzy heard the question and was so excited that she choked as she tried to answer. She coughed quite hard until she was finally able to clear her throat. "Yes! I would love to help!" Again, Izzy was

embarrassed by her sudden burst of emotion.
Usually she was very calm and collected, but these
were not usual circumstances.

Hal was pleased that something so simple brought so
much joy to her. She reminded him of his youngest
sister, Philippa. He was the only one of the brothers
who still called her by her pet name of Pippa, even
though she was a Queen. Pippa had been married
young, at just twelve to King Eric, but was now
eighteen; just about Izzy's age. Hal smiled thinking
of the trouble that he and Pippa used to get into when
they were kids. He could imagine that Izzy and
Andy were very much the same. Lost in thoughts of
his youth he did not notice that he was being studied
by Izzy.

Izzy watched Hal as he got lost in his own thoughts
of a place or time that was not here or now. She
watched a soft, thin lipped smile soften his angular
features and wondered what his thoughts were. She
looked away when she felt Henry stir at her side.
Returning her attention to the sick man, she felt his
forehead again. His fever had finally broken.

Hal snapped back to the present when he saw Izzy
move from the corner of his eye. He watched her
face relax as she laid a hand on Henry's forehead.
"How is he?"

Izzy smiled. "His fever has broken, but do not get
too excited. His recovery will be long, there may be
setbacks, and until the infection has cleared his body,
he will fever again. For now, though, we can both

get some rest. Help me to reapply some oils on his feet and spine, then I should get what little sleep I can before the camp begins to wake. I will want to see everyone who has injuries tomorrow.

Hal did as he was told and then left the tent. It was predawn, and the dark night sky was beginning to lighten. Soon the burst of colors that teased of sunrise would appear and the camp would begin to awaken. He stretched and breathed in the cool spring air. He wondered if Henry would recognize Izzy or if Izzy was correct and she would be a stranger to him. Hal walked to his tent and saw that the fire had been kept well fed through the night. He entered his tent, took his boots off and collapsed into bed, dragging a blanket over his body and surrendering to sleep.

Izzy listened to Hal walk away before she busied herself prepping herbs for the morning. She knew that she should be resting, but it would be horrible to wake up in the morning and not have everything that she would need to treat the men in the camp. She would get rest later.

Hal woke up to the same sounds and smells as he always did. The sound of steel clashing with steel, and grunts from blows either deflected or taken. He could smell meat being cooked over a fire and felt his stomach rumble. Stiff, he rolled from the cot, found his boots and laced them up, then stepped out of the tent. The bright morning sky blinded him for a moment. When his eyes adjusted, he was surprised by what he saw. In front of him, was a line of twenty or so men standing patiently. He followed the line until he found Izzy. It was almost comical; there she was, short and curvy standing before a large battle-scarred man. He watched Elliot wince as Izzy squeezed his hand. Quietly chuckling to himself and shaking his head, he turned and walked towards Henry's tent.

Henry was being tended to by the woman from the night before, Sadie, if he remembered her name correctly. She was petite, plain and polite. She barely spoke except to ask Henry to roll over as she applied a cold poultice down his back. Henry startled when Hal came in. Struggling, he attempted to sit up only to have the timid Sadie bark an order at him to lie back and rest. Not daring to question her authority, and slightly fearful of her as well, he did as he was told and laid back.

"He is not allowed to get out of that bed unless it is to relieve himself." Sadie paused as she walked past Hal. Turning around, she faced him, "I will know if he has gotten out of bed, and I will tell Lady Isa-"
Hal could not let her blurt out Izzy's name. "I understand, Sadie. I believe Lady Bird is waiting for a second set of hands. I promise to keep him in bed."

Sadie was bothered that she had been interrupted but found herself more curious as to why he referred to Izzy as Lady Bird. She would ask Izzy later.

Nodding to Hal, she turned and left the tent in search of 'Lady Bird'.

Hal moved a stool next to Henry's cot. "How are you feeling?"

"Tired. Strange." Henry thought for moment. "I feel like I have forgotten something. Something very important. The more I struggle to figure out what it is, the more exhausted I become. How long have I been asleep?"

"You have been asleep for nearly three days. How do your wounds feel?" Hal was curious how effective the herbs that Izzy had used really were.

"Sore. Like I had a spike lodged in my side," Henry attempted to joke. "How did you manage to get it out, everything we did seemed to have driven it deeper."

Hal waited a moment before replying. "I sent for a healer. It took her less than one minute to extract that spike. She is very knowledgeable. I am sure she will be in sometime today to check on you personally." Hal could not imagine anyone forgetting Izzy and was curious how Henry would act when he was introduced to his wife. "Are you hungry?"

"I am famished. Do you really think the boss will know if I get out of bed?" Henry half asked, and half teased.

Hal smiled. "As vicious as Sadie seems, she learned her skills from the healer. I would be more worried about what the healer would do if I were you." Hal did not have to imagine too hard to envision Izzy's pretty face turning cold and getting mean. He was certain she had faced her fair share of skepticism and whining people with injuries and ailments of all kinds.

"A healer huh? A healer is a woman from the nunnery, correct?" Henry could only imagine how old the woman was and how jaded she was from a life of servitude.

"Usually, but not this one. She is a smart, young woman. She reminds me quite a bit of Pippa actually," Hal reflected.

"Young, smart, pretty? Are you not worried that the men in camp would try and take advantage of her?" Henry was curious how Hal intended to protect this young woman.

"Something tells me that she will be well protected. I will speak with everyone and explain my expectations, and consequences should those expectations not be met. However, I believe she will be safe here with us." Hal wondered when Izzy would be in to check on Henry and how Henry would react. The suspense was killing him! "Well, I am going to go make my rounds, I will come check in on you later. Stay in bed. I do not want to be in trouble with Sadie or Lady Bird."

Henry nodded and felt his body grow heavy with sleep. Just then Sadie came back in with a tray of food.

"I am not a servant, do not get accustomed to me bringing you food. I am doing this as a favor to

Lady Bird and Hal. You need to eat as much of this as you can, your body needs to heal. I will return later with some help so that you may relieve yourself, and then return straight to bed. Lady Bird will be in later to check on your wound as well." Sadie did not wait for Henry to respond or ask any questions before she left the tent.

Alone again, Henry ate the food that had been brought to him. There was bacon, porridge and two boiled eggs. Devouring everything, he carefully set the empty tray on the stool that Hal had left next to the bed. Leaning back against the pillows, Henry fell asleep within moments. As he slept, he was transported back to the castle in Era. He could hear James saying something but could not quite discern the words being spoken. He could hear Jayde laughing, but could not see her face. There was another woman laughing, but he did not recognize her laughter. She sounded so young and happy. He walked through the castle searching for the voices, never quite able to reach them. Henry jolted awake, feeling frustrated and lonely.

"Hal, do you have a moment to spare? I am about to scc to Lord Henry and his wound. Would you like to join me?" Izzy asked.

"Of course. Where has Sadie disappeared to? I thought she was to assist you with Henry?" Hal asked.

"She was, however, there were a few more men that decided that they needed some attention to their injuries." Izzy said with a chuckle pointing towards the group of men that had been training all morning. Those same men were now gathered together listening and watching Sadie explain how they could help themselves to keep minor injuries clean and when to ask for help.

Smiling, Hal nodded and led the way to Henry's tent. Pulling back the tent flap, he waited for Izzy to enter first.

"Good afternoon Lord Henry, how are you feeling? I see that you were able to eat something this morning," Izzy said as she walked into the tent and pulled some more herbs from her apron pocket. She pulled out a tied bunch of Rosemary and handed them to Hal. "Please take these to the fire and light just the tip on fire, then bring it back here."

Henry waited until she was done giving orders to the crown prince and facing him before he answered her question. If the prince did not disobey her, then he was not about to cause any problems either.

Izzy moved the tray, then sitting down on the stool next to Henry, she began to grind lavender, peppermint, and lemon leaves. She sat there silently grinding the leaves and herbs, waiting of Henry to say something.

Henry sat silently in bed staring at his clasped hands waiting for Hal to return, hoping and praying that he would know how to speak to this tiny powerful creature sitting next to him.

Hal finally got the damned bunch of rosemary lit and carefully shielding the flame with his hand, slowly walked back to the tent holding his breath. This was his fourth attempt. Each time he lit the green needles of the plant, the flames would immediately go out. Walking into the tent, this time proud of himself he gently handed the still flickering rosemary to Izzy. "It took me four times, but I finally got it!"

Izzy smiled at Hal as she took the burning rosemary, then blew out the flame and carefully set it on a stone near the head of the bed.

"Why did you blow that out? Did you not hear me when I said that it took me four, FOUR, times to light that thing and then walking slower than the dead to get it to you still lit? Why would you do that?" Hal was upset and confused and did not even try to hide his agitation.

Henry had never seen the prince like this before and was both amused and startled by the outburst. Hal almost looked as though he could cry.

"Oh, Hal, I appreciate your time and effort! It was so thoughtful and sweet that you wanted to keep the rosemary actually on fire, but I simply need it to smoke. It helps to clear the air and it will help to keep Lord Henry from getting sick while he is healing," Izzy clarified. "It is okay, truly, I appreciate your help!" She waited a moment before speaking again. "Are you angry?"

Hal could hear that Izzy's words were genuine. He felt embarrassed by his outburst and worse that she thought he was angry with her. "No, of course not. I am not angry. I was just confused and ignorant of what the herb was for and how it was used." Hal smiled. He hoped it was a convincing smile and that Izzy would leave his embarrassment and him alone. Izzy nodded and went back to grinding the herbs. After a minute, Hal and Henry began to converse. Izzy listened to their conversation, keeping herself busy so that she could learn how Henry was actually feeling, and more about who he was. She thought that she was going to hear nothing but war talk between the two men until Hal asked Henry about the family.

"Have you spoken to either of your brothers recently?" Hal asked.

"No, I have not been keeping in touch with them," Henry kept his answer short and sweet.

"Why not? Do you not want to learn if you have any nieces or nephews? Has Raymond married yet?" Hal pushed.

Henry hesitated before finally answering. "I do not keep in touch with my family because," again Henry hesitated. "...because I made several problems for myself at home before you sent for me. If I just leave everyone alone, maybe they will forget me and then they will not have to deal with the problems that I created."

"What about a woman? Do you not have a sweetheart or someone at home that you miss?" Hal pressed again.

Suspicion crept up Henry's neck. His eyes shifted to the last place he left his letters and seeing that they were all still there stacked neatly and seemingly undisturbed, he relaxed. "Why do you ask?" Henry asked slowly.

"I am merely curious. We will be taking a longer break and I must travel back to my father for a few days. Several men are also choosing to return home for a break for the next two weeks. I think it would be a good idea if you returned home to heal during that time as well. As soon as you are healed, you may return and we can go back to squashing these rebellions. What do you think, will you return home?" Hal asked.

Henry looked towards the healer. "I might just stay here and let the healer care for me. No use worrying or bothering them over me."

"I believe that Lady Bird was intending to return to her home once you were no longer on bed rest. Unless you can convince her otherwise, you will be on your own or you can return home." Hal stipulated.

Izzy cleared her throat. "Excuse me, Hal, I need your help to apply more poultice to his back."

Henry objected, straining to move his own body as Hal tried to help him roll to his side.

"STOP! If I wanted your help, I would have asked," Izzy ordered. "Your job is to not use your abdominal muscles at all if it can be helped. If you rip your wound open, not only will you experience extreme pain, but then I will have to try and fix you again.

Now sit back, and relax while Hal and I work."
There was authority in Izzy's voice that impressed
and shocked both men. She commanded their
cooperation and compliance and left no room for
disobedience.

Henry relented and let Hal roll his body as Lady Bird
applied the cool poultice. When Henry was lying on
his back again he thanked her.

"I am going to gently remove the linens and look at
your wound. Okay?" Izzy said.

"Oh, I think I am fine. You do not need to bother
with checking my wou-" Henry stopped mid word
after looking into Lady Bird's face.

Izzy glared at Henry as he spoke and was about to
give him another tongue lashing when he stopped
speaking and slowly pulled back his shirt to expose
the bandage. Raising one eyebrow, Izzy began to
peel back the layers of linen. Henry had opted to
look away while Hal seemed glued to Izzy's side,
wanting to get a closer look at the wound. Hal
sucked in his breath when Izzy finally removed the
last layer of linen exposing the wound to the air.
Henry heard Hal suck in his breath and felt Lady
Bird's cool fingers gently touch his skin. He
flinched as her fingers touched him, sending fire
across his stomach. It surprised him that the fire
came from her mere touch, and not from any pain.

"Did I hurt you?" Izzy asked. His wound looked
remarkable, with very little redness, no heat, and the

skin was not peeling back. She was impressed by her own work.

"Um, no, it just, um, tickled a little. I am okay now." Turning his head to look at his wound, he did not remember it being so big. The stitches were straight, evenly placed, and the wound looked clean. "Wow, who stitched me up?"

Izzy hesitated, then squinted her eyes defensively before replying, "I did. Do my skills not meet your expectations?" She thought for sure that her skills were being scrutinized.

"Truly? You did an incredible job. I am very sore though. Is there anything you can do for the pain?" If he were honest, he was not just sore, the inside of the wound was throbbing and he simply wanted to die.

"I will give you something for the pain, but eventually I will not give you anything and you will have to learn to deal with it. For now, I will give you a small amount of opium, and I will rub a blend of oils around the wound as well. The opium will make you very drowsy. Do not fight it. Just close your eyes and try to rest. It can cause you to have very vivid dreams, but either myself, Hal or Sadie will be here with you." Izzy stood and searched in her satchel for the small dark bottle. Carefully, she pulled out one opium seed and handed it to Henry to take. Then she returned to her satchel and found the large brown bottle that contained the blend of oils she used to ease the pain of wounds, muscles or joints. Izzy put the bottle in her pocket, took a clean, dry linen and left the tent with a small bucket. Going out to the fire she filled the bucket with some of the water that was boiling and returned to the tent. Sitting back down at Henry's side, she took the linen and dipped it in the steaming water and squeezed out the excess. Gently, she wiped the poultice from yesterday off, trying her best not to hurt Henry. After removing all of the old poultice, she let the wound air dry as she mixed up a new poultice to apply to the wound. While Izzy worked, Henry and Hal continued to discuss what Hal's plans were and where they would attack next and when. Izzy continued to work silently, listening to the two men talk and hoping to understand more about the person that Henry was. Izzy picked up the brown bottle from the ground and using another small, dry, clean linen, she smeared her blend of oils around the wound, careful to not get the oil on the wound itself. Finally, she applied the new poultice, and layered on the fresh linens. Izzy stood again and turned to the table behind her, grabbing the mug that she had cleaned that morning. She added chamomile, lavender and a small amount of peppermint. Adding hot water to the mug, she began to clean up her herbs while the tea steeped.

"Okay gentlemen, it is time to say goodbye. Hal, I must ask you to leave now and let Lord Henry get some rest. Go on, I promise that he will still be right here later when it is time for the evening meal." Izzy waited for Hal to leave before picking up the mug and handing it to Henry. "Here, careful, it is hot. Drink all of this. It will help you to relax and sleep." Izzy sat back down on the stool with a stack of linen in her lap and began to tear them into strips. After Henry had taken a few sips, she asked, "What will you do when Hal does not have any more rebellions to fight?" Izzy watched as Henry thought about his answer.

Henry had not put much thought into the idea of not being needed by Hal. After all, there was always a battle to fight, right? "There are always knights needed to fight someone," Henry finally answered. "Yes, this is true, but what if Hal decides to not fight those battles, or you become permanently injured and are no longer able to fight?" Izzy pushed. Taking a deep breath, Henry hesitantly answered, "I suppose if I were horrifically injured and could not find any way to assist in battle, I would have to return home."

"It almost sounds like you are avoiding home. Is there a reason that you do not want to return?" Izzy asked.

Henry's eyes jolted up from staring at his hands to meet hers. Her eyes were intense, almost as though she could see right through him. Her face questioned him softly but her words cut right to his heart. He was a monster, a monster that did not deserve the comforts of home. "I do not go home because I do not think I would be welcome there." He watched her emotions play across her face, but could not quite discern what they were.

"I see, so rather than try to fix whatever the problem is, you would rather hide from it. What did you do that was so awful that your family would not welcome you home?" Izzy tried not to be so blunt with him, but it was such a part of her personality that she knew no matter how she tried, whatever she said would come out that way.

Henry was amused by her honest assessment of him. He studied her face again while she continued to strip the linens. Her lips were full, but her mouth petite and her nose were delicate and straight. For some odd reason, he had the urge to reach out, pull her close and kiss the tip of her nose. Her eyelashes were long like feathers fluttering over her eyes, and he could see that across the bridge of her nose and decorating the top of her cheeks, were faint freckles. He felt his pulse quicken, and suddenly he fantasized tangling his hands in her hair and pulling her head back while he kissed her neck down to her collarbone. He would then push the dress off her shoulder to continue the trail of kisses down her body. He could almost feel her hands digging into his shoulders as he cupped one breast in his hand and his mouth –

"Henry, are you okay? You look quite flushed." Izzy reached her hand out and felt his forehead. He did not feel fevered, but his skin still had a pink glow to it.

Henry realized that his palms were sweaty as well, and he could not shake the vision of her body melting into his. "I, uh, I am fine. I think I just need some rest."

"Close your eyes then, and rest. Just remember, the opium can cause vivid dreams. I will stay here while you rest, and Hal is just a shout away," Izzy reassured him.

Vivid dreams? If only she knew! Henry licked his lips remembering his fantasy. He took a deep breath and tried to clear his mind. The images kept coming back to him making it impossible to relax and rest. Henry opened his eyes and peered at Lady Bird. Her back was to him and he had a perfect view of her shape. She was perfectly petite, with broad shoulders, a small waist, flared hips and a what hinted at a very round butt that he desperately wanted to cup in his hands. Her shape was gorgeous and sensual. He could see himself walking up behind her, reaching his hands out and resting them on her shoulders, kissing her ear, neck and shoulder then letting his hands slide down to her waist. My God, her waist and hips, his mouth went dry. He stared at her waist as it cut in slightly before her full hips curved out and the rest of her body disappeared under her skirts. He turned her around and could see her blue eyes staring right into his. He smiled softly and wondered why she did not smile back, and instead was turning bright red.

147

Izzy had turned around to see Henry staring at her openly, his eyes roaming her body, undressing her. She felt nearly naked under his gaze. What on earth could he be thinking? "I think it is time that Hal comes in to watch over you while you rest." Izzy spun on her heals and nearly ran out of the tent to look for Hal.

Hal was training with his knights when he saw the tent flaps to Henry's tent fly open and Izzy dash out looking as red as a rose. Chuckling to himself, he guessed that he was right and that Henry did indeed remember his wife. "Excuse me men, I have to tend to something." Hal announced as he left the group and walked over to Izzy. "Lady Bird, I take it that Henry's memory was not faulty after all. I told you that you would be hard to forget! Well, what did he say?"

"You must watch over him. It felt as though he was undressing me with his eyes! I knew that opium could cause vivid dreams, but this is a bit much for me to handle right now. If you don't mind, I think I am going to lay down and rest. I stayed up through the night to prepare for the morning, and I will most likely do the same this evening as well. I really should rest and avoid Henry for now. Please, I am asking you for your help," Izzy prattled with frustration. Never in her life had she felt so vulnerable, wanted and sexy. She knew she should feel improper but she loved the feeling!

Hal was shocked. He struggled not to laugh and agreed to go watch over Henry while Izzy rested. He wanted to hear about this from Henry himself. As he walked towards the tent, he could not resist laughing to himself. "Henry, are you awake?" Hal asked as he walked into the tent.

"Yes," Henry answered gruffly.

"You have managed to chase off our sweet and innocent healer. Whatever did you do?" Hal baited Henry.

Henry rubbed his face with his hands and groaned. "How can any woman be so damned gorgeous? I tried to not see myself touching and kissing her, but she was there and her eyes, God they are endless pools of blue and her hips..." Henry groaned again. He was still feeling quite relaxed from the opium.

"So why not charm her and let her fall madly in love with you. Ask for her hand in marriage and make love to the woman?" Hal proposed.

Henry was finally succumbing to the opium induced sleep that he so desperately needed. As he drifted off, he answered Hal. "I do not think my wife would like that very much..."

Hal sat on the stool in disbelief that Henry had just admitted to having a wife. He would have to handle this very carefully. He would need to consider if it would be better to confront him on his secret or to leave it alone and wait for Henry to bring it up again. Hal ate his evening meal alone in Henry's tent, then continued to wait and watch over Henry until Sadie came to the tent to take over watch. "Please call for me when he wakes and I will help him to stand and relieve himself, then help him back to bed. Do you know when Lady Bird will be returning to watch over Henry?"

"I suspect she will return once the camp has gone to bed for the night. There is not much more for her to do in the camp right now, and I know she will be anxious to return home. Despite what she says, she has grown to love Adonia and its people." Sadie took Hal's seat and began to grind up cat's claw for a tea for Lord Henry to drink later. Izzy would mix the cat's claw and the calendula together to make a tea for Lord Henry.

Hal thought for a moment about what Sadie had said. He wondered if Izzy loved Adonia and its people solely for them or because she felt this would be as close to loving her husband as she would ever get. He nodded to Sadie, then left the tent to tend to business that he had forgotten about these past few days.

Izzy woke and found a tray of stew, and a loaf of bread under a linen cloth on the table left for her. After eating the rabbit stew, she finally changed from her yellow linen gown into one of the two garden gowns that she had brought. Then she sat down at the table and wrote two notes.

Hugh,

> *I arrived at camp yesterday evening and was able to help Lord Henry. He is recovering now and as long as he follows instructions, he should heal quickly. His Royal Highness has asked that I stay here as a healer and I have agreed, although I intend to return home to Adonia within the next week or two. Please make sure that the ladies in town have the quilt finished. I will be home to help prepare for the festival but will need to leave shortly after to return here to the camp. Please tell Sir Merek's wife that he is well and will be accompanying me home. I am sure she misses him a great deal. I am sending word to Lady Jayde and Lord James of the situation, so that should they require me for any reason, they will know where to find me. I hope that everything is going well for you, but I have no doubt that you will keep everything running smoothly. Take care, I will be home soon.*

> *Sincerely,*
> *Lady Isabel*

Izzy folded and sealed the note before starting the second one.

Lady Jayde and Lord James,
I want to inform you that Lord Henry
was injured in battle this past week. His
Royal Highness sent for me, and Sadie and I
were able to recover the lodged spike in
Lord Henry's side. He is healing, but we
will be here at this camp for another week
before we return to Adonia. I will be in
Adonia for the festival and then will be
returning here to the camp at the request of
His Royal Highness as a healer. Should you
need anything, please send for me. There is
nothing more important than family! Give
Ellyn, Dario and Edward hugs and kisses
from me and tell them I miss them dearly!
My love to you all,
Izzy

Izzy folded the second note and sealed it as well. Taking both notes with her, she went to Hal's tent and seeing the light was still on, called out to him. "Hal, are you still awake?"
Hal was startled hearing Izzy's voice calling to him from his tent. "Yes, come in."
Izzy opened the tent flap but did not tie it shut. "I wanted to use a messenger to take these two notes to Era and Adonia. Would that be possible?"

Hal took the two notes. One had *Era* written on it and the other *Adonia*. "Of course. Are they urgent or can they wait until dawn to leave?"

"Neither are urgent, I just need the note to Adonia to be delivered first," Izzy instructed.

"Then I shall send it out with the messenger in the morning. Are you going to Henry's tent now?" Hal asked.

"I am. Are you up for a while longer or are you retiring for the evening?" Izzy inquired.

"I will be up for quite a while longer. I have some business to attend to for my father, then travel plans to make. I must leave camp in three days. But will return seven days later. My father has requested that I stay home longer, but I know that you have business to tend to back home as well, and so I plan to return early. Will you be able to stay and tend to Henry while I am away?" Hal shuffled papers on his desk.

Izzy answered, "I shall be able to stay while you are away, however, I will need to leave as soon as you return. As you know, I do have obligations to go home to. I will be gone for about ten days, but will come back as you requested. Will camp still be here or will you have moved?"

"By that time, we will be tearing down the camp and moving. There is *another* rebellion that we must squash, but I fear that it will take quite a bit of time to deal with. So, we will move camp closer. Is there anything you will need while we travel?" Hal readied his quill to write anything that Izzy might require for their traveling.

"I will carry whatever herbs I need, although it would be nice to have some linens on hand should we need to bandage anyone up," Izzy conceded.

Hal made a few notes on the paper, then returned the quill to the desk. "I will be sure that we have plenty of clean linen to travel with. Thank you again for agreeing to travel with us and stay as our healer. You are a tremendous help." Hal paused a moment before speaking again. "Would you like some company again tonight or do you wish to be alone?" He hoped that she would want his company. She was unlike any other woman he had ever met. He could only imagine if she were his, taking her in his arms and kissing her soft pink lips.

"If you are awake and would like to visit for a while, I would love the company and am sure that if Henry is awake, he would prefer to speak with you rather than me." Izzy stood to leave the tent.

Hal laughed softly as he spoke to her, "Do not count on that. He continued to talk about you when I went to the tent. In his delirious state, he even admitted to having a wife. I think I will keep that a secret unless he brings it up, but I am curious to see if he remembers what he said as he drifted off to sleep. I need to finish these papers, but I shall visit you and Henry shortly."

Izzy blushed remembering the scene earlier in Henry's tent. She could see the twinkle in Hal's eyes

154

as she left his tent and walked over to Henry's. She slowed her steps as she approached, his tent and hesitated before entering. Taking a deep breath, she stepped inside. She had a job to do, and falling in love with her husband was not that job. Inside she saw Henry quietly sitting in his cot and bringing his finger up to his lips he signaled her to be quiet. Confused at first, Izzy did not notice the slumped over sleeping figure at the desk. Poor Sadie was sound asleep in what looked to be the most uncomfortable position. Laughing softly at her dear friend, Izzy turned and poked her head out of the tent to see if Hal was on his way yet.

Hal decided to head over right away to visit with Henry. He had been exhausted the entire day and desperately needed sleep. This way he could visit, then retire to his tent in hopes of getting some rest. As he strode up to Henry's tent, a head suddenly peaked out of the entry startling him so badly he nearly fell backwards.

Izzy let out a sharp yelp as she shoved her head out of the tent and nearly collided with Hal. As Hal jumped backwards and nearly fell over, Izzy could barely contain herself. Gasping for a breath as she laughed, she clutched the flaps of the tent to keep from falling over herself.

"You deserve to topple over for scaring me so badly!" Hal said while laughing as he regained his composure and pushed past Izzy into Henry's tent.

Izzy and Hal immediately sobered with concern when they saw Henry clutching his side with one foot swung over the edge of the bed.

"What are you doing?" Hal asked rushing forward. "Are you trying to kill yourself? What are you thinking? Lay back and let me take a look. I hope you haven't ripped a stitch!" Izzy immediately started to remove the layers of linen from his wound.

"I heard you scream and was trying to get up to protect you." Henry winced painfully.

"I mean no offense Henry, but I think that Lady Bird could defend herself better than you right at this moment," Hal teased as he helped to situate Henry back in bed.

Sadie remained sound asleep slumped over at the table.

"I told you to stay quiet, but you obviously did not understand such a simple message," Henry fired at Izzy with a smile on his lips.

Izzy paused her inspection of his wound to look up at his face. Once she realized that he was teasing her, she rolled her eyes, and smiled back. Sitting up, she spoke quietly. "I think you were very lucky Lord Henry. Your wound is a little red, but the stitches held out." She sighed with relief. She could not imagine the pain he would be in if he had ripped a stitch or if she would have had to re-stitch his wound. "Hal, I need your help with Sadie. I do not want to startle her, but I know she would be far more comfortable in a bed."

"I can carry her, and hopefully she will stay asleep. If she can sleep through your fit of giggles, then she should be able to sleep being carried to her tent," Hal said as he stood up.

"I will walk with you, then when we return, you can assist Henry to stand to relieve himself." Izzy stated as Hal bent forward and scooped Sadie into his arms. Quietly the two left Henry alone to his thoughts. His heart was still racing from her smile. When she first looked up at him, he thought for sure she would be offended and not understand his joke, but then her eyes had sparkled and a smile had spread across her face. It was true that she was quite beautiful, and obviously she was smart. Was she good and kind though? He thought back to three Christmas's ago and to the bride that he left behind. Try as he might, he did not remember what she looked like. Did she have brown hair or blonde? Was she pretty or smart? What they had was not a marriage, and he would talk to Hal privately about requesting an annulment from the King. It was not fair to trap either of them in a marriage, especially one that was still only recognized in the eyes of the law and not in the eyes of God. Maybe it was time to stop punishing himself. Henry quickly banished his thoughts as Izzy and Hal walked back in, talking and laughing quietly. She was like a light in a sea of darkness, truly breathtaking.

"I will step outside to allow you some privacy. Just let me know when you are finished. Then we will get you settled back in bed and let your wound air out a little longer before reapplying the poultice. I am surprised that you have not fevered again. I thought for sure that it would take your body longer to fight the infection but am pleased that it is not the case." Izzy smiled again at Henry before she left the tent.

Once outside, Izzy wondered how deep Henry's humor went. His face had been so relaxed when she had looked up at him earlier. It had felt so good to laugh and to laugh as much as she had today was exhilarating. Her mind wandered to Adonia and how everyone was doing these past few days. Only another ten until she could return. Her thoughts were interrupted by Hal announcing that Henry was finished.

Henry watched Lady Bird closely when she came back into the tent. He could see that her mind was elsewhere and wondered what or who she was thinking of. She was quite young to be a healer, he would be sure to ask her about it later.

Hal stayed for a short time more before finally retiring to his tent. He hoped that sleep would come quickly for him and grant him sweet, peaceful rest. Henry tried to relax and rest but his body ached to get up and move about again.

"I can only imagine how difficult it must be to stay in bed, but you are healing quickly and should be off of bed rest soon. If you keep up the good work, I think that by the time Hal leaves, you should be able to at least get up and walk around." She smiled gently at him.

"It is quite difficult. Thank you for understanding that. Lady Bird, may I ask you some questions?" Henry was hoping she would not get cold and shut him down.

Izzy grabbed a handful of rosemary twigs and began to organize them and tie them together. "Of course, you may, but please, just call me Izzy."

A smile spread across Henry's face at learning her first name. Izzy, it seemed to suit her perfectly.

"Izzy, what do you do for fun when you are not taking care of careless Lords like myself?"

"Lord Henry, I would not call you careless, maybe reckless though," she teased him as she continued to bunch and bind rosemary.

"You can call me Henry. No need to keep the formalities," Henry interjected.

"Very well Henry, hmm, let me think... fun... I love to garden, visit family... oh! I have these new cards! Would you like to try them with me? I got them during a festival from a merchant from Italy!" Izzy pulled the cards from her bag. She had forgotten until that moment that she had placed them there when she bought them. "See, they have numbers and symbols on them called suites." She showed Henry the cards.

"I have never seen these before. What do we do with them?" Henry asked as he passed the cards back to Izzy.

"The merchant said you mix the cards, then divide them between two people. Then each person turns one card over at a time. The higher card wins and that person gets to keep both cards. The person with the most cards wins!" Izzy was thrilled to actually get to use these. Hugh had teased her, saying that she was being robbed. She could not wait to tell him that they turned out to be quite handy!

"Izzy, if I may be so bold to say, you are quite attractive. Why did you choose to join a nunnery?" Henry hoped that he was not so bold as to offend her, but he wanted to know who she was.

Izzy was flattered at first, then shocked by his question. It took her a moment to gather her thoughts. "I did not choose to join a nunnery. I was orphaned at the age of twelve, and the nuns took me in."

Henry thought carefully before speaking again. His impulsiveness and impatience often got him into trouble and he felt in his heart that whatever relationship this would be was one that he did not want to destroy. "The nuns took you in, and taught you everything you know?" Henry felt awkward but desperately wanted to learn more about her.

"Yes, pretty much. It took a few years, but eventually, I was considered a healer." Izzy kept her answer short. She did not want to confess any information that would give her true identity away.

Henry watched her face attentively, for any sign that could help him understand her better. "Have you never wanted to be married, or have a family?" As soon as he spoke, he regretted his words. There was his impulsiveness and impatience again. "Please excuse me. I fear that it has been a very long time since I have been around a Lady and my manners are boorish at best."

Izzy turned a card over and waited for Henry to do the same. They played in silence for five more turns when finally, Izzy spoke. "I always dreamed of being swept off of my feet, to fall in love, and to be loved. I used to dream of not just being married, but actually being friends with him. Such a silly girl's fantasy." Izzy turned another card. "As the years went by, I settled on the fact that the magical moment I had dreamed of would never exist for me. I was prepared to devote my life to the nunnery when a marriage to a man in a good family was arranged."

Henry stared at her, taking in what she was saying. What he hoped she was not saying. Henry had to choke out his question. "Are you married then?"

Izzy turned another card over. "Indeed, I am." She waited for him to turn another card over as well. The tent felt oppressive, and Izzy avoided looking Henry in the eye for fear that he might see the truth in hers. Henry felt as though his heart was being crushed. "So your husband, is he um, is he, kind?"

Startled, Izzy looked up into Henry's eyes. She was entranced and felt like she was being pulled into something. She studied the green flecks in his irises that seemed delicately placed just to tease anyone who got close enough to notice them. She could feel the hair on the back of her neck stand up and managed to bring herself back to the present. Blinking rapidly, she sat up straight and cleared her throat. How could she answer that question?

Henry could still feel every tense muscle in his body that refused to relax. Her face had been so close to his. He could have reached out, entwined his fingers in her hair and leaned forward. He could have softly let his lips press against hers, before letting his tongue slip into her mouth and taste what sweetness was hidden. Izzy's voice interrupted his fantasy and he regretfully turned his attention back to reality.

Izzy's heart was still racing as she forced herself to answer his question. "My husband, he is a very loyal man, devoted to family and image. He trusts me to manage his estates while he is away… and, well, I think he wants to be kind."

Henry's fantasy shattered, immediately feeling on edge and thinking the worst of this 'husband' of hers. "Does he hurt you?"

Izzy was confused before realizing that her words were misconstrued. "No, he would never, I mean, he, well, it is complicated. You see, he is really never around. I do not know much about him. His family is wonderful, so I can only hope that he is like them, but I do not have any firsthand experience or knowledge."

"So he married you, but has abandoned you?" Henry felt wave after wave of guilt roll over him. He could only imagine how Lady Isabel, his own abandoned wife, must feel. If she was half as good and kind as Izzy, then she must feel responsible for his poor behavior. She truly deserved someone better than him. He imagined that she could be like Izzy, and dreaming of having a husband that was a lover and friend. All the more reason to petition the King for an annulment of their marriage. He would need to speak with Hal before he left in a few days. Sighing, Henry suddenly felt tired. He set the few cards that he had left in his hands down on the table and leaned back, closing his eyes. "Will you be here all night or retire to your tent?"

Izzy gathered the cards and carefully placed them back in her bag. "I will remain in here with you through the night. Then in the morning, I will tend to the men we took care of today. I will lay down to rest in the afternoon just as I did today. Do you need me to help you to stand so that you may relieve yourself? I will leave the tent so that you may have privacy, or you will have to wait until morning when Hal returns."

Henry thought about it before deciding that he was fine to just go to sleep and wait for Hal in the morning.

"Sleep well then Henry." Izzy pulled the covers up and tucked them around Henry's chest, then turned around and moved the candles away from him to the table to allow him to fall asleep easier. After a while, Izzy found herself staring at Henry thinking back on their conversation. Sometimes he seemed to be very closed and pushing the world away. Other times he seemed to be on fire and trying to draw her near. Which Henry was the true and real Henry; or was he somewhere in between? Izzy returned her focus to preparing herbs for the morning rounds with the men in the camp.

As dawn began to light the sky, the silhouettes of trees against the painted heavens made Izzy's heart flutter. Suddenly, she felt homesick for Ackerley and her mind became anxious for the days to pass quickly so that she could leave. She decided in that moment that she would spend a day or two in Ackerley before returning to the camp. She stood outside the tent and watched the early morning fog slowly retreat back into the tree line while the sun continued to wake up the world with its grace. Finally, the bright rays crested the tree line and bathed her in its intoxicating warmth. Izzy closed her eyes and took a deep breath. The morning air was still cold despite the warmth coming from the sky and Izzy felt her soul flutter to life. Birds all around the camp began to chirp, singing their praises for the new day and men began to emerge from their tents and stretch, reaching their hands towards skyward. Izzy returned to the inside of the tent and gathered her supplies to set them on a table in the camp. Hal stepped out of his tent and walked over to her.

"How did Henry do last night? Did he behave himself?" Hal teased her.

Izzy laughed softly. "He was a gentleman. If it is alright with you, I would like to set up my supplies here at this table and treat the men here."

"Of course, where ever works best for you," Hal said before he slipped into Henry's tent. "Good morning Henry. How did you sleep?"

"Good morning. Better than the night before. I am restless though." Henry accepted Hal's help to stand and walk to the chamber pot. Henry waited for Hal to step out of the tent while he relieved himself then called out to him. Once he was back in bed, Henry asked Hal about Izzy. "Did you know that Izzy is married?"

"Yes, I did. Were you unaware of this?" Hal was shocked that Izzy said anything about being married.

"I learned this from her last night. I have never seen a ring on her finger. I would have expected a Lady to have a ring to wear. Do you know why she does not wear one?" Henry was still troubled by the unexpected news.

"I had never thought about it before, but no, I have not seen her wearing a ring. Does that somehow make her marriage less real or sacred?" Hal responded nonchalantly.

Henry made sure to keep his emotions and heart well hidden. "No, I suppose not. Do you think she is happy with her marriage?"

Hal smiled at his friend, and hesitated before answering. "I do not believe that she is unhappy, but I know that she wishes her marriage was better. That the relationship she has with her husband was more honest and loving. Again, why does that matter?"

"Hal, I have a confession to give you. I, myself am married." Henry looked up at Hal to see shock cross his face. "I do not love her, and she deserves better than me. I have realized these past couple of days, well, if I am completely honest, I realized this back in October, on my birthday. Anyway, I have realized that my wife deserves a husband who loves her. I cannot give her that love, but I can give her the chance to find that love." Henry stopped speaking and looked again at Hal.

"How exactly do you intend to do that? Allow her to take a lover?" Hal was annoyed with where he knew this conversation was going.

"No, I would like to request an annulment of my marriage from the King. Would you bring my request to your father for me?" Henry asked nervously. Hal looked quite upset.

Hal struggled to control his temper. "Have you even tried to be better for your wife? I will take your request to my father, but you should know, my father rarely grants annulments."

"It is complicated Hal. I just know that she would be happier without me." Henry was hoping that Hal would not ask more questions.

"Have you asked her if she would be happier without you? How would you know anything, if you have not been home in over two years?" Hal boomed before storming out of the tent.

Izzy and half of the camp were outside eating when they heard Hal yelling and then watched as he thundered out of Henry's tent off toward the training grounds. Curious, Izzy picked up her meal, and bringing it with her, walked into Henry's tent. "Is everything okay? Hal seemed quite angry just now." Henry was startled when his tent flaps opened and the bright light shone in. When he realized it was Izzy, he was even more surprised. No doubt half of the camp was eating their morning meal and heard Hal's outburst. Sighing heavily, he answered, "Yes, just a personal disagreement between Hal and I."

Izzy sat down on the chair next to Henry's bed. "I believe your meal should be arriving shortly. Tell me a little about yourself while you wait."

Henry frowned. He did not like to discuss his personal life with anyone and was struggling to make an exception for her. "What exactly would you like to know? Are you wanting to know if I have all of my ten toes or if I name my war horse?"

Izzy could hear the pretense in his voice and wondered what had happened to give him reason to doubt peoples' interest in his personal life. "I was merely curious if you had siblings. Is that something I am not allowed to ask?"

Henry contemplated her question, avoiding eye contact. How could she use this information against him? Who could she hurt?

Izzy saw his hesitation and again wondered who he was protecting. "I have one brother, two brothers-in-law and one sister-in-law." She offered, coaxing the information from him with her own. "I had always wanted a sister. I just had to wait until I married to get one!" Izzy smiled and took another bite of the food on her plate. Her mind wandered to Jayde and James and how they were doing. Ellyn was nearly identical to Jayde but instead of dark ringlets framing her face, she had bouncy golden curls. She would be turning two soon. The twins, Edward and Dario, would be one in a few months and she missed their sweet chubby cheeks, big kisses and fierce hugs. She wondered if they would all be joining her at the festival next week.

Henry felt slightly more at ease to answer her questions, but still worried. Maybe he could just avoid the whole thing if he asked her questions about herself. "Is your brother older or younger than you?"

Laughing gently, Izzy objected to his question. "Oh no, you get answers when you give answers. Do we have an agreement?"

Henry groaned because he knew that she had won this time. "Fine, but I swear, if someone does not bring something in for me to eat soon, I might start eating my own shirt!" As if it had been planned and rehearsed the tent flap opened and food was brought in.

Izzy simply smiled and thanked the woman before turning back to Henry with one eyebrow raised.

Henry waited for the servant to leave the tent before he tore into his bread. "I am one of five brothers." He ate a hardboiled egg before repeating his question to Izzy. "Is your brother older or younger than you?"

Izzy was grateful he finally answered her question. She knew about Geoff and Thomas and their passing, as well as their parents, but if she wanted information, she would have to play the game and feign the ignorance an outsider should have. "He is older, but only by a couple of years. What is your favorite season of the year?" Izzy hoped that she could learn much more about him in the short amount of time she had with him.

"I think my favorite season is summer; the warmth in the air, the sun shining down, and the many parties." Henry smiled thinking back to the grand parties his parents used to throw. He would like to do that one day. He could see the party in his mind as though it were a memory, until he saw himself dancing with Izzy in his arms.

Izzy waited while Henry silently ate his meal until her impatience grew to be too much for her to contain. "No more questions for me?"

Henry once again snapped out of his fantasy and back to reality. A question for her, but he had so many! The only problem is that none of them were appropriate. "What is your favorite flower?" "Hmm, that is a great question. Well, I love roses, lavender, lilac, and foxgloves, but my absolute favorites are Felicia daisies and chamomile. I love the many uses of the chamomile and the beautiful delicate flowers, but the daisies, although they look delicate, are strong. My father always said that they reminded him of me. He would go on trips and say that anytime he saw a field of Felicia daisies, he knew I was thinking of him." Izzy struggled to not let the past haunt her yet again. "Okay, now my turn to ask a question. What are your parents like?" Henry involuntarily flinched, as though someone had struck him in the stomach. It had been three years since he had gathered with his brothers to remember and honor their parents as well as Geoff and Thomas. His heart broke a little realizing that he had allowed personal problems to interfere with visiting his parents' grave site. He needed to take a few days to visit, hopefully without having to run into James or Jayde. What if Isabel was visiting at Era? She and Jayde seemed to be good friends, at least it sounded that way from her letters. He missed home. "My parents are deceased. They passed in one of the bouts of plague." Henry needed to get out of the tent. "When will I be trusted to walk around?" Izzy sensed that Henry was done playing this game. "I will have a look at your wound after the evening meal. If it is still looking good and healing well, then Hal and I will take you for a short walk this evening."

"Why do you and Hal need to walk with me? Do you not trust that I will obey your instructions?" Henry felt irritated at the idea that he was being babysat and that he could not find any privacy to be alone with his memories and thoughts.

Izzy smiled patiently and left the place where she felt like she might be becoming a friend to Henry and went back to the cold and lonely place of being the healer. "I will be there to observe your wound to make sure that it does not tear open while you are walking and Hal will be there to make sure that if you do need assistance to walk you will have a strong shoulder to lean on."

"Ha! A strong shoulder, I am far stronger than -" Henry started to say before he was interrupted by Izzy.

"I am the healer, not you. You will do as I say or I can leave and you can die from secondary infection. The choice is yours. I will send someone in to assist you to relieve yourself in a bit, and then I will return later." Izzy shut down all further conversation with Henry and left the tent carrying both her plate and his. She brought the dishes to the cook and then went to the table where she had set up her supplies to check on the other men in camp.

A few men cheered when they saw her approaching the table. Hal had said that only she could give them the all clear to return to duties.

"Healing Bird has arrived!" One of the men called out which was then followed by applause. Izzy blushed before reaching the table and seeing the first man.

"Your wound is looking wonderful. One more day of rest, then I think you should be able to return to training. Just remember to keep it clean. Any redness or pain, come see me immediately." Izzy smiled as the knight walked away with a smile on his face. It felt amazing to be so useful and needed. She continued to look at each wound for the line of men through the midday meal.

"Izzy, you are going to push yourself too hard. Were you up all through the night again?" Hal asked as he approached with a plate of food.

"I was up through the night. I find that when I am tending to someone, that if I work through the night while they rest, I can get more accomplished. Unfortunately, it leaves me exhausted in the afternoon. Is this plate of food by any chance for me?" Izzy's stomach rumbled loudly as she finished her sentence.

Hal laughed and pushed the plate towards her.

"Indeed it is. I watched you work through the meal and thought you might be hungry."

"I am famished! Thank you so much!" Izzy sat down and began to eat quickly, forgetting her manners.

"Henry asked if he could walk about soon and I said that I would check on his wound later. If it looks good, I will need your help to accompany him on a walk with me. I need strength in the event that he needs assistance walking back. Would you mind terribly?"

"I was going to mention something similar to you actually. I was about to inquire about his wound and when he would no longer be restricted." Hal seemed pleased that they were all thinking the same thing. "If everything goes well, I will make sure to teach him how to properly get out of bed so that he does not reinjure himself. Then he will no longer need aid throughout the day to relieve himself. Once he is able to walk, he will need to walk multiple times daily to help strengthen his muscles around the wound. However, because he is so robust, it should not be too long for him to return to normal training and activities." Izzy took a chunk of bread and layered some of the pork on it before taking a bite. "I wanted to discuss with you my future with the camp. I know that you have asked for me to return and I am thrilled to be of use, however, I also have my duties at home to keep up. I would like to be able to return home frequently to care for Adonia and keep up on Ackerley. Will I be able to come and go as needed?"

Hal could not imagine there being a problem with her traveling to and from. Granted it did put her in more danger traveling so frequently, but he knew that her knights would give their lives for her. "I do not see a problem with this at all. As long as you and I keep our communication with one another open, I think it will be fine."

Izzy smiled, relieved that there would be no problems and that she could continue to uphold her duties to the two towns and Jayde. Finally, she felt full and in the place of her hunger she felt exhaustion trying to take hold.

"You look like you are ready to rest. You should go. I will have a plate saved for you this evening and then we can go tend to Henry together." Hal smiled and stood, walked around the table and offered his arm to Izzy.

Izzy stood and wrapped her hands around Hal's forearm as he escorted her to her tent. "Well, my fair prince, this is where I must bid you farewell." Izzy teased Hal who in turn bowed deeply to her. She giggled before turning into her tent, then laying down, she fell asleep within minutes on her bed.

Izzy woke to the soft voice of Sadie.

"Izzy, Izzy, are you awake? I am coming in." Sadie pulled a tent flap back and walked in.

Izzy pushed herself up off of her stomach from the bed. She still felt drained, but knew that it was time for her to return to duty. Hopefully Henry would be able to get up and start walking around a bit and that would free up some of her time to actually sleep when normal people sleep, in the dead of the night. Doing her best to straighten her dress and tidy her hair, the involuntary yawn that escaped gave away her true state of being.

Sadie smiled at Izzy. "Here I brought your meal in to you. Hal said that you and he were going to see if Henry could handle walking about this evening?"

"Yes, I think it will do Henry so much good, and if he can walk on his own, then the evening watch can be eliminated. It will do us all good," Izzy said between bites.

"So, you are Lady Isabel de Seaton at home, Izzy to Henry and now Healing Bird to the entire camp. You are leading quite the complicated triple life! May I ask how long you plan to keep up the different characters?" Sadie was laughing at her friend as she spoke. She knew that Izzy would rather not lie, but she had also learned that Izzy had an uncanny ability to know when the right time to lie was.

Izzy started to laugh with her friend. "Goodness, what have I gotten myself into? Healing Bird? Where on earth did you hear that?"

"That is what all the men in the camp call you. They are sharing with each other the amazing work of Healing Bird and showing off how well their wounds have healed. A few of the men were even saying that when they return home that were going to teach 'those hygiene tricks to all the other men and women who will listen'. You have made quite an impact in their lives." Sadie then looked at Izzy quite seriously. "My Lady, you have done so much good here already. Will you be content to return home or will you miss this adventure?"

"Actually, I plan to return after the fair. I wanted to ask you if you wanted to return with me or if you would prefer to stay at home. I would not be upset if you chose to stay home. It is far cleaner there than here, and does not smell quite so. Not to mention how quiet it can be." Izzy saw that Sadie was about to answer, but she held up her hand to stop Sadie from speaking. "I do not need an answer now. Please just think about it. Wait until it is time for me to return, give me your answer then." Izzy smiled before taking another bite.

Sadie smiled in return. How could Izzy even ask her such a question? She would not leave Healing Bird's side until they were no longer needed. She was grateful for the opportunity to travel and be so useful. Sadie told Izzy about the drama that had unfolded while she rested and laughed when Hal had stepped in and scolded the two men like a mother would her two young boys. Both ladies laughed enjoying the brief break from work. When Izzy was done eating, Sadie took her plate back to the cook and helped clean up.

As Sadie left the tent, Izzy stood up and stretched before leaving her tent to walk to Henry's. She was caught by surprise when she saw Hal walking towards her.

"My Lady, may I?" Hal said offering his arm to her again. As though they were walking through the gardens at court, they took their time walking to Henry's tent. Hal looked forward to moments like this when he could be alone with her. He loved touching her skin and loved feeling her body next to his. "Where do you plan for us to walk with Henry?"

"I was thinking that we should stay close to the tables with seats available. I want him to be able to stop and rest as he needs to rather than try and push himself. We will walk no farther than the main path leading out of camp before turning around. Lord Henry not so inconspicuously hides his pain. He is a true knight and very noble." Izzy sounded somewhat disappointed with her last statement and it showed on her face as well.

"That sounds like a perfect plan. May I ask you why you still call him Lord Henry rather than just Henry?" Hal was amused by her formality toward Henry around him. He knew that in Henry's presence she dropped his title because he had overheard her speaking to Henry informally when they were alone.

"I suppose it is because we are discussing his rehabilitation. I had not thought about it before though. Interesting indeed…" Izzy let her sentence trail off without further effort to understand the change.

Henry sat restlessly in his bed waiting for Hal and Izzy to arrive so that he could show them how strong he was. He was so tired of being inside his tent! What would he do if they told him that he needed to remain in bed longer? He might go crazy, is what he would do. No, he had to prove to them that he was better.

Hal held the tent flap open for Izzy. "Good, you are awake! Are you ready to take a walk about?"

"More than ready!" Henry began to get out of bed.

"Stop. Until your wound heals completely, let me explain and show you how you need to get in and out of bed. First, I want you to roll to your side, then drop your feet to the ground. Good! Next you can stand straight up! To get back into bed you will do exactly the same, but backwards. Go on, sit down. Now lie on your side, pick your feet up off of the floor, and roll back. Great! Now do it all again, by yourself and let us take a short walk!" Izzy was ready for Henry not to need round the clock care. If he managed to successfully walk about, she planned on sleeping though the night for the first time since she arrived.

Hal and Izzy walked with Henry to the path through the camp then back. Henry walked slowly, but was strong.

"I am impressed my friend!" Hal said. "It looks like it was a good thing that I called for a healer. Lady Bird, my deepest gratitude for saving my best knight."

"Over the course of the next week you should continue to get stronger and by the time you are facing your next rebellion, you will be ready to be injured again." Izzy tried to smile to show that she was joking, but the truth behind her words prevented her from doing so. "I am very glad that I was able to be here. I appreciate you sending for me Hal. Henry, how is your side feeling?" she added as they arrived back inside Henry's tent.

"A little tense and sore, but much better than when I first woke up. You have done a wonderful job, thank you." Henry was serious for a moment. For once, instead of cracking jokes, he understood how very different everything could have been had Hal not known this healer and called for her.

Izzy smiled back at Henry and for a brief moment forgot that Hal was still in the tent with them. "On that note, I will let you rest alone tonight. Remember how to get in and out of bed and I look forward to seeing you impress everyone by joining us for the morning meal."

"You are not staying with me tonight? No card games or rounds of questions?" Henry was a bit disappointed. He had enjoyed the other night and her company.

"I am sorry to disappoint you, but I am looking forward to sleeping through the night," Izzy said as she imagined her bed, waiting for her to fall into for a dreamless sleep. An awkward silence fell between the three until Hal finally spoke.

"I should walk you back to your tent. After the meal in the morning, I will be leaving. Henry, as always, I will leave you in charge, but I expect that Lady Bird will have her own orders for you. Please, do as she says. I would hate to think of what she could do as

punishment for men who do not follow her rules."
Hal winked at Henry and laughed at Izzy as a look of
disapproval fell across her face.

"Sleep well Henry. If you have any problems in the
night, please come get Hal and myself. Good night."
Izzy turned and left the tent standing outside of it and
waited for Hal to join her.

As Hal walked Izzy to her tent he asked, "How do
you intend on hiding Calvin and Merek from Henry
now that he is allowed to be mobile?"

"The same way they have stayed hidden thus far.
They take shifts keeping watch at the rear of the
camp, sleep while I am working in the mornings, and
the cook has a servant who brings them food. When
I return, I might need to bring a couple of knights
from Ackerley instead." Izzy had already thought of
this and had discussed the plans with Calvin and
Merek. All three agreed upon the change of knights
when they returned to Adonia.

"I am glad to know that you were already on top of
this, but I must say, I am not surprised. You remind
me so much of my baby sister, Pippa. She was
always one step ahead of the rest of us," he
reminisced as they walked to Izzy's tent.

"When we have both returned from our homes, I
would love to hear more about the adventures that
you and Pippa had growing up. Sleep well Hal.
Thank you for everything," Izzy said as they reached
her tent, and stifled a yawn.

"Good night Izzy, and truly, thank you again for rushing here and working so hard to not only help to heal Henry, but the other men in camp as well," Hal said, holding her tent flap open for her. Without thinking of his actions, Hal leaned forward and quickly kissed Izzy on the cheek.

Izzy pulled back, startled by Hal's bold gesture. Blushing fiercely, she pulled her arm and body away from Hal and quickly rushed into her tent. She waited until she heard Hal's footsteps retreat from her tent before letting her guard down. Although she was troubled by Hal's actions, exhaustion took over. Quickly undressing, she climbed into bed and fell asleep immediately. The morning came too quickly, and just as quickly, she was left in camp with only Sadie as a friend, a wounded knight leading the group, and two secret knights to protect her and her secret identity.

The week that Hal was gone passed quickly though. Henry made incredible progress and had even started light training again by the time Hal was to return. At each meal, he sat next to Izzy and tried to learn more about who she was, and who this mysterious husband of hers. At night he had dreams of holding Izzy's hand, caressing her cheek and kissing her innocent lips. He had spent so much time watching her mouth move while she spoke to him, or to the other people in the camp, that he could not shake their image from his mind. In truth, he actually enjoyed the conversations they shared. He both loved and was intrigued by her brutal honesty and how she was not afraid to argue with him. A few times during the week while Hal was away, he had sat around the fire at night quietly talking and laughing with her. She spoke so highly of her family and of the traditions they all took part of that it made him miss his own family. Maybe he could find a way to go home to Era and visit James and Jayde. He would wait to visit Adonia until he knew that Lady Isabel would be visiting Jayde. He missed his own room quite a bit. The day prior to Hal's return, Sadie had packed Izzy and her own belongings, and collected dried meats, cheese and fruit from the cook for their journey home. Izzy had spent most of this last day preparing supplies for Hal should he need something while she was away. She was excited to return to Adonia and the preparations for the festival. At the midday meal, Izzy did not sit down to eat. Instead, she found Sadie and informed her that they were to be ready to ride before dawn and were going to leave immediately after Hal arrived. Hal had already sent word that he would arrive before the morning meal. In his note, he seemed as anxious to return to camp as Izzy was to return home. Izzy was so busy preparing to leave, that she did not notice Henry's curiosity or disappointment at her absence. Both she and Sadie took their evening meal early and in their tents so that they could go to sleep early and be rested for their early morning departure.

Henry watched as Izzy flew about the camp all day, disappearing from his sight completely for most of the afternoon. He wondered if she was privy to information that he was not, especially when she stood at a table with Sadie cutting linens. Later, he noted that the two women were making salves and wondered what they were preparing for. Tomorrow Hal would return, and hopefully he could sit down with Izzy and enjoy a conversation, maybe even a picnic. That evening, when Henry had finished his watch duties, as he was climbing into bed, he imagined having some private time with Izzy. He imagined her sitting beside him under an oak tree, leaning against him and his arms wrapped around her body. He imagined his fingers tracing her arms while he whispered sweet things in her ears and nibbling on them. Smiling, Henry shook his head at himself. She was married and had expressed her loyalty to her husband already. She would never behave like that with him - but what if she would? Henry closed his eyes and drifted off to sleep with a smile on his face and the fantasy of tomorrow. Izzy and Sadie were awake and waiting for Hal well before dawn. Both Calvin and Merek waited anxiously just outside of camp to start their journey as well.

When Hal returned, he seemed surprised that both ladies were awake and waiting for him. "I am a lucky man indeed to be greeted by two beautiful ladies!" Hal teased as he dismounted his horse inside the camp. "I see that you are eager to return home?" Izzy smiled. "I am ready for a true bath and to hear how my townspeople are faring. I find that I miss all of the wonderful things they do for one another." "You will keep in touch with me and return after your festival still?" Hal asked. He knew he would miss her and looked forward to her returning. "Yes, of course!" Izzy reassured him. "Henry is doing well. I gave him the go ahead to return to training but to take it easy and listen to his body. Please do not let him push himself too hard just yet. Give him several more days to heal as much as possible." "I promise to make him take it easy. Please, ride safely and send word to me when you arrive home. If you need anything, do not hesitate to send a message. I shall do whatever I can to assist you. Ride safely, Godspeed." Hal said as Izzy and Sadie mounted their horses and quietly left the camp. After his behavior the night before he left, he was sure to keep his distance. Watching her leave, a torrent of unexpected emotions rose within him. He wanted her to stay; to take her into his arms, kiss her, make love to her and make her forget Henry, but he knew she would never allow such a thing. The group of four rode home to Adonia with only stops to rest once every couple of hours. They arrived at the castle gates at sunset. Izzy was in awe of how beautiful Adonia was. She had not realized how much she had truly missed it until she arrived back to it. What a breathtaking town it has truly become. Finally reaching the stables, the four riders slowly dismounted while the stable boys came and took their horses for brushing and a bucket of oats. Hugh was waiting for them as well.

"I have trays of food for you waiting in the Hall. How is his Lordship?" Hugh asked as he escorted the group into the Hall.

"Thank you Hugh. We are famished! Lord Henry is doing much better. We were able to extract the spike tip from his side and managed to get rid of the infection. When we left, he was already getting back to training for their next battle," Izzy said as they all sat down at the table and waited for the meal to be served to them.

"My Lady, that is wonderful news. Would you like for me to have a hot bath sent up for you?" Hugh asked as he stood up.

"Oh yes, please Hugh. That would be amazing!" Izzy could not decide if she was more excited to sleep in her own bed or about taking a hot bath. The group ate in silence truly enjoying the warm, clean Hall and quiet sounds. Izzy finished eating first and excused herself to her room.

Once in her room, she quickly undressed and sank into the hot water that awaited her in front of the fire. She completely submerged under the water letting all of the accumulated filth release its grip from her body and hair. Using a bar of her lavender rose soap, she scrubbed every inch of herself until her skin and scalp stung. After climbing out of the tub and putting on a clean chemise, she sank into her bed and pulled the covers up to her chin falling fast into a deep and much missed sleep.

Chapter 7
Adonia

Izzy awoke long after the sun had risen. She stretched in bed feeling rested and excited for the new day. She could hear the knights already up and in the training fields hard at work. She could hear the call of goats, horses and milk cows and the happy sounds of birds chirping from the garden down below made the day even more glorious. Izzy got up and floated across the room to her wardrobe. Oh, how wonderful it was to put on a clean dress! The next time she traveled to camp, she would bring more than two dresses and find out who was washing the garments for the knights. She was sure that Hal had some women in the camp that tended to laundry. She would need to be careful when speaking of his Royal Highness around others and not use the nick name he gave her to use except in camp. Quickly, she put on a white under tunic and a deep purple over tunic. It was one of her favorite simple gowns to wear. The purple gave her pale complexion a warm glow and it made her blue eyes sparkle. She felt so happy to be home. Home? She had not truly ever considered Adonia her home, until now. What changed that, she wondered to herself. Sitting down on the bench, she grabbed her brush and began to brush the long fine strands of blonde hair. Working quickly, she gave herself a braid that wrapped around her head like a crown and tied it with a thin leather ribbon. Moving to her desk, she grabbed a paper and quill and sent a quick note to Hal informing him of her safe return and asking him to keep her up to date about when to return and where. After sealing the letter, she put it in her pocket to give to Hugh when she saw him later.

Izzy ran down the stairs and found Bess setting a bowl on the table. "Good morning Bess!" Izzy called as she raced past.

"My Lady, you must stop and eat," Bess called after her. "It is not healthy to miss the morning meal. I even made sure it was your favorite! Oatmeal with cinnamon and honey. Hugh would be mighty upset with me if he knew you did not eat." Bess pulled every reason she could think of to get her Ladyship to sit and eat. She knew that Lady Isabel would push herself beyond a reasonable point for others here in Adonia and it was her sole job to make sure that Lady Isabel was taken care of too.

Izzy stopped when Bess mentioned the cinnamon and honey. "Cinnamon and honey? Mmm, well, if you insist. Who can say no to cinnamon and honey?" Izzy came back to the table and gave Bess a quick hug before sitting down. "Thank you."

"You are welcome My Lady. I'll have a cup of mint tea out to you in just a minute as well." Bess hurried back to the kitchen to prepare the mint tea and then carefully carried a tea cup and saucer in one hand

and a tea pot in the other back into the hall. "Here we are Lady Isabel. If you need anything else, just call for me. I will not be too far." After setting the tea pot and tea set down, she hurried off to keep the daily chores organized and to help the kitchen staff prepare for the midday meal.

Izzy waited a few minutes before pouring herself a cup of mint tea. Surrounded by so much masculinity, her tea cup was a bright touch of delicate femininity. After she finished her oatmeal, she sat back in her chair and held her cup with both hands. Her mind drifted back to the camp and Henry. He was more handsome than she had remembered. He seemed intelligent, modern, and even funny. She knew that due to his pain and injury that she was not seeing all of the man he was. Curious, she would have to ask Lord James more about Henry should they visit Adonia for the festival. Oh! The festival! She would need to check in with the ladies from town to ask about the progress of the head wreaths that they would sell; ribbon braided with strips of leather to make a crown and tails of curling ribbon hanging down the back of the crown. There were also to be delicious sweets, foreign foods, and games for everyone to enjoy.

She poured herself one more cup of tea. It was cool enough to drink rather quickly now, and she preferred it that way. Taking large, unladylike gulps, Izzy drank the second cup of tea and left to search for Hugh. She needed to know everything that had happened these past two weeks while she was away and then she wanted to plan for the next few days leading up to the festival.

Izzy stepped outside of the Hall and into the courtyard where the sun was already high in the sky. The sun instantly warmed her face and the clothes that she wore. She could feel it all the way to her bones. She took a deep breath of the Adonian air and smiled. When she opened her eyes, she saw Hugh, Sir Calvin and Sir Merek looking at her, smiles on their faces. Calvin shook his head and called out, "And you thought you would never miss this place you considered prison," Hugh laughed as his smile grew even bigger. Izzy approached Hugh who was already walking her way.

"What is so very funny?" Izzy asked in jest, happiness bubbling up from inside of her.

"My Lady, you have the look of either someone who has fallen in love, or someone who has never experienced happiness until now. Tell me friend, which is it?" Hugh led Izzy around to the herber where she preferred to have their meetings when the weather allowed for it.

Love? She had not considered that before. Perhaps she had finally fallen in love. Who could blame her?

"Hugh, I believe you are right. I never once thought I could fall in love with Adonia, but truth be told I missed it and all of its wonderful people so very much! Happiness, well, it has been far too long since I have experienced true happiness and it has been at my feet all along." Izzy smiled at Hugh with hope in her eyes and her heart exposed for all to see should they pass by. She was vulnerable, and that was something she had not been in eight years. She felt a shiver run up her spine remembering that dark time, struggling to push the cold away and grasping at the warmth from the sun.

Hugh and Izzy spent the rest of the morning reviewing all of the news of the town, then finalizing plans for the remainder of the week until the festival. After their meeting and the midday meal, Izzy handed the note she had written to Hugh to send with a messenger to Hal, then walked over to the blacksmith where she left her dagger to be sharpened and picked up before evening. As she walked through town, she greeted everyone and asked how they were doing with the preparations for the festival. Three days of fun, laughter, friends and family; Izzy was beyond thrilled and even more excited for progress in Adonia.

On her way back to the blacksmith, Izzy passed the field of Felicia daisies that they had grown specifically for the festival. Each morning of the festival they would pick bundles of the beautiful blue daisies to sell. Smiling, she remembered her family before the plague. She drove the sad memories away and continued walking to the blacksmith. When she reached the shop, everything was quiet. The fires were no longer blazing and she did not see Baxter anywhere. She waited a moment longer, and then noticed that there were some beautiful pieces of metal work hanging on the wall. Slowly walking towards them, she became mesmerized by the complex details of each piece. They were incredible and Izzy wondered who they were being made for. There was a sound from behind her and Izzy jumped, spinning around quickly. It was just a cat jumping from a shelf. "Baxter? Are you around?" Izzy called out. She left the shop and walked over to Baxter's home. Hesitantly, she knocked on the door and called out again, "Baxter, are you home?"

There was a shuffle of feet and the sound of a chair sliding back. The door swung open as Baxter wiped his mouth. "My Lady, my apologies! I was grabbing an early meal, so that I could work on some pieces in the shop. I was not expecting you back so soon. I have your dagger right here." Leaving the door open he rushed to a shelf behind him and quickly picked up a sheathed dagger. "Here you are My Lady. Please be sure to check the blade to see that it meets your requirements. It is truly a beautiful dagger. Is it a family heirloom?"

Izzy inspected the blade. It was perfect. The hilt was magnificent; she could not remember ever seeing it shine so beautifully. "Did you shine the hilt as well?"

"I did My Lady. It was so carefully sculpted and carved; I took the liberty to clean it properly. Now the gems catch the sunlight as well. I did not recognize the crest on the hilt, which is why I suspected it to be passed down in your family. I hope I did not overstep."

"Oh no, quite the opposite. It is incredible. Thank you so very much for your extraordinary work." Beaming, Izzy paid him for his services and a little extra for the additional services rendered. Izzy quickly put on the belt with the sheath and dagger and left to return to the hall.

Upon arriving in the hall, Izzy was greeted by the room filled with knights. Oddly, she felt alone. She missed laughing with Henry and Hal. She and Hal teased and played the way she used to with Andy. Once their parents had passed, Andy did not want anything to do with Ackerley, or anything that reminded him of their parents, including her. People always commented on how she looked exactly like her mother, except for her blue eyes that were like her father's. Andy had their father's eyes too. It was the only feature that Andy and Izzy had in common; otherwise, no one would ever have realized they were related at all.

Izzy made it through the evening meal making small talk with the knights around her. Her mind was elsewhere and those around her noticed. Izzy excused herself afterward and retired early. She was still craving the softness and warmth of her own bed and could not even bear the idea of returning to that bed in camp.

The next three days passed so quickly, no one in town had a moment to breathe. The morning of the festival arrived and Izzy, like most everyone else in Adonia, was up before dawn to prepare for the day. She ran from vendor to vendor assuring that everything was perfect. The entire scene looked like it belonged on a painting. As the vendors were setting up, children ran around laughing and screaming. The sun lit up the trees and fields, and the low-lying fog slowly creeping back gave everything a romantic feel. Izzy had begun to retreat to the castle when she turned around to look at everyone below. It was breathtaking and she wished that Henry was here to be a part of it. She was jolted out of her daydream when she heard her name called. "Izzy!" Jayde called out and waved while holding one of the twins in her arms.

"Iz-Iz!" Ellyn called out as she ran as fast as her little toddler legs could carry her with her arms held high in the air towards Izzy.

Izzy ran towards Ellyn and scooped her up in her arms, spinning her around as she squealed in delight. "Again! Again!" Ellyn pleaded.

Izzy of course complied; she could not resist her darling little niece. Finally, Izzy made her way to Jayde and James giving them both affectionate hugs and inviting them inside where Izzy hoped that Bess had tea waiting for her.

Bess was just setting the table for Lady Isabel to sit down to the morning meal when she noticed Lady Jayde and her family come in as well.

"Oh! Lady Jayde! It has been too long!" Bess called out as she ran back into the kitchen grabbing another cup for tea and bringing it out for Lady Jayde as well. Bess was a few years older than Lady Jayde and she remembered the darkness that took over the castle when Lady Ethna moved in. Quickly, she and two other maids brought out oatmeal for the whole family to enjoy together.

"When did you arrive?" Izzy asked as she sat down and stirred her oatmeal.

"It was quite late last night. Hugh was so kind. He showed us to our room and offered to wake you, but I know how busy you have been and said we would announce ourselves in the morning," Jayde said. Izzy laughed as James struggled to keep the twins nearby.

"You laugh now Izzy, but a time will come when you are chasing after your own children and then we shall see who has the last laugh," James teased.

"James!" Jayde reprimanded giving him a stern look. Laughing, Izzy asked, "Is there something I should know or that you know and I do not?"

"I just do not want him to bring up something so sensitive. It is rude and I am still very cross with Henry for leaving like he did. He still has not written or visited anyone of us. You are his wife, and I expected better from him." Jayde spoke in the same tone any scolding mother would use.

195

"Do not be too tough on him Jayde. I think he feels far guiltier than any of us can imagine," Izzy said softly.

"Have you gone soft on us Izzy or are you in love?" James teased again.

Laughing with a sparkle in her eyes, Izzy said, "Hugh asked something like that of me the other day. I must confess that I feel a love for Adonia that I never realized was there before. As for Henry, he does not realize that his healer is also his wife." Izzy saw the shocked look on both James' and Jayde's faces.

"How does he not know who you are? Has he gone blind?" James asked.

Smiling gently Izzy explained, "He truly does not remember me. He is an interesting man and is very guarded about sharing information about any of you to anyone. I had to bargain with him to get him to even mention Geoff and Thomas. When I asked about his parents, he flinched as though I had hit him."

"When will you tell him who you really are?" Jayde asked curiously.

"I am not sure to be quite honest. I would really like to take this opportunity to get to know him more. I fear though, that the price I will pay to learn about who he really is will be losing his trust. I do not know if I could bear that either. At least this way, I can have a small taste of friendship with him, and that is something that I have always wanted." Izzy was thoughtful as she answered. She wondered just how fragile his heart was and if a friendship between them would be strong enough to survive the half-truths and lies that she was casting. An awkward silence fell across the group.

"You said in your message that Henry had been injured but was recovering well. How is he doing now?" James broke the silence.

"He is doing incredibly well! I was able to sew his wound up nicely, so as long as he takes it easy another few days and does not rip it open, there should be very little scar to show for his injury. He was up and doing light training and duties when I left. I am expecting a message from Prince Henry in the next couple of days." Izzy immediately looked down to her oatmeal. It almost felt too intimate to be expecting a note from Hal.

"Will you be returning to see Henry again sometime soon?" James asked Izzy, watching her face closely. He caught the flicker in her eyes and the slight upturn of her lips before she hid her face again.

"Yes, eventually. Prince Henry will be requesting me as a healer again when they ready for the next rebellion," Izzy said while staring into her bowl of oatmeal. She was afraid to look James in the eye because she worried that he might see something on her face that she was not ready to confront yet. There was something about Henry that made her want to know him more. Not just as her husband, but as a person. He appeared so tough, almost forsaken but when he watched her, when he did not think she could see him, there was a tenderness in his eyes that he kept hidden from the world.

James and Jayde watched Izzy, lost deep in thought as they finished eating in silence. They both glanced at each other, James with questions written across his face and Jayde with hope embracing her heart.

Izzy sat back, drinking her tea while she watched James and Jayde persuade the kids to eat their oatmeal. Smiling she could not help but feel a tightness in her chest, a longing for a family of her own that she very much doubted she would ever have. Just then Hugh walked in with both excitement and anxiety written across his face.

"Lady Isabel, there is a line of people already arriving and waiting at the gate! Should we open early, or make them wait?" Hugh asked excitedly.

Izzy smiled comfortingly at Hugh. "Just breathe, are most of the vendors ready?"

"Yes, nearly all of them are." Hugh struggled to contain himself.

Izzy was confused at his unrestrained excitement, so unusual for him. "Then, we should open the gates. Try to relax; we have three entire days to enjoy!"

"Lady Isabel, there is a very unusual pair of guests! You will never guess, let me just tell you! It is King Henry and Queen Joan!" Hugh said breathlessly.

Izzy sputtered, choking on her tea as she shoved her chair back and stood up. "Heavens above, please, I pray that you have not left them at the gate!"

"No, Lady Isabel, he most certainly did not," Queen Joan said as she and King Henry entered the hall hand in hand.

Immediately Izzy and Jayde curtsied deeply while James bowed with humility before the King and Queen.

"I truly hope it is not a bother to you that we stopped by. We were actually on our way to visit Ackerley, but remembered Hal saying that you were having a festival here in Adonia. Funny, we have never visited either estate." Queen Joan said as Ellyn wriggled free of Jayde's arms and ran to her wrapping her arms around her skirts. "My goodness, what a beautiful little girl!" Then bending over slightly, she asked, "What is your name darling?" Ellyn beamed up at the Queen. "Ellyn. You are so pretty! I like your dress!"

Jayde was purple with embarrassment. "Ellyn dear, come to mommy please."

Queen Joan smiled sweetly first at Ellyn then at Jayde. "She is no bother at all; she makes me miss when my daughters were so young. Lady Isabel, would you mind taking us about Adonia?"

"Yes of course Your Majesties. Would you like to start now or would you like to enjoy a cup of tea first?" Izzy asked.

"We can enjoy tea later while we talk. Henry darling, did you want to walk with us or would you rather Hugh show you the more masculine qualities of Adonia?" Queen Joan asked King Henry.

"Honestly my dear, I would like to go back to where I could see and smell the food. Hugh, could you show me around to the vendors?" King Henry asked already turning away from the ladies and heading back to the festival with two knights closely following behind him.

"As you wish dear. I will catch up with you soon!" Queen Joan said as she waved goodbye to his back. "Good, now we can talk freely."

Izzy felt quite awkward. In her many years of training with the nuns, she was far from prepared to entertain a Queen. "As you can see, we are in Adonia's Hall. For both the midday and evening meals, all of Adonia's knights share their meals together in here. It helps to bring about a sense of family and loyalty for one another." Izzy continued on sharing as much about the castle, its history and the wonderful people of Adonia as she could.

"While there are many amazing places here in Adonia, my garden and herber are my favorite places. My herber has all of the herbs I use to heal with. During the late spring, summer and fall, I typically like to eat my morning meal and drink tea out here." Izzy led the Queen into the heart of the garden.

Queen Joan inhaled sharply. It was beautiful. There were benches spaced around the garden, plants with no flowers and plants with flowers smaller than her pinky nail. She saw bushes of lavender far in the corner, and stepping stones weaving throughout the garden. Above the small table and two chairs, there was a sturdy trellis with healthy grape vines woven through. "Lady Isabel, was all of this here when you arrived?" Queen Joan finally managed to ask after taking in the natural splendor.

"No Your Highness. This was a barren space when I arrived, but with the help of the townspeople, it has become a beautiful and productive space. The stones there that make that wall were dug out of the fields by the farmers, and then the knights took shifts carrying them up here. Several knights and farmers helped me build that wall. Baxter, our blacksmith took each of the stepping stones and made sure they were smooth enough to walk on, barefoot even. He is a kind and gracious man and very artistic. I had the opportunity to see some of his carvings on some hilts and swords earlier this week. They were breathtaking." Izzy paused admiring her beautiful garden. "Oh, here is Bess. Your Majesty, would you like to take our morning tea out here or should we return to the hall?"

"Oh, let us take our tea out here. This is far too stunning to walk away from," Queen Joan gushed. Izzy and Queen Joan sat at the table while Bess brought out two elegant tea cups and a pot of tea. Bess poured the Queen a cup of tea first, and then poured one for Izzy while another servant brought out tea cakes.

Queen Joan waited for the servants to leave before speaking again. "Lady Isabel, Hal tells us that you are an amazing healer. Do you agree?"

"I am flattered that his Royal Highness spoke so highly of me. I do believe that I am very good, as that is what I was so meticulously trained for. I know that the people of Adonia trust me and that speaks volumes," Izzy said as she admired the tea set that she had never seen before. She would be sure to ask Bess about the tea set after the King and Queen had left.

"Hal said that you took care of the many knights in the camp as well, always putting their health and comfort before yourself. He was quite impressed." Queen Joan spoke matter-of-factly. "May I ask how it is that you were trained by nuns to be a healer, and then came to be married? I was under the impression that when you were trained by nuns it was because you were intending to enter the convent. Am I mistaken?"

Izzy took a sip of her tea now that it was cool enough to actually drink. "You are not mistaken, but I was not intending to join the convent. My parents passed when I was twelve and my brother abandoned me so that he could go train with the knights. After spending nearly every day at my parents' grave markers for a month, the nuns took pity on me and began to teach me about herbs and flowers and how to grow them. Eventually they taught me of healing and midwifery. I was a good pupil. I did as I was told and I learned quickly. After a few years, my people in Ackerley began to trust me as a healer. By the time I was eighteen, I had decided that my time to marry was likely past and with my parents gone and my only guardian afraid of being reminded of what we had lost, I did not think I was considered eligible any longer. I was preparing to go to the nuns and pledge to them when I received an urgent note from my brother requesting my presence in Era for a marriage," Izzy smiled softly, taking another drink of her tea.

Queen Joan thought about this young lady's story and found herself still not understanding everything. "Then how did you come to know Hal?"

Izzy explained the notes she had written to her husband, and how when he was injured, Hal had read those notes and realizing that Henry had a wife, sent for her.

"Oh, that explains it all now. Hal says that your husband does not recognize you, is that due to an injury?" Queen Joan asked.

Izzy smiled and laughed gently. "Unfortunately no." She then went on to describe her wedding day and Henry being whisked away at Hal's request. When she got to the part where she reprimanded her intoxicated husband, Queen Joan burst into laughter.

"Your Majesty, may I ask why you are traveling to Adonia and Ackerley?" Izzy ventured.

"Hal spoke so highly of you, Adonia and Ackerley that I was curious to see what was so intriguing. Hal said that the way you described Ackerley made him feel as though he had actually grown up there with you," Queen Joan replied.

"Ackerley is a sight to behold. It has nothing like your royal gardens or grounds I am sure, but I promise, it will not disappoint," Izzy said confidently.

Queen Joan smiled and asked, "Are you able to visit Ackerley often?"

"I try to visit as often as possible, although it is usually only once every two or three months. I usually stay there for three to five weeks at a time and do occasionally visit for a few days here and there, especially if there is an urgent matter to attend to." Izzy made a note to send a messenger to Ackerley as soon as possible to give her servants advance notice of the King and Queen's impending visit. She knew that they would be sure to dress the bed with clean sheets, open the windows to air it out, and pick fresh flowers for the bedside tables. She was confident that Myles would take care of anything the King and Queen might need and that there would be succulent meals planned.

"I hate to leave your little corner of paradise, but I must go find my husband before he becomes too tired to travel. Thank you for the wonderful tea. Is it a blend that you made yourself?" Queen Joan asked as she stood.

"It was my pleasure to share tea with you Queen Joan. Yes, the blend is one that I created. It is lemon and rose. I am so pleased to know you liked it! Thank you." Izzy stood with her and led the way through the garden and down to the festival.

The festival was already filled with people from many different nearby estates and as soon as people recognized the Queen, they stopped and bowed or curtsied to her.

"Izzy, what are your intentions for Adonia with this festival?" the Queen asked nonchalantly.

"Adonia has a unique charm to it do you agree?" Izzy asked. Then without waiting for an answer she continued on. "I want to help the people here by showing them that they have something to offer to all of England, but to also help it to grow. Adonia has been in such a bad state for so long and needs to be self-sufficient again. I would like to open up more trade between our neighbors too."

"What will you do when Adonia grows and you suddenly have more finances and power?" Queen Joan pushed on. She knew that Adonia could flourish, and with enough power, if they banded together with other estates, they could harm the already fragile monarchy.

"Power? Oh gracious, Adonia does not need power. We are a confident and small community and are finally starting to help each other. I cannot imagine having power to do anything with. I suppose that if we were a powerful enough community then we could be of great benefit to the monarchy. I know that Lord Henry believes in the crown and would forsake all else to support it. As for the finances, Adonia is still a struggling estate, recovering from the hell it had been put through when Lady Ethna resided here. I do not know all of the details, but the townspeople were terrified of her. When I arrived, I was shut out, feared, and not trusted. The people of Adonia have grown to not only trust in me during the last two years, but to trust one another as well. It is incredible to watch, almost like watching a child grow up."

Queen Joan relaxed knowing that it was not Lady Isabel's intentions to create more problems. "What will you do Lady Isabel, when your husband learns the truth about who you are?

"I do not know. It is something I think about and fear nearly each night. It is too late for me to tell him who I truly am, and yet it is too early as well. All I ever wanted was to be his friend. I remember him from when I was a young girl. Our families were friends, and we would often spend a week at their estate visiting each summer. In turn they would visit us each fall. I was always tagging along with my brother and I remember that he and Lord Raymond would get so annoyed by me. They used to push me down and run away, desperate to leave me behind, as many brothers do. I remember one time in particular, because Andy pushed me down into the mud. I sat there in my new lavender dress crying. That was the last summer that any of us would visit. The plague began to pick at our families one by one. I remember the hot angry tears streaming down my mud-covered face and through the blur I saw a hand extend out to me. Looking up, it was the second oldest of the five de Seaton boys, Lord Henry. He pulled me up and wiped my face with the edge of his shirt. He said that purple made my eyes even more blue than before. Then he made a plan to help me get back at both Andy and Raymond, promising that they would never push me down again. He was right. We played a prank on them the next day and Andy never pushed me around again." Izzy laughed a little of the memory of Andy and Raymond running from the woods screaming like little boys while she and Henry were doubled over laughing. How could Henry not remember her? Izzy and Queen Joan found Hugh with King Henry sitting happily in the shade biting into the last of a chicken breast. "Oh, my love! You must taste this, it is absolutely delightful. The man says it is cooked with cumin, garlic, and pepper," King Henry hummed as he chewed, handing a piece of the fried meat to his wife.

"It is quite delicious. We will mention it to the cooks when we get home. Are you ready to travel to Ackerley now? We will not make to our camp before nightfall if we do not leave now," Queen Joan reminded her husband.

"Ah yes, I suppose. Lady Isabel, it was a pleasure to see your little town and partake in your festival. I hope that we enjoy our visit to Ackerley just as much." King Henry stood, cleaning his hands and handing the soiled linen to a servant next to him. Izzy curtsied deeply to the King while saying the pleasure was hers and that she hoped they enjoyed their visit to Ackerley as much as she always did. As soon as the King and Queen were in their carriage and on their way, Izzy grabbed Hugh. "Hugh, I need to send a messenger to Ackerley immediately to give them notice of the King and Queen visiting."

"I already sent a messenger this morning and sent it urgently. I knew you would expect no less of me." Hugh said with a tender smile. He understood the love for the land that Izzy had. Ackerley was like a child to Izzy, much like Adonia was to him and now to Izzy as well.

Izzy was so relieved she let out the pent-up breath that she had been holding. Smiling and thanking Hugh, she began to walk about the festival assessing how each stand and vendor were doing. She quietly listened to the conversations between guests and vendors, as well as patrons that were relaxing in the shade of the trees. When she came upon Baxter's table, her breath was taken away. On the table were a few of the incredible masterpieces she had seen on shelves in his shop earlier that week. Also on the table were a few pieces of jewelry. "Oh my goodness! Baxter, these are beautiful!" Izzy said as she gently touched the bracelet and matching necklace.

The color rose in Baxter's cheeks. "My Lady, you flatter me. Thank you."

"Oh no Baxter, I am quite honest. Could you possibly add some gems to these for me?" Izzy inquired.

"Of course, My Lady. What stones would you like?" Baxter asked.

"I would like the pale blue zircon paired with imperial topaz. Could you please leave two blank links between the pairs?" Izzy requested.

"Yes, of course Lady Isabel. I will finish it as soon as possible. It will take a few days so that I may acquire the perfect stones," Baxter said as he smiled. The two stones would be beautiful together and he realized that they represented the colors for Adonia and Ackerley. He was touched that she wanted something to wear to show everyone the pride in her estates. Only people from Adonia or Ackerley would understand and that, he felt, was more important and intimate than any banner or flag. He was thrilled that she would choose his work to wear. Izzy smiled and continued on searching for Jayde, James, and the children as she excitedly thought about the jewelry she was purchasing. This way she would always have a piece of Adonia and Ackerley with her where ever she went.

Finding Jayde and James nowhere in sight she made her way back up to the castle. She found Jayde and James sitting alone in the quiet hall. James appeared almost asleep himself. "My, it is quiet in here. Are the children napping?" Izzy whispered, almost afraid of disrupting the calm atmosphere.

Jayde smiled and quietly stood to link her arm with Izzy's and turned them towards the gardens. "We will just leave James there to rest. The boys wear him out easily these days."

Once back in the garden and sitting at the table where Izzy had sat with the Queen just hours before, Jayde inquired about the meeting with the Queen. Izzy and Jayde talked about the visit while enjoying tea from Bess until the afternoon began to cool down.

"Well, I suppose the children will be awake soon, I should go and make sure they are ready for the evening meal." Jayde spoke as she stood up and began to walk inside.

Izzy noticed that Jayde rested her hand across her midsection. "Jayde, how are you feeling?"

Jayde stopped and looked back at Izzy. She should have known that Izzy would know nearly as soon as she herself had realized it. She smiled sheepishly at Izzy. "Are you ready to deliver another niece or nephew?"

Izzy jumped up and gave Jayde a huge hug. "Oh Jayde! I am so excited for you! When do you estimate that you are due?"

"Sometime around Christmas I think. Do you think you would be home then?" Jayde asked. Izzy had delivered Ellyn, Edward and Dario and she could not imagine anyone else being there for her.

"I promise I will be there no matter what. Does James know yet?" Izzy whispered.

"I have not told him yet. I will tell him when we get back home. Oh Izzy, how am I supposed to manage four young children! I do not know how we will survive!" Jayde said, her voice laced with worry. Izzy smiled, "You are such a strong woman and amazing mother, you will do just fine. Until you tell James, your secret is my secret."

"Come on, let us go inside. Poor James is likely losing his mind already!" Jayde said with a giggle.

Chapter 8

The festival had been a tremendous success and before Izzy knew it the week was almost finished. Hugh and Izzy had agreed that there should be five new homes built before the end of summer. They would contract with the current residents for time, labor and supplies and pay them accordingly. This would keep money from Adonia stay in Adonia and help its current residents at the same time. To keep from putting too much strain on the town, Hugh agreed with Izzy that they needed to limit the number of new families moving in. Just as they had hoped, there were several families that requested permission to relocate to Adonia and Izzy decided that they would accept petitions for relocation through the end of June when they would give their decisions. This would also allow them to see what trades could be filled. After their meeting, Izzy spent the remainder of the morning and most of the afternoon picking herbs and preparing them to be dried.

It had been a long day and she was beginning to wonder if she would hear from Hal sometime soon. The castle had been too quiet after Jayde, James and the children had left and Izzy felt an emptiness that was slowly encroaching on her soul. After the evening meal, she decided to take a walk-through town to occupy her mind on anything other than the family that she would never have. Izzy passed the

Felicia daisy patch and leaned down picking several flowers. Continuing through town she was on her way back up to the castle, when she heard her name being called. Stopping, she turned and looked to see who it was. It was Baxter!

Izzy placed a hand on his shoulder as he caught his breath. "Baxter, what is the matter, is everything okay?"

"Yes My Lady, I was trying to catch up to you because I have your bracelet and necklace completed," Baxter panted, still stooped over slightly with his hands on his thighs.

"Really? I will walk with you back to your shop to pay you and pick them up then!" Izzy exclaimed happily.

"Oh, that will not be necessary. I brought them with me!" Baxter held up a box.

"Please, let us go into the hall then." Izzy turned to lead him to the hall. Once inside, Baxter set the box down on a table. Izzy looked at it and traced the intricate carvings she found. Tracing each image, she came across two words on the bottom. Her breath caught in her throat and she felt tears slowly fall down her cheeks.

Quietly, almost sacredly, Baxter began to speak. "The oak tree is obviously representation of Ackerley. The Goddess is Adonia, the Lamb represents you, a symbol of gentleness and patience under suffrage, and of course the Staff of Asclepius is symbolic of the healer."

 "And the name at the bottom, where did you get that from?" Izzy whispered, afraid of breaking the unspeakable beauty with her words.

Once again Baxter spoke, whispering as if he was in church, "My Lady, word of Healing Bird travels quickly; especially when the King and Queen of our country take a trip specifically to meet her just for the sake of meeting her. I am honored to have had an opportunity to make something for our Healing Bird. It is an honor that I will cherish as long as I am alive."

Izzy looked up to meet his gaze and when their eyes met, Baxter bowed deeply and graciously before her. "My Lady, you might not wear a crown, but you deserve no less respect." Baxter praised.

When Baxter stood upright again, Izzy reached forward and hugged him with all of her might. Finally letting go, Baxter spoke again. "Healing Bird, would you like to inspect the jewelry?"

"Yes." Izzy's breath caught again in her throat. As Baxter opened the box, the sunlight glinted off of the stones, reflecting their brilliant colors.

"Baxter, these are incredible!" Izzy exclaimed as she lifted the long necklace out of the blue velvet lined box and put it on over her head. Baxter helped her to put the bracelet on and then took a step back smiling.

"Baxter, your work is impeccable. I am privileged to wear these pieces. Thank you." Izzy paid him for his work and watched as he humbly left the hall. She stood there staring at the box. It held more sentiment than anything else she had ever seen or owned. Despite Baxter saying the honor was his, she knew that truly, the honor was hers.

"Pardon me My Lady, the evening meal is nearly ready. Would you like for me to carry the box for you and help you to change?" Bess asked, startling Izzy out of her reverie.

"Yes, thank you, I would appreciate the help." Carefully, she handed the box over to Bess as she made her way upstairs to her chamber. She removed her new jewelry only long enough to change her dress, and then put her necklace and bracelet back on.

Bess left the room for the kitchen where the meal was being placed on platters while the knights filed into the hall.

Izzy admired the jewelry again before finally leaving her room and returning downstairs. Everyone was already seated and waiting for her as she walked to her seat., Outside, the sound of a single horseman could be heard galloping into the courtyard.

Immediately every knight in the room stood, placing their hand on their daggers and swords prepared for anything that was about to come rushing in.

Izzy held her breath waiting for what she assumed was a messenger. Would it be from Jayde or Hal? The messenger came in breathless. "Excuse me, I am searching for Healing Bird?"

Instantly, every knight relaxed. As everyone else reseated themselves, she remained standing. "I am Healing Bird," she announced nervously.

The room erupted in cheers, shocking the messenger and causing him to jump. The messenger proceeded to walk unsteadily to the one woman standing. "My Lady, I was given strict orders to hand this directly to you."

"Thank you very much," Izzy said accepting the message and paying the messenger. "Go to the kitchen and Bess will prepare a plate for you." Izzy signaled to Bess to serve the meal while she retreated to the study upstairs to read the note in privacy.

Healing Bird,

 I hope that your time off has been well served and you are rested. We have moved our camp finally and are preparing for another battle. Please leave by dawn tomorrow and return to us. The knights are healthier than ever and everyone has healed beautifully. I know you must be curious about your most injured patient. He is doing quite well physically, although it seems as though something else is wrong and he is taking his frustration out on everyone in camp. I am sure that as soon as our healer has returned, she will be able to diagnose

*and treat his 'affliction' and our camp as a
whole will be much happier.*
                    Yours Truly,
                         Hal

Izzy folded the message back up and placed it in the
desk drawer. Locking the drawer, she took a sheet of
paper and quill and wrote a note to Sadie.

> *Sadie,*
>   *Our services have been requested
> again. Please be ready to travel in two
> days. A second messenger and a knight will
> arrive then to travel with you and bring you
> to our location. I hope that your family and
> Ackerley are doing well. See you soon my
> friend. Be well and safe travels.*
>   *Izzy*

Folding and sealing the note, Izzy returned
downstairs to find Hugh waiting for her. "I travel by
dawn with two knights and the messenger. Would
you please send an Adonian messenger in the
morning to Ackerley and have this note delivered to
Sadie please?"
"Yes, of course Lady Isabel." Hugh took the note
and placed it in his pocket. "My Lady, will our
Healing Bird need anything for her travels in the
morning?" Hugh asked.

Izzy could see the sparkle in his eyes as he called her Healing Bird. She could see the pride exuding from his body and she could not stop the blush that crept into her face. "I will pack after the evening meal. I will request your help gathering items then." Hugh nodded at Izzy as she turned away and sat down again to finally enjoy her meal.

Not more than five minutes had passed when another set of hooves could be heard racing into the courtyard. Izzy's heart sank as the whole room grew quiet. If Hal had already sent his message, then this one could only be from Jayde, and something must be wrong at the speed of the rider. Standing, waiting for the urgent message, Izzy cried out when she saw the rider walk into the hall.

"Raymond!" Izzy cried out racing across the room to him.

Raymond was exhausted from riding so hard for so long but when he saw Izzy running toward him, he opened his arms, lifting her up and spinning her around as he hugged her. "Sweet little sister! I have missed you! I beg of you, tell me there is a seat for me at your table. There is so much to discuss and I am famished. I hear there is a mysterious healer living nearby…" The room once again erupted in cheers. "I do believe I have found her!" Raymond said, following Izzy to the table while Bess brought out another place setting and Hugh pulled up another chair for Lord Raymond.

"Raymond, what brings you to Adonia? Is everyone well?" Izzy asked still too nervous to eat.

"Yes, actually I have just left them in Era. I swear, Ellyn will have all of England wrapped about her finger should she choose too," Raymond laughed. "She already has every maid in Era and Adonia at her beck and call and not a single person can seem to say no to her except Jayde. She has her work cut out for her raising that little angel. What brings you to Adonia so urgently?"

He smiled. He could always count on Izzy for getting straight to business. It was truly one of his favorite qualities about her. "How is Henry? Jayde says he still has not come to his senses."

Izzy sighed deeply. Raymond was unlike either of his brothers. He might not be able to keep a secret, but he would only answer her questions when he was ready. James and Henry would collapse like a deck of cards, but Raymond could withstand her interrogation for much longer. "Henry is doing well. He healed quickly but is still quite guarded against me."

"Jayde said that you have kept your identity as his wife a secret from him. He only knows you as Lady Bird. Why is that?" Raymond asked before taking a spoonful of the chicken and dumpling soup and shoving it into his mouth.

"I went because His Royal Highness sent for me but then, well, Henry did not remember me." Izzy began to explain.

219

"Oh, yes, Hal told me everything but he could not, or would not, explain the reason for the secrecy. He said it was a matter of the heart, but would say nothing more," Raymond stated, continuing to eat. Izzy considered his words and Hal's statement. A matter of the heart, huh? "I just wanted to know who he was, I wanted him to at least be my friend. Adonia has become a place that I love and cherish and a place I call home. I cannot imagine existing here if he hates me." She looked at Raymond hoping he could understand. In response, she saw softness in his eyes, something she had never seen, not in any of the de Seaton brothers.

Raymond listened carefully to her words and watched the expression on her face change into hope as she spoke about Adonia, then change again to a gentleness he had not witnessed on a woman's face since his mother was alive. Without thinking, Raymond asked, "Do you care for him Izzy?" Izzy was shocked at the uncharacteristically blunt question from Raymond. She blinked her eyes rapidly to clear the shock from her mind before answering. "I do not know. He still will not open up to me, and I fear that even if he does, when he learns the truth, he will shut me out again."

"Izzy, Henry is not like that. He wears his heart on his sleeve. If he opens up to you, he will never truly be able to shut you out. He was so hurt by James' decision to marry the two of you without his consent that rather than retaliate, he simply fled. He will never stop loving our brother no matter the cost to himself. Right now, the cost of loving his family is to sacrifice the opportunity for his own happiness and you." Raymond paused, wondering if he should continue on. "Izzy, I read the letters that you wrote." He saw the look of shock on her face. "He willingly showed them to me. He said he hates how he has treated you, but does not think he can ever earn your forgiveness. He told me about this healer that everyone in camp loves. They call her Healing Bird." He saw the gentle smile on her face. "He talked about her a lot. He said that she is beautiful, strong, witty, and not afraid of a single man in that camp, including him." Raymond chuckled at Henry's story about her ordering him about. "He was quite amused at how this Healing Bird gave him strict orders and how he was even slightly terrified at what she might do to him should he disobey her. It sounded like Henry had possibly met his match, his equal. Someone that he wanted to know more about, wanted to fall in love with. Someone who could love him unconditionally." Raymond watched Izzy's face as she listened to him without meeting his gaze. Softly, he asked, "Do you know where I might be able to find her?"

Izzy looked up finally meeting his gaze, fighting the tears that welled up in her eyes, threatening to fall down her cheeks.

Raymond saw what he hoped were tears of hope and promise. He smiled and sighed, setting his spoon down on the table. "Izzy, do not give up on him. Let him fall in love with you."

"And what am I to do when he realizes that he loves his Healing Bird and cannot bear to be without her. What do I do when he wants to cast his wife, Lady Isabel de Seaton, aside?" Izzy asked struggling to restrain her emotions.

"You just be the beautiful, strong woman that you have always been and you show him who you really are. He might be angry, he might laugh at himself for not seeing it sooner, but do not give up. He needs you," Raymond tried to encourage her.

Izzy and Raymond ate the rest of their meal avoiding the subject of Henry all together. After the hall had cleared out, they moved to the chairs near the fireplace. "Bess, would you bring us a pot of tea? No ale for us tonight. I suspect there is business for us to tend to," Izzy announced while looking at Raymond who turned his face from her to gaze into the fire. His simple gesture confirmed that her suspicions were right. Once Bess had returned with the pot of tea and two cups, Izzy excused her for the night. The two sat in silence for quite some time waiting for the tea to steep and cool off a bit.

"Well, Raymond, while I enjoyed our conversation earlier, I assume it is not Henry that you came here to discuss. What is going on? Are you in trouble?" Izzy cut right to the chase.

Without looking up, Raymond answered. "No, I am not in any trouble, but I am going to be leaving soon.

Very soon actually." He took a deep breath and looked up, meeting Izzy's gaze. "I am going to be gone for quite some time."

Izzy felt confusion and a hint of fear in the pit of her stomach. "Does James know?"

"Yes, I needed his blessing for what intend to do." Raymond took another deep breath. "You see Izzy, where I am going, I might not ever make it back. It is risky, and Iole, well that was my mother's estate."

Izzy was starting to understand what Raymond was doing.

"Iole is breathtaking, and it was such an important place to my mother. When James gifted it to me after he married Jayde, I was honored. Not just honored, but I felt as though I was getting one more chance to be with mom. To be surrounded by the halls, trees and flowers that she grew up with was truly a gift. So you understand that I cannot let Iole fall to ruin and abandonment?" He watched as Izzy nodded. "I needed James' blessing because I am not going to be asking him to accept responsibility for it." Again, Raymond paused before speaking again. "Izzy, I need for you to accept responsibility of Iole. I know that you can take care of it better than I and I know that should I not come back, that you will love it as dearly as you love Ackerley and Adonia. Please, do this for me."

Izzy looked into Raymond's eyes. She could see the love in his eyes for his mother and Iole and also the desperation in them. "You are sure that James agrees to this?"

"Yes, I have his signature right here, in fact." Raymond pulled the document out of his leather bag and set it on the table. "I wanted his signature on it as well because I need for you to know that we both feel that you are the right person to continue to care for Iole. Please Izzy, will you say yes?"

Izzy could not believe what she was hearing. "Raymond, of course you will come back. This is silly! Where on earth could you possibly be going and not coming back?"

Raymond held his breath and released it, words spilling out in one breath. "Izzy, I am going on a sailing vessel. I am going to explore."

Izzy felt her shoulders sink. "So, it is the sea that is calling to your heart, not a woman." Izzy stood silently staring at the document. "May I read the document in full?"

"Yes, of course." Raymond smiled and said, "I would not expect any less from the brilliant woman that you are, little sister." Raymond waited while Izzy read the document. It was quite a straightforward document. It ensured that should he die, no one else could try to claim the estate, lands, farms or people as their own. It stated that should he survive and return, he could not take Iole back. It also guaranteed that in the event that Henry tried to annul their marriage that he could not take possession of Iole and if Henry died, that Iole would remain hers. The document specifically stated that Iole belonged solely to Isabel de Seaton, and no one else. Any profits that were made through Iole belonged to Izzy.

Izzy picked up the quill and ink that Raymond had already laid in front of her. She signed and dated the document. "Raymond, when do you leave for your port?"

"I leave at dawn. It is a half day's ride there." Raymond became choked up. "My horse, though, I will have to sell him when I arrive. There is no place for a horse on the vessel. He is a good horse. He will make someone else very happy."

"Thank you for entrusting Iole to me. I promise to care for her and protect her as I do Ackerley and Adonia." Izzy watched as Raymond nodded and tucked his quill and ink back into his bag. "You should go upstairs and get some rest. Dawn will come faster than you are prepared for. Good night Raymond." Izzy hugged him tightly and watched as he left her alone in the hall, disappearing upstairs to his chamber. Izzy immediately went to find Hugh and wake him.

"Hugh, I am sorry to wake you but this is urgent and I need your help," Izzy called as she knocked on his door. There was a shuffle of feet and the sound of something knocking over. Izzy cringed. The door finally opened and Hugh stood before her with his sleeping gown on. "Hugh, I hate to wake you, but I need your help."

225

"Of course, Lady Isabel. Let me dress and I shall meet you in the hall in just a moment." Hugh wiped the sleep from his eyes and stifled a yawn.
Nodding in agreement Izzy turned on her heal and hurried back to the hall, out of the cold night.
Izzy sat down immediately at the desk in the hall and wrote a note to Hal.

> *Hal,*
>
> *An urgent family matter has arisen and I must delay my travel to camp by one day. I do hope that you understand and know that I will explain everything in great detail when I arrive.*
> *Your Friend,*
> *Healing Bird*

Izzy folded and sealed the note. Hearing footsteps behind her, she turned around to see Hugh quickly walking towards her. After explaining to him Raymond's situation, he understood exactly what she needed without her saying much to him.
"Have you already written a note for His Royal Highness?" Hugh asked.
"I have, here it is." Izzy handed the sealed note to Hugh.
"I will wake the messenger and send him on his way immediately. He has already given a detailed description of where the camp is to Calvin and Merek, as well as your two knights from Ackerley. I

shall wake Calvin and Merek in a few hours to ready them for your journey with Raymond. When you return, your knights from Ackerley, Sir Wade and Sir Randall will be waiting with a fresh horse for you and will take you to the camp," Hugh confirmed. "Have you packed for camp yet?"

"I have packed some items, but still have much more to do," Izzy said feeling the effects of an already long day becoming longer.

"My Lady, you should try and rest before your ride in the morning. I will take care of packing some dried staples for your journey. Is there anything else I can pack for you?" Hugh asked waiting to be dismissed.

"No, I am going to go finish packing and then prepare for my journey to port with Lord Raymond. Thank you, Hugh. I could not have prepared for the morning and the evening journeys without you." Smiling, she placed her hand on his forearm before turning toward her chambers to finish packing for travel to the camp. She already knew that there would be no rest for her this night, and it was nothing new, but she did worry about going two days without rest. She suspected that by the time she arrived in camp that there would be many people waiting for her services. Quickly packing dresses for herself, she went and dug into a trunk that she had brought over from Ackerley last year. Opening it up, she smiled touching the beautiful quilt of light blue, lavender and white. Her mother had made this for her when she was still a baby. Sometimes still, Izzy would pull out the quilt and hold it tight finding comfort in knowing her mother had made it. Carefully lifting it out of the trunk, she picked up the next quilt. It was a quilt that her mother had made for her father. He took it with him anytime he had to travel for long periods of time. It was a deep blue with dark orange accents of small oak leaves bordering the edges. The best thing about this quilt was that it was a summer quilt and much lighter than the others that her mother had made. It could be folded up quite compactly and being mostly dark blue, it would not show dirt as easily as it would if it were white. Izzy pulled it out and laid it on the bed. Carefully she returned the other quilt to the trunk then walked over to the small desk in the corner. Sitting down, she wrote a note for Raymond. After folding the note, she laid it on top of the quilt. Then she took one of the Felicia daisies that she had picked and tucked it into the folds of the note. Quietly, she went down stairs to search for twine and wrapping paper. She began looking in the kitchen hoping that she would find it quickly. Instead, Hugh found her.

"My Lady, I see that you are not getting any rest. What can I help you to find?" Hugh asked as he set down travel bags.

"I was hoping to find twine and wrapping paper. I have something that I want Raymond to have but I need to wrap it first," Izzy said still opening and closing cabinets.

"This way My Lady," Hugh directed as he walked toward the bakery. Opening the last drawer in the kitchen, he pulled out thick brown twine. Then continuing on to the large pantry, he pulled down a roll of brown wrapping paper. "Will these do?"

"Oh Hugh! Thank you!" Izzy said as she took the items and rushed back upstairs. She was running out of time and knew that Raymond would leave earlier than he planned. He hated goodbyes and avoided them at all costs. She wrapped the quilt and note and rushed back down to the hall where Hugh was waiting for her, holding her riding cloak. Hugh handed Izzy her leather travel bag and waited for her to place the wrapped package inside it. She put the strap over her shoulder and neck and let the bag rest against her right hip. Then, taking her riding cloak from Hugh, she fastened it and walked out to the stables where her horse was waiting along with Sir Calvin and Sir Merek. The three of them waited for Raymond who came sneaking into the stable from the back. They waited until he had mounted his horse and was quietly walking him from the stable.

"As I live and breathe!" Raymond shouted, startled, as three cloaked riders appeared from the outside of the stable in front of him. He was about to draw his sword when Izzy pulled her hood back.

"You did not honestly think for one minute that you would ride alone, did you?" Izzy asked.

"I had hoped that I would not wake you and would not have to say it. You know I hate the finality of that word," Raymond said.

"Then when we get to port, we will be sure to not say goodbye. Instead we shall say, 'see you soon.' Does that sound better?" Izzy asked even though it was more of a statement. She saw Raymond nod his answer.

Raymond could say nothing. He knew that like Jayde, there would be no argument and that Izzy would not change her mind. In truth, he was grateful that he would not ride alone and maybe they would even stay to watch him depart.

"If we intend to get far before the heat of the sun begins, we should go now." Izzy turned her horse towards the gate.

Raymond spurred his horse forward quickly alongside Izzy's, Calvin and Merek close at his heals. They rode hard for hours, only stopping only once to water the horses and eat a snack of dried fruit. They arrived in Tenby just in time for the midday meal. The group of four tied their horses in the shade, sat under a tree and enjoyed bread, meat and wine. As they were finishing their meal, a bell began to toll.

"Well, this is it, here I go." Raymond stood up and stared towards the sea unsure of how to say goodbye.

"Come on, let's ride to the pier. From there you can hand me the reins to your horse. I will bring him home and keep him for you. I promise I will not let

Orion get fat," Izzy said as she mounted her own horse. "Is this still what you want to do?"

"Yes, it is still something I want to do," Raymond said confidently. The four of them rode to the pier where the crowd was beginning to thicken. There were wives and children crying, supplies being loaded onto the ship, dogs running around barking, and younger women being kissed goodbye.

Izzy could see the thirst for adventure in Raymond's eyes. "Will you promise to write to us every few months?"

Raymond smiled as he climbed off his horse and handed the reins to Izzy. "I promise to write as often as I can."

"I look forward to hearing of your adventures and the places you go. We will see you soon Raymond! Godspeed brother!" Izzy called out waving her hand high in the air while smiling.

Raymond walked around all of the people, grabbing a sack of grain on his way to the ship. After he crossed the gangway, he signed in with the Captain. Looking back to where he left his horse, Izzy and the knights, he could see them all waving, Izzy waved the fiercest of them all. Even from here, he could see the smile on her face. Smiling back, he gave a short wave before turning around and getting to work. Suddenly Izzy realized that she had forgotten to give him his gift. Jumping from her horse, she pulled the package from her bag and ran screaming at the top of her lungs, "Raymond! Raymond wait! I forgot to give this to you! Raymond!" She continued to yell as she ran with her skirts hitched high up to her knees. Raymond heard Izzy calling for him frantically. Racing back up on deck, he saw her running towards him. Worried that something could have gone wrong so quickly he ran across the gangway and grabbed her. "What! How could something have already gone wrong?"

Trying to catch her breath, she saw the captain staring at them. "I forgot to give you this." Izzy shoved the package into his hands with relief. "Open it later, when you can."

Raymond took the gift and looked as his sweet little sister. He grabbed her and hugged her tightly. He could feel Izzy's body shaking.

Izzy began to cry on his shoulder holding on to him as tightly as she could. "Raymond, promise me that you will come home! Promise!"

Raymond held her tighter and whispered in her ear, "I promise I will do everything within my power to return home to all of you."

"I love you Raymond de Seaton, do not ever forget that," Izzy whispered fiercely as she pulled back from him and wiped her face.

"I will never forget." Raymond said finally letting go of her.

The captain bellowed, "Let's go!"

Raymond crossed the gangway again and boarded the ship. "Take care Healing Bird!" Raymond called as the gangway was pulled back, the sails dropped and the anchor pulled up. Raymond turned to go below deck and leave the package on his bunk when the captain grabbed him.

"Raymond, I know that this is your first major sail, but as my second in command, you do not sleep below and do not leave your personal belongings about. Your cabin is next to mine. Go get your bags and bring them up."

"Yes sir." Raymond went below and gathered his belongings. When he came back out on deck, he could still see Izzy standing at the edge of the pier looking out to them.

She stood at the edge of the pier watching the ship sail away with Raymond on it, knowing it would be quite some time before they would see him again - if they ever saw him again. She would find out from Hal where the vessel was going, what it was intended to do and ask him to keep her informed should anything happen. Finally, she turned around and solemnly walked back up the pier to where Calvin and Merek were waiting. The two knights watched as Izzy grabbed her horse and mounted it. They could see the tear stains on her cheeks and her slumped shoulders. Without another word, the three of them began the long ride home to Adonia with Orion, Raymond's horse, with them.

Chapter 9

The group arrived in Adonia long after the evening meal had been eaten. They were exhausted and practically fell off their horses as they arrived at the stables. Stumbling into the hall, Hugh and Bess quickly brought out warm biscuits, rabbit stew, cold ale and grapes. Izzy had managed not to shed a single tear the entire ride back and decided that she would not allow herself to cry here either. She could cry later, when she was alone.

Hugh and Bess left the three of them to eat alone and retreated to the kitchen. "Did you see how swollen her sweet little eyes are Hugh? Oh, the poor dear must be so sad."

"I know, I saw. She will handle this in her own time. I must go and wake Sir Wade and Sir Randall for their ride with Lady Isabel. Unfortunately, she has left herself no time to rest." Hugh left to go wake the knights and tell the stable boys to have three rested horses saddled and ready to go shortly. Upon returning to the hall, he saw Bess clearing the table as Calvin and Merek we leaving. Standing at the fireplace, stood Izzy with her hands stretched out towards the warm fire.

"Lady Isabel, when you are ready, your horse is ready as well. Is there anything I can get you?" Hugh asked.

Izzy shook her head no. Sighing, she turned from
the fire and giving Hugh a faint smile, she walked
out to the stables while fastening her cloak on once
again. She could see that her horse had saddle bags
on it, stuffed with her belongings. She took the new
leather bag filled with herbs from Hugh and tied it on
under her cloak. She was as ready as she was ever
going to be. "Hugh, thank you again for your help. I
should return home within two or three weeks. I will
send word and keep you updated." Then, without
another word, she mounted and spurred her horse
forward into a gallop and raced to the camp where
Hal and Henry were waiting with her two knights on
her heels.

They reached camp a little after dawn and she could
hear the moans coming from within. There were not
even guards to protect the soldiers or the wounded as
their horses came thundering in, she tried to scan and
assess the situation. She searched for Hal, Henry and
Sadie. Sliding off of her horse, she threw the reins to
her knight and shouted, "Tie them up and come back
to help me! Quickly now!"

Izzy turned around and ran right into Henry. It
seemed as though time stood still. Their eyes met as
he steadied her with his hands on her hips. Her
breath caught in her throat and she could hear
nothing else but the sound of her own beating heart.
Henry saw the riders coming in and hoped it was
Izzy. He was so thankful that his prayers had been
answered he rushed over to her but when she turned

around without warning and nearly collided with him, he involuntarily had reached out to grab her waist to buffer the impact. He felt fire shoot up his fingers and through his arms. She was more beautiful than her remembered.

The moment ended just as quickly as it began. "We need you Healing Bird," Henry whispered still staring deep into her eyes.

Izzy blinked when he called her Healing Bird, bringing herself back to reality. "Where? Where can I begin?"

Henry led her to the tables farthest from the entrance. "These are the men that are hurt the worst."

Izzy held on to Henry's arm. "Henry, where is Hal?" She held her breath waiting for his answer.

"He has not returned from the battlefield yet. He is uninjured as far as I know though," Henry informed her.

Izzy walked to the first man. She looked at his grey skin. There was no breath in his body. Henry was at her side as she walked from table to table. "Henry, these six men are no longer living. They are grey, cold, and the breath has long since left their bodies. There is nothing that I can do for them. Their bodies need to be prepared for burial or taken to their homes. I am sorry." She waited a moment to let her words sink in. "Henry, where are the next critically injured men?"

Henry quickly led her to the next row of men. Izzy worked hard, ordering Henry, Wade and Randall about, instructing them on what to do. She was so busy that she did not notice Hal return and immediately jump into action, helping to manage the injured. More than half of the men in camp were injured, and ten were dead. The morning seemed as though it would never end. Izzy moved by memory through to the end of the day when everyone had finally been treated. She stopped for a moment looking over the scene at the camp and noticed for the first time that it was once again dark. She had spent the entire day treating the wounded and praying for peace for the dead.

Hal had spoken with Lord Raymond before he had traveled to Era for James' signatures and then to Adonia for Izzy's signatures. He was not prepared for Izzy to delay her travels to camp, but when she had, he knew exactly why. She would never allow her brother-in-law to leave alone especially when the risks were stacked so high against him returning. He had known the de Seaton brothers all of his life. He remembered how devastated he was when he learned of Thomas and Geoff's passing. He had hand selected the men he wanted on that vessel and he knew that Raymond, if he were up to the task, would be fundamentally useful on this trip.

Izzy began to wash her bloodied hands when she felt the world begin to spin about her. 'Get a grip Izzy,' She told herself, taking a deep breath and focusing on something stationary. She sighed and wiped her hands on a dry linen that she had tucked into the waist of her over tunic. Finally, she saw Hal walking towards her. He had a look on his face and in that instant, she realized, he had known all along that Raymond would go. As quickly as she realized he had known all along, she felt both anger and sadness course through her veins. Her sadness and anger began to overwhelm her and she struggled to stay on her feet.

Henry was about to walk over to Izzy and offer her some water when he saw Hal approaching her as well. He waited to watch their interaction. There was something strange about their relationship, as though there were too many secrets for there to be just a friendship. He felt his chest tighten as he watched Hal open his arms and Izzy collapse into them.

Izzy looked into Hal's eyes as she fell into his open arms and there was a silent understanding. Before she could stop it, the sobs that she had been suppressing since yesterday escaped her mouth, her knees buckled, and the world around her began to spin violently.

As soon as Izzy's legs gave out from beneath her, Hal scooped her up into his arms. Her body shook from the weeping that seemed to be emanating from deep in her soul. Quickly, he took her into Henry's tent; it was closer to him than either his or hers and he knew that she would feel safe there.

Henry rushed forward getting to the tent and holding a flap back as Hal carried Izzy inside. Henry followed closely behind, letting the tent flap fall back into place. "What is going on?" he asked.

"Sit there and just hold her while I get her cool water to drink and damp linens for her neck," Hal ordered. As soon as Henry sat down on his bed, Hal thrust Izzy into his arms and ran from the tent.

Henry held Izzy and she clung to his neck as though her life depended on it. Her small body shook so fiercely, it was almost as though someone were actually shaking her.

Izzy cried harder once she realized she was in Henry's arms. Did he even know that his brother had left? Did Raymond say anything to Henry or did he just pretend like nothing had happened? She was exhausted and that fueled her emotions. Suddenly something cool was laid across her neck.

"Here, drink this." Hal held a cup with a splash of brandy in it for her to drink. It was as if it became a magical liquid. He watched as she quickly quieted and then slipped into a deep sleep.

"Is she asleep or did you kill her?" Henry asked, half joking.

"She is sound asleep," Hal answered with sadness in his tone.

"What happened? Was all of this blood and injury too much for her to handle?" Henry pressed Hal for information.

Hal considered what Henry knew. "There was an urgent family matter that required her to delay her travels out to us and it seems that emotionally, it has taken its toll on her. Stay here with her please and just - just keep her safe." Hal left the tent without another word. He had to step out of the tent and walk away from her. When he was near her, it took everything in him not to touch her, taste her or kiss her, and when she was away, he dreamed of her walking into his arms and laying next to him at night. He wiped the sweat from his brow and continued to walk away.

Henry held Izzy in his arms for as long as he could. When his arms began to fall asleep, he laid himself down on the mattress with her still in his arms. Slowly, rolling to his left side, he let her lay on the pillow beside him. He looked at her to make sure she was still asleep. He could still see the tears that stained her cheeks, and the dark circles under eyes hinted that she had not slept in quite some time. Her blonde hair, despite being pulled back into a braid had strands of hair that had come loose and framed her face. He noticed for the first time that even though her hair and eyes were light, that her eyelashes were as black as night and long. Her skin was lightly golden, and her cheeks gently pinked. He laid there as she slept, simply watching her and eventually dozed off as well, facing her, with his arm draped across her waist and his hand splayed at the small of her back. It was well into the early hours of the morning when Henry woke and sitting on the stool next to him was Hal.

"How long have you been sitting here?" Henry asked quietly, trying to not wake Izzy up.

"Not too long. Sadie arrived a few hours ago and began doing checks on everyone that Izzy treated." Hal quietly bunched together some dried lavender that Izzy had given him before she had left.

"I do not understand why a family matter would cause so much exhaustion in her. If she becomes this overwhelmed, is she the right person to be the healer for this camp?" Henry questioned. He saw the tension tighten Hal's expression and again wondered if there was something more that he wasn't being told.

"She had been without sleep for nearly three days. She has journeyed across the country to the coast and back, switched horses and rode here. Then she spent an entire day treating the wounded and declaring others dead. Some of these men she had laughed with, shared stories with and listened to stories about their families. I would say that she has earned some sleep. Do not question her abilities as a healer. Had it not been for her, you would be dead right now." Hal took a deep breath and tried to calm himself.

"Did you and Raymond have a good time visiting?" Henry rolled onto his back to face Hal easier. "We had a pleasant visit. He talked about Jayde and James, and their three children. He said that Adonia was flourishing and that there had been a festival there recently." Henry turned his head back towards Izzy as she adjusted her head on his arm.

241

"A festival?" Hal asked raising his eyebrows, feigning surprise. "My parents recently traveled to a festival. I wonder what the odds are that it was the one at Adonia. The Queen did mention meeting a healer there. She said that she was beautiful and smart. I shall have to ask the next time I write." Hal halfheartedly hoped to get Henry stirred up and interested in wanting to know more about Izzy. It had been something that he had promised to Raymond before he left. Raymond had requested that Hal do everything that he could to try and help Henry to see what an incredible woman Izzy was. Hal's problem would not be in helping Henry fall in love with Izzy, but rather keeping himself from falling in love with her anymore himself. He had hoped that Henry would correct him or ask a question, but Henry remained silent and staring at Izzy. Hal sighed, he would make good on his promise to Raymond to invoke Henry's interest but he couldn't just sit and watch them lie together in bed. He stood and sparing himself anymore torture, he left the tent without any parting words.

Henry laid on his back for a short while after Hal left thinking on his words. The King and Queen traveled to a festival? At the same time as a festival happened to be going on in Adonia. What were the odds? He could not help but wonder if Izzy lived nearby Adonia and if she had been at the festival. Why was there a festival at Adonia? For a brief moment he considered writing to Lady Isabel, but when Izzy stirred in his arms, all thoughts of his wife left him. Henry looked back to Izzy as she stirred next to him. On her face was a frown, her lips turned slightly downward and fresh tears gathered on her eyelashes like dew on the petals of a flower. A few strands of hair had fallen forward across her cheek. Without another thought, he reached out and tucked the strands of hair behind her ear. Her cheek was so soft against his fingertips that he rested his hand against the skin there with his thumb barely brushing her pale pink lips. He could feel excitement race up his fingertips and course through his body. His arms tensed as he sucked in air and for once in the past two years he felt something that he could only call 'life' stir within him. He had shut out the world, all emotions, hope, and trust for so long and now, involuntarily, it all came back to him.

Izzy felt warmth on her cheek and slowly woke up. Her eyes fluttered open to find herself staring into Henry's eyes just inches from her face. Struggling to focus and come out of her sleepy state, she tried to wrap her mind around the situation, but finally gave up. She did not care anymore. She just needed warmth, and an end to the isolation she carried with her everywhere she went.

Henry froze when Izzy opened her eyes and stared right into his. Looking at him, the tears that had been sitting on her lashes fell against her cheeks and slid down to her chin. Henry could feel his heart breaking for a reason that he had no answer to.

243

Bending his head forward, he rested his forehead against hers for a moment before softly kissing her lips. Initially Izzy's body tensed in his arms. Henry gently pulled her bottom lip into his mouth with his teeth, then he heard the quiet moan escape her lips as her body relaxed completely in his arms. Henry pulled back from her face, struggling between returning to reality or succumbing to this pocket of time, this secret between them. He searched Izzy's eyes to determine what she wanted from him.

Izzy nearly melted when Henry kissed her, but when he pulled her lip between his lips, she could not contain the thrill that exploded within her, setting all of her senses on fire. Henry pulled away from her and was searched her eyes for an answer to something. She felt his hand slide behind her head and gently pull her towards him, tucking her face against his chest, and resting his chin on top of her head. Again, the overwhelming sadness and hurt that she constantly carried consumed her.

He felt her silent sobs shake her body once again as he held her tightly, giving her the silent promise of protection and support the only way he knew how to. Eventually, her body went still and he heard the even rhythm of her breathing as she fell into what he hoped was a peaceful sleep.

Izzy woke up to the sounds of camp life and the smells of breakfast being cooked. Looking around she realized that she was not only in Henry's tent, but his bed as well and from the looks of it, he had shared his bed with her, literally. Sitting up, she stretched and saw that she was still in the dirty dress that she had put on four days ago. Standing slowly, she quietly slipped out of Henry's tent and went in search of Hal so that she could be directed to her own tent. She desperately needed to clean herself and change into clean clothes. When she finally found Hal, he was sitting with Henry at a table with mugs of hot black tea in their hands. Izzy approached shyly, until Hal looked up at her. Henry's back faced her, and when he turned around, it looked as though he had not slept at all.

"Good morning, are you feeling better?" was all that Henry could say. He had barely slept after he had kissed her. He had held her tightly through the night trying to imagine what family matter had been so urgent and heartbreaking. He kept thinking that if only her husband was around, he might be able to be the kind of man that would have been there to support her so that she did not have to bear whatever burden alone.

Izzy turned a deep red as she answered Henry. "Yes, um, I did. Thank you. Did you, um, sleep, very well?" Henry looked at her, his eyes filled with something she could not name. They were deep and intense and it felt as though he could undress her with a simple glance.

"I slept as well as I could," Henry finally answered. Hal began to choke on his tea. As well as I could? Seriously, Henry looked as though he had not slept in days. Both Henry and Izzy were looking at him now.

"Are you alright?" Izzy asked.

"I am fine, thank you." Hal responded still coughing. Once he had recovered, he asked, "Is everything okay? Is there something you need?"

"Yes actually. First, I have no idea where my tent is, or my herbs, or my clothes. Secondly, I desperately need a bath. Finally, I need to get my dress laundered. So, either I am going to need to use the river or need to find someone in camp who has been laundering clothes and ask to add to her work load." Izzy had regained her composure now that she was focusing on speaking to just Hal.

"Ah yes, your tent. I had it set up on the far side of the camp, however, Henry and I both agree that you should not be so far from one of us. So, we looked at the options and the space available and your tent, herbs and belongings are being moved as we speak. As to a bath, it will be several hours before your tent is set up. I can have one sent to Henry's tent. I do not believe he will mind sharing for one more day, will you Henry?"

Henry could not believe what he was hearing. Izzy taking a bath in his tent, naked, in his tent. He slowly looked up to meet Hal's gaze. His desire, and torture must have shown because Hal smiled smugly at him before continuing to address Izzy.

"Your dress, I do not think a lady should be laundering anyone's clothing. I will speak with the women in camp who are employed to clean the camp's clothing and bedding. I am sure that it will not be a problem. If you can give me half an hour, I will have everything set up for you." Hal cast a sideways glance in Henry's direction to see how he was recovering. "Henry, can you find Izzy's bag of clothes and bring them to your tent? I am sure that she would rather get washed up sooner rather than later."

Henry went over to where the tent sat in a pile next to Hal's tent and picked through it until he found saddle bags and a large messenger's bag. Grabbing them he returned to his tent where there was a large tub already nearly filled with steaming hot water. He set the bags down on his bed and turned to leave slamming into Izzy who stumbled backwards. Reaching out, he grabbed her by the waist and pulled her to him to keep her from falling backwards to the ground.

Izzy placed her hands out in front of her as she went from falling in one direction to falling in the other direction. Her hands landed on Henry's chest, her chin down, and her entire body pressed firmly against Henry's. Looking up, Izzy found Henry staring down at her. There was an infinite depth to his dark eyes that captivated her, swallowed her whole. She did not want to resist him, she wanted to feel his eyes, hands and mouth devour her soul. Henry had been staring into her eyes since the moment that she looked up at him. His pulse quickened, his chest tightened, and he held on tightly to her waist, keeping her body close to his. The sound of laughter from outside abruptly broke the spell and Henry let go before anyone could walk in. Hal knew that Henry and Izzy were alone in the tent, so he wanted to give them warning before he entered, just in case. He cleared his throat and asked, "Izzy, may I come in?"

Izzy cleared her own throat and smoothed her dress out of habit. "Yes of course!"

Hal walked in and the tension in the air nearly choked him. He smiled tightly, glancing from Izzy to Henry and back to Izzy again. "I wanted to make sure that you had everything you needed for your bath. I see that Henry brought some of your bags here. If you need something else, just shout. Both Henry and I will be outside the tent to ensure your privacy." Hal saw Izzy flush pink and Henry look away. "Come on Henry, let us sit outside and give her a chance to clean herself. Izzy, I spoke with the head servant for laundry. She said that she would personally wash your garments and keep them separate from the men's clothing both to wash and dry." Hal smiled as he and Henry left the tent. They both sat on stumps outside of the tent in silence until they heard the sound of Izzy climbing into the tub. Hal leaned forward and rested his elbows on his knees, then turned his head to look at Henry. "Henry, tell me, how well did you really sleep last night?"

Henry looked over to Hal, then ran his hands over his face. "Honestly Hal, I barely slept. After kissing…" Henry suddenly stopped and looked over at Hal. He had told Hal that he was married, he had told him everything.

Hal burst out in laughter. "Yes, please go on, after you kissed that evil temptress in there, what?"

Henry looked down at the ground. "After that, I just held her in my arms until she stopped crying and fell asleep again. She just looked like she needed something besides my hands all over her," he said the last sentence quietly, tenderly.

Hal continued to watch Henry while he spoke. He had known Henry for many years and he had never seen him or heard him talk about a woman this way, ever. His heart warmed at the idea of helping his friend and keeping his promise to Raymond and yet he could feel the cold fingers of jealousy grip his heart as well.

Henry expected Hal to laugh at him or at least tease him. He looked over to Hal, hoping to assess his silence and saw a slight smile on his face. "What? What are you smiling at?" Henry asked.

Hal looked down to his feet and said, "I just think it is amazing that our hearts know what they want long before our minds catch up."

Henry frowned to himself. What is he talking about, our hearts? Did he think he was falling in love with Healing Bird? "Hal, do not forget that I am a married man."

"Yes, Henry, you are married in the eyes of the laws, just not the church. Your young bride is still as innocent and pure as the day she married you. Unless she has taken a lover? Do you forget so easily that our Healing Bird is a married woman?" Hal calmly asked.

"No, I do not forget that she is a married woman. What makes you believe that Lady Isabel has taken a lover? And Izzy's husband does not love her like a husband should, he was not even there for her when she needed support for the urgent family matter. What does it matter if I provide some kindness and comfort to her? At least then she would know what love is," Henry spat, upset at the idea of Izzy being alone and realizing that he himself was no better than the husband he so despised.

"How do you know that her private affairs had nothing to do with her husband?" Hal waited for Henry to answer. When he did not, he continued. "Henry, what do you know about how to love a woman? I am not talking about lust and sex, but *love*. When she is more important than just what happens between the sheets. Knowing her favorite color, flower, and season. Knowing what will make her smile and doing everything you can to earn that smile… and never forgetting what makes her sad and moving heaven and earth to never give her reason to shed a tear again. To be willing to turn a blind eye to society for her happiness, to sacrifice yourself for her, always. That is love. Maybe her husband does not stay with her because there is a sacrifice that he must make for her; for her to be happy." Hal stared out towards the woods where able bodied men were training.

Both men sat in silence until Izzy emerged from the tent dressed in a clean gown. Her skin glowed still from the hot water, and her hair was combed and tied back at the nape of her neck. At the sound of the fluttering tent flaps, both men jumped up.

Hal grinned. "Feeling better? More rested?"

"I do, thank you," Izzy glanced at Henry who was looking away from her. She felt her heart sink a little. What did she expect, for him to rush over to her and kiss her passionately?

Hal watched the small and seemingly insignificant interaction between Izzy and Henry and knew that he needed to do more to help push Henry in the right direction. "Izzy, would you mind taking a walk with me. I would like to accompany you while you look over the injured. Sadie arrived last night and immediately began to check everyone. I know she is exhausted as well. I am sure she would appreciate some rest. There are also some private concerns that I would like to discuss with you." He held out his arm for Izzy to take just as she had before she left for Adonia, when they were less burdened and could laugh more easily.

Izzy nodded and took Hal's arm walking away with him without looking back.

Hal felt every fiber in his body light up when Izzy held on to his arm. If only this was not to help a friend, he would cast aside everything for her. Henry's head snapped up as he heard Hal walk away, shocked that Hal could be so bold. He had practically confessed to him that he cared for Izzy in some way. He thought for sure that Izzy would at least look back to him, but she did not. Instead, he saw Hal tip his head toward Izzy as they walked away. It was a good thing that neither of them turned back to look at him for he was sure that he would not have been able to hide the anger and jealously that he knew was displayed on his face. "Just keep walking with me. Do not look back and try to relax," Hal whispered as they walked away from Henry. When they were far enough away he spoke again, "I made a promise to Raymond that I have every intention to keep. I need for you to play along though. I am going to become friendlier with you." Hal chuckled when he felt Izzy tense a little and saw her look up at him with a stern look on her face. "Do not worry. I have no intentions of causing you to break your vows to your husband," Hal lied. He wanted so much more from her. "I might hold your hand, ask you to take walks with me, whisper so that only you can hear me. I might even go so far as to place my hand at your waist if you are comfortable with that. I need you to trust me though. Will you do that; will you trust me?"

Izzy thought about what he was saying. He wanted to help her make Henry fall in love with her. "Hal, how will this help you to keep a promise to my brother?"

"Raymond came to me the day after you left. I arranged for his voyage; actually, I hand selected him for the vessel and had asked him months ago," Hal said.

Izzy froze and looked at Hal with a mixture of contempt and pain. "Hal, how could you?" Izzy began, fresh tears threatening to fall down her cheeks again.

Hal turned to her and took both of her delicate hands in his own large battle-hardened ones. "Izzy, it was either him or Henry, and I knew that Henry had more responsibilities here. I just did not realize that he was married. I also knew that Raymond was not settled here and was looking for a change. I made the best choice and knowing everything that I know now, I would make the same choice again." He saw her shoulders drop and he reached out and hugged her. From the corner of his eye he caught Henry watching. "Come, let us continue to walk, we are being watched by your husband," Hal whispered in her ear. He took Izzy's hand and laid it on his arm again as they started walking once more.

"He was going to leave alone, in the darkness; just slip away like a thief in the night. I could not let him leave thinking that no one cared. What if he does not come back? I wanted him to have a reason to fight and come back to his family. They have already lost so much, to lose Raymond too would be too much to bear. I hope you are not upset," Izzy softly said. "Angry? Absolutely not! I knew when I received your note that you were going to see him off. I also knew that your swollen eyes were not from the horrors of our battle, but the sorrow in sending a loved one out to the unknown." The two of them walked to each tent where there laid an injured knight. Each man had been well cared for by both Izzy and Sadie. Some of them would have long recoveries.

"Hal, for the men with longer recoveries, it might be best for them to return home where they can heal without the pressure of war. It would be wise to consider requesting healthy, well rested replacements. Honestly, some of the more injured men might not be able to fight again. They will need to heal and start anew."

Hal considered what she was saying. "How many men do you think I should be sending home?"

"Honestly, I would send four maybe five of them home immediately. There are another five that once their injuries heal, and the risk of infection is practically nonexistent, I would send them home as well."

"I will take that into consideration. Thank you for your honesty." Hal said to Izzy.

The two of them had turned back toward the main part of camp when Izzy suddenly stopped. "Hal, where is my tent? I cannot share a bed with Henry again tonight."

Hal smirked and raised an eyebrow at her. "You cannot? Please, explain to me why, I did not think that Healing Bird, a married woman had temptations!" Hal teased.

Turning a deep shade of red, Izzy slapped his arm playfully. "Oh stop you! You are incorrigible!"

Hal laughed at her before saying, "Fear not little healer, I have had your tent set up while we were gone. I believe it to be in a much better place. I am sure that you and Henry will agree."

"Hal! What have you done?" Izzy asked in an accusing tone.

As they returned to Henry's tent, Izzy noticed a second tent, a tent that was not there the hours before, practically touching Henry's tent. "Hal…" Izzy said as she looked up at him with the face that any scolding mother would show.

"Healing Bird, I have had your tent relocated to be closest to my most trusted knight, Lord Henry de Seaton. It is my most firm belief that there is no other place in this camp where you will be safer unless you are in his arms at night." Hal patronized her.

"Hal, do you really believe this is necessary?" Izzy asked with a worried tone.

Hal noticed Henry passing them nearby. Grabbing Izzy's hand and bringing it to his mouth he kissed her knuckles and said, "If you would feel safer, you can share my tent with me."

Henry's mouth fell open as he watched the scene before him, but had to suppress the laughter from exploding from his mouth when he saw Izzy's face and her polite attempt to remove her hand from Hal's. Henry shook his head as he walked on towards the training field with a huge smile on his face.

That evening, as Henry tried to sleep, he could hear Izzy moving about in her tent, then leaving, coming back, knocking something over, cursing out loud, leaving again and finally returning to her tent for the night. He could see the glow from inside her tent and he wondered what it was that she was doing so late.

Izzy was finally in her tent for the night. Two knights from Ackerley stood guard through the night with strict instructions that only Sadie, Hal or Henry were permitted to enter her tent. Anyone else was considered to have malicious intentions. She felt quite tired but knew that she needed to write a note to Jayde. Sitting down at the little desk, she pulled out her quill and ink and began her note.

> *Jayde and James,*
>
> *I spoke with Raymond and accepted his request. I signed the paperwork he presented with his, Prince Henry's and James' signatures and added my signature*

to it as well. I am honored to accept Iole as my own. Thank you so much. I hope I make you all proud. I wanted to tell you that I am at the new camp. I arrived a day later than planned. I just could not allow Raymond to leave without anyone to see him off and give him a proper 'see you soon.' When I arrived here at camp, it had been a brutal defeat. Although everyone here seems to think it was a victory. There were already several men dead on tables when I arrived and so many more close to death. Miraculously, only ten men perished. I am settling in much more quickly this time, and will return to Ackerley when I leave. My next trip home after that, I will travel to Iole. I am eager to see the beautiful place where Lady Catherine grew up. I will keep you posted when I travel home again. Stay safe, be well and I look forward to when we are all together again. Give everyone my love!

Izzy

Izzy folded and sealed the note setting it aside. She would give it to Hal in the morning to send out with messengers. Just then, she heard some whispers outside, then her tent flaps parted and Henry's head appeared.

"I saw that you were still up. May I keep you company for just a little while?" he asked.

"If I say no will you just stand there all night with your head in my tent but the rest of you outside?" Izzy asked giggling a little. She watched a smile light Henry's face. "Yes, you may come in. I was about to combine some oils for treatments."

Henry entered the tent letting the flaps close behind him. "How are you feeling? Better I hope."

Izzy smiled sweetly. "I am better now that I have rested. It has been quite some time since I went that many days without rest. Thank you for um, well, for letting me cry on your shoulder all night."

"Oh, yes, well of course," Henry said. Silence fell between them for several moments.

Izzy sighed. "I really hate awkward, and this is awkward." She saw the surprise in Henry's face. She could not stop now. "Last night, was I dreaming or did you and I kiss?"

Henry's face warmed as blood rushed into his cheeks. She was quite forward and he was not sure if he liked that or not. "That was you and I kissing. Would you have rather it been a dream?" If she chose to be that bold, then he would be just as bold in return.

Izzy hesitated. She was not prepared for him to meet her audacity with his own. "No, I think I rather preferred that it was not a dream," she admitted softly. She lifted her eyes to meet his gaze. "Would you rather that it was just a dream?" she asked him in return.

Without looking from her, he answered, "No, I would not." He felt his palms begin to sweat, and his chest constrict again. Excitement coursed through his body slowing time. "I saw you walking with Hal today."

Izzy finished counting the drops of oil that she was transferring from one jar to the next before answering him. "Yes, we walked around the camp. He showed me where everything was and accompanied me to check on all of the men who had been injured. Hal is a nice man. He really trusts you and respects you, it seems."

Henry raised his eyebrows. Respect? Is that what it was called to behave the way that Hal did today? "You seem to like him quite a bit."

Izzy could hear the jealousy in Henry's voice despite him trying to hide it. She remembered what Hal had said, to trust him and to play along. She took a deep breath, "Yes of course, he is a good man, and we get along quite well actually. He can be quite funny. It is nice to laugh again." She was careful to not lie yet not let Henry feel quite at ease just yet.

Henry could not help but wonder why he felt so territorial over Healing Bird. After all, Hal did know her first. "You said you do not like awkward, did you mean that?"

"Yes, I do not like awkward silences. I do not like being spoken to as though I am simple minded or need to be protected. I prefer that if you have something to say, that you just say it. Is there something that you wish to say to me, Lord Henry?" Izzy was curious where this was leading. She set her oils down and turned her full attention to Henry.

"Please, I thought that you and I were beyond labels, I thought it was just Henry and Izzy," Henry stated.

He watched Izzy's face soften as she nodded. He stood up finally and turned to leave. He stopped when he heard her get up as well. Turning around to face her again he extended his hand out to her. Izzy saw his outstretched hand and delicately placed her hand in his unsure of what the meaning of this was. Suddenly, he pulled her firmly to him.

Henry pulled Izzy bringing her body against his. He reached around her and placed his hand at the small of her back, feeling her breath quicken against him. With his other hand he guided her chin up so that she would meet his gaze. When her eyes met his, he brought his mouth down to hers and slowly kissed her. She began to relax in his arms and he parted her lips with his tongue, twining his with hers. A soft moan passed through her lips and she grabbed hold of his arms where her hands had been resting. He deepened his kiss, tightening his arm around her waist. Then he pulled his mouth away from her and placed hot kisses on her throat. With his hand that had been resting on her shoulder, he delicately pushed the fabric aside and trailed his kisses to her shoulder, then in towards her collarbone.

Izzy was dizzy with pleasure. His mouth trailed down her neck and shoulder to her collarbone and she thought she might die from desire. She let him slide the gown off of her shoulders and to the floor. She felt his hand pull the front of her kirtle down just enough to expose the soft curve of her breasts. There he followed his hands with his mouth and nibbled the inside of her breast before sucking on it. Izzy could take no more and her legs crumpled from under her.

Henry caught her full weight with the hand at the small of her back as he brought his mouth back up to her neck where he kissed her again before hoarsely whispering in her ear, "Remember me when Hal walks with you and whispers sweet nothings in your ear." He let go of her then and immediately turned, leaving her tent and returning to his own.

Izzy stood still not trusting her legs to move just yet. After a minute, she walked to the tent and tied it closed. Turning, she saw the gown on the floor. Walking to it she picked it up and shook it off before laying it on the back of the chair at the little desk where she had been sitting. Her hands still shook as she changed into her chemise. Izzy blew out all of the oil lamps except one. She climbed into bed and laid on her left side facing Henry's tent. His words echoed in her mind as she tried to drift off to sleep, still feeling his hands on her back, shoulders and breast. It was as though they had burned a trail in her skin. Her neck was still on fire as she tried to fight the memory and succumb to sleep. Finally, she relaxed enough to fall asleep only to be haunted in her dreams by Henry's hands and mouth again. "Remember me..." was all that he kept saying in her dream.

When morning came, Izzy emerged from her tent feeling as rested as she looked. Making her way to the fire, she found a pot of black tea sitting on the table. She poured herself a cup of the strong tea and waited for it to cool as the fog began to retreat into the woods. A plate filled with two eggs, bacon, and cheese was set in front of her. Looking up, she saw

Henry. Memories from the night prior flooded her mind and she blushed intensely.

Henry smiled when he saw her blush and set his plate down across from hers. He poured himself a cup of the black tea as well and quietly, the two of them sat across from each other eating the morning meal.

Hal saw Henry bring a plate over to Izzy then sit down across from her. He watched a moment more realizing that they were not talking at all. He went over to the table and sat down next to Izzy and looking from one to the other. "Izzy, how did you sleep last night?"

"Very well, thank you. I felt very, safe." Izzy's gaze shifted up to Henry then quickly back down to her cup of tea.

"Henry, how did you sleep? It looks as though you had a difficult night last night. Anything wrong?" Hal questioned. Something was going on and neither of them looked as though they had slept very soundly.

"I tossed and turned a bit, but I slept fine I think. What shall we train on today Hal?" Henry asked curtly. He was both amused and bothered by how close Hal was sitting to Izzy. He thought back to last night and remembered Izzy's moan followed by her legs giving out beneath her at his kiss. He smiled while looking at his plate of food and thought to himself. Good luck Hal for beating that. Hal was a skinny man and a woman with the curves that Izzy had needed a strong, robust man who knew how to handle those curves. His thoughts of holding Izzy against him again were interrupted by Hal's voice. "Izzy, I thought that you might like to join me for a picnic at the river today for our midday meal. We can talk about something beside the injured. I can tell you more about the city. Maybe you would even like to join me there sometime."

Izzy again glimpsed up to Henry who seemed unaffected by Hal's invitation. Without taking her eyes from Henry, she accepted Hal's offer to join him for a picnic. Only then did she see him react, clenching his jaw repeatedly. Pulling from her pocket the note she had written she handed it to Hal. "Do you think a messenger could take this to my sister today?"

"Of course, anything for you Izzy." Hal rather enjoyed seeing Henry irritated. It was going to make training together this morning so much better.

Hal waited for Henry to finish his food and tea before bantering him to get up and get moving to the training fields.

Izzy made her rounds with Sadie. Most of the injuries were minor, and this time none of the injured men required constant care. When the midday meal was served, Hal appeared and escorted her away from everyone else. There was a quilt laid out next to the river bank, and a tray of fruits, cheeses, cold meats, and bread. There was a decanter of wine as well as two cups sitting on the quilt as well. Izzy felt uneasy at the sight of such an intimate setting.

"Relax, it is for appearances only. Henry is a skilled soldier, he moves through the woods unseen." He led her to the quilt. "How long do you think you will need to stay this time?" Hal asked.

"Honestly, I could leave now. Sadie can handle the injuries on the other men, there is nothing here that needs my immediate attention," Izzy answered.

"If you do not mind wait until tomorrow then before you leave. Which estate will you be at?" Hal asked Izzy as she put a piece of cheese in her mouth.

She waited until she had finished chewing before answering. "I will be in Ackerley. How long until your next attack?"

"We will attack in about one week. Will you be able to return by then?" Hal asked Izzy then popped a grape into his mouth.

"Yes, if I leave tomorrow, then I will spend five days in Ackerley before returning. Will you be here at this camp for long?" Izzy questioned.

"Yes, we will be here for several months I will continue to try and work this out between rebellions. I dislike the battle unless it is necessary." Hal said leaning in closer to her. Izzy looked down at her hands feeling uncomfortable with the situation. Hal and Izzy finished eating and Hal escorted Izzy back to camp and to her tent.

Sitting down at the desk, Izzy wrote a quick note to Jayde telling her of the days she was traveling. Folding and sealing the note, Izzy searched for the messenger. When she could not find one, she walked out to the training field. She watched as the men sparred with one another until she found Hal sparring with Henry. Henry's shirt clung to his body, wet with sweat. She could see every muscle flex as he moved. It was almost graceful, the way he moved. She approached the two men not seeing the danger in it. Hal lunged at Henry who blocked his advance sending Hal's sword flying through the air right at Izzy. In one fluid motion Henry pivoted forward towards her and grabbed her hand as he pulled her towards him. Their faces were inches from each other when Hal began to yell.

"What are you doing? You could have been killed! Are you okay? Are you hurt?" Hal left his sword on the ground where it landed and ran over to Izzy. He pulled Izzy from Henry's embrace and looked her over.

"I am fine. I am sorry, I did not know it would be dangerous to walk out here. I simply needed to find a messenger, and when I could not find one, I came to ask you. I am not hurt, I promise," Izzy insisted, though she was breathless.

"You are shaking, I will take you back to camp," Hal said as he began to lead Izzy away.

Henry stood for a moment wondering what he should do when he caught Izzy looking back at him. Sheathing his sword, he was at her side in three strides, "I will take her to camp. You should stay and help the other men train." He did not give Hal the opportunity to object as he took Izzy's hand in his, placed his other hand at the small of her back and led her out of the training fields. Once they arrived at Izzy's tent, he did not bother to ask if he could come in, he simply followed her in. "Are you sure you are not injured?" he asked again holding her shoulders so she was facing him.

265

Izzy was still in shock, but not because a sword went flying at her. She was in shock that Hal had yelled at her.

Henry placed a hand on either side of her face and drew her to him. He kissed her gently at first, then deeply. He felt Izzy's hands run up his arms and then wrap around his neck tangling in his hair. Izzy felt all of her senses ignite and her only thoughts were to draw Henry closer to her.

He slipped his left hand behind her head and let his right hand drop down to her hip. He spread his hand wide so that his thumb was at the front of her hip and his fingers wrapped around to her butt cheek. When he felt Izzy stand on her tiptoes he dropped his left hand to wrap around her waist as well.

Izzy moaned softly knowing she wanted more, but not sure what that would exactly be. Henry brought his mouth to her neck, then again down to her shoulder and then in towards her breasts. Her breath caught and she dug her nails into his soft flesh just slightly.

Henry thought he might lose his mind when she dug her nails into him. Without hesitation, he lifted her up as she wrapped her legs around his waist, still supporting her weight under her butt with one arm while the other untied the string at the top of her kirtle. The front of the kirtle fell open exposing her breasts to him and he took full advantage of their availability. Sitting down in the chair with Izzy still in his arms and her legs still wrapped around him, he cupped her breast and lifted it up as he brought his mouth down. His lips trailed across her breast until he reached the pale rose toned nipple. Taking the nipple in his mouth he sucked it, hearing her gasp and feeling her dig her nails into his back.

Izzy did not think there was any more that she could take after he had put his mouth on her breast, but when he took his mouth and drew her nipple in, her world exploded with pleasure. Then, as though to prove that he could give her more pleasure, he took her other breast in his mouth tracing the tip of her nipple with his tongue, toying with it, before sucking on it again as she leaned her head back and arched her back.

Henry ran his hand down her leg grabbing the hem of her dress and pulling it up as he caressed her toned legs. Kneading her thigh with one hand, he brought his mouth back to the top of her breast, nibbling and sucking on the inside curve leaving a red mark.

Then he sought her mouth again, thrusting his tongue deep into her mouth while his other hand trailed down her other leg and brought up her dress on that side as well, until her skirts were bunched up at the top of her thighs exposing her naked legs.

Izzy could not think straight and desperately grasped at anything to draw her back to earth. When Henry finally began to kiss her mouth again she was able to draw in a deep breath. She had to get her head on straight. Placing her hands on either side of his face, she slowed him down. Pulling her face from his, she rested her now sweaty forehead against his, both of them breathing ragged breaths.

Henry squeezed the bunched-up skirt that he had in each hand trying to regain his composure. "I am sorry," he said softly. Releasing her dress, he wrapped his arms around her and lightly caressed her back. He wanted to take her right now and hear her call out his name, dig her nails into his flesh, and cry out in ecstasy. He wanted to lay her down and make love to her, to trace every inch of her skin with his hands, then his mouth. He wanted to taste her sweetness, hold her through the night again and wake up next to her warm naked body. Supporting her body, he stood up and set her on her feet. "I need to leave. See you at the evening meal." He saw embarrassment cover her face as he walked past her. He could not let her feel embarrassed by something as beautiful as what he felt. Stopping he turned around and walked to her turning her around to face him. Tilting her chin up to face him, he brought his mouth to hers and kissed her tenderly. "I hope that I am not out of line in asking to please be allowed to kiss and hold you again. You leave me breathless. I spend my days thinking of you, wondering what Hal says to you and loathing the idea and images of Hal touching you at all. I spend my nights dreaming of you, desiring you, and imagine bringing you pleasure. I want to know who you are, physically and emotionally. Will you deny me?"

Izzy drew in a ragged breath. Tenderly, she said, "I will not deny you Henry."

"Will you deny the company of Hal? Or will I need to compete for you?" Henry asked.

Izzy did not know what to say. Compete for her? Poor Hal, he was simply trying to make Henry fall in love with her, not get into a duel over her. Before she could find any words to say to Henry, he kissed her mouth firmly, then brought her hand to his mouth and kissed the back of it lightly.

Reluctantly, he let go of her hand and left the tent leaving Izzy alone to pull herself together. His heart raced as his skin still burned from their tryst.

Walking briskly back to the training fields, he knew he was willing to fight his King and country to win her love.

Izzy spent the entire afternoon checking on the injured men and explaining to Sadie what each man needed. "Sadie, are you sure you are comfortable being here alone? I will only be gone for one week." Sadie smiled. "Yes Healing Bird, I will be fine while you are away. If their injuries were any more severe, or we were to be going to battle again then I would be worried, but the hard work has already been done."

"Sadie," Izzy said blushing slightly. "You do not have to call me Healing Bird. I am still Izzy. The same girl you played in the mud with. The same girl you used to catch lady bugs with."

"I know, but it is truly special that you are respected by so many for your skills in healing. I am proud to get to work alongside you." Sadie smiled. She knew that Izzy was a humble woman and would never think of herself so pretentiously. "What time will you leave?"

"I was going to leave tomorrow, but I think that I will make use of the daylight and leave during the evening meal." In truth, Izzy needed to step away from Henry. She needed to clear her head. Yes, she wanted to love him and for him to love her, but she wanted to know who he was, not just if he was extraordinary in bed. Although after this afternoon, there was little doubt in her mind that being loved by this man physically would be no less than marvelous. Sadie could see that Izzy was lost in thought and it was rare for Izzy to lose focus. "Thinking about a certain gentleman?"

Izzy turned red and could not resist smiling in response. "Really Sadie, you imagine some of the wildest things!"

"Somehow I doubt that it is *I* imagining the wildest things right now My Lady," Sadie teased. Both ladies giggled as Izzy relived the afternoon in her mind. Izzy sighed as the giggles began to lessen between them. "Will you be giving him a proper goodbye?"

Again, Izzy turned red. Then bashfully she asked, "What exactly would be a proper goodbye?"

Sadie laughed out loud. "Oh Izzy! You must give him something to remember you by! Give him a memory so that while you are gone he will think of no one else!"

"Oh, I am pretty sure that I have already done that," Izzy said sarcastically.

"Izzy! What did you do?" Sadie squealed

"A lady never tells!" Izzy gathered her messenger bag. "I must find Hal and my knights and let them know of my change of plans."

"Please say goodbye before you leave," Sadie called after Izzy, but she was already off and searching for her knights and Hal.

Izzy had found her knights and told them to go eat something now and to pack some dried meats. Izzy did not see Henry or Hal and decided to see if she could sneak up on them and watch them train without being noticed. As she approached the field where she had found both men earlier, she could hear the sound of their steel swords making contact. Walking behind the shrubs until she had found them, she hid crouching low, watching the two men. "Henry, what has changed? You are training harder than I have ever seen you train before. Did you get into an argument with our sweet Izzy?" Hal baited Henry. He wanted to know how far he could push Henry before he let his temper control him. When Henry said nothing, Hal decided to push him some more. "Speaking of Izzy, have you ever noticed the curve of her hips? I do enjoy taking walks with her. She is beautiful. I wonder if she is as feisty between the sheets as she is when ordering people about…" Hal stopped speaking because Henry's fist slammed into his jaw sending him sprawling to the ground. When he came to his senses, he saw Henry striding away towards camp. Then out of the corner of his eye, he saw Izzy come forward.

"You got what you deserved. You should not torment him like that. Let me look at your face. Can you move your jaw, like this, and like this?" Good, it is not broken. You will be sore for a day or two, but I am sure you can handle it." Izzy stood up and waited for Hal to come to his feet as well. "Why would you tease him like that?"

Still rubbing his jaw, Hal said, "I wanted to see if he cared for you at all."

"Did you get the answer that you were looking for?" Izzy asked dryly.

"Yes indeed I did. I am not sure what you have said or done to him or if it was just me making him see that he was not the only man capable of taking your attention, but he is quite protective and possessive of you." Hal smiled to himself. He wondered what exactly Henry would do if he saw Izzy being kissed by him.

"Stop. Whatever it is that you are thinking, you need to stop." Izzy could see mischief cross his face and did not like it. "I wanted to hand this to you to send out with a messenger tonight. Also, I am leaving now to return home. I do not think it will hurt any to leave now instead of tomorrow."

"Will you be saying goodbye to Henry before you go?" Hal asked with one eyebrow raised.

Izzy hesitated and looked to the ground before looking back up at Hal.

"I see. You intend to leave without saying anything to him?" Hal asked, surprised that she would not want to at least say goodbye.

"I have left him a note, and I have left it in his tent for him to read tonight," Izzy said quietly.

"Why do you not want to say it in person?" Hal asked, quite confused.

Izzy bit her lip then whispered, "If I say goodbye in person, I might not be able to leave."

"What did you say?" Hal thought he heard, but then again, he could have been imagining her words.

Izzy groaned. "I said that if I say goodbye in person I might not be able to leave!"

Hal loudly laughed while doubling over bracing himself on his knees with his hands.

"If you are done making a scene and howling like a dog, I must hand this to you and leave." Izzy thrust the note in his face.

Henry had gone to search for Izzy, consumed by jealousy, intent on demanding to know if she was as forward with Hal as she was with him. He could not find her in her tent, walking the camp or at the tables. The only place left was the training fields. He saw Hal standing with Izzy before him, facing Hal. He could not make out what they were saying but Izzy must have said something amusing because Hal bent forward laughing. Izzy did not seem to find her own words funny as she thrust a piece of paper in his face. She had her riding cloak on. Suddenly she turned his way, so he hid in the brush and sat motionless. He watched as both Izzy and Hal walked passed him. Quickly, he followed behind them and was confused when Hal walked Izzy out of camp where two knights and a third horse were waiting. He was still not close enough to hear what they were saying.

"Hal, please ensure that this goes out this evening. It goes to my sister-in-law. I worry about her health and need for her to know where I am in the event that there is a crisis," Izzy said.

Hal held the reins while she mounted her horse. "I will see to it that the messenger leaves just after you do. And what about Henry?"

Henry saw Izzy's body tense.

"Hal, watch over him. Do not let him get hurt. Will you promise that there will be no more rebellions to be squashed until I return?" Izzy asked.

"I promise, no rebellions," Hal replied.

"Hal, thank you. I will return shortly."

Just then Hal saw something from the corner of his eye, something that did not belong. Glancing in that direction, he realized it was Henry. He wondered if Henry could hear what they were saying, but he doubted it. Just to torment him a little more, he took Izzy's hand in his own, placed his other hand on her thigh just above her knee and kissed the back of her hand.

Henry could feel his blood boil. He wanted to run over and tackle Hal, but before he could even move Izzy spurred her horse forward kicking up dirt with her two knights alongside her. He held still waiting for Hal to pass.

Hal walked directly to where Henry was hiding. "If you were only wearing a shirt that blended in better with the shrubbery, I might not have noticed you." Then he walked away from Henry and found the messenger finishing his meal. "I need you to ride to Era immediately.

Henry was frustrated. He was angry at himself for allowing his emotions to control him, angry at Hal for having a close relationship to Izzy and somewhat angry at Izzy for just leaving. Standing, he made his way back to the heart of the camp where the evening meal was being served. After eating he decided to isolate himself. He went to the river, and stripping down to nothing, waded into the frigid water. He scrubbed his head and body trying to scour his feelings away. Finally, he climbed out of the river and put on the clean pants that he had brought with him. Returning to camp, he dropped his clothing into the pile of his other dirty clothing for the laundress to collect in the morning. He sat down in the chair at his desk and saw the letters from his wife. Carefully, he picked them up and read each one again. He studied them, hoping to find a reason in them for him to go to her, but could not find any. Finally, he got up and laid down on his bed. As he laid back, something sharp scratched the back of his neck. He sat up and reached for the object realizing it was a note.

> *Henry,*
>
> *I wonder if by now you have realized that I am nowhere to be found. If you did not realize this until now, then I am quite the fool. I did not want you to worry. I was only staying in camp until I was not needed any longer. Sadie has everything under control and most of the men that are injured will only need care for another day or so. I have business to tend to at my family estates but intend to return in seven days. Should you need anything, I am sure that Sadie is quite capable of helping. You must think I am a coward for leaving without saying goodbye or explaining myself, but I hope*

you can understand. I worried that I would not be able to leave if we shared another tryst, and I could not delay my obligations any longer. I seem to lose my senses when you are around and all will power the moment your hands touch me. I hope that while I am away, you will not forget me or replace me with another. I know that each moment that I am gone, I will think of your kisses and your hands that leave me so vulnerable.

See you soon,
Izzy

Henry read the note twice. He smiled at the thought of her coming to say goodbye only to end up in his arms again. He fantasized his mouth leaving hot kisses up her legs as he slowly exposed her soft flesh, to hear her moan and watch her arch her back again. He wanted to watch her squirm with pleasure at his hands, and feel her hands touch him, leaving him vulnerable only to her. Feeling relief wash over him, he quickly fell into a deep sleep.

Chapter 10

Izzy, Sir Wade and Sir Randall arrived in Ackerley just before the night sky began to brighten the day. The three quickly and quietly departed each other's company, Wade and Randall going to the stables and Izzy to her chamber where she fell asleep quickly, dreaming of Henry's hands wandering her body. Izzy woke up mid-morning excited to tend to Ackerley. She dressed quickly, braiding her hair and tying it with a red ribbon that matched the delicate red embroidered flowers along the hem of her skirt, collar and sleeve cuffs. The dress was a pale blue, and the red flowers stood out distinctly. She left the hall unseen and began to walk the road leading out of the castle courtyard. May in Ackerley was incredible; the oak leaves were big and green, giving plenty of shade to anyone who traveled the road. Izzy took her time walking the street. Her first stop would be the nunnery. There she would visit with Sister Ava and listen to everything that had happened since she had visited last and discus herbs and poultices. Sister Ava and Izzy walked the multiple herbers while talking until well after the hour for the midday meal had passed. Sister Ava showed Izzy the records of births, deaths, baptisms, and marriages. Izzy was thrilled. In the past six months four babies had been born, two widowers with children married each other, and sadly, the retired cobbler and his wife passed away the month before.

"Come with me Lady Isabel. We all have many questions for you! When Sadie was back, she told us how you have been helping His Royal Highness! The King and Queen even visited us here and spent an entire day in the nunnery asking questions about you! You have been a very productive lady." Sister Ava led Izzy into the hall where many other ladies were reading.

She was thrilled to see the beautiful and familiar faces in the nunnery. They asked questions about the wounds she treated, how they healed, what her role was in Adonia and why everyone was calling her Healing Bird rather than Lady Isabel de Seaton. Sighing, Izzy explained some of the story to them. She started where she had arrived at camp to treat Henry and told only the minor details leading to the men in camp giving her the nickname. Izzy could see the look on Sister Ava's face. It was a look that Izzy had seen many times in the past when Sister Ava would ask how the injured got the wound and knew that they lied to her for one reason or another. Finally, after visiting for quite a while, Sister Ava offered to walk her back up to the castle.

"Lady Isabel, how are you and your husband getting along?" Sister Ava asked. She had watched Lady Isabel's face while she spoke to the other sisters, and knew that there was something amiss.

Izzy took a deep breath. "Oh Sister Ava, it is quite complicated." Izzy proceeded to explain in detail from the moment she arrived in Era for her wedding to her most recent trip to the battle encampment. She noticed the older woman covering her mouth desperately trying not to laugh. "Please Sister Ava, why are you laughing so and what am I supposed to do?"

Sister Ava could not contain herself any longer and burst out laughing with Lady Isabel joining in on her laughter shortly after. Finally sighing heavily, Izzy said, "I am in over my head Sister Ava!"

"Oh my child, you are far from being in over your head. You are simply courting your husband. I find it amusing though, that he does not remember someone of your grace and beauty. If he had spent any time with you, he would never have left you alone so long and he would never have forgotten you. Do not fret dear, it will happen with time and from the sounds of it, he already wants you as his own, so why are you so worried?" Sister Ava asked.

"Sister Ava, what happens when he falls in love with me, and wants to annul his marriage?" Izzy implored. "Everything is simple until then. If I wait to tell him the truth until then, I risk losing everything I will have earned, and if I tell him now, I will lose the opportunity to get to know and love him at all."

Sister Ava took Lady Isabel's hands in her own. "Sweet child, if your mother were here, she would have the wisdom of the saints to give you. You are the closest thing I have ever had to a daughter and I love you as though you were my own. I do not have the experience of a married woman and can only give you words from the Lord. Have faith in God's plan. He will not guide you wrong, but you must have trust in Him. If you are scared of having your heart broken, you will never be able to love completely." Sister Ava saw a flash of emotion cross Izzy's face. "Lady Isabel, do not fear what goes on between a man and wife, I have heard that it can be quite enjoyable."

"Sister Ava!" Izzy burst out laughing. "I do not fear the physical comforts of being with my husband, just that I might lose a friend in gaining a husband."

Sister Ava smiled. Lady Isabel was never one to trouble herself over the notion of personal discomforts or problems. She had always put the comfort and emotions of others before herself, even as a child. It was of no surprise that she would value a friendship over physical pleasures. Sister Ava reached forward and hugged Izzy "You have grown into such a fine young woman. I am blessed to have had the opportunity to help raise you and educate you. Your Lord Henry is the luckiest man. Give him time to recognize that."

Izzy kissed the older woman's cheek, returning the hug. "Thank you for your kind words and all of your time and effort that you put into me. I hope that I make you proud."

"I am proud of you every day," Sister Ava said before finally turning and leaving Izzy to walk through the courtyard alone.

Izzy watched as Sister Ava slowly walked down the oak lined road back to the nunnery for a minute before turning and seeking out Myles, her constable. She was only home for a few days before returning to the camp and wanted to make good use of her time.

Myles arranged for the people of Ackerley to come
to court to give any requests that they might have so
that Lady Isabel could tend to the needs of her town
quickest. There was not much else to plan, as she
had already had meetings with Myles and plenty of
correspondence regarding the running of the estate.
The day after, she walked the fields with the farmers
and saw that all of their needs were being met to care
for Ackerley. On her third day home, she went back
down to the nunnery and visited the hall where, once
a week, the nuns gathered all of the children in town
to make sure they learned to read, write and do
arithmetic. It was something that Izzy's mother
made sure of when she was still living. She
informed the church that it was their Christian duty
to dedicate a place where the children could learn.
After Lady Ryia discovered that the priest was
beating the children, she requested the nuns take
over. The nuns never asked for the families to pay
for the education of the children and never harmed
them either. As a result, Ackerley had the highest
literacy rates of the lower class of any place in all of
England. Izzy spent the next three days inspecting
the castle and leaving a list of things to be mended or
replaced before summer was over. On what was to
be her final night in Ackerley, Izzy was anxious to
return to camp and dare she admit it, back to Henry.
Rather than waiting until dawn, she did exactly as
she had done when leaving for Ackerley and
departed immediately after the evening meal.
Izzy knew that Hal had been planning another attack,
but it was to happen after she arrived at camp, and

she was arriving half a day earlier than they expected. Just as the early morning sky was beginning to lighten, the moon still in the sky, Izzy, Sir Wade and Sir Randall came out of the woods and into the clearing outside of camp. Unprepared for the scene they came upon, they halted their horses. Before them were men fighting, cursing, and screaming. There had been a surprise attack against Hal and his men.

"Lady Isabel, run for cover!" Sir Wade called out. Izzy heard his command but was already halfway off of her horse and turning to face the injured. There was a curse from behind and the sounds of steel clashing with steel as Izzy ran forward to the first of Hal's injured men lying on the ground. The gash in his leg went clear to the bone and blood was pulsing rapidly out of the wound. Izzy opened her messenger bag and pulled two strips of linen out. Quickly, she tied them together and grabbing a stick from the forest floor, she tied the linen around his leg, then using the stick, she tied another knot around it and began to twist the stick until the bleeding nearly stopped. Another man injured nearby began to crawl to her.

"Healing Bird, please, help me!" he called out inching closer.

"Here, sit next to him and hold this stick just like this. Very good. Let me look at your other shoulder." She hurriedly made a rough sling, looped one end around his wrist, and slipped the other end over his head. "Do not let go of that stick, do you understand? He will bleed out and die." She jumped

to her feet and began to move towards the next man.
By the time Izzy had reached the eighth man, she had
run out of clean linen strips from her bag. She only
traveled with enough for her and her knights.
Pulling her dagger out, she began to cut the men's
shirts from their bodies and began to tear them into
strips. Everywhere she turned, men called for her.
The attack was horrific. She could see Henry
fighting in the distance but could not see Hal.
Working her way closer to Henry, she hoped she
would find Hal as well and at least know that both
men were safe. On the ground, literally rolling
around was Hal fighting with another man, neither of
them using their swords.
Izzy continued to treat the wounded, occasionally
glancing up to keep her eyes on Hal and Henry.
There was a loud commotion behind her and she
could hear Henry calling out her name in a panic.
Henry was running as fast as he could, trying to
dodge the swords and the occasional spinning mace.
He could see the rider coming straight for the figure
that he was sure was Izzy. It had been running from
body to body, looking as though it were cutting
shirts. He knew in his heart it was her.
Izzy heard him call her name again. She looked up
to see both Henry and Hal running at her and in that
split second she heard the hooves approaching fast.
Suddenly she was flying into the air and being
thrown over a saddle on her stomach, holding on for
dear life as the rider spurred the horse forward faster.
Izzy heard a gasp and then a body slumping forward
over her. Struggling to hold on, Izzy felt the body

begin to slide off of the saddle. The horse was still running, and Izzy was losing her grip. At last, Izzy lost her grip and she and the body dropped to the ground.

Henry watched with horror as an enemy knight had reached down and lifted Izzy, throwing her over the front of his saddle. He was not close enough to throw his sword and felt a sickness grip the pit of his stomach as he realized there was nothing he could do. Then from the corner of his eye, he caught one of Izzy's knights draw a cross bow, load, aim and release, striking with incredible accuracy. Running after the horse he watched as the slumped over body dragged Izzy off of the horse with it to the ground. Izzy tried to get her bearings again but was too afraid to sit up. She screamed when the shadow of a large man came running to her.

Henry drew his sword ready to finish the job when he heard Izzy scream. He reached her side expecting to see a man still trying to attack her, only to discover a dead man and Izzy with her eyes squeezed shut. "Izzy, Izzy, are you hurt?" Henry asked as he knelt down beside her.

Izzy felt Henry's warm, strong hand on her shoulder and his voice, thick with concern and affection, speaking to her. She opened her eyes and pulled herself up to her knees holding onto his arm. Facing him, she threw her arms around his neck and hugged him as tightly as she could, closing her eyes. The sounds of steel clashing on steel had since lessened and opening her eyes again she looked around, still afraid to let go of Henry.

In a quiet and deep voice Henry asked, "Are you hurt?" He felt Izzy shake her head, no. "Good. When we return to camp, and you have done your job, I swear to God, I am going to yell at you for doing something so stupid as to run into a battle. Do you understand?"

Izzy nodded, still holding tightly to Henry. "If I had not run into battle and started to treat men, several of them would be dead already, just so you know," Izzy said quietly, hoping this might calm him down. Instead it seemed to make it worse.

In an even deeper tone Henry answered, "I do not care. All of their lives are not worth yours." Hal finally made his way over to them.

"Is she okay?" Hal asked Henry.

"She is for now," Henry replied.

Hal just shook his head and chuckled. "We need to get our men back into the camp."

Everyone who was lucky enough to be able to walk helped to carry others that were not so lucky. Izzy and Sadie worked through the morning with everyone who was able to lend a hand to bandage wounds. Izzy had to make the call to amputate the leg of the first man she treated. It was awful. She gave him whiskey and belladonna, but nothing could dull the pain. Henry held the man down until he fainted from the pain. The sound of his scream stained Izzy's memory as she began to cut. She had managed to find the vessel that was bleeding and stitched it tightly. If she had not found the vessel, he would have died without question. Now, the second fight for his life would begin. If they could keep his

285

wound clean, keep infection away, then he would have a chance. When Izzy and Sadie had treated everyone, Izzy searched for Hal.

Approaching him, she saw he had blood soaking through his shirt. "SIT!" Izzy commanded. "Sadie! I need you here please!" Izzy ripped open his shirt to expose the large gash across his chest. "Sadie, I need a clean needle, and silk thread. Also, please get this dagger wet, then hold it in the fire." Izzy was so mad at Hal that she had no words and so remained silent.

Hal knew she was angry. He wanted to defend himself, but he also knew that she needed to yell. He watched as she internalized everything and knew that she very rarely shed a tear. So if screaming at him would help her to let it all out, then he could let her do that.

Sadie returned to Izzy and waited with a red-hot dagger in one hand and a clean needle and silk thread in the other. Izzy checked for debris in the wound and found it to be sufficiently clean. Izzy took the silk thread, and using the hot dagger, cut several pieces of silk thread, carefully setting them on a clean swatch of linen. Taking the first piece of thread, Izzy began to stitch Hal's open wound closed. "You are lucky this is not any deeper. You will bear a scar from this. I will add an oil that helps to heal the skin to your poultice, but I can only do so much." Izzy did not say another word until she was done stitching him closed. Taking the still hot dagger, she said, "This will hurt badly" as she quickly laid the edge of the still red steel along the wound to cauterize it. "Go put on a clean shirt, I will check on you this evening." Izzy left Hal to return to his own tent and for Sadie to clean up.

Izzy returned to her tent, still next to Henry's and began to violently blend herbs and oils for poultice that she would apply later tonight. How could he? He had promised to wait to fight until she had returned. Those men were butchered. Well over half of the camp required stitching. So deep in thought, she did not hear Henry slip into her tent.

"Izzy, are you okay?" Henry asked as he watched her viciously attack the herbs. He walked over to her and gently laid his hands-on top of hers. When he felt her muscles relax, he trailed his hands up her sleeved arms until he reached her shoulders. Gently he rubbed them feeling her let her guard down just a little more. Finally, he saw her bring her hands to her face, felt her shoulders begin to shake, and heard the familiar sound of her quietly crying. He turned her around to face him and was startled at the anger in her eyes as large hot tears fell down her cheeks.

"What were you thinking? Hal promised that he would wait until I had returned! How can I do my job properly if I am constantly arriving and immediately repairing men? I even returned half a day early! Can you imagine the casualties if I had not been there!" Izzy was yelling at Henry.

Hal was searching for Izzy to try to explain when he heard the yelling coming from her tent. She must be yelling at Henry. Poor guy. Then he heard Henry yell back.

Henry tried to shush her, quietly tell her that it is not how it appears, but Izzy just kept yelling at him. This was not his fault! "That is enough! First of all, it was a surprise attack against us! Secondly, you, you… you!" Henry was livid at the fact that she so carelessly ran into battle.

"Me! I what?" Izzy yelled back.

"You cannot go running into a battle! You are going to get yourself killed!" Henry exploded at her.

"I can do as I please! You are not my King, and I am not your property!" Izzy yelled even louder.

"Dammit Izzy, no you cannot! What if you died?" Henry countered.

"Then I guess you would have to find a new healer!" Izzy was not going to back down.

Hal still stood outside of Izzy's tent and smiled to himself. He and Henry had spoken while Izzy was gone and agreed Hal would no longer pursue Izzy unless he was willing to duel with Henry. Turning around and walking away from Izzy's tent, he knew that he was successful in keeping his promise to Raymond. As that thought sank in, sadness and frustration filled his head. He had fallen in love with someone who would never love him in return. This was a battle that he had lost, one that he was never destined to win.

"I do not want a new healer!" Henry yelled at her.

"Really Henry? Are you sure? Do you even know what you want?" Izzy shouted back.

"Yes, I do know what I want. I know exactly what I want!" He barked.

"Please enlighten me then Henry!" Izzy roared back.

Henry stopped. He looked at her and saw so much
passion. She was angry that they had been hurt. She
was angry that she thought Hal had lied and put them
all in danger by not securing a healer before battle.
And she was breathtakingly beautiful. Quietly,
nearly in a whisper, he said, "You. I just want you.
Izzy's heart beat wildly in her chest. What did he
just say?

Henry took a step closer to her and setting his hand
on her hips he said again, "Izzy, I want you."
Instantly Izzy felt all of the pent-up anger melt away.
She could feel the tears welling up in her eyes.
Embarrassed, she dropped her chin to look at the
floor. She had not cried this much since her parents
had passed.

Henry kissed the top of her head, then her forehead.
Tilting her chin up to him, he slowly kissed her soft
lips. Carefully, he unbuttoned the front of her gown.
He slid her arms out of the sleeves. When her gown
hit the floor, he stepped out of his boots. Taking a
step forward, Izzy took a step back. Henry kissed
her neck while his hands untied her kirtle. He slid
the kirtle down, trapping Izzy's hands at her sides,
leaving her breasts and stomach exposed to him.
With the kirtle situated at her hips, he pulled his shirt
up over his head and let it fall to the floor next to her
gown. With one hand he pushed the kirtle down as
his other hand pulled Izzy's now nearly naked body
to him. Unlacing his breeches, Henry let them fall to
the floor and taking another step towards Izzy, he

stepped out of them, again causing Izzy to step back again.

Izzy's legs hit the edge of the bed as Henry stood before her without any clothes on. Never taking her eyes from his, she felt her body tremble as Henry unlaced her drawers. He slid them off of her hips and let them fall to the ground.

Henry placed one hand at the back of her head and kissed her deeply. Keeping his other hand at the small of her back, he slowly laid her down on the bed, bracing himself above her body. He kissed her mouth again before standing up. Her body was even more exquisite than he had imagined. Henry kissed the back of her left hand then gradually moved his mouth up her arm tasting her skin. He felt her shiver as he passed the inside of her elbow and could not help but to smile. Reaching her collar bone, he was delighted and thrilled to hear her breath quicken as he neared her breast. Taking her full breast in his hand he teased her with his tongue tracing her nipple. As she softly moaned he could not help but to chuckle softly.

Izzy waited for the familiar pleasure of Henry taking her nipple in his mouth and felt an energy build within when he teased her instead. Her hands were at his shoulders, and she dug her nails into his shoulders trying to pull him to her.

Henry moved away from her breast and began to touch and kiss her smooth stomach. He felt her squirm a little as he kissed then blew on the delicate skin across her ribs. His hand followed the shape of her body running down each leg before returning to her full hips. Coming back to her breast, he took the other breast in his mouth and sucked firmly on her nipple feeling her arch her back to him. Henry was enjoying knowing how much he affected her. He was between her legs and kissed her as he entered her finally.

Izzy was lost in a sea of desire and pleasure. Henry touched, kissed and caressed every inch of her body, setting her on fire. She was not prepared for him to enter her, nor was she prepared for the stinging pang that accompanied it. As he penetrated her, she gasped in pain and tucked her head into his chest. Henry froze. He could feel her legs shaking tightly against his own legs as she curled against him in obvious discomfort. She was married, how could she still be innocent? Balancing on one arm, he smoothed her hair back. "Izzy," he crooned. Slowly she laid her head back against the bed again. Tears formed at the corners of her closed eyes. "Izzy, look at me," Henry requested.

Izzy opened her eyes, quickly blinking away the tears. At last, she looked up and met his worried stare.

"Izzy, is this your first time?" Henry could not believe what he was asking.

Izzy could only nod to him in response, blushing deeply.

Henry sighed and rested his forehead against hers.

"Are you angry?" Izzy asked, her voice filled with distrust.

"No! No, I am not angry. I wish you would have told me, I would have been gentler. I would have done everything I could to make sure that you did not feel any pain." He sweetly kissed her lips again. "But now I know and I will go slowly. I will be careful." Slowly, Henry began to pull back, then tenderly thrust forward again and again until Izzy's body relaxed around his, and he heard her sigh. The sting went away and Izzy closed her eyes, laying her head back against the bed and felt the absolute pleasure that was building up inside of her. As Henry began to thrust fast and deeper into her, she matched his rhythm with her hips until she felt like she was going to explode. "Henry!" she called out, opening her eyes nearly in a panic at the intense explosion of pleasure that ripped through her body. Henry waited until he could feel that she was close before he relaxed and allowed his orgasm to come to him as well. He came with her, calling her name out softly as he felt his body shudder with relief. "Izzy," he said again.

"Yes?" Izzy softly replied.

"That was incredible. It was beautiful." Henry slowly pulled out and rolled off of her, drawing her body against his.

Izzy smiled, then kissed his shoulder and Henry grabbed her leg at the back of the knee and drew it across his waist. "Yes, that was incredible and beautiful." Henry pulled a blanket over them and held on tightly as both of them fell asleep.

Chapter 11

Izzy awoke to Henry gently rubbing her arm and waist. The sensation caused her to shiver.

"Are you cold?" Henry asked. "I can fix that for you if you would like," Henry said seriously despite the lust that lit his eyes.

Izzy blushed deeply as Henry pulled her on top of him. Lifting her by her hips, he slid her back until she gasped, feeling the tip of his erect penis start to penetrate her again. He could feel the excitement already building up inside himself again as he guided her hips into a rhythm that quickly became too fast. Sitting up, Henry rolled Izzy onto her back again and together they exploded with pleasure.

After catching her breath, Izzy sighed as she caressed the taught skin across Henry's back. "I need to get up and get dressed. I need to go check on injuries.

Henry was afraid of letting her step out of the tent for fear that this was a cruel joke; only a dream and he would wake up alone in his own tent. Sighing at last and admitting defeat, he reluctantly let go of her.

"Izzy," he called.

Izzy turned to face him. There was something in his voice that left him sounding vulnerable.

His eyes met hers and he took a deep breath.

"Please, do not ever leave again without saying goodbye to me. It killed me knowing that I did not get to tell you how I felt before you left."

Izzy sat on the edge of the bed half dressed in clean clothes. "How exactly do you feel about me Henry?"

Henry almost drew back at her question. What was he supposed to say? Love? That was quite a strong word… "Izzy, I care for you."

He cared for her? That was it? She gave herself to him, she gave him her innocence and all he could say is that he cares for her? Izzy raised her eyebrows and a small, fake, smile spread across her face. She quickly stood up and finished getting dressed, leaving her dirty dress in a basket near the tent flaps. "Izzy?" Henry called to her again. Something was wrong. He just did not understand what. When she turned to face him, he saw the anger flash in her eyes like bolts of lightning and Henry instantly knew that he had said something wrong. "Izzy wait!" He called once more as she left the tent.

"He cares about me. My heart is nearly beating out of my chest. I might swoon at his sweet words," Izzy muttered sarcastically to herself through clenched teeth. Running into Hal, she practically barked at him to sit down.

"Sure, Izzy, um, is everything okay?" Hal asked cautiously.

"Okay? Of course everything is okay. He cares for me you know. Cares. I care for most of my patients. I care for the children in town. Care. He 'cares for me'," she said in a mocking tone dripping with sarcasm.

Just then, Hal saw Henry come from Izzy's tent with only his breeches on running his hand through his hair scanning the camp for her. 'Oh no, Henry, what did you do?' Hal thought to himself. He winced slightly as Izzy inspected his wound none too gently. Watching Henry spot Izzy, he saw Henry's chest swell with a deep breath then deflate as he exhaled. "I am going to put this salve on your wound. I will look at it again tomorrow. You will need to take it easy for about a week. Since the gash is not very deep, it should heal considerably faster than other wounds." Izzy did not even wait to see if Hal had any questions. She grabbed her jar of salve and left Hal sitting with his shirt open.

Hal watched as Izzy stormed off and Henry approached him. "What did you do? What did you say to her?"

Henry groaned as he rubbed his hands over his face. "I do not know what I did. I do not know what I said! Everything was wonderful. Then she got up to get dressed. She asked me how I felt and I told her I cared for her. Then she got this weird smile on her face and left."

Hal sighed heavily, dropped his chin and shook his head. Henry was hopeless. "You said, 'I care about you?' Was there anything in particular that happened prior to you telling her that you cared for her?"

Henry looked at Hal with both embarrassment and pride. He could never bring embarrassment down on Izzy by telling Hal of what they did last night, but he could see that Hal understood exactly what had happened.

"I see. So, you were with her, a married woman, who broke the vows she took before God and her husband, to give herself to you, and when she asked you how you felt about her, you told her you cared for her. Yet, you do not know what went wrong." Hal looked at Henry with disappointment. "I thought you were a smart man. Had I known that this is how you felt about Izzy, I would have accepted your offer to a duel, as I know that I would have treated her better." Hal saw the silent shock on Henry's face. He stood up, and walked away saying over his shoulder, "Good luck Henry. I hope you can fix this before it is too late."

Henry stood alone outside as the sun was setting. Returning to Izzy's tent, he gathered his clothes and boots and returned to his own tent. Changing into a clean shirt, he thought about what Hal had said; to fix it before it was too late. It was already too late, he had broken his vows to his wife, and Izzy had broken her vows to her husband. What he could not understand though, was why she was still untouched if she was married. What if she were widowed? He saw Izzy walking back to camp looking defeated. He watched as she turned away from his direction and started walking towards Hal's tent.

Hal was leaving his tent to go sit down for the evening meal when he saw Izzy approaching him. He could see the tears that fell down her cheeks.

297

Immediately worried, he rushed to her, holding her while she cried.

Izzy quickly silenced her tears. Taking a deep breath, she spoke in a hushed voice and explained that the knight whose leg they had amputated had passed.

"Izzy, none of us expected him to make it. He had lost so much blood, you cannot blame yourself," Hal comforted her.

Izzy looked up at him in disbelief. "*I* expected him to make it. I did everything I could, everything that I knew how, and them some extra. He did not die from blood loss. I believe it was infection. Still, I cleaned my tools first, this should not have happened. He was so kind and gracious. How will you tell his family?"

Hal smiled sympathetically. "I will take care of having his body brought home and informing his family. I do not want you to worry another minute about it. You did everything you could."

"Yes, but I am the healer. I do not deserve the title of Healing Bird if I cannot even stave off a simple infection."

Henry watched as Hal and Izzy spoke quietly with one another, their bodies close, nearly touching. He felt jealous that Izzy had turned to Hal to calm her and listen to her problems rather than him.

The sound of a galloping horse echoed through the camp. Everyone in camp that heard it stood, ready to fight again.

Izzy and Hal were closest to the gate and
instinctively Hal pushed Izzy behind him and drew
his sword. Henry was next to them, his sword drawn
and ready to fight alongside Hal once again. The air
was thick with tension and fear as the solo rider
came racing in.

"I need Healing Bird. Please, it is urgent!" the
messenger cried, out of breath. Izzy pushed past
Henry and Hal.

"I am Healing Bird," Izzy said, her hand outstretched
as she approached the messenger.

Thrusting the note into her hand, the messenger said,
"Please, you must hurry, she will not make it." Izzy
turned around as her two personal knights went
racing back to where they kept their two horses and
Izzy's. Rushing to her tent, she tore open the note.

> *Healing Bird,*
>> *Jayde has lost the baby, she is*
>> *hemorrhaging. The midwife here*
>> *cannot stop it. Help.*
>> *James*

Izzy dropped the note to the table, grabbed her bag
and stuffed it full of Lady Mantle, Garden Sage,
Shepherd's Purse, and a bottle of Cypress oil.
Henry ran after her throwing open the tent flap
seconds behind her. He watched as she frantically
began to move bottles that were sitting on top of the

table. Grabbing a leather bag from the corner of the tent, she dumped the contents on the bed.

"Damn it! Where is it?" Izzy screamed. Turning back around, she threw the dried herbs on the floor and opened the small chest that she had been using as a shelf. There in the chest was the bottle filled with chokecherry juice. She stuffed it in her bag and put the bag on. She grabbed her cloak and ran past Henry and out of her tent to where Sir Wade and Sir Randall were waiting with her horse. Swinging her leg over the saddle, they kicked their horses forward to a full gallop as they raced towards Era. Veering off of the road, they cut through the woods desperate to shave off as much time as they could.

Henry picked up the note and read it. It was from his brother, and Jayde was in trouble. He had no idea that she was even pregnant again, and now they were all about to lose her too. Running outside, he ran to his horse calling to Hal as he ran. "It is Jayde, I have to go!" He did not even wait for Hal to answer as he kicked his horse forward trying to catch up to Izzy. Not knowing that they cut through the woods, he followed the road.

Izzy and her knights rode through the evening and arrived at Era when the full moon was high in the sky above them, illuminating the rolling hills and casting large shadows down in the valleys. Izzy was already half way off of her horse when a midwife came to her.

"Are you Healing Bird?" When Izzy nodded she grabbed her hand and running back in the midwife said, "Lord James has not left her side."

Izzy could only nod. She ran past the midwife and up the stairs to Jayde and James chambers. Without knocking, she pushed the door open and was startled at the gray lifeless body in the bed.

"My God, help me," Izzy prayed as she rushed to Jayde's side. "Jayde, I am here." Turning, she said to Maggie, "Maggie, bring me hot water in a tea pot, run!" Opening her bag, she pulled out several herbs, then grabbed hold of the bottle of Cypress. Pulling the covers down to expose Jayde's naked form, she carefully poured a small amount of the oil on Jayde's stomach rubbing as gently as she could. Maggie came back into the room with the pot of hot water. Quickly, Izzy began to add dried Lady Mantle, Garden Sage and Shepherd's Purse to the hot water. She waited a few minutes then poured a cup. Adding some cool water to the cup to help reduce the heat, she turned to James. "I need for her to drink this. You will need to help me. This is a tea with three herbs that help to stop the bleeding, but James, you must be prepared for any outcome."

"Maggie, help me to clear the blood-soaked linen from under her." Then turning to the midwife, she said, "Grab those clean linens over there and lay them under her body when we lift her up. James, come help me by lifting Jayde very slightly." Everyone began to move, each doing their part and taking orders from Izzy. "James, go wash your hands, then get Izzy to finish that tea. I have some juice that she must drink as well. I must look at her, do you understand James?"

James nodded as Izzy began to palpate Jayde's stomach, then examine her. "What the hell is this?" Izzy growled as she began to pull blood soaked linens from inside Izzy.

"I was simply trying to soak up the blood," the midwife said quietly.

"Do not ever do that again. Even if this antiquated idea worked, which it will not, you will instead kill her with an infection. When will people begin to understand that cleanliness is one of the best paths to health?"

"She has finished drinking the tea," James announced, still holding the cup.

"James, reach into my bag and pull out the large bottle. It is filled with a red juice. Pour a cup and get her to drink it. When she is done, give her another. Then keep alternating between the tea and the juice."

Izzy racked her brain trying to understand what was going on. "James, you saw the fetus?"

"No, we were eating this morning, and she said she did not feel well. When she stood up, she doubled over in pain and has been bleeding heavily since. Did I do something wrong?" James answered, his voice wracked with worry and fear.

"Oh James! That's it!" Izzy exclaimed. Izzy began to massage Jayde's stomach. "I am so very sorry Jayde," Izzy lamented as she helped Jayde's body expel the now dead baby and placenta.

Suddenly the door flew open and Henry burst in to see blood soaking the bed, covering Izzy nearly to her elbows and part of her dress. "Oh God, James, what can I do?"

Izzy looked up to see anger flash across James' face before he looked back down to Jayde without answering. Izzy focused again on Jayde. "Henry, get me a wash basin now. Maggie get me fresh water please." Both bolted into action. Henry found a wash basin and brought it to Izzy's side. He noticed that she still had her cloak on and it seemed to be in the way. He reached around her neck from behind and unclasped the cloak handing it to the midwife. "Here, do something with this." He then took a step back to get out of the way. He had been working alongside Izzy long enough to know that the biggest help was to move back and give her space. "Thank you," Izzy said quietly to Henry. Finally, she finished helping Jayde's body do what it had been struggling so long to do by itself. Standing up, she turned to the midwife who was now ghost white, leaning against the wall on the far side of the room. "Here, please get a cedar box and prepare him for burial." Maggie and the midwife left together with the baby. Izzy then turned back to Jayde, and noted that the bleeding was not as heavy as it had been.

She continued as she had been taught for post births and soon the bleeding stopped. Sitting back on the stool, Izzy rested her elbows on her knees, closed her eyes and said a silent prayer. She waited another minute to see that the bleeding had indeed stopped. She stood up again and walked over to the wash basin that had been replaced with Henry close on her heels. Picking up the pitcher, he slowly poured fresh water over her hands as he had done many times before. Once her hands were clean, she dried them on the clean linen.

"James, come lift Jayde so that I can once again change the linens beneath her. She is going to need several days to recover. Do not push her to get up and move around. Let her lead the way," -Izzy said softly as she changed the linens again.

"Wait, are you leaving right now?" James asked, hoping she would stay.

"No, I will stay for at least a day, maybe two to make sure she is recovering well. Then I must return to camp." Izzy walked to the door, then turned, "I will ask Maggie where I can rest." Then she left the room expecting to go and search for Maggie. Instead, Henry left the room with her and placing a hand at the small of her back, he guided her to his chamber. Once the door was closed he grabbed her and pulled her close, kissing the top of her head. He had no words to say to her. She had dropped everything for his family. She had raced across the countryside, after tending to a camp full of inured and dying to save Jayde. Turning her to face him, he unbuttoned her dress, then untied her kirtle letting all of it fall to the floor. Then undressing himself, he carried her to his bed. Laying her down on the bed, he laid down beside her and as tenderly as he could, he kissed her sweet soft lips. Each part of Izzy's body that his hands touched, he gently kissed. He kissed the skin between her breasts, kissed down her naval and her belly button. After kissing her from her mouth to her ankles, he crawled over her until he was kneeling over her hips, gently, he rolled her over to her stomach and moved her hair to the side so that he could kiss the delicate skin at the back of her neck. As he kissed her, he saw goose bumps rise up on her arms and neck. He smiled to himself, kissing her back, down her spine to the top of her round bottom. He rolled her back over to face him, her eyes staring at him trying to see to his soul. Slowly he lowered himself down on her. Kissing her mouth, to her earlobe where he nibbled as he gradually entered her. Thrusting forward as far as he could, he stopped moving, grabbing her hands in his and pinned them down at either side of her head. He left her ear and trailed down her neck and bending his back he circled her nipple with his tongue, gently, slowly, then blowing on it as it became a firm peak. Izzy's entire body ached, feeling the torturous pleasure that Henry continued to bring her. He took his time with each movement, deliberately going slow and ignoring her plea for him to go fast. When he took her second breast in his mouth nibbling the soft flesh to the underside of her nipple she arched her back, almost in a primal state and moaned a soft, guttural noise that she herself had never heard before. Finally, when Henry encompassed her nipple in his mouth again, she gasped and squeezed his fingers entwined with hers.

Henry felt her entire body tense beneath him. Her legs were bent, hugging his hips tightly. It was agonizing to go as slow as he was, but he wanted more from her than just sex. He wanted it to be more meaningful, to have an impact on her and himself. He began to pull back and thrust forward at a leisurely pace, letting go of her hands and feeling her trace her fingers down his neck, across his shoulders and down his arms. Every few strokes, he thrust a little harder, then returned to the even rhythm they were moving to. When he felt Izzy's hands caress his back, down his ribs and to his hips, he nearly lost his mind. His began to breathe harder, struggling to maintain control of his speed. Izzy splayed her hands on his butt cheeks and dugs her nails in. Bending his head forward to her shoulder, he bit the soft flesh as he thrust into her hard. He heard her moan again, and knew that he was losing control. Lifting his head so that he could watch her, he started to quicken his rhythm, watching as she closed her eyes, and tilted her chin up. He watched as she began to climax, realizing that he was seeing the most vulnerable beauty that a human could ever expose to another. Thrusting harder and faster, he climaxed just after she did collapsing onto her, both of their bodies shaking and wet with sweat. He rolled over pulling her to him. He pulled her right hand to his chest and laid it over his heart, where even he could feel through his own fingertips his racing heart. He wrapped his right hand around her waist and rested his hand on her butt cheeks.

Izzy could barely move. She lay still in Henry's arms feeling his heart beating wildly in his chest. There had not been a single word spoken between them; it was beautiful. Izzy's mind drifted back to the camp and as she succumbed to the sweet darkness of sleep, she was even more confused by her feelings for Henry and how he felt about her.

Henry listened as Izzy fell asleep in his arms. After a half hour or so, he slipped out from under her and dressed. Then, taking the covers, he pulled them up to her shoulders and tucked a strand of hair behind her ear. In a whisper, almost as though he was trying to keep a secret from himself, he said, "I love you Izzy." Getting up, he stoked the fire and then sat down at the desk to pen a note to the King.

> *King Henry,*
> *I have been loyal to our country all of my life, and loyal to you and your son, His Royal Highness. I was married to a beautiful woman two and a half years ago*

and have not yet taken her as my bride as I was summoned on my wedding day to fight beside Prince Henry. I have done so without complaint or request for anything, but today, I have learned that I love another woman. A married woman and I know that I will never give my bride the kind of love that I have for this woman. Lady Isabel de Seaton, my wife, deserves a happy life, and no matter how much I provide, I will never be able to provide that to her. I am beseeching you to grant me an annulment, so that I may set her free. This is not a decision that comes lightly. Please consider my request.

Forever Loyal,

Sir Henry de Seaton
of Adonia

Henry folded the note and sealed it. Turning to Izzy, he saw she was still asleep. He smiled and quietly left the room. As he walked down the hall he ran into Maggie. "Maggie, will you be sure that Izzy gets a bath later?"

"Yes, of course My Lord." Maggie watched him knock quietly before entering Jayde's room.

"James, how is she?" Henry asked, closing the door behind him.

James looked up to see Henry standing before him. Looking back to Jayde, he felt hot tears streak down his face.

Henry looked to Jayde and saw that there was color in her cheeks once again. He was relieved and knelt down beside his brother. "Her skin is looking pinker. I am so sorry that you and she are going through this. I cannot imagine the pain and fear you feel now, but I want you to know, that I love and support you James. I know that my behavior has been cowardly at best, and for that I am sorry. I hope that you and Jayde will find a way to forgive me in time. Until then, just know that I am here for you should you need anything." Henry saw tears rolling down James cheek. "James, are you okay? Would you like me to leave you now?"

James picked up his head and faced Henry. "She saved her. Your Healing Bird saved Jayde. Thank you."

Henry gave a confused smile before standing and leaving the room. Down in the hall he found Sebastian, the constable at Era. "Sebastian, please see to it that this note leaves with a messenger immediately."

"Yes, of course Lord Henry." Sebastian looked down to the note and saw that it was addressed to King Henry. Surprised, he looked back up to see Henry leaving the hall.

Henry went to the stables and prepared his horse to ride back to camp. As he trotted out of the stable in the courtyard, he glanced back up to the window at his room where Izzy rested. The window to Jayde and James's room opened and he saw James wave goodbye to him. Waving in return, Henry left the courtyard. Once at the top of the hill, he urged his horse forward into a canter and began his ride back to camp. Henry arrived in time for the evening meal. Hal had watched him ride into camp and waited for him to take care of his horse prior to checking on him.

"Henry, is Jayde okay? Where is Izzy?" Hal asked confused and concerned.

Henry took a deep breath. "Walk with me while we get something to eat. I have not eaten since yesterday morning." The two of them walked to get a plate of food for the evening meal. Sitting down together Henry told Hal about what he walked into and how Izzy saved Jayde's life. "Hal, she was incredible. She stayed calm, she delegated tasks to everyone, including the midwife, she figured out what was wrong and took care of Jayde. I was so grateful and proud."

Hal watched Henry as he spoke about the situation. "I am so glad to hear that Jayde is better. Do you know how long Izzy will be gone for? Did you fix your problem?"

Henry had forgotten that there was even a problem. "No, I do not think I fixed the problem. But I am working on it. It is going to take some time." Henry thought back to the note he sent to the King. "Izzy said she planned to stay for another day or two. Then she would return to camp."

Henry and Hal sat together in silence for the rest of the meal. As Hal stood up he asked, "Henry did you get any rest last night?"

"No, I was up through the night. Why?" Henry asked.

"I want you to rest tonight and start fresh tomorrow." Hal put his hand on Henry's shoulders. "Sleep well my friend."

"Thank you Hal." Henry said as he yawned and walked to his own tent. Laying down, Henry could still smell lavender, as though Izzy were laying next to him. He felt his chest tense at the thought of her and his mind immediately wandered, wondering what she was doing in that exact moment. Finally, Henry drifted to sleep with a smile on his face and knowing that an annulment was the right choice.

Chapter 12

It had been three days since Izzy had arrived in Era. Jayde was still weak but recovering well. Izzy was checking in on Jayde when James stopped her in the hallway.

"Izzy, you are sure you must leave today?" James asked.

Izzy smiled and hugged her brother-in-law.

"Unfortunately, yes. I must return to the camp, collect my belongings and return to my other life; the one where I am simply Lady Isabel de Seaton, not Healing Bird. It will not last long though. His Royal Highness will call for me again, but it seems like this is one of the last rebellions that he will be tending to. Then I believe he will be disbanding the group. That will be good. From what I have learned about Iole, there are quite a bit of herbs that I really should harvest and dry before it is too late. Raymond said that there are fields of lavender and chamomile! What a wonderful natural resource for Iole!"

James smiled at Izzy with a love she had never seen from him before. "You remind me so very much of my mother. Henry is very lucky."

"I am like your mother? I cannot think of a greater compliment. Thank you." Izzy blushed.

"Has Henry come around? He seemed very familiar with you," James said.

"Oh, well, yes, but no. I still have not said anything to him about being his wife. I am at a complete loss as to what to say or how to tell him. I am sure that when the time presents itself that the right words will come to me. I hope…" Izzy bit her lip as her words trailed off.

James sighed and placed a hand on her shoulder. "Do not wait until it is too late little sister." James smiled before changing the subject. "Are you on your way to check on Jayde once more?"

"Yes, I am very pleased with how she is recovering." Izzy stepped back into her role as healer again. "Give her at lease twelve weeks of rest before trying for another child. The children can visit with her, but no lifting for two weeks, then let her go at her pace. If she says she is too weak or looks faint, do not let her continue with whatever task she is doing. Have her drink one cup of the chokecherry juice each day until it is gone and drink one pot of the tea each day until it is gone as well. I have left enough herbs to make the tea for one week, which should be enough to help her. But if anything happens, if you have any questions or concerns, please send for me immediately." Izzy turned toward Jayde's chamber, but stopped and turned back to James. "James, one more thing, please. I am begging you; do not call for that midwife again. Ever."

James nodded as Izzy walked away into Jayde's chamber, closing the door behind her.

"Good morning Jayde. How are you feeling this morning?" Izzy asked as she felt Jayde's forehead for any sign of fever.

"I am feeling well. I am so grateful to you Izzy. James explained everything that you did for me. Izzy, you saved my life. Thank you." Jayde choked back the tears. She could not help but to think about her beautiful children not having a mother, and the possibility that they would end up with a stepmother like she had.

"Jayde, I would have given my life to save yours. I am so thankful I was able to get here in time." Izzy grabbed her oil and put it in her bag, then poured Jayde a cup of tea. "Jayde, I have already explained everything to James, but I want to make sure you understand too. No sex for twelve weeks. I want to make sure that your body has ample time to fully heal. Drink the chokecherry juice until it is gone and a pot of tea every day for a week. No picking up the children for a minimum of two weeks. Send for me if there are any pains, sudden bleeding, problems or questions. Do not send for the midwife. That is it. Take it easy. I think that James is going to get your little angels. They have missed you so much!" Izzy hugged Jayde before putting her messenger bag on and leaving the room. She met Wade and Randall at the stables. Fastening her cloak, she then mounted her horse. "Are we ready to travel?" The two knights nodded their heads and they made their way through town and up the hill before galloping away to camp.

The afternoon was just setting in when Izzy, Wade and Randall arrived at camp. She immediately performed wound checks on everyone, and then went back to her tent to start cleaning up the mess she left three days earlier. She had not been in her tent for more than a few minutes before Hal arrived and requested permission to come in.

"Yes, of course! I apologize for the mess. I left in haste." Izzy felt embarrassed by the disarray but continued to clean as Hal came in and sat on a chair.

"How is Lady Jayde?" Hal asked. He had not spoken about her since Henry returned.

"She is doing much better. I think she will recover well, but it will take some time before she has fully healed. She is in good spirits though," Izzy said as she finished organizing her bottles. "How are talks going? Any more rebellions in the foreseeable future?" she asked.

"Actually, that is what I came to talk to you about. I am in the midst of talks and things seem to be going well. While I do not think that there will be any more rebellions, would you allow for me to call upon you should we have an urgent need?" Hal asked.

"Of course you may. I will be in Iole for the next couple of weeks, then returning to Adonia. I will likely be spending most of the summer in Iole with frequent trips back to Adonia. When do you expect to be disbanding the camp?" Izzy questioned.

Taking a deep breath, Hal answered. "As long as talks go well, we will begin to disband within a month, and everyone will be dismissed within six weeks." Hal waited for this to fully sink in and when she did not react as he had expected, he continued on. "Izzy, that means that in six weeks, Henry will be sent home, to Adonia…Do you understand?"

"I understand," was all that Izzy could say. She bit her bottom lip, considering everything before her.

"Well, I should get back to my duties. I will see you later." Hal stood and left the tent.

Izzy began to pack up her oils and herbs into the crates stacked in her tent. She would send a wagon for the rest of her belongings as soon as she arrived in Iole. She would make sure the wagon brought everything back to Adonia. When she had finished packing her oils, she went to find Sadie.

"Sadie," Izzy said, when she found her mixing oils on a table outside in the shade. "Sadie, I am going to pack up and leave tonight. I will send a wagon for my things once I reach Iole. Will you be okay here treating minor injuries?"

"Yes My Lady. If I need anything, I can send for you though?" Sadie asked.

"Always, you can always send for me or send me a question!" Izzy said and hugged her friend.

"Lady Isabel, will you be okay without a lady's maid though?" Sadie asked.

"Oh Sadie, you are so sweet! I will be fine. I am going to be returning to Iole this time. So if you

need anything, send a messenger to Iole first." Izzy
felt the butterflies in her stomach of getting to go and
see the beauty that Raymond had cared for.
"Do you know how much longer I will be here
before I will be able to return home?" Sadie asked.
"I believe only until everyone is healed, unless there
is another rebellion, then we will both be here
awhile. Well, I am going to prepare to leave again. I
have most of my things packed up, so I will plan on
leaving either late tonight or early in the morning. I
should go pack up my clothing. I want to make sure
that items need only be loaded and brought to
Adonia." Finally, Izzy said goodbye and left.
Izzy went back to her tent and finished packing the
rest of her belongings before sitting down to write a
note to Henry.

> *Henry,*
>
> *I am leaving again, but cannot
> imagine saying goodbye to you once more,
> especially since I do not know when we will
> see each other next. I hope that you know
> how much I have enjoyed getting to know
> you, and care for you. Laughing over cards,
> sitting quietly around the fire and working
> beside you were wonderful. I found a
> friendship with you that I have dreamed of
> finding and it literally is breaking my heart
> knowing that I am going to lose that. I hope
> that when you return home to your wife, that*

you find a way to forgive yourself for the
burden that you carry and that you seek out
a friendship with her. I am sure that she will
feel just as lucky as I have at getting to know
you. I hope that you find her to be a kind
woman as well. I have learned a great deal
about trust and love and hope that you did
too. Take what you have learned and move
forward, do not look back. Life has too
much to offer to keep wishing for yesterday.
All my love,
Izzy

Izzy folded the note and sealed it. She picked it up and placed it in her pocket. It was almost time for the evening meal. She hurried to find her two knights before she lost them to the evening meal. Izzy found Sir Wade and Sir Randall leaving their tents and walking towards her.

"Healing Bird is everything okay?" Sir Wade asked.

"Yes, I wanted to let you know that we will be leaving in the morning, predawn, and we will be traveling to Iole."

"Of course," Sir Randal said. Izzy then walked behind the two men making their way back to the center of camp. She parted ways with them and walked to Hal's tent. Calling out, she requested to come in and speak with him.

Hal cleared his throat and answered her, "Yes, come in Izzy." As Izzy walked into his tent, she was startled to see Henry standing there. Hal looked less than pleased.

"I am sorry, I did not know that you were busy. I will come back later," Izzy said and turned to leave.

"No, that will not be necessary Izzy, Lord Henry was just leaving. We can continue our conversation later or tomorrow." Hal waited for Henry to leave before speaking again. "Izzy, what can I do for you?" Hal struggled to not let his exchange with Henry affect his conversation with her.

Izzy pulled the note that she had written to Henry out of her pocket. "I was wondering if you would give this to Henry tomorrow morning some time. I do not have the strength to give it to him myself." Izzy held the note out for Hal to take as silence fell between them.

Hal took the note from Izzy, "Yes of course. Have you told him yet?"

Izzy gave a sad smile and shook her head before turning and leaving the tent. She was tired and only wanted to go home, where life was predictable. Izzy skipped the evening meal and instead went to her tent and quickly fell asleep.

The time came for Izzy to leave and as she quietly rode out of camp, she felt her heart break. She pulled her hood up onto her head and rode to Iole without a single word spoken between her and her knights.

Iole was beautiful. Just as Raymond had said, the fields were covered with wild lavender and chamomile. It was incredible to see the purple flowers swaying in the wind and the chamomile bouncing as if to its own beat. They followed the road through the town seeing many people stop to stare at them. Izzy smiled and nodded to as many people as she could. There were so many children, it was wonderful! What a thriving town! They continued down the road until they reached the gates to the courtyard. Pausing they looked up at the formidable wall that surrounded the castle. Hesitantly, the trio continued forward through the gates and into the courtyard. As they reached the stables, an older, plump woman came rushing over to them.

"You must be Lady Isabel! I am Millie, head servant here at Iole. Lord Raymond told us so much about you. I even had the pleasure of visiting Adonia and the festival that you held. His lordship described you perfectly!" Millie waited for the group to dismount. "Please, follow me inside. We make a lavender lemonade. Have you ever tried it? It is delicious and quite a refreshing change to wine and ale." She continued to talk and walk as she led the group into the great hall.

Izzy walked into the cool hall and gasped. It was exquisite! The walls were covered in murals, sprawling across the ceiling. The windows were large with multiple panes of glass and each window had a few select panes of colored glass that created small pictures. The tables were beautiful and well oiled, keeping the wood vibrant. It was truly a beautiful estate.

"Lady Isabel, Lord Raymond spoke so highly of you and said that you had done so many wonderful things to Adonia. He said that you would only bring good fortune and progress to Iole. Would you like to sit? I will have the kitchen bring out the midday meal," Millie said before leaving the group.

One servant carried out a pitcher and cups, while two others carried out trays. One filled with carved meat, the other with cheese and grapes. Millie then reappeared pouring three glasses of the lavender lemonade. "I will leave you to enjoy your meal. Should you need anything, just signal to one of the women. Simon will probably come in soon to meet you as well, show you around and answer any questions that you have."

"Thank you very much," Izzy said before turning and tasting the lavender lemonade. "Mmm, this is wonderful." Both Wade and Randall tried the lemonade as well and nodded in agreement. "Wade, Randall, will you both be able to stay here with me for two weeks or would you like to return to Ackerley? I am sure that the knights here in Iole can take your position if you wish. I know that you must be missing Ackerley as much as I am." Izzy spoke while they ate.

"We will manage and stay with you until you return to Ackerley," Sir Randall said while Sir Wade nodded in agreement.

"Really? Thank you very much! I feel grateful to have you both by my side. We shall only stay in Iole for two weeks or less," Izzy said.

Izzy noticed a tall man who looked to be not much older than Henry walk into the hall and cross the room towards her.

"Hello, I am Simon. I am the constable here at Iole. Millie said that you are Lady Isabel, am I correct My Lady?" Simon asked.

"Yes, you are correct. It is a pleasure to meet you Simon," Izzy gave Simon her brightest most confident smile.

Simon gave a courteous smile in return. Lord Raymond had promised that this 'Lady Isabel' would not change anything unless it was necessary. That she would preserve the character and charm that was the soul of Iole, but they all knew what happened when new nobility took over; they changed everything.

Izzy could see by the tightness in Simon's face that he did not trust her. She took a deep breath. Adonia greeted her with a similar caution. Izzy hoped that she would have the fortitude to work with the resistance that was presented to her now as well.

"Simon, can you tell me what is most special about Iole?" Izzy wanted to dispel the distrust and build up his confidence in her.

"Most special about Iole, My Lady? Everything about Iole is special," Simon said stiffly.

Izzy could tell that this was going to be harder than she hoped. "I see." She realized that she would have to break down the walls that were already built up against her. "Simon, I need for you to specifically tell me just one thing that I must not change about Iole," Izzy said refusing to break eye contact with Simon. She watched Simon's expression change from ice cold to fearful. She narrowed her gaze slightly, waiting for Simon to answer her question. He could not believe what he was hearing. He knew that Lord Raymond had been wrong. This woman was going to ruin Iole.

"Simon, I am waiting for you to pick only one thing about Iole. You want to push me away and tell me that *all* of Iole is special, yet you can find nothing that is so special and important that it would be the demise of Iole should I change it. When Lord Raymond approached me, and asked me to care for Iole, he assured me that Iole was a place that I would love and would love me. He promised me that its people were kind, generous and would not make assumptions of me. He promised me that it would not be more work for me to take on Iole. Are you prepared to make a liar out of Lord Raymond?" Izzy challenged Simon.

Simon blinked rapidly, startled by how assertive Lady Isabel was. "No, My Lady, Lord Raymond is not a liar! I would never do anything that would make a liar of his Lordship!"

"Wonderful. Let me tell you something about myself, Simon. I have spent the last two months riding back and forth between my estates, a battle camp and rushing in the middle of the night across the countryside to save my sister's life. I have spent the last two and a half years helping my husband's estate to recover from the hell that was brought down upon it from its previous nobility. I built trust between the servants and myself. I earned the trust from my farmers and their families. I went down into town and built homes with my own hands for the families that live in my town to move into because their homes were awful and no one should have to live in a home of such poor quality. I did that not because I was asked to, but because they deserved it. I have spent countless sleepless nights in their homes holding their children's hands because they had horrific fevers and everyone else was terrified that they had the plague. I have helped to bring life into this world and watched life disappear before my eyes. I am tired, but if pushing myself beyond exhaustion is what it takes to prove to you that I have no ill intent towards Iole, then I will. If I truly must go back down into town, and build new homes with my bare hands, then I will. If I must put my own life at risk to prove to you, the servants and townspeople that I will only do what I can to help, then I will. Do you understand? I gave my word to my brother, Lord Raymond, that I would love and care for Iole the way that he did, the way his mother did and I never go back on my word. I will do whatever is required of me for Iole to continue to be the beautiful place that it is. Yes, I will eventually make changes, but only if they help the people of Iole, not the nobility. Now, I am going to find Millie, ask her to show me to my chamber, and I am going to rest for the entire day. Tomorrow, after the morning meal you will have to make a choice. You will either be here, with a change of mind and attitude and you will want to show me everything there is in Iole; the beautiful rolling hills of lavender and chamomile, the church, the fields, the market, everything, or you will not show up and I will take it upon myself you walk the streets of town with my knights without you. I will learn about Iole and I will earn the peoples' trust, but you choose how difficult you will make it for me. Good day Simon. Sir Wade, Sir Randall, I hope that you enjoy your day of rest. I will be taking my meals in my room the rest of the day. I will see you both here, in the morning." Izzy stood and began to walk to the kitchen when she heard Simon begin to speak. "My Lady, I apoligi-" Simon began but stopped when Lady Isabel turned around.

Izzy turned to face Simon and held her hand up in the air at him and said in an authoritative tone that she rarely needed to use, "That will be enough Simon. Return to your duties. Good day!" She then turned back around and walked towards the kitchen where Millie and two other servants stood staring.

"Millie, would you kindly show me to my chamber? I think I would like to rest. Also, would you please have a pot of hot water sent up for tea, and I would like to eat the evening meal in my chamber, alone."

"Yes of course Lady Isabel. Right this way please." Millie led Izzy down a hall, then up a set of winding stairs while the other two servants rushed to get the tea pot ready. Millie was still in shock at how Simon behaved downstairs. Reaching the chamber directly across the hall from Lord Raymond's chamber, Millie opened the door. "Lady Isabel, this was Lady Catherine's chambers. It still has her feminine touches, so it is not nearly as dark as Lord Raymond's. Although, if you would prefer that chamber I will take you there instead."

"Oh no Millie, thank you though. That is Lord Raymond's chamber. It will always be waiting for him. This is lovely, thank you." Izzy looked around the room decorated in so much pink. Although Izzy was not in love with the color, it was definitely a beautiful room.

"Lady Isabel, if you would prefer different colors, or furniture, let me know, and we will see what we can change immediately, and what we will need to build or purchase." Millie hesitated before speaking again, but she could not hold her tongue. "My Lady, I pray that you do not think that we all behave and think like Simon. Truth be told, I am embarrassed by his behavior. I cannot apologize enough for how he spoke to you."

Izzy watched Millie's expression and body language as she spoke about Simon. She could see the sudden change from kindness to anger. "Millie, I am not judging you or anyone else and will not even judge Simon. I understand that you are all scared. I am scared too. I am scared that I will not be everything that Lord Raymond promised that I would be or that you all hoped I could be. I worry that I will fail Lord Raymond. Tomorrow will be a new day." Izzy smiled at Millie, suddenly feeling the exhaustion from so little sleep the past week. There was a knock at the door and a servant brought in the teapot and teacup.

"Thank you My Lady. Thank you for having faith in us." Millie took the teapot and cup and set them on the table.

"I beg your pardon My Lady, but you did not say what kind of tea you wanted, so I brought up a chamomile blend and a lemon blend," the other maid chimed in.

"That is so kind of you, I actually have a blend that I want, but after the midday meal, would you bring up another pot of tea using the lemon blend? By any chance does it have lavender in it as well?" Izzy asked kindly.

"Of course, My Lady and yes, the lemon blend does have lavender in it as well," the servant answered with a warm smile.

"Wonderful, I will look forward to it. I did not get your name. Would you tell me your name?" Izzy inquired.

"Yes My Lady, my name is Julianna." She liked Lady Isabel already. She did not care what Simon had said before she arrived. She thought that Lady Isabel seemed as beautiful inside as she was outside. Julianna then turned and left the room, returning to the kitchen and her duties.

"My Lady, are you always this kind when speaking to servants?" Millie asked. Lady Isabel spoke to them as though they were her equals.

Izzy tilted her head to one side for a moment before she answered. "I suppose. I had just always considered it to be respectful. Everyone deserves respect," Izzy said as she walked to the shuttered window and opened it, allowing the early summer air to flow into the chamber. "Millie, have you ever looked at the view from here? It is incredible! Look! You can see the town from here! Oh! And the lavender and chamomile!" Izzy and Millie talked for just a moment more before Millie left to tend to her duties again, leaving Izzy alone to rest.

Izzy waited for her tea to steep, then poured herself a cup. She sat at the window seat watching the town below and enjoying the wonderful summer air. Finally, she lay down and closed her eyes, hoping to rest a bit. Taking a deep breath, she tried to clear her mind, but kept thinking of the fact that in six short weeks, she would be face to face with Henry and

have to tell him the truth. What would she say?
'Surprise, I am your wife,'? She did not think that
would be taken too well. She could not relax, so she
got up and walked over to the window seat and sat
staring out the window at the town below. Slowly,
she relaxed enough that she fell asleep leaning
against the wall facing the window.

Battle Camp

Henry had heard Izzy leave early in the morning and had not thought anything of it until now. It was evening and she and her knights had still not returned. He saw Sadie in passing and stopped her. "Sadie, do you know when Izzy will be returning?" "Returning? Lord Henry, I was under the impression that Healing Bird would not be returning. I can ask Hal for you if you would like. It seemed as though it was decided very last minute." Sadie hoped that she was not saying more than she should.

"No, I will go speak with him myself. Thank you Sadie," Henry said with a smile on his face, but fire in his heart. He walked back to Izzy's tent and walked in. Her herbs and bottles were packed up, her personal belongings gone. Henry left the tent and went straight to Hal, who was coming in from the training field. "Where is Izzy?"

Hal looked to Henry from the man he had been talking to. "We can talk more tomorrow." Hal said to the knight and turned towards his tent, motioning for Henry to follow him. Once inside, he offered Henry a seat, but Henry declined. "It was her choice to go without speaking to you." Hal saw something that resembled a vehement emotion flicker across Henry's face. Turning to his desk, Hal picked up the note that Izzy had given him for Henry. Turning back, he held the note out. "She left this for you.

What will you do? Will you chase after her? You should be free to go in six weeks when we are completely disbanded."

Henry took the note from Hal, he would wait until he was back in his tent before he opened it. "Thank you." There was nothing else that he could say. She left again, without saying goodbye. He would read her note, then just try to forget about her. He needed to deal with his own problems.

Chapter 13
August 1410
Era

Henry rode through the gates of Era slowly. The last
time he had been here, Jayde had been on her death
bed, and Healing Bird was saving her life. He
remembered the smell of lavender in her hair and on
her skin, and her beautiful blue eyes that could see
deep into his soul, if he would have only let her in.
He had held her in his arms until she fell asleep, and
then disappeared. If he had only known then that he
would never hold her again, he might have told her
that he loved her while staring into her beautiful blue
eyes, and that he would be willing to give up
everything for her. Maybe then she would have left
everything behind and started a new life with him.
He could dream. Riding into the courtyard, he saw
James waiting for him. Climbing down from his
horse, he handed the reins to the stable boy. Henry
stood still in front of James awkwardly. Finally,
James stepped forward grabbing Henry and hugging
him.

"Henry, thank you for coming home. I am glad that
you and I have finally been able to put the past where
it belongs, behind us. Have you gone home to your
wife yet? Does she know that you are coming
home?" James fired questions to Henry as they

walked together into the hall and then up to James' study.

Sitting down Henry took a deep breath. "I have not gone home to Adonia yet and have not sent any word to her." Henry could see the tension begin to build up between himself and James yet again. "Let us discuss something else. How are the kids?"

James worried for Henry and Izzy. He could not help but think that something terrible was coming and he wondered if there was something that he could do to prevent it. "The kids are doing wonderfully. They should be out with Jayde, walking through the town, but will be home in time for the evening meal. What will you do when you go home to Adonia?" James could not leave the conversation alone. What was Henry's plan?

"I do not know. I guess I will figure it out when I get there." Henry could not tell James that he had petitioned King Henry for an annulment. He was simply waiting here in Era until he heard from the King, then he would travel to either the King's Court, or to Adonia. James and Henry continued talking, James asking about the battles that Henry had fought in, and in turn Henry asked James what changes and growth that Era had gone through. When Maggie knocked on the door to the study, the two men stood and followed her downstairs to the hall where Jayde, Ellyn, Dario and Edward were all waiting on them. For the first time since Izzy had left, Henry laughed again. Dinner with the twins was more entertainment than Henry had seen in years. Eventually, the evening wound down and Henry, along with everyone else, retired to their own chambers.

As Henry lay down for the night and closed his eyes, Izzy's smile and body haunted him as she did each night. He struggled to escape the memory of her in his bed, the sweet lavender scent that clung to her skin and hair and stained his senses. Eventually, he fell into a dark tormented sleep, the same as always. When he woke in the morning, he would try and recall the dreams over and over, trying to solve the mystery that plagued him. There was something that he knew but could not quite remember.

Mid-August 1410
Adonia

Izzy was tending to the herber, when Bess brought
out her morning pot of tea. Izzy arched her back,
and stood slowly, stretching once she stood up. The
nausea had not been as bad today, but then she had
also skipped the morning meal. Sitting down just as
Bess poured her a cup of tea, they both heard the
rider galloping into the courtyard.
"You just rest Lady Isabel, I will go and see what
needs to be handled and come back to update you."
Bess walked away from Lady Isabel and towards the
courtyard when Hugh came around the corner nearly
knocking Bess over. "Heavens Hugh! You need to
slow down."
"I am so sorry Bess. This just came for Lady
Isabel." He walked quickly past Bess and straight out
to the herber where Lady Isabel was sipping on the
sweet mint tea. "Lady Isabel, this arrived for you
from a royal messenger.
Izzy froze and felt the color drain from her face.
Recently she had written to Hal requesting any
information regarding Raymond and his vessel. She
stood up and took the note from Hugh. Slowly, with
trembling fingers, she opened the note and read it.
Hugh watched, filled with anxiety hoping that it was
only good news. As he watched the letter flutter to

the ground and Lady Isabel begin to sway he knew there was no hope for it to be anything but terrible news. Rushing forward to Lady Isabel he caught her just before her entire body crumpled to the ground. He called out for Bess.

Bess heard the distress in Hugh's voice and came running. She saw Hugh sitting on the ground with Lady Isabel motionless in his arms. Turning around she ran to the stables and sent one of the stable boys to fetch Sir Calvin and Sir Merek from the training fields, then returned to the herber. Merek arrived first and had Izzy in his arms by the time Calvin arrived.

Lady Isabel was carried up to her chamber while Hugh followed with the letter in his hands. As Bess took a clean linen, soaked and wrung it, then placed it on Lady Isabel's forehead, Hugh read the note.

> *Lady Isabel de Seaton,*
>
> *Your immediate presence is required at court. A request to annul your marriage has been made by your husband, Lord Henry de Seaton, declaring your marriage to have not been consummated. You have ten days to arrive in court.*
>
> *King Henry IV of England*

Hugh carefully folded the letter back up and tucked it into his pocket. He had made a promise to Lord James and Lord Raymond to watch over Lady Isabel and he considered this something that would require help. "Bess, keep me updated on her status, I must tend to an urgent matter. I will return shortly." He left without waiting for an answer. Going down the hallway, he entered the study and quickly wrote a note.

> *Lord James,*
> *This arrived from the King today.*
> *Lady Isabel was completely taken off guard.*
> *I worry for her health and the baby's health.*
> *Please send word of what you would like for*
> *me to do.*
> *Hugh*

Hugh then folded the note he had just written around the note received from the King, sealed it and rushed down to their messenger. "Take this to Lord James at Era. If you get there before nightfall, I will double your pay." The messenger nodded and sprinted to the stable, leaving within minutes. Hugh returned to Lady Isabel's chamber in time to see her coming to and sitting up in bed. "Everyone leave please. I have an urgent matter to discuss with Lady Isabel." Bess was shocked that Hugh would need to address business at a moment like this. "Hugh! She needs to rest, now is not the time for business!"
Hugh remained calm but spoke again in a lower tone of voice. "Bess, leave now. The two of you need to

leave as well," Hugh said looking at Calvin and Merek.

"We shall wait in the hall below." Both men stood and walked out of the chamber without another word followed by a very cross Bess.

Hugh waited for the door to close before he began to speak. "How are you feeling?"

Izzy took a moment to answer. "I am not sure." Did he read the note? What must he be thinking?

"Lady Isabel, I have sent word to Era. I did not want you to handle this alone and, at the risk of you dismissing me, I have already sent a messenger." Hugh waited for the blow of dismissal. He would not break a promise to watch over and protect her even if the cost was his position. He watched as he witnessed something resembling anger pass over Lady Isabel's face for the first time.

"What did you say in your note?" Izzy asked.

"I explained that I was worried about your health and the baby's health. I sent the letter as well." Hugh could feel his heart pounding in his chest.

"I see. Thank you," Izzy said tightly. "Please send Sir Merek and Sir Calvin up."

Hugh stood up with a knot in his stomach. Quietly, he did as he was asked.

"Hugh, this is a private conversation that I need to have with my knights, please stay down stairs," Izzy said as Hugh opened the door to leave.

"Yes, of course My Lady," Hugh said quietly.

Izzy waited for Hugh to leave before she stood up. She was still a little dizzy, but she knew that it would pass soon. She walked over to her chest and found her yellow dress. Carefully she rolled it up then pulled out the yellow sleeveless jacket with matching ribbon that zigzagged down the sides. She rolled that up as well, then pulled out a blue gown, purple gown and finally a brown silk gown. Each dress was rolled up carefully and two gowns were placed in one side of a saddle bag and the other two gowns were placed in the other side. Izzy wore a pale rose colored dress with small flowers embroidered with beige thread along the hem of the skirt, the cuffs of the fitted sleeves, and across the square collar. The bodice was flared under an empire waist that was also embroidered with the beige flowers. It was a very simple and elegant dress. She pulled out a white kirtle and dark green over tunic. As soon as she was finished talking with Merek and Calvin, she would change.

Calvin and Merek walked into Lady Isabel's chambers expecting to see her still resting in bed. Everyone in Adonia knew that she was pregnant and everyone also knew that it was supposed to be kept a secret. They did not understand the reason for the secrecy but supposed it was related to her being a healer.

The truth was that if word got back to Henry that his wife was pregnant, it would implicate her in an affair. He could then petition for an annulment, which he had done anyway. The only person in all of Adonia who knew the entire truth besides Izzy was Hugh.

Izzy asked them to close the door before she began to speak. "I have been summoned to the King's court. I must leave immediately and I do not know when I will be returning. I need to know if one or both of you are able to travel with me."

Calvin and Merek glanced at one another. "Lady Isabel, we would travel with you anywhere you have to go. You never need to ask," Merek said while Calvin nodded in agreement.

Izzy smiled weakly. "Thank you both. We need to leave now then. I am only bringing this saddle bag so that we may travel quickly. I will change my dress and then be waiting in the stable."

Both men nodded and left the chamber quickly. Izzy closed the door behind them and changed her clothing. She wanted to be gone before James had some crazy idea to come to her or send Henry to her. Changing her dress quickly, she rolled and tucked the dress she had been wearing into the saddle bag as well. She grabbed her bag and cloak and snuck out to the stable where Calvin was waiting with her horse and Merek's. They waited another minute before Merek joined them and they left making their way to the King's court.

Era

James had already gone to bed. He and Henry had spent the day training exceptionally hard. Jayde was sitting up in the hall enjoying the peace and quiet that came with the solitude that only the late hours in the evening could give. The quiet was shattered by the sound of hooves racing through the night. Jayde stood up and quietly walked to the courtyard where she recognized the rider, a messenger from Adonia. Her heart froze. Why was a messenger racing through the night to get to her? What if Izzy was hurt? The messenger jumped from the wet and panting horse and hurried straight to her.

"Lady Jayde. Hugh gave this to me with strict orders to get it to Lord James with haste." The messenger held out the note, panting for breath.

"I will take it to him. You should go and rest for the night in the loft. You can get a fresh start in the morning," Jayde insisted as she went back inside to the hall where she had been relaxing. She grabbed a candelabra and sat down using it for light. She read the note from Hugh, and the enclosed note from the King. Her hands shook as she gathered her chemise and robe in her hands and with the letter, ran up the stairs. Bursting into her chamber and scaring James awake she handed James the note with still shaking hands.

James took the note from her and read it and the enclosed note twice. "I cannot believe this. What has he done Jayde? What are we supposed to do? I am going to kill him."

"James, re-read Hugh's note." Jayde could tell that he had not comprehended Hugh's words.

He read the note again then looked up at Jayde confused. "What am I missing?"

"He said he is worried about Izzy and the baby." Jayde looked at him with anger beginning to simmer through her veins. "Izzy is pregnant. Henry still does not know that Izzy is his wife. Neither of them have been completely honest with either of us as to the extent of their relationship. He has fallen in love with Izzy, Healing Bird. He has fathered a child with her. Now he has petitioned to annul a marriage due to failure to consummate the marriage, however, he is wrong. They have consummated their marriage and are about to have a baby! Do you understand now?"

James ran his hands over his face. "Come, lay down with me. There is nothing that I can do tonight. Let me sleep on this and calm my temper. We can figure out what we will do in the morning." James set the note on the table next to the bed, then held his arms open to Jayde.

Neither of them slept much, both tossing and turning, fighting to get what little sleep they could while their minds struggled to prepare for the next day.

When morning came, Jayde and James sat in bed longer than usual. "James, what are you going to do?"

"I do not know. I will figure it out. Come on, let us get dressed and go down for morning meal." Exhaustion laced in James' voice.

"James, I do not know if I can look him in the face, let alone eat a meal with him! How could he do this?" Jayde implored.

"Jayde, I do not believe that he knows that Izzy is pregnant. I doubt he would be here if he knew any of the truth. Come on." James untangled himself from his wife.

They dressed and went down the hall where Henry was waiting for them with a huge grin. "You two took long enough to get down here!"

Jayde looked down at the floor, too upset to look at him.

"Yes, well, you look mighty cheerful so early in the morning. What brings you such happiness?" James asked.

"A messenger from the King arrived just a few moments ago bringing me news that I have been waiting and hoping for," Henry replied, elated.

"I see. Have you spoken to Izzy, the healer recently?" James baited Henry.

Henry answered with sadness in his voice, "I have not heard from her in eight weeks. Why?"

"Jayde was saying last night, that she had received word that our sweet Healing Bird was pregnant! Can you believe it? Did she let on that she was pregnant when she was in camp?" James watched Henry very carefully as he spoke.

Henry sat down heavily as James spoke. Izzy was pregnant? With his child? Did her husband know and if so, how angry was he? He was going to be a father. Wait, another man would raise his son or daughter?

James watched as shock rolled over Henry's face like waves rolling up on the beach. "I thought the two of you were pretty close?" James waited a moment before speaking again. "Are you well Henry?"

"How did you learn this information?" Henry asked looking directly at Jayde.

"I received a note from a friend. Apparently Healing Bird has been summoned to the King's court for an annulment. I wonder what the King will do knowing that she is pregnant." Jayde said, her heart betraying her and the sadness showing in her eyes.

Henry felt sick to his stomach. "Where does she live, so that I can go speak to her? Please." His voice gave away his feelings.

"Henry, you should stay out of her personal affairs. I am sure she will be fine. The King is not likely to grant the annulment unless the child is from an affair." James watched as Henry's panicked gaze shot from Jayde to him. Henry's face was white and he looked desperate.

"James, please, I am begging you to tell me how I can find her," Henry implored hoarsely.

"Tell me why it is so important to you first." James stared at him coldly.

Henry took a deep breath and looked at the floor. Finally, he looked James in the face and said, "I need to know that she is okay, and that the baby is okay." Henry took another breath. "The child she carries is mine."

James was shocked that Henry admitted it so quickly. "The messenger that came with the news last night is leaving in a moment. I will ask him to take you to her. When you arrive, simply ask the constable for 'Healing Bird' and he will be able to help you from there. You should get ready to leave. I will be sure to have your horse waiting for you in the stable." James waited for Henry to prepare to leave before running out to the stable and asking the messenger to ride without Adonia's colors, and to not speak to Henry except to tell him they must hurry before she leaves. When James saw Henry approach, he handed him a bag with some dried meat and bread.

"Godspeed brother and good luck. Send word when you can." James left and went back inside where Jayde was waiting.

"Why did you not tell him the whole truth?" Jayde hissed at James.

"Let him figure out his mistake on his own. Let him fully understand what he has done. It will give him an opportunity to value the love a woman gives him. Izzy has given Henry love from the start. She cared for and loved that land because she saw that he loved Adonia and she wanted to share that love with him." James was angry with Henry but refused to involve himself any more than he already had.

Henry recognized the landscape as they rode across the country but was growing more confused as they drew closer to Adonia. When they arrived late that night, everyone was already asleep. Henry quietly made his way upstairs and opened the door to his room. He found it empty and looking as though no one had been in the bed at all that day. Henry did not even think twice as he kicked off his boots and laid down on the bed, falling into an instant sleep. For the first time in weeks, he did not dream. Henry woke up the next day feeling rested and confused. Izzy was a Lady, married to a Lord, but here they were at Adonia. Perhaps this was a resting point? Quickly, Henry got up and changed his clothes, then went down to find his constable, Hugh.

Hugh saw Henry coming down the stairs and his surprise was apparent.

"Hugh! How wonderful it is see you. You look wonderful. Can you tell me where the messenger is? I rode in with him last night and I believe we need to continue on our journey," Henry said not wanting to explain more.

"The only messenger that came in last night was ours, but I had no idea that you had ridden with him.

My deepest apologies My Lord. Where were you intending for your journey to continue? Perhaps I can help?" Hugh realized that Henry still had no awareness of the truth.

"I am searching for Healing Bird. Have you heard of her?" Henry asked in earnest.

"Yes, Lord Henry. I am very familiar with Healing Bird. She is truly amazing," Hugh responded.

"Where does she live? I must find her with great urgency," Henry nearly begged with anticipation of seeing his Healing Bird.

Hugh fought the urge to yell at his Lordship. "She left yesterday without word of where she was going, but that happens often. She usually returns within a few days or sends word. Can I get you anything until then?" Hugh asked.

Henry thought about it for a moment then declined. He watched as Hugh turned to walk away and realized he did have questions. "Hugh wait! Can you answer some questions for me?"

"Of course My Lord," Hugh answered dryly.

"Hugh, have you had the opportunity to truly get to know Lady Isabel, my wife?" Henry began.

"I have My Lord. She is a motivated and gifted woman. She has worked very hard to help Adonia and her people to heal." Hugh answered.

"Hmm, I see. Do you know where she is at the moment?" Henry asked while looking around expecting Lady Isabel to appear from out of nowhere.

"Unfortunately, I do not know where Lady Isabel is at the moment. She has a tendency to disappear for days at a time. She will return in a day or two I am sure." Hugh waited for several moments before speaking again. "Will that be all My Lord?"

"Yes, of course. Thank you for your time Hugh." Henry watched as Hugh hurried away, seeming eager to return to his duties. Henry ate the morning meal, then began to wander the castle and town. He spent the entire day walking through town, speaking with the residents, inspecting crops, homes, and the overall health of the town. He was incredibly impressed with how literate everyone was becoming. Everyone seemed to sing praises of his wife and asked how her health was. Upon returning to the castle for the evening meal, Henry asked Hugh why people questioned him about her health.

Hugh was caught off guard by the question. He had not realized that people in town had found out that Lady Isabel had fainted yesterday. "Lady Isabel is fine. She received a note from a messenger two days ago and fainted. She recovered and left without word."

Henry thought about Isabel and wondered what it was that caused her to have such a spell. He sat quietly through the evening meal, deep in thought. He was tired and retired earlier than the room full of knights. "Hugh, notify me at once when Lady Isabel returns, as well as Healing Bird." Hugh nodded as Henry left the hall and retired to his chamber. Henry undressed and without another thought, once again climbed into bed and fell fast asleep.

Henry awoke with the sun. He stood up and stretched, then dressed himself. Opening the shutters, light cascaded into the room illuminating everything. He looked around. His wife had not changed any of the décor in the room, which surprised him. As he took in everything though, the hair on his arms and back of his neck prickled. There were dried herbs everywhere he turned, and brown bottles exactly like the ones that Izzy traveled with. Is it possible that his wife was ill and Izzy had been treating her for some time? Henry went downstairs to search for Hugh again. Henry saw Hugh directing the kitchen servants about. He waited patiently for Hugh to finish.

"Lord Henry, how did you sleep? What can I help you with this morning?" Hugh asked, wondering if his lordship would ever figure out the truth on his own.

"Hugh, was Lady Isabel ill?" Henry asked.

"She has been ill for the past several weeks, but herbs and teas seemed to be easing her symptoms slightly." Hugh offered.

"So Healing Bird has been here. I wonder if she knows…" Henry trailed off wondering if that is what Izzy's last letter had meant.

"My Lord, if I might be so bold to say something?" Hugh asked.

Henry raised his eyebrows. Hugh rarely spoke out to anyone. "If you feel that you must, then go ahead and say it."

"You are not very observant. You sleep in a room filled with herbs from Healing Bird. You question your wife's health after nearly three years of not giving a damn about her, and both women are gone, leaving without saying a word on the exact same day. Your wife's name is Isabel, and everyone fondly refers to Healing Bird as Izzy. Do you even know what your wife looks like? I have seen Healing Bird. She is incredible, beautiful and smart. She sees no class barriers when she is treating people. She puts her own life at risk to save others and somehow finds an infinite amount of love to give. Your wife, is like no other noblewoman that I have ever met. When the messenger comes, she does not think twice to jump into action. It does not matter if she is eating or has not slept in two days. She gives of herself until she collapses. Even now, after everything that she has gone through, she continues to give. She received a note from his Majesty two days ago. Sir Merek had to carry her to her chamber since the shock of the note caused her to faint. You see Lady Isabel, is with child. She was summoned by the prince several months ago because her husband was injured in battle and on his death bed. She had not even had her morning meal yet and she left, racing to be by his side; a man who had never bothered to reply to any of her letters. She returned here, continued to care for the people of this town, pushing herself to give even more than before. Traveling back and forth between here and the battle camp, she also traveled to the sea to see that Lord Raymond was not alone when he left on one of His Majesty's ships. She has divided her time between Adonia, Ackerley and now Iole as well. You see, Lord Raymond gifted Iole to her. He knew that she would give more than she had to keep Iole the way your mother remembered it." Hugh took a deep breath and watched as the pieces were falling into place for Lord Henry. "You see My Lord, your wife was sent to you so that she could be there when you died from infection. Instead, she saved you. There was a problem though. You did not recognize her. She stayed in that filthy camp to make it better for everyone, and she fell in love with a man married to another woman, a woman that although existed, was not truly alive. She had no way to tell you the truth. So now, she is pregnant, and has received a summons from the King stating that her marriage is to be annulled due to it not being consummated." He saw the shock on Lord Henry's face. "Yes, I read the note, I had to. I had promised Lord James and Lord Raymond that I would watch out for her as much as she would allow me to. Those were the King's exact words: 'failure to consummate the marriage.' Can you just imagine seeing her pretty face blanch and then her body crumble? Someone as strong as her, so dedicated and giving, being struck down by words penned on paper." Hugh suddenly felt old and tired. Finally expelling the truth, he no longer felt the need to be strong.

Henry dropped down into the chair feeling as though his world was spinning out of control. Izzy, Healing Bird, was his wife? He looked up at Hugh, anger filling his soul. "She lied to me. She knew the entire time who I am. She let me feel guilty about cheating on my wife. She lied to me about her husband, telling me he was never around! She-" Henry stopped. She had not lied to him about her husband. She said that he was a good man, dedicated to his country and family. She knew who he was and that is what she said about him, her husband. She said he would never hurt her, yet he did. He failed her because he was selfish. She ran to Jayde's aide, oh God, Jayde. Did she know the truth? She must have. She told him to let go of his guilt, to not look back. She loved him despite believing he loved another woman? What was she going to do when he came home though? How was she planning to explain it to him? Oh no, the annulment. The King was granting him the annulment. He had to go. "Hugh, did she leave with a wagon?" Henry asked as he strode toward the stable.

"No My Lord, she left with a saddle bag. Nothing more," Hugh said with a slight smile. Henry was going to go do what was right, he just prayed it would not be too late

"Of course she did not take a wagon. Why would she do anything the way that a proper married noblewoman should? She has probably already arrived. I am going to lose her. Hugh, get two horses, you are traveling with me. I have a feeling there is so much more that you need to tell me and I will likely need your help." Henry ran to his chamber to grab two riding cloaks, one for him and one for Hugh. He raced back down and to the stable where Bess had two bags filled with provisions for their ride.

"Bess, what are you doing?" Henry asked.

"I apologize Lord Henry, but I heard everything. You cannot travel on an empty stomach. Hurry! Bring Healing Bird home!" Bess spoke as she handed the bags to him and Hugh.

Henry thanked her as he accepted the bag. He put it on before putting on his riding cloak then handed Hugh the other riding cloak. Together, the two men mounted their horses and began the long journey to Windsor Castle.

Windsor Castle

Henry and Hugh arrived at Windsor Castle late in the night. A guard addressed them, asking their business at the castle. Henry explained that he was here to speak with the King; that he had fought with Prince Henry and was requesting a room and an audience. The guard stayed with him while another disappeared into the castle. Returning shortly, the second knight directed Hugh and Henry to the stables where there would be someone waiting to show them a room.

Once in a room, Hugh fell fast asleep. Riding so intensely was not something he did regularly. Henry on the other hand, tried to clean himself up as best as he could with only a wash basin. It did not matter, he knew that come morning he would still look as terrible as he felt. Maybe that was a good thing. Henry laid down on the bed but found that still, sleep evaded him. He paced the floor, practiced what he would say, and changed what he said, practiced again, contemplated begging and still could find no peace in the night. When morning at last arrived, he was already dressed and ready to meet with the King. Surprisingly, the King agreed to meet with him immediately. The King and Queen were seated eating breakfast when Henry was brought to them. "Your Majesties," Henry said bowing deeply before them.

"Lord Henry, did I not just send you notice that I would be granting your request for an annulment?" The King asked.

"Yes Your Majesty, you did," Henry said.

"Then what are you doing here, bothering me in my court?" The King grumbled

"I am here in hopes of begging you to-" Henry was not able to get another word out of his mouth because a fist slammed into it knocking him to the floor.

"How dare you come here? I told you not to petition for an annulment. You could not listen, could you? LEAVE! You are not welcome here!" Hal growled at Henry.

"Hal, that will be enough. You should prepare a plate and take it to our guest in her chamber. Let your father handle this," Queen Joan scolded gently. Hal looked at his step mother, then turned with a servant following him closely. Soon they left the room with two large trays of food.

"Do you plan to stay on the floor or return to your feet?" King Henry questioned blandly.

Henry rubbed his jaw, then stood up trying to grasp the entire scene that had just played out. Hal had seemed more than angry. He seemed as though he had wanted to kill him.

"Tell me why you are here," King Henry ordered.

"I am here to beg you to reconsider my request for an annulment. I have made a terrible mistake. I was wrong on every account. I have to try and fix this," Henry groveled.

The King looked thoughtful as he took another bite of his food. "I have already granted your request, there is no reason to be here."

"Yes your Majesty, you did. However, I also learned that you summoned my wife to court regarding said annulment and I am praying that this means that your final decision has not been made. Please your Majesty. If I must beg, I will." Henry waited quietly as the King continued to eat.

"I will take this into consideration. However, I do not like to go back on my decisions. You may stay here until I decide." The king then dismissed Henry. Henry bowed deeply and left the hall. He returned to his chamber where Hugh was waiting for him.

"Well My Lord, what did the King say?" Hugh asked.

"He said to wait." Henry felt frustrated. "I need to walk." Henry left the room again and went to the gardens. He walked himself dizzy in the garden before returning to the castle for the midday meal. As he was leaving the hall again, he saw Hal escorting a blonde woman wearing a familiar purple dress. He could not see her face but recognized the way she walked. The memory of the purple dress suddenly struck him, nearly as hard as Hal's fist had that morning. He could see Izzy's scared face standing before him the day after Christmas wearing that dress. He flinched at the memory of his crudeness. "Izzy!" he called out, but it was too late. The doors closed behind them.

Izzy spun around to face the closed doors as she heard Henry's voice calling out to her. She felt anger course through her body at the thought that he had come here. "Why is he here, Hal?"

"I am not sure Izzy, but if you do not want to see him, I can arrange that," Hal said softly.

Izzy did not answer. She let Hal take her hand and rest it on his arm as he led her forward to where the King and Queen sat. This time a chair was offered to her.

"Hal, I want you to leave. You are far too emotionally involved to be of any use in this meeting. I will be sure that Lady Isabel is taken care of." King Henry waited for his son to take his leave.

Hal bowed to his father, then turned to Izzy. "I will be waiting just outside of those doors," he said pointing to a set of side doors. "When you are finished, you will be dismissed and will exit there." He kissed the back of her hand, then left.

The King watched his son fawn over Lady Isabel before finally leaving. "Lady Isabel, do you have any romantic notions with my son?" King Henry sounded tired of the game before him. His health was beginning to fail him and he was feeling it.

"No your Majesty. I look to Hal as a friend, even a brother, but not a lover," Izzy replied.

Relieved, the King and Queen began to question Izzy, finally hearing the entire story. "My Dear, you mean to tell me that you lied to your husband about your true identity for four months?"

Izzy looked ashamed as she answered, "Yes your Majesty. I wanted to tell him, but could never find the right words or time or way to tell him. This mess is all my fault." Izzy saw the Queen smile at her as the King spoke again.

He spoke gently this time. "Healing Bird, may I call you that?" When Izzy nodded he continued. "Healing Bird, this is not your fault. Yes, you could have told him the truth right away, but I can understand why you did not. Lord Henry failed to be a proper husband to you which forced your hand down this path. I have it in mind to deny the annulment, but I will do whatever it is that you prefer. I know that my son thinks highly of you. I can see that he cares for you deeply, more than he should. I must warn you though that under no circumstances will you be permitted to marry my son." He was reassured by her smile and small giggle that Hal was not the object of her affections. "What would you like for me to do? I personally believe that you should make him suffer. He seems to be quick to make decisions and needs a level-headed wife to guide him."

"Your Majesty, I do not wish to have my marriage annulled. I want to return home, to raise a family and happily fight with my husband," Izzy said with tears in her eyes. "I am beyond angry with him right now and have no idea how to recover from this. I would accept any advice that you should be so kind to give me."

"Let me think on it. Enjoy the grounds and I will have an answer for you tomorrow. My advice for the moment is that you avoid your husband until we speak again at that time," King Henry advised. "I believe my son has been pacing outside those doors waiting to learn your fate. If you would, please let him down gently. I have never seen him so protective of anyone before."

"Yes your Majesty," Izzy said quite solemnly. She stood and curtsied deeply before exiting the hall through the side doors as she was instructed.

As soon as the side doors opened, Hal was on his feet. "How are you feeling? Would you like to walk the grounds? I will take you to the Queen's rose garden."

Izzy smiled. "Thank you, that would be lovely."

Izzy and Hal walked the grounds together for quite some time until Izzy asked if they could sit down. She was tired and needed to rest.

"Izzy, what did my father say?" Hal asked.

"He said he would make a final decision tomorrow, but that ultimately it was my choice," Izzy answered. The gardens were well manicured, but everything was very bland. There were very few bright colors and what patches of color there were, were very small.

"Izzy, is there anything that I could say to persuade you to consider the annulment?" Hal asked softly.

Izzy was startled. She had not expected this from him. "No Hal, I do not think that there is anything that you could say to change my mind. You are very sweet to think of me and want to care for me though. Thank you."

Hal thought seriously, then said, "Perhaps something I could do?"

"Hal, I know where my heart lies," Izzy maintained. Henry had watched as the couple walked the grounds from the balcony. He watched in panic as Hal behaved far too friendly with Izzy, his hands constantly touching her, holding her. When they finally sat down he began to feel relief. The guards were coming out to bring him before the King when he saw Hal reach forward and tilt Izzy's chin up. When his lips met hers he nearly lost him mind. Without thinking, he started to climb over the wall of the balcony until the guards grabbed him. He watched as Izzy jumped up and Hal grabbed her hand. The guards were dragging him away from his wife, who was being wooed by the future King of England. He had no chance.

The King watched as the guards dragged Henry into the hall and down to him. Finally, Henry quit struggling, and stood on his own two feet. The King looked upon Lord Henry's face and saw a defeated man. "Lord Henry. You had an affair, is that correct?"

"Yes and no your Majesty," Henry answered desolately.

"Explain to me how you did and did not have an affair," the King instructed patiently.

Henry explained a nearly identical story as Izzy had related earlier, but this time with the torment and guilt of betraying a wife he chose not to love. "Your Majesty, I did not believe I could love someone I did not choose. What is worse is that now that I realize that the woman I love has been waiting for me all along, it looks as though I am about to lose her to someone else."

"Why do you think that you will lose her to someone else?" King Henry asked with interest and concern.

"What woman would refuse an offer from the Prince? Especially when he has known all along what and who he wanted," Henry responded.

"My son has made an offer to your wife?" the King asked cautiously.

"Well, if by kissing her in the gardens then holding her back when she tried to walk away is not an offer, then I would be curious to know what it was," Henry answered with both sadness and anger. He could feel for the first time in years, tears well up in his eyes.

The King and Queen watched as the man before them realized that he could lose everything. The King took his Queen's hand in his own and kissed the back of it. While land determined power, love could conquer anything, and drive a sane man mad.

"I will make my final decision in two days." The King dismissed Lord Henry.

"Dear, why did you give him a different time frame than you did Lady Isabel?" Queen Joan asked him. "I wanted to give Lady Isabel a head start home. I have a feeling she will return to Iole, the estate that her brother-in-law gave her, rather than return to either of Lord Henry's estates," King Henry predicted.

"You think she would return there rather than Ackerley where she was raised?" The Queen questioned again.

"No, Ackerley holds her past, and Henry will look for her there when he realizes that she is not at home in Adonia waiting for him. I do not think that he knows that Iole was given to her. This will give her some time to gather herself and figure out how she will deal with his desire of an annulment. I do not envy that man. I imagine that she can be as ill-tempered as she is calm." King Henry chuckled at the thought of the sweet little Healing Bird losing her temper. "Guard, bring my son to me immediately." Henry ran back out to the balcony where he had spotted Hal and Izzy earlier. He saw Hal sitting alone on a bench and was about to go down there to fight him when he saw the royal guard approach him. The group walked together and disappeared out of sight.

It was time for the evening meal and Henry went to the dining hall where he waited, hoping to see Izzy. He watched as a servant prepared a platter of food, and left the dining hall with it. He followed the

servant, hoping she would lead him to Izzy. He
waited around the corner and listened as the servant
knocked.

"Lady Isabel, I have brought you your meal," the
servant called out.

"Are you alone? Prince Hal did not accompany
you?" he heard Izzy answer.

"No My Lady, I am alone," the servant assured her.
He closed his eyes, grateful to hear the worry in her
voice. She did not want Hal! He took a deep breath.
His eyes shot open when he heard a second knock on
a door in the hallway.

"Izzy? It is me, Hal. I just wanted to talk to you.
Please, let me in, please hear me out." Henry heard
Hal call out. Then he heard Hal let out a deep
breath.

Henry held his own breath when he heard the door
open, then close again.

"Excuse me Your Highness. Lady Isabel is not
feeling well and requests no visitors this evening,"
the servant said placing her body against the door as
a barricade.

Henry heard as Hal walked away without another
word. Henry left from the direction he came before
the servant could find out that he had followed her.
Returning to the dining hall, he absently ate then
retreated outside where he thought he could be alone.
Hal watched as Henry left the hall. Quietly he
followed him outside. When he knew that they were

alone he came up from behind and said in a flat tone, "You do not deserve her you know."

Henry sat very still. He had heard the footsteps approach from behind.

"I could give her so much more than you ever will," Hal continued.

"Money cannot buy you love Hal. Especially a woman like Izzy, she is not fooled easily," Henry spoke through gritted teeth, reining in his temper.

"My father has left the decision up to her. Do you truly believe that a woman like her would settle for a boy like you, one who cannot even admit his love?" Hal snorted. "She will be well provided for with me."

"How soon after you take her will you get bored with her and take a mistress? Izzy is not the kind of woman to be pushed aside." Henry retorted. "And if you think that you can buy her with jewels and fancy gems, then you do not know anything about my wife." Henry stood up and walked away from Hal before he said something that would get him in trouble. He returned to his guest chamber where Hugh was waiting for him again.

"My Lord, forgive me, but you look terrible. You must sleep. I brought a tea with herbs in it from the dining Hall for you. Lady Isabel sometimes drinks it when she is having a difficult time resting at night. Drink it and get some rest. Sitting up through another night will not help the days pass any faster." Hugh handed Lord Henry the cup of tea.

Izzy was awake and had dressed in the brown dress she had brought, before the sun rose over the castle walls. She had packed up her dresses and sent word to her knights to prepare their horses to begin their journey home. Izzy ate her morning meal alone again, then was taken to the Great Hall where the King and Queen both waited for her.

"Lady Isabel, did you make your final decision?" King Henry asked.

"Yes your Majesty. I would like to remain married to Lord Henry de Seaton. I would like to leave today, and return home. I left many things undone and would like to figure out how to begin to build a life with Henry. I imagine that he will be upset at the annulment being denied and will be even more upset when he learns who I am," Izzy sighed apprehensively.

King Henry and Queen Joan smiled.

"Lady Isabel, give him a chance when he comes to his senses, would you?" Queen Joan asked.

"Yes your Majesty, I will." Izzy agreed.

"Well, if that is all, then it is my official declaration that your annulment shall be denied. If there is nothing else, you are dismissed and free to return home. Just one question though. Where do you think you will return to first?" the King asked.

"I will return to Iole first, then to Adonia." Izzy answered.

King Henry looked at Queen Joan. "I told you so." Then looking back to Izzy, "Safe travels my dear."

Izzy curtsied deeply then left the hall through the side doors. She half expected to see Hal again, but instead was greeted by Calvin and Merek.

"We are ready to travel Lady Isabel. Are you ready as well?" Merek asked.

Smiling, Izzy answered, "Yes, let us go home."

Chapter 14
Adonia

Henry jumped from his horse and went running into the hall. "Izzy! IZZY!" he called running up to their chamber, then down to the hall again.

Hugh was just coming into the hall when Henry was coming back down. Bess walked out of the kitchen, and looked at Hugh, slowly shaking her head.

"Is she not here? Where is she?" Henry asked frantically.

"I am sorry Lord Henry, but Lady Isabel has not returned to Adonia," Bess relayed sadly.

"Where else could she be?" Henry asked.

"My Lord, she could be at Ackerley, or in Iole," Hugh suggested.

"Iole, why would she be at Raymond's estate?" Henry asked pained at the thought that every other person in his family was more of a comfort to his own wife than he was.

"Iole is no longer Lord Raymond's estate. He signed it over to her when he set sail," Hugh informed Henry.

"What do you mean he signed it over?" Henry asked, shocked by the information.

Hugh sighed. He had already explained this once before and was becoming tired of repeating himself. "I will explain it to you as we ride to Iole. She will be there. She has been working hard to gain the trust of the people there." The two men first went into the kitchen to eat before leaving for Iole.

Iole

Izzy, Calvin and Merek were preparing to leave after having spent the past two days in Iole. Everything was going as planned; the town was beginning to trust her. She had made very few changes to Iole. The biggest change being the way they harvested the lavender. The new way preserved so much more of the plant, making it usable to create oils to sell. This could be quite profitable for them. The oil could be used for health and wellness, in baths, and for overall scent. Simon seemed to be coming around most of all and not fearing the horrible person that he thought she would be. He even joked with her the day before. Izzy, Calvin and Merek were about to mount their horses when Simon appeared. In his hand he held a large bunch of lavender and chamomile. "Lady Isabel, I thought you might enjoy these; a reminder to come back and visit us soon. I look forward to working with you more and continuing to keep Iole a wonderful place." Simon handed Izzy the flowers.

Izzy smiled and thanked him while putting the flowers in the saddle bag. She then mounted her horse. She was tired and wanted to go straight home to Adonia. Simon had told her the day before of a shorter route to take them home. He said the road was smooth and well used. They were going to take that route today and see just how much shorter it truly was.

Stopping for the midday meal by a creek, Merek cautiously asked Izzy about the baby. "Lady Isabel, I hope that I am not out of line, but when is the baby due?"

Izzy automatically placed her hand on her stomach. "I had not realized that many other people had noticed. The baby should arrive in March sometime. How long have you known?"

Merek smiled. "I noticed shortly after we arrived home from camp. Your symptoms were the same as my wife's symptoms."

"Oh Merek! How exciting! When are you expecting the baby to be born?" Izzy exclaimed.

"We think near the end of January. I told my wife that I would ask if you would mind coming to check on her when we get home. If you have the energy of course. We are very excited," Merek said proudly.

"Of course! I will come by tomorrow. Would the morning be okay?" Izzy asked.

"Tomorrow morning would be fine." Merek began to pack up their food and drink.

"We should get going. I think we will be home in time for the evening meal! I was worried that Simon was sending us astray," Calvin admitted.

The small group mounted their horses again and continued their trip home. As the gates of Adonia came into view for Izzy, Calvin and Merek, Henry and Hugh were arriving at the gates of Iole.

Simon heard the horses running up the road and went out to greet them. He was concerned that it was Lady Isabel and her knights coming back. He knew the directions he gave them were accurate, and he hoped that something had not gone wrong. As he went out to the courtyard, he saw the two men. He immediately recognized one of them as Lord Raymond's brother, Lord Henry, but the other man was unfamiliar. "Lord Henry, what a pleasant surprise. Please, come inside. The evening meal is about to start."

Henry and Hugh followed Simon into the castle. "Simon, I am looking for Lady Isabel. Have you seen her?"

"Of course! She left here today," Simon served the two men, and then served himself before sitting down.

"When did she leave?" Henry asked still not having touched his meal. Hugh on the other hand had already started to eat. He was famished as neither of them had thought to bring any food before they left Adonia.

Simon looked at Hugh curiously as the man ate, still not having spoken a single word. Then he looked back to Lord Henry. "She left just after the morning meal. She is as wonderful as Lord Raymond promised. I was especially apprehensive about her at first, but she has proven that I was just being paranoid. Lord Raymond did not say how she was related, I only know that she has the same surname. Is she a cousin?"

Henry looked sad and defeated yet again. "I am never going to catch up to her, Hugh." Taking a deep breath, he looked up at Simon. "Lady Isabel is my wife."

"Oh! I did not realize! You are truly a lucky man Lord Henry!" Simon said, before taking a bite of his food.

Slowly, Henry began to eat the food before him. "Thank you for your hospitality Simon. We should be getting back on the road as soon as we are finished."

"Lord Henry, I know that you are a skilled knight, but Lord Raymond would never forgive me if I did not absolutely insist that you stay the night. The roads are not safe in the dark. There are several bandits that group together near here. Please, for your safety, stay the night." Simon looked Henry in the eyes with absolute honesty and sincerity. "I will wake you with the sunrise if you would like so that you can get back to her that much sooner, but I beg of you, stay safe tonight," Simon pleaded.

Henry sighed deeply. It would do him no good to be taken by surprise by a group of bandits. "We will stay tonight but leave with the sunrise."

"Oh! Thank you so much!" Hugh said before he could control himself.

Henry looked at him with raised eyebrows.

372

"I beg your pardon My Lord, my body is just getting old and I am incredibly sore from riding for so many days," Hugh relented.

"We should be getting to bed. I want to be riding out of the gates at predawn. Simon, would you show me to my chamber?" Henry stood from the table.

"Of course. Right this way Lord Henry." Simon stood as well and led Lord Henry up the stairs to the chamber where Lady Jayde stayed.

As Henry stepped into the room, he saw that it was exactly how it had been when they were children; just as his mother had left it. He saw dried bundles of lavender and chamomile hanging near the window. "Is this the room that my wife stays in always?"

"Yes, Lord Henry. I thought you would rather stay in her chamber rather than a guest chamber," Simon answered.

"Has she not wanted to change the room at all?" Henry asked again.

"No, when Millie asked Lady Isabel what she wanted to change, Lady Isabel said that she did not want to change anything. She told Millie that this room was perfect just the way it was. Why do you ask?" Simon inquired.

"I find it interesting, since my wife only likes dusty rose as a shade of pink. This room is drowning in pink and I can only imagine what my wife thought when she first came in here." In his mind's eye, Henry could see Izzy's nauseated expression being surrounded by so much pink. Laughing out loud, he turned to Simon. "Thank you Simon. We will see you early in the morning. I appreciate everything. Good night." He waited for Simon to leave before undressing and climbing into the bed. As he pulled the covers up, he could smell the lavender and he suddenly realized that back in Adonia, the covers smelled of lavender as well. He wondered if that was why he had not dreamed of Izzy when he was in Adonia. Everything smelled like lavender, like her. Henry smiled and closed his eyes. For the first time in nearly a week, he slept soundly.

Henry awoke to the sound of knocking on the door. "Come in," he called out.

Simon walked in. "Good morning Lord Henry. The sky is starting to change color, and you asked to be wakened to leave at predawn."

Henry woke up fully. "Thank you Simon. Have you wakened Hugh yet?"

"Yes Lord Henry, he is awake and getting your horses ready," Simon replied.

"Thank you, I will be ready momentarily." Henry jumped out of bed and hastily dressed before racing down the stairs. The smell of biscuits filled the air and Henry felt his stomach growl. Before he could say a word, Simon came from the kitchen carrying two messenger bags in one hand and a smaller linen bag in the other. He followed Henry out to the stables where the horses were pawing at the ground anxiously.

Simon handed one messenger bag to Lord Henry and the other to Hugh. Then he opened the linen bag and pulled out two large biscuits. "These are sweet biscuits. They are the best in all of England. Travel safe Lord Henry. I hope that you find what you seek, and I hope that we see you and Lady Isabel again soon." Simon waved as the two men left the courtyard eating their sweet biscuits.

Adonia

Izzy woke and dressed in the same dusty rose dress that she had worn that awful day two weeks ago. She loved this dress too much to let the bad memory taint it. She finished her morning meal out in the herber as she liked to do each morning during the summer. Then she walked the herber inspecting the herbs, picked some fresh lavender and walked down into town to meet Merek and his wife. She arrived at the small house where Merek and his wife lived and knocked on the door. A young woman with red hair answered.

"Hello Lady Isabel. I am Erin, Merek's wife. Thank you so much for coming down to see me. Would you please come in?" Erin gestured Izzy into the house.

Izzy smiled and stepped inside. "It is a pleasure to meet you Erin. Merek is a wonderful man. I wish you could hear the way he speaks about you! He was bursting with pride when telling me about your pregnancy. He said that you think you are due sometime near the end of January?"

"Yes, that is correct. This is our first child and I have no idea what to expect!" Erin gushed.

"I will need to examine you. Will you be comfortable with that?" Izzy asked. Erin nodded as she walked over to the bed and sat on the edge of it. "Go ahead and lie down and get comfortable. I am

going to set these down on the table first." Izzy laid
the lavender on the table then sat on the edge of the
bed next to Erin. She began to feel Erin's stomach
and ask questions. She was reminded of when Jayde
was pregnant with the twins, and Erin's stomach felt
the same. Izzy experimented and pushed on one side
of Erin's stomach. She felt the baby beneath her
move, then saw the other baby move in response.
She helped Erin sit up and retie her dress.
"Well, am I healthy? I am pregnant and not crazy
right?" Erin laughed.
Izzy smiled at her. "You are indeed healthy and very
pregnant. I do not believe that you will give birth in
January though. I expect Christmas babies instead."
Erin froze. "Wait, did you say babies? As in two?"
Izzy's smile grew even bigger. "I did.
Congratulations Erin! If you head out now, you
could probably catch Merek before he starts training.
I believe they are working on archery today."
Erin hugged Lady Isabel before running out of the
house and down the road not even saying goodbye or
closing the door. Izzy shook her head, laughing at
the joy Erin exuded as she ran to tell Merek. Izzy
closed the door behind her and walked back up the
hill to the herber where she knew that her tea would
be waiting. She sat down and rubbed the small bump
that was still easy to keep hidden. In another few
months, it would no longer be a secret, but she did
not mind. As she settled in the chair, and drank her
tea, she wondered where Henry might be now. She

still had not received an official note from the King
denying the annulment, but she knew it would arrive
soon. Izzy poured her second cup of tea and took a
sip. The grape vines climbing the trellis provided
shade from the morning sun and absorbed some of
the heat. Izzy heard the rider coming into the
courtyard and assumed it was the messenger she had
just been thinking of. Hugh would get it and bring it
to her. Izzy closed her eyes and enjoyed the sounds
surrounding her. It had been so long since she had
just closed her eyes here in the herber and listened to
the sounds around her. It was comforting and
relaxing at once.

"What are you seeing right now Healing Bird?"
Henry asked. She was sitting there with her eyes
closed, face tilted up to the sky in the only pink dress
she owned.

Izzy gasped and smiled at the sound of his
unexpected voice. She instantly felt the tears start to
slide down her cheeks. The voice was closer this
time, so close that his breath tickled her ear.

"Izzy, tell me, are you wishing you had a knight on a
white horse holding you right now?" he whispered.
Izzy could only shake her head no as she squeezed
her eyes even tighter, afraid that if she opened them,
this would only be a dream.

Henry walked around her chair and dropped to his
knees. "Izzy, Lady Isabel, my wife. Do you think
that there will ever be a day when you can forgive
me for all of the wrongs that I have done to you and

the pain that I have caused you? If you say no, I
understand, but should warn you that regardless, I
will spend every single day for the rest of my life
striving to make it up to you."

Izzy sat up and brought her hands to her face to hide
the ugly tears that cascaded down her face. She felt
his hands brush hers away and then pull her forward
to him where he rested her head on his shoulder.
"Izzy, please…" he waited for her tears to subside.
Finally, she sat back and opened her eyes to look at
him. "Isabel de Seaton, I love you. I love you with
every fiber of my body. I promise to you right now
that I will always drive you crazy with my stubborn
streak, always do everything wrong the first time and
only listen to you the second time, and if it is the
only thing I ever do right, I promise to love you as
fiercely as you love me. I ask you again, will you
deny me?" He remembered asking her the same
question in camp and prayed that her answer would
be the same.

Izzy searched his eyes for truth. "I will not deny you
Henry de Seaton."

Henry placed a hand on either side of her face and
kissed her. He did not think there were any words
that could say as much as their kiss did. When he
finally pulled his mouth from hers he looked into her
eyes. "Izzy, will you ever be able to forgive me?"
"Kiss me like that every day and I think I will
manage to forgive you," Izzy teased through her
tears.

Henry grabbed her and kissed her again letting his hands slide to her hips. Pulling back, his thumbs caressed her hips. "Izzy, someone mentioned that you are expecting my child. Is there any truth in that?" he whispered with his forehead pressed against hers and his gaze lowered to her lips. When she did not answer him, he lifted his gaze and searched her face for the answer.

Izzy waited for Henry to meet her gaze before she answered. Taking both of his hands, she laid them on her stomach. "You cannot feel it now, but in another two or three months you will be able to feel the baby kick, stretch and even roll over."

Henry smiled so big that tears came to his eyes. He felt his heart skip a beat and his chest tighten. Reaching up, he caressed her cheek. "I love you Izzy. I will never leave your side or doubt my love for you again. I cannot wait to meet our little baby. I hope that he or she looks just like you."

Epilogue
Adonia
March 31st

Sister Ava arrived in Adonia by mid-afternoon. She quickly climbed the stairs and knew which door to open. She could hear Lady Isabel moaning with the pains of labor. "Breathe Izzy, deep breaths, there you go." Sister Ava saw Henry at her side. "You should leave now. I will send for you when your child is born." Sister Ava smiled reassuringly at Henry.

"I respect your knowledge and authority, but I made my wife a promise several months ago that I would never leave her side again and that includes now. My family will be waiting in the hall when they arrive and I will only go down then to show them our little baby. So, make use of me as you need, but I will not leave this room," Henry asserted kindly yet firmly. Izzy squeezed his hand again and screamed out in pain.

Sister Ava smiled at the couple. This was a love that would last a lifetime.

Jayde, James and the kids were eagerly waiting in the hall when the evening meal was served. Every knight waited anxiously for any news. Each of them cringed at the sound of Lady Isabel's screams followed by absolute silence. After several minutes the sound of a baby crying echoed through the hall followed by the roar of the knights cheering. The mood in the hall lifted and laughter began to spread. Henry looked upon the blond-haired baby boy lying on Izzy's chest. He kissed Izzy then his newborn son. "He is beautiful Izzy. You are amazing! Have you anymore thought of a name for him now that you are holding him?"

"Yes." Izzy said softly. "I think his name should be Geoffrey Thomas," Izzy said as she stroked his sweet chubby cheeks.

Henry sucked in air as his chest swelled with pride. His brothers would have been honored that their names were passed down to their little nephew. Henry's voice broke as he said, "I think Geoffrey Thomas is a strong name." He watched as Izzy nursed Geoff for the first time. When he had finished, Sister Ava took him and swaddled him, then laid him in Henry's arms. Henry looked at his son's face and smiled with pride. Looking over to Izzy, he saw her smile at them. There were no words to give justice to the flood of emotions he felt. Turning, he quietly left the room and took Geoff down the stairs stopping four steps from the bottom. Holding up his son, he announced, "I present my first born, a son. His name is Geoffrey Thomas de Seaton."

The walls seemed to shake with the vibrations from the cheering. Izzy could hear the roars of excitement from below. She smiled when the hall grew quiet

Lady Ryia Bird – Isabel's mother. B: January 4th, 1365 d: 1401

Lord Andrew Bird (Andy) : b Feb 20 1383 (24 yrs.)

Lord Dario – Jayde deceased father

Lord Dario de Seaton (B: June 20th 1409)

Lord Edward de Seaton (B: June 20th 1409)

Lord Geoffrey Thomas de Seaton (b: March 31st, 1411)

Lord Henry de Seaton – b Oct 13 1378 (29 yrs.)

Millie –head servant at Iole

Myles – Constable of Ackerley

Orion – Raymond's war horse

Queen Joan of Navarre, Queen of England

Queen Philippa of Pomerania, Denmark, Norway and Sweden, youngest sister to Prince Henry (b 6/4/1394)

Sadie – Lady Isabel's lady's maid

Sarah– servant at Adonia

Simon – Constable at Iole

Sir Calvin – head knight at Adonia

Sir Fendrel - Era

Sir Luther - Era

Sir Merek – head knight at Adonia

Sir Peter - Era

Sir Randall – knight from Ackerley

Sir Wade – knight from Ackerley

Sister Ava – head nun in Ackerley, helped to raise Izzy

www.ingramcontent.com/pod-product-compliance
Lightning Source LLC
Chambersburg PA
CBHW031419240626
47154CB00001B/118

* 9 7 8 0 9 9 9 8 2 9 4 6 3 6 *